The Nibelungenlied

Translated into Rhymed English Verse
in the Meter of the Original

The Nibelungenlied

Translated into Rhymed English Verse
in the Meter of the Original

Translated by
George Henry Needler

Associate Professor of German in University College, Toronto

ÆGYPAN PRESS

Originally written in Middle High German (M.H.G.), sometime
around 1200 A.D., although this dating is by no means certain.
Author unknown.
The text of this edition is based on that published as *The Nibelungen-
lied* in 1909.

The Nibelungenlied
A publication of
ÆGYPAN PRESS

www.aegypan.com

Preface

This translation of the Nibelungenlied is published with the simple purpose of placing one of the world's great epic poems within the reach of English readers. Translations are at best but poor substitutes for originals. A new translation of a poem implies also a criticism of those that have preceded it. My apology for presenting this new English version of the Nibelungenlied is that none of those hitherto made has reproduced the metrical form of the original. In the hope of making the outlines of the poem clearer for the modern reader, I have endeavored to supply in the Introduction a historical background by summing up the results of investigation into its origin and growth. The translation itself was begun many years ago, when I studied the original under Zarncke in Leipzig.

G.H.N.
University College, Toronto, September, 1904.

I. The Nibelungen Saga

1. Origin of the Saga

All the Aryan peoples have had their heroic age, the achievements of which form the basis of later saga. For the Germans this was the period of the Migrations, as it is called, in round numbers the two hundred years from 400 to 600, at the close of which we find them settled in those regions which they have, generally speaking, occupied ever since. During these two centuries kaleidoscopic changes had been taking place in the position of the various Germanic tribes. Impelled partly by a native love of wandering, partly by the pressure of hostile peoples of other race, they moved with astonishing rapidity hither and thither over the face of Europe, generally in conflict with one another or buffeted by the Romans in the west and south, and by the Huns in the east. In this stern struggle for existence and search for a permanent place of settlement some of them even perished utterly; amid the changing fortunes of all of them deeds were performed that fixed themselves in the memory of the whole people, great victories or great disasters became the subject of story and song. We need only to recall such names as those of Ermanric and Theodoric to remind ourselves what an important part was played by the Germanic peoples of that Migration Period in the history of Europe. During it a national consciousness was engendered, and in it we have the faint beginnings of a national literature. Germanic saga rests almost entirely upon the events of these two centuries, the fifth and sixth. Although we get glimpses of the Germans during the four or five preceding centuries, none of the historic characters of those earlier times have been preserved in the national sagas.

With these sagas based on history, however, have been mingled in most cases primeval Germanic myths, possessions of the people from prehistoric times. A most conspicuous example of this union of mythical and originally historical elements is the Nibelungen saga, out of which grew in course of time the great national epic, the Nibelungenlied.

The Nibelungen saga is made up of two parts, on the one hand the mythical story of Siegfried and on the other the story, founded on historic fact, of the Burgundians. When and how the Siegfried myth arose it is impossible to say; its origin takes us back into the impenetrable mists of the unrecorded life of our Germanic forefathers, and its form was molded by the popular poetic spirit. The other part of the saga is based upon the historic incident of the overthrow of the Burgundian kingdom by the Huns in the year 437. This annihilation of a whole tribe naturally impressed itself vividly upon the imagination of contemporaries. Then the fact of history soon began to pass over into the realm of legend, and, from causes which can no longer be determined, this tradition of the vanished Burgundians became united with the mythical story of Siegfried. This composite Siegfried-Burgundian saga then became a common possession of the Germanic peoples, was borne with many of them to lands far distant from the place of its origin, and was further molded by each according to its peculiar genius and surroundings. In the Icelandic Eddas, the oldest of which we have as they were written down in the latter part of the ninth century, are preserved the earliest records of the form it had taken among the northern Germanic peoples. Our Nibelungenlied, which is the chief source of our knowledge of the story as it developed in Germany, dates from about the year 1200. These two versions, the Northern and the German, though originating in this common source, had diverged very widely in the centuries that elapsed between their beginning and the time when the manuscripts were written in which they are preserved. Each curtailed, re-arranged, or enlarged the incidents of the story in its own way. The character of the chief actors and the motives underlying what we may call the dramatic development assumed widely dissimilar forms. The German Nibelungenlied may be read and appreciated as one of the world's great epic poems without an acquaintance on the part of the reader with the Northern version of the saga. In order, however, to furnish the setting for a few episodes that would in that case remain either obscure or colorless, and with a view to placing the readers of this translation in a position to judge better the deeper significance of the epic as the eloquent narrative of a thousand years of the life of the people among whom it grew, the broad outlines of the saga in its Northern form will be given here.

2. The Northern Form of the Saga

Starting at the middle of the fifth century from the territory about Worms on the Rhine where the Burgundians were overthrown, the saga soon spread from the Franks to the other Germanic peoples. We have evidence of its presence in northern Germany and Denmark. Allusions to it in the Anglo-Saxon poem, the *Wanderer*, of the seventh century and in the great Anglo-Saxon epic *Beowulf* of a short time later, show us that it had early become part of the national saga stock in England. Among the people of Norway and Iceland it took root and grew with particular vigor. Here, farthest away from its original home and least exposed to outward influences, it preserved on the whole most fully its heathen Germanic character, especially in its mythical part. By a fortunate turn of events, too, the written record of it here is of considerably earlier date than that which we have from Germany. The Eddas, as the extensive collection of early Icelandic poems is called, are the fullest record of Germanic mythology and saga that has been handed down to us, and in them the saga of Siegfried and the Nibelungen looms up prominently. The earliest of these poems date from about the year 850, and the most important of them were probably written down within a couple of centuries of that time. They are thus in part some three centuries older than the German Nibelungenlied, and on the whole, too, they preserve more of the original outlines of the saga. By bringing together the various episodes of the saga from the Eddas and the Volsung saga, a prose account of the mythical race of the Volsungs, we arrive at the following narrative.

On their wanderings through the world the three gods Odin, Hönir, and Loki come to a waterfall where an otter is devouring a fish that it has caught. Loki kills the otter with a stone, and they take off its skin. In the evening they seek a lodging at the house of Hreidmar, to whom they show the skin. Hreidmar recognizes it as that of his son, whom Loki has killed when he had taken on the form of an otter. Assisted by his sons Fafnir and Regin, Hreidmar seizes the three gods, and spares their lives only on the promise that they will fill the skin, and also cover it outwardly, with gold. Loki is sent to procure the ransom. With a net borrowed from the sea-goddess Ran he catches at the waterfall the dwarf Andvari in form of a fish and compels him to supply the required gold. Andvari tries to keep back a ring, but this also Loki takes from him, whereupon the dwarf utters a curse upon the gold and whosoever may possess it. The ransom is now paid to Hreidmar; even the ring must, on Hreidmar's demand, be given in order to complete the covering of the otter's skin. Loki tells him of the curse connected with the ownership of the gold. When Hreidmar refuses Fafnir and Regin a share in the treasure, he is killed by Fafnir, who takes possession of the hoard to the exclusion of Regin. In the form of a dragon Fafnir dwells on Gnita Heath guarding the hoard, while Regin broods revenge.

From Odin is descended King Volsung, who has a family of ten sons and one daughter. The eldest son is Sigmund, twin-born with his sister Signy. King Siggeir of Gautland sues for the hand of Signy, whom her father gives to Siggeir against her will. In the midst of King Volsung's hall stood a mighty oak tree. As the wedding-feast is being held there enters a stranger, an old man with one eye, his hat drawn down over his face and bearing in his hand a sword. This sword he thrusts to the hilt into the tree, saying that it shall belong to him who can draw it out again; after which he disappears as he had come. All the guests try their strength in vain upon the sword, but Sigmund alone is able to draw it forth. He refuses to sell it to Siggeir for all his proffered gold. Siggeir plans vengeance. He invites Volsung and his sons to Gautland, and returns home thither with his bride Signy, who before going warns her father to be upon his guard.

At the appointed time King Volsung and his sons go as invited to Gautland. In spite of Signy's repeated warning he will not flee from danger, and falls in combat with Siggeir; his ten sons are taken prisoners, and placed in stocks in the forest. For nine successive nights a she-wolf comes and devours each night one of them, till only Sigmund remains. By the aid of Signy he escapes. The she-wolf, it was said, was the mother of Siggeir.

To Sigmund, who has hidden in a wood, Signy sends her eldest boy of ten years that Sigmund may test his courage and see if he is fit to be a helper in seeking revenge. Neither he, however, nor his younger brother stands the test. Signy sees that only a scion of the race of Volsung will suffice, and accordingly disguises herself and lives three days with Sigmund in the wood. From their union a son Sinfiotli is born, whom also, after ten years, she sends out to Sigmund. He stands every test of courage, and is trained by Sigmund, who thinks he is Siggeir's son.

Bent on revenge, Sigmund repairs with Sinfiotli to Siggeir's castle. After Sinfiotli has slain the king's two sons, he and Sigmund are overpowered and condemned to be buried alive. With Sigmund's sword, however, which Signy has managed to place in their hands, they cut their way out, then set fire to Siggeir's hall. Signy comes forth and reveals to Sigmund that Sinfiotli is their own son; and then, saying that her work of revenge is complete and that she can live no longer, she returns into the burning hall and perishes with Siggeir and all his race.

Sigmund now returns home and rules as a mighty king. He marries Borghild, who later kills Sinfiotli with a poisoned drink, and is cast away by Sigmund. He then marries Hjordis. Lyngvi, the son of King Hunding, was also a suitor and now invades Sigmund's land. The latter hews down many of his enemies, until an old man with one eye, in hat and dark cloak, interposes his spear, against which Sigmund's sword breaks in two. Sigmund falls severely wounded.

In the night Hjordis seeks the scene of the combat and finds Sigmund still alive. He refuses to allow her to heal his wounds, saying that Odin no longer wills that he swing the sword. He tells Hjordis to preserve carefully the pieces of the broken sword; the son she bears in her womb shall yet swing the sword when welded anew, and win thereby a glorious name. At dawn Sigmund dies. Hjordis is borne off by Vikings and, after the birth of her son, she becomes the wife of the Danish prince Alf.

The son of Hjordis was called Sigurd. He grew up a boy of wondrous strength and beauty, with eyes that sparkled brightly, and lived at the court of King Hjalprek, the father of Alf. Regin, the dwarfish brother of Fafnir, was his tutor. Regin welds together the pieces of the broken sword Gram, so sharp and strong that with it Sigurd cleaves Regin's anvil in twain. With men and ships that he has received from King Hjalprek Sigurd goes against the sons of Hunding, whom he slays, thereby avenging the death of his father. Regin has urged him to kill Fafnir and take possession of the hoard. On the Gnita Heath he digs a ditch from which, as the dragon Fafnir passes over it, he plunges the sword into his heart. The dying Fafnir warns him of the curse attached to the possession of the gold; also that Regin is to be guarded against. The latter bids him roast the heart of Fafnir. While doing so he burns his finger by dipping it in the blood to see if the heart is done, and to cool his finger puts it into his mouth. Suddenly he is able to understand the language of the birds in the wood. They warn him to beware of Regin, whom he straightway slays. The birds tell him further of the beautiful valkyrie Brynhild, who sleeps on the fire-encircled mountain awaiting her deliverer. Then Sigurd places Fafnir's hoard upon his steed Grani, takes with him also Fafnir's helm, and rides away to Frankenland. He sees a mountain encircled by a zone of fire, makes his way into it and beholds there, as he deems it, a man in full armor asleep. When he takes off the helmet he finds that it is a woman. With his sword he cuts loose the armor. The woman wakes and asks if it be the hero Sigurd who has awakened her. In joy that it is so, Brynhild relates to him how Odin had punished her by this magic sleep for disobedience, and how that she had yet obtained from him the promise that she should be wakened only by a hero who knew no fear. She now teaches Sigurd many wise runes, and tells him of harm to fear through love of her. In spite of all, however, Sigurd does not waver, and they swear an oath of mutual faithful love.

Next Sigurd comes to King Gjuki at the Rhine, and joins in friendship with him and his sons Gunnar and Hogni. Queen Grimhild gives Sigurd a potion which causes him to forget Brynhild and be filled with love for her own daughter Gudrun, whom he marries. Gunnar now seeks Brynhild for wife, and Sigurd goes with him on his wooing-journey. They come to the castle encircled by fire, where Brynhild lives. She will be wooed only by him who will ride to her through the flames. Gunnar tries in vain to do this, even when mounted on Sigurd's steed Grani. Sigurd and Gunnar then exchange shapes and the former spurs Grani through the flames. He calls himself Gunnar the son of Gjuki, and finally Brynhild consents to become his wife. Three nights he shares her couch, but always his sharp sword lies between them. He takes the ring from her finger and places in its stead one from Fafnir's treasure. Then he exchanges form again with Gunnar, who is soon after wedded to Brynhild. Only now does Sigurd recollect the oath that he once swore to Brynhild himself.

One day Brynhild and Gudrun are bathing in the Rhine. A quarrel arises between them when Brynhild takes precedence of Gudrun by going into the water above her in the stream, saying that her husband is a braver and mightier man than Gudrun's. Gudrun retorts by revealing the secret that it was Sigurd in Gunnar's form, and not Gunnar himself, who rode through the flame, and in proof thereof shows her the ring taken by Sigurd from Brynhild's finger. Pale as death, Brynhild goes quietly home: Gunnar must die, she says in wrath. Sigurd tries to pacify her, even offering to desert Gudrun. Now she will have neither him nor another, and when Gunnar appears she demands of him Sigurd's death. In spite of Hogni's protest Gunnar's stepbrother Gutthorm, who has not sworn blood-friendship with Sigurd, is got to do the deed. He is given the flesh of wolf and serpent to eat in order to make him savage. Twice Gutthorm goes to kill Sigurd, but cowers before the piercing glance of his eyes; at last he steals upon Sigurd asleep and thrusts his sword through him. The dying Sigurd hurls the sword after the fleeing murderer and cuts him in two. To Gudrun, who wakes from sleep by his side, he points to Brynhild as the instigator of the crime, and dies. Brynhild rejoices at the sound of Gudrun's wailing. Gudrun cannot find relief for her grief, the tears will not flow. Men and women seek to console her by tales of greater woes befallen them. But still Gudrun cannot weep as she sits by Sigurd's corpse. At last one of the women lifts the cloth from Sigurd's face and lays his head upon Gudrun's lap. Then Gudrun gazes on his blood-besmirched hair, his dimmed eyes, and breast pierced by the sword: she sinks down upon the couch and a flood of tears bursts at length from her eyes.

Brynhild now tells Gunnar that Sigurd had really kept faith with him on the wooing journey; but she will live with him no longer and pierces herself with a sword, after foretelling to Gunnar his future fate and that of Gudrun. In accord with her own request she is burned on one funeral-pyre with Sigurd, the sword between them as once before.

Atli,* king of the Huns, now seeks Gudrun for wife. She refuses, but Grimhild gives her a potion which causes her to forget Sigurd and the past, and then she becomes the wife of Atli. After Sigurd's death Gunnar had taken possession of the Niflungen hoard, and this Atli now covets. He treacherously invites Gunnar and the others to visit him, which they do in spite of Gudrun's warnings, first of all, however, sinking the hoard in the Rhine. On their arrival Atli demands of them the hoard, which, he says, belongs of right to Gudrun. On their refusal he attacks them. Hosts of fighters on both sides fall and in the end Gunnar and Hogni, the only two of their number remaining, are bound in fetters. Gunnar refuses Atli's command to reveal the hiding place of the hoard, bidding them bring to him the heart of Hogni. They kill a servant and bring his heart to Gunnar; but Gunnar sees how it still quivers with fear, and knows it is not the heart of the fearless Hogni. Then the latter is really killed, and his heart is brought to Gunnar, who cries exultingly that now only the Rhine knows where the hoard lies hidden. In spite of Gudrun Atli orders that Gunnar be thrown into a den of serpents. With a harp communicated to him by Gudrun he pacifies them all but one, which stings him to the heart, and thus Gunnar dies. Gudrun is nominally reconciled with Atli, but in secret plans revenge for the death of her brothers. She kills Atli's two sons, gives him at a banquet their blood to drink and their hearts to eat. In the night she plunges a sword into his own heart, confesses herself to him as his murderer, and sets fire to the castle, in which Atli and all his remaining men are consumed.

---

* That is, Attila; the Etzel of the Nibelungenlied.

3. *The Saga as Preserved in the Nibelungenlied*

*T*he saga as we find it in the German Nibelungenlied differs very
widely in form and substance from the Northern version which has just
been outlined, though the two have still enough points of similarity to
indicate clearly a common origin. Each bears the stamp of the poetic
genius of the people among whom it grew. Of all the sagas of the
Germanic peoples none holds so prominent a place as the Nibelungen
saga, and it may safely be said that the epic literature of the world,
though offering poems of more refined literary worth, has none that
are at the same time such valuable records of the growth of the poetic
genius of two kindred peoples through many centuries of their early
civilization as the Edda poems of this saga and the Nibelungenlied. It
is impossible here to undertake a comparison of the two and point out
in detail their parallelism and their respective significance as monu-
ments of civilization; suffice it to indicate briefly the chief points of
difference in the two stories, and note particularly those parts of the
Nibelungenlied that have, as it were, suffered atrophy, and that point
to earlier stages of the saga in which, as in the Northern version, they
played a more important rôle.

First, as to the hoard. The Nibelungenlied knows nothing of its being
taken by Loki from Andvari, of the latter's curse upon it, and how it
came finally into the possession of Fafnir, the giant-dragon. Here it
belongs, as we learn from Hagen's account (strophes 86–99), to Siegfried
(Sigurd), who has slain the previous owners of it, Schilbung and
Nibelung, and wrested it from its guardian the dwarf Alberich (Andvari).
From this point onward its history runs nearly parallel in the two
versions. After Siegfried's death it remains for a time with Kriemhild
(Gudrun), is treacherously taken from her by Gunther (Gunnar) and
Hagen (Hogni), and finally, before their journey to Etzel (Atli), sunk in
the Rhine.

The protracted narrative of Sigurd's ancestry and his descent from
Odin has no counterpart in the Nibelungenlied. Here we learn merely
that Siegfried is the son of Siegmund. His father plays an entirely
different part; and his mother's name is not Hjordis, as in the Edda,
but Siegelind.

Of Siegfried's youth the Nibelungenlied knows very little. No men-
tion is made of his tutelage to the dwarf smith Regin and preparation

for the slaying of the dragon Fafnir. The account of him placed in the mouth of Hagen (strophes 86–501), how he won the hoard, the *tarnkappe,* and the sword Balmung, and slew the dragon, is evidently a faint echo of an earlier version of this episode, which sounds out of place in the more modern German form of the story. From the latter the mythical element has almost entirely vanished. It is worthy of note, moreover, that the very brief account of Siegfried's slaying of the dragon is given in the Nibelungenlied as separate from his acquisition of the hoard, and differs in detail from that of the Edda. Of Sigurd's steed Grani, his ride to Frankenland, and his awakening of Brynhild the Nibelungenlied has nothing to tell us. Through the account of Siegfried's assistance to Gunther in the latter's wooing of Brunhild (Adventures 6 and 7) shimmers faintly, however, the earlier tradition of the mythical Siegfried's awakening of the fire-encircled valkyrie. Only by our knowledge of a more original version can we explain, for example, Siegfried's previous acquaintance with Brunhild which the Nibelungenlied takes for granted but says nothing of. On this point of the relation between Sigurd and Brynhild it is difficult to form a clear account owing to the confusion and even contradictions that exist when the various Northern versions themselves are placed side by side. The name of the valkyrie whom Sigurd awakens from her magic sleep is not directly mentioned. Some of the accounts are based on the presupposition that she is one with the Brynhild whom Sigurd later woos for Gunnar, while others either know nothing of the sleeping valkyrie or treat the two as separate personages. The situation in the Nibelungenlied is more satisfactorily explained by the theory that they were originally identical. But we see at once that the figure of Brunhild has here lost much of its original significance. It is her quarrel with Kriemhild (Gudrun) that leads to Siegfried's death, though the motives are not just the same in the two cases; and after the death of Siegfried she passes unaccountably from the scene.

But it is in the concluding part of the story — the part which, as we shall see, has its basis in actual history — that the two accounts diverge most widely. So strange, indeed, has been the evolution of the saga that the central character of it, Kriemhild (Gudrun) holds a diametrically opposite relation to her husband Etzel (Atli) at the final catastrophe in the two versions. In the Nibelungenlied as in the Edda the widowed Kriemhild (Gudrun) marries King Etzel (Atli), her consent in the former resulting from a desire for revenge upon the murderers of Siegfried, in the latter from the drinking of a potion which takes away her memory of him; in the Nibelungenlied it is Kriemhild who treacherously lures Gunther and his men to their destruction unknown to Etzel, in the

Edda the invitation comes from Atli, while Gudrun tries to warn them to stay at home; in the former Kriemhild is the author of the attack on the guests, in the latter Atli; in the former Kriemhild is the frenzied avenger of her former husband Siegfried's death upon her brother Gunther, in the latter Gudrun is the avenger of her brothers' death upon her husband Atli.

4. Mythical Element and Historical Element

A sifting of the Nibelungen saga reveals a mythical element (the story of Siegfried) and a historical element (the story of the Burgundians and Etzel). How, when, and where these two elements were blended together must remain largely a matter of conjecture. This united central body received then from time to time accessions of other elements, some of them originally historical in character, some of them pure inventions of the poetic imagination.

The Siegfried myth is the oldest portion of the Nibelungen saga, and had already passed through a long period of development before its union with the story of the Burgundian kings. Like so many others of its kind, it is part of the spiritual equipment of our Germanic ancestors at the dawn of their recorded history. It grew gradually with the people themselves and has its counterpart among other peoples. Such myths are a record of the impressions made upon the mind of man by the mighty manifestations of the world of nature in which he lives; their formation may be likened to the unconscious impressions of its surroundings on the mind of the child. And just as the grown man is unable to trace back the formation of his own individuality to its very beginnings in infancy, so is it impossible for the later nation in its advanced stage to peer back beyond the dawn of its history. It is in the gloom beyond the dawn that such myths as this of Siegfried have their origin.

Though modern authorities differ greatly in their conjectures, it is generally agreed that the Siegfried story was in its original form a nature-myth. The young day slays the mist-dragon and awakens the sun-maiden that sleeps on the mountain; at evening he falls a prey to the powers of gloom that draw the sun down again beneath the earth. With this day-myth was probably combined the parallel myth of the changing seasons: the light returns in spring, slays the cloud-dragon, and frees the budding earth from the bonds of winter.*

In the course of time this nature-myth became transformed into a hero-saga; the liberating power of light was humanized into the person of the light-hero Siegfried. This stage of development had already been reached at the time of our earliest records, and the evidences point to the Rhine Franks, a West Germanic tribe settled in the fifth century in the country about Cologne, as the people among whom the transformation from nature-myth to hero-saga took place, for it is among them that the saga in its earliest form is localized. By the Rhine Siegfried is born, there he wins the Nibelungen hoard, and in Frankenland he finds the sleeping valkyrie. By the Rhine, too, he enters into service with the Nibelungen kings and weds their sister.

The Franks had as neighbors up-stream in the first half of the fifth century the Burgundians, an East Germanic tribe. These Burgundians, who were closely allied to the Goths, had originally dwelt in the Baltic region between the Vistula and the Oder, whence they had made their way southwestward across Germany and settled in the year 413 in *Germania prima* on the west bank of the Rhine about Worms. Here a tragic fate was soon to overtake them. In the year 435 they had already suffered a reverse in a conflict with the Romans under Aëtius, and two years later, in 437, they were practically annihilated by the Huns. Twenty thousand of them, we are told, fell in battle, the remainder were scattered southward. Beyond the brief record by a contemporary, Prosper, we know but little of this event. It has been conjectured that the Huns were on this occasion acting as auxiliaries of Aëtius. At any rate it is fairly certain that Attila was not personally on the scene.

We can easily imagine what a profound impression this extinction of the Burgundians would produce upon the minds of their neighbors the Rhine Franks. Fact, too, would soon become mingled with fiction. This new feat was ascribed to Attila himself, already too well known as the scourge of Europe and the subduer of so many German tribes. A very few years later, however, fate was to subdue the mighty conqueror himself. With the great battle of Châlons in 451 the tide turned against him, and two years afterwards he died a mysterious death. The historian Jordanes of the sixth century relates that on the morning after Attila's wedding with a German princess named Ildico (Hildikô) he was found lying in bed in a pool of blood, having died of a hemorrhage. The mysteriousness of Attila's ending inspired his contemporaries with awe, and the popular fancy was not slow to clothe this event also in a dress of fiction. The attendant circumstances peculiarly favored such a proc-

---

* For the Siegfried saga in general see Symons in Paul's Grundriss der german-ischen Philologie, 2d ed., vol. III, pp. 651–671.

ess. Historians soon recorded the belief that Attila had perished at the hands of his wife, and it was only a step further for the imagination to find the motive for the deed in the desire of Hildikô to avenge the death of her German kinsmen who had perished through Attila. The saga of Attila's death is before long connected with the growing Burgundian saga, Hildikô becomes the sister of the Burgundian kings Gundahari, Godomar, and Gislahari, and her deed is vengeance taken upon Attila for his destruction of her brothers. As is seen at once from the outline I have already given (*Chapter 2.*) of the saga as we find it in the Edda, this is the stage of development it had reached when it began to find its way northward from the Rhine country to Norway and Iceland.

It is unnecessary here to record the speculations — for beyond speculations we cannot go — as to how the union of this historical saga of the Burgundians and Attila with the Siegfried saga took place. In the course of time, and naturally with greatest probability among the Rhine Franks who followed the Burgundians as occupants of *Germania prima,* the two were brought together, and the three Burgundian kings and their sister were identified with the three Nibelungen kings and their sister of the already localized Siegfried saga. It is also beyond the scope of this introduction to follow the course of the saga northward or to note its further evolution during its wanderings and in its new home until it was finally recorded in poetic form in the Edda. We have now to consider briefly the transformation it passed through in Germany between this date (about 500) and the time (about 1200) when it emerges in written record as the Nibelungenlied.

An account has already been given (*Chapter 3.*) of the chief features in which the Nibelungenlied differs from the Northern form. As we saw there, the mythical element of the Siegfried saga has almost entirely evaporated and the historical saga of the Burgundian kings and Attila has undergone a complete transformation. That the originally mythical and heathen Siegfried saga should dwindle away with the progress of civilization and under the influence of Christianity was but natural. The character of the valkyrie Brynhild who avenges upon Sigurd his infidelity to her, yet voluntarily unites herself with him in death, as heathen custom demanded, is no longer intelligible. She recedes into the background, and after Siegfried's death, though she is still living, she plays no further part. The Nibelungenlied found its final form on Upper German, doubtless Austrian, territory. Here alone was it possible that that greatest of all transformations could take place, namely, in the character of Attila. The Franks of the Rhine knew him only as the awe-inspiring conqueror who had annihilated their neighbors the Burgundians. In Austrian lands it was quite otherwise. Many Germanic tribes, particularly the East Goths, had fought under the banner of Attila, and in the tradition handed down from them he lived as the embodiment of wisdom and generosity. Here it was impossible that epic story should picture him as slaying the Burgundian kings through a covetous desire for their gold. The annihilation of the Burgundians is thus left without a motive. To supply this, Kriemhild's character is placed upon an entirely different basis. Instead of avenging upon Attila the death of her brothers the Burgundian kings, Kriemhild now avenges upon her brothers the slaying of her first husband Siegfried. This fundamental change in the character of Kriemhild has a deep ethical reason. To the ancient heathen Germans the tie of blood-relationship was stronger than that of wedlock, and thus in the original version of the story Attila's wife avenges upon him the death of her *brothers*; to the Christianized Germans of later times the marriage bond was the stronger, and accordingly from the altered motive Kriemhild avenges upon her brothers the slaying of her *husband.* In accordance, too, with this ethical transformation the scene of the catastrophe is transferred from Worms to Attila's court. Kriemhild now looms up as the central figure of the second half of the drama, while Etzel remains to the last ignorant of her designs for revenge.

This transformation of the fundamental parts of the saga was accompanied by another process, namely, the addition of new characters. Some of these are the product of the poetic faculty of the people or individuals who preserved and remolded the story in the course of centuries, others are based upon history. To the former class belong the Margrave Ruediger, the ideal of gentle chivalry, and Volker the Fiddler-knight, doubtless a creation of the *spielleute.* To the second class belong Dietrich of Bern, in whom we see the mighty East Gothic king, Theodoric of Verona; also Bishop Pilgrim of Passau, a very late importation, besides several others in whom are perpetuated in more or less faint outline actual persons of history. This introduction of fresh characters from time to time as the saga grew has led to some strange anachronisms, which however are a disturbing element only to us readers of a modern day, who with sacrilegious hand lift the veil through which they were seen in a uniform haze of romance by the eye of the knights and ladies of seven centuries ago. *They* neither knew nor cared to know, for instance, that Attila was dead before Theodoric was born, and that Bishop Pilgrim flourished at Passau the trifling space of five hundred years later still.*

---

* Attila lived from about 406 to 453; Theodoric, 475 to 526. Pilgrim was Bishop of Passau, 971 to 991.

II. The Nibelungenlied

1. The Manuscripts

Among the German epic poems of the Middle Ages the Nibelungenlied* enjoyed an exceptional popularity, as is evident from the large number of manuscripts — some thirty, either complete or fragmentary — that have been preserved from the centuries immediately following its appearance. Three are of prime importance as texts, namely, those preserved now in Munich, St. Gall, and Donaueschingen, and cited as A, B, and C respectively. Since the time when Lachmann, about a century ago, made the first scientific study of the poem, a whole flood of writings has been poured forth discussing the relative merits of these texts. Each in turn has had its claims advocated with warmth and even acrimony. None of these three principal manuscripts, however, offers the poem in its earliest form; they all point to a still earlier version. It is now generally admitted that the St. Gall manuscript (B), according to which the present translation has been made, contains the best and most nearly original text.

---

* The closing strophe of MS. C calls the poem der *Nibelunge liet*, or Nibelungenlied, i.e. the lay of the Nibelungen, and this is the title by which it is commonly known. MSS. A and B have in the corresponding strophe *der Nibelunge nôt*, i.e. the 'need', 'distress', 'downfall' of the Nibelungen. In the title of the poem 'Nibelungen' is simply equivalent to 'Burgundians': the poem relates the downfall of the Burgundian kings and their people. Originally the Nibelungen were, as their name, which is connected with *nebel*, 'mist', 'gloom', signifies, the powers of darkness to whom the light-hero Siegfried fell a prey. After Siegfried obtains possession of the treasure the name Nibelungen is still applied to Alberich and the dwarfs who guard it and who are now Siegfried's vassals. Then after Siegfried's death the name is given to the Burgundians. It is a mistake to suppose that the name was applied in each case to those who became possessors of the hoard, for Siegfried himself is never so designated.

2. Stages in the Evolution of the Poem

Hand in hand with the discussion of the relative authenticity of the manuscripts went the consideration of another more important literary question, — the evolution of the poem itself. Even if we knew nothing of the history of the Nibelungen saga as revealed in the Edda and through other literary and historic sources, a reading of the poem would give us unmistakable hints that it is not, in its present form, a perfect literary unit. We detect inconsistencies in matter and inequalities of style that prove it to be a remodeling of material already existing in some earlier form. What, then, has been the history of its evolution? How did this primeval Siegfried myth, this historical saga of the Burgundians and Attila, first come to be part of the poetic stock of the German people? What was its earliest poetic form, and what series of transformations did it pass through during seven centuries of growth? These and many kindred questions present themselves, and the search for answers to them takes us through many winding labyrinths of the nation's contemporary history. Few products of German literature have so exercised and tantalized critics as the Nibelungenlied.

In this connection we have to remind ourselves that comparatively little of what must have been the large body of native poetry in Germany previous to the eleventh century has come down to us. Barely enough has been preserved to show the path of the nation's literary progress. Some of the important monuments have been saved by chance, while others of equal or perhaps greater value have been irrecoverably lost. The interest in the various incidents of the Nibelungen story was sufficient to keep it alive among the people and hand it down orally through many generations. If we could observe it as it passed from age to age we should doubtless see it undergoing continuous change according to the time and the class of the people that were the preservers of the native literature in its many ups and downs. Lachmann in the year 1816 was the first to bring scientific criticism to bear on the question of the Nibelungenlied and its origin. Applying to it the same methods as had recently been used by Wolf in his criticism of the Homeric poems, he thought he was able to discover as the basis of the complete epic a cycle of twenty separate *lieder*, ballads or shorter episodic poems, on the strength of which belief he went so far as to publish an edition of the poem in which he made the division into the twenty separate lays and eliminated those strophes (more than one third of the whole number) that he deemed not genuine. It is now generally admitted, however, that the pioneer of Nibelungen investigation fell here into overpositive refinements of literary criticism. Separate shorter poems there doubtless existed narrating separate episodes of the story, but these are no longer to be arrived at by a process of critical disintegration and pruning of the epic as we have it. An examination of the twenty *lieder* according to Lachmann's division convinces us that they are not separate units in the sense he conceived them to be. Though these twenty *lieder* may be based upon a number of earlier episodic poems, yet the latter already constituted a connected series. They were already like so many scenes of a gradually developing drama. Events were foreshadowed in one that were only fulfilled in another, and the incidents of later ones are often only intelligible on the supposition of an acquaintance with motives that originated in preceding ones. It is in this sense only, not according to Lachmann's overwrought theory, that we are justified in speaking of a *liedercyclus,* or cycle of separate episodic poems, as the stage of the epic antecedent to the complete form in which we now have it. But beyond this cycle we cannot trace it back. How the mythical saga of Siegfried and the Nibelungen, and the story of the Burgundians and Attila, were first sung in alliterative lays in the Migration Period, how as heathen song they were pushed aside or slowly influenced by the spirit of Christianity, how with changing time they changed also their outward poetical garb from alliteration to rhyme and altered verse-form, till at last in the twelfth century they have become the cycle of poems from which the great epic of the Nibelungenlied could be constructed — of all this we may form a faint picture from the development of the literature in general, but direct written record of it is almost completely wanting.

3. *Character of the Poem*

T he twelfth and thirteenth centuries witnessed far-reaching changes in the social and intellectual life of the German lands, the leading feature of which is the high development of all that is included under the name of chivalry. It is marked, too, by a revival of the native literature such as had not been known before, a revival which is due almost entirely to its cultivation by the nobility. From emperor down to the simple knight they were patrons of poetry and, what is most striking, nearly all the poets themselves belong to the knightly class. The drama has not yet begun, but in the field of epic and lyric there appear about the year 1200 poets who are among the greatest that German literature even down to the present time has to show. The epic poetry of that period, though written almost entirely by the knights, is of two distinct kinds according to its subject: on the one hand what is called the Court Epic, on the other hand the National, or Popular, Epic. The Court Epic follows for the most part French models and deals chiefly with the life of chivalry, whose ideals were embodied in king Arthur and his circle of knights; the National Epic drew its subjects from the national German saga, its two great products being the Nibelungenlied and the poem of Gudrun. Court Epic and National Epic are further distinct in form, the Court Epic being written in the rhymed couplets popularized in modern times in English by Sir Walter Scott, while the National Epic is composed in four-lined strophes.

Though we know the name and more or less of the life of the authors of the many court epics of the period, the name of the poet who gave the Nibelungenlied its final form has not been recorded. As we have seen, the poem is at bottom of a truly popular, national character, having its beginnings in mythology and early national history. For centuries the subject had been national property and connected with the name of no one individual. We have it now in the form in which it was remodeled to suit the taste of the court and the nobility, and like the court epic to be read aloud in castle hall. That it is written in four-lined strophes* and not in the usual rhymed couplets of the court epics is doubtless due to the fact that the former verse-form had already been used in the earlier ballads upon which it is based, and was simply taken over by the final molder of the poem. This latter was probably a member of the nobility like the great majority of the epic poets of the time; he must at least have been well acquainted with the manners, tastes, sentiments, and general life of the nobility. Through him the poem was brought outwardly more into line with the literary ideals of the court circles. This shows itself chiefly in a negative way, namely, in the almost complete avoidance of the coarse language and farcical situations so common with the popular poet, the *spielmann.* Beyond this no violence is done to the simple form of the original. The style is still inornate and direct, facts still speak rather than words, and there is nothing approaching the refined psychological dissection of characters and motives such as we find in Wolfram von Eschenbach and the other court writers.

---

* For description of the Nibelungen strophe see below, *Chapter 7.*

When we look to the inner substance we see that the ground ideals are still those of the original Germanic heroic age. The chief characters are still those of the first stages of the story — Siegfried, Brunhild, Gunther, Kriemhild, Hagen. The fundamental theme is the ancient theme of *triuwe,* unswerving personal loyalty and devotion, which manifests itself above all in the characters of Kriemhild and Hagen. Kriemhild's husband Siegfried is treacherously slain: her sorrow and revenge are the motives of the drama. Hagen's mistress has, though with no evil intent on Siegfried's part, received an insult to her honor: to avenge that insult is Hagen's absorbing duty, which he fulfils with an utter disregard of consequences. Over this their fundamental character the various persons of the story have received a gloss of outward conduct in keeping with the close of the twelfth century. The poet is at pains to picture them as models of courtly bearing, excelling in *höfscheit, zuht, tugent.* Great attention is paid to dress, and the preparation of fitting apparel for court festivities is described and re-described with wearisome prolixity. A cardinal virtue is *milte,* liberality in the bestowal of gifts. Courtesy toward women is observed with the careful formality of the age of the minnesingers. It was above all Siegfried, the light-hero of the original myth, whose character lent itself to an idealization of knighthood. Ruediger holds a like place in the latter part of the poem. In the evident pleasure with which the minstrel-knight Volker of the sword-fiddlebow is depicted, as well doubtless as in occasional gleams of broader humor, the hand of the minstrels who wrought on the story in its earlier ballad stages may be seen. And the whole poem, in keeping with its form in an age strongly under church influence, has been tinged with the ideals of Christianity. Not only does the ordinary conversation of all the characters, including even the heathen Etzel, contain a great number of formal imprecations of God, but Christian institutions and Christian ethics come frequently into play. Mass is sung in the minster, baptism, marriage, burial are celebrated in Christian fashion, the devil is mentioned according to the Christian conception, we hear of priest, chaplain, and bishop, Christians are contrasted with heathen, and Kriemhild, in marrying Etzel, has a hope of turning him to Christianity. In Hagen's attempt to drown the chaplain whom the Burgundians have with them as they set out for the land of the Huns we have perhaps an expression of the conflict between the heathen and the Christian elements, possibly also a reflection of the traditional animosity of the *spielmann* to his clerical rival.

The Nibelungenlied and the Iliad of Homer have often been compared, but after all to no great purpose. The two epics are alike in having their roots deep in national origins, but beyond this we have contrasts rather than resemblances. The Iliad is a more varied and complete picture of the whole Greek world than the Nibelungenlied is of the German, its religious atmosphere has not been disturbed in the same way as that of the saga of early Germanic times projected several centuries into a later Christian age, and it possesses in every way a greater unity of sentiment. In the varied beauty of its language, its wealth of imagery, its depth of feeling and copiousness of incident the Iliad is superior to the Nibelungenlied with its language of simple directness, its few lyrical passages, its expression of feeling by deeds rather than by words. Homer, too, is in general buoyant, the Nibelungenlied is somber and stern. And in one last respect the two epics differ most of all: the Iliad is essentially narrative and descriptive, a series of episodes; the Nibelungenlied is essentially dramatic, scene following scene of dramatic necessity and pointing steadily to a final and inevitable catastrophe.

4. Later Forms of the Saga

In the Northern Edda and in the German Nibelungenlied the Nibelungen saga found its fullest and most poetic expression. But these were not to be the only literary records of it. Both in Scandinavian lands and in Germany various other monuments, scattered over the intervening centuries, bear witness to the fact that it lived on in more or less divergent forms. The Danish historian Saxo Grammaticus of the latter part of the twelfth century has a reference to the story of Kriemhild's treachery toward her brothers. About the year 1250 an extensive prose narrative, known as the Thidrekssaga, was written by a Norwegian from oral accounts given him by men from Bremen and Münster. This narrative is interesting as showing the form the saga had taken by that date on Low German territory, and holds an important place in the history of the development of the saga. It has much more to say of the early history of Siegfried than we find in the Nibelungenlied, and yet in the main outlines of the story of Kriemhild's revenge it corresponds with the German epic and not with the Northern Edda. A chronicle of the island of Hven in the Sound, dating in its original form from the sixteenth century, as well as Danish ballads on the same island that have lived on into modern times, tell of Sivard (Siegfried), Brynhild, and also of Grimild's (Kriemhild's) revenge. In Norway and Sweden traces of the saga have recently been discovered; while songs that are sung on the Faroe Islands, as an accompaniment to the dance on festive occasions, have been recorded, containing over six hundred strophes in which is related in more or less distorted form the Nibelungen story.

In Germany the two poems known as the *Klage* and *Hürnen Seyfrid* are the most noteworthy additional records of the Nibelungen saga, as offering in part at least independent material. The *Klage* is a poem of over four thousand lines in rhymed couplets, about half of it being an account of the mourning of Etzel, Dietrich, and Hildebrand as they seek out the slain and prepare them for burial, the other half telling of the bringing of the news to Bechlaren, Passau, and Worms. The poem was written evidently very soon after the Nibelungenlied, the substance of which was familiar to the author, though he also draws in part from other sources. Compared with the Nibelungenlied it possesses but little poetic merit and is written with distinctly Christian sentiment which is out of harmony with the ground-tone of the Germanic tragedy.

The *Hürnen Seyfrid* is a poem of 179 four-lined strophes which is preserved only in a print of the sixteenth century, but at least a portion of whose substance reaches back in its original form to a period preceding the composition of the Nibelungenlied. It is evidently, as we have it, formed by the union of two earlier separate poems, which are indeed to a certain extent contradictory of each other. The first tells of the boyhood of Seyfrid (Siegfried) and his apprenticeship to the smith; how he slew many dragons, burned them, and smeared over his body with the resulting fluid horny substance (hence his name *hürnen*), which made him invulnerable; how he further found the hoard of the dwarf Nybling, and by service to King Gybich won the latter's daughter for his wife. The second part tells how King Gybich reigned at Worms. He has three sons, Günther, Hagen, Gyrnot, and one daughter, Kriemhild. The latter is borne off by a dragon, but finally rescued by Seyfrid, to whom she is given in marriage. The three brothers are jealous of the might and fame of Seyfrid, and after eight years Hagen slays him beside a cool spring in the Ottenwald.

The poem *Biterolf,* written soon after the Nibelungenlied, and *Rosengarten* of perhaps a half-century later, represent Dietrich in conflict with Siegfried at Worms. The famous shoemaker-poet Hans Sachs of Nuremberg in 1557 constructed a tragedy, *Der hörnen Sewfriedt,* on the story of Siegfried as he knew it from the *Hürnen Seyfrid* and the *Rosengarten.* A prose version of the *Hürnen Seyfrid,* with free additions and alterations, is preserved in the *Volksbuch vom gehörnten Sigfrid,* the oldest print of which dates from the year 1726. Of the vast number of Fairy Tales, those most genuine creations of the poetic imagination of the people, in which live on, often to be sure in scarcely recognizable form, many of the myths and sagas of the nation's infancy, there are several that may with justice be taken as relics of the Siegfried myth, for instance, The Two Brothers, The Young Giant, The Earth-Manikin, The King of the Golden Mount, The Raven, The Skilled Huntsman, and perhaps also the Golden Bird and The Water of Life;* though it would seem from recent investigations that Thorn-Rose or the Sleeping Beauty, is no longer to be looked upon as the counterpart of the sleeping Brynhild. Finally, it is probable that several names in Germany and in Northern countries preserve localized memories of the saga.

5. Poem and Saga in Modern Literature

*F*undamentally different from the foregoing natural outgrowths of the Nibelungen saga are the modern dramas and poems founded upon it since the time of the romanticists at the beginning of the nineteenth century.† Nearly all of these have already vanished as so much chaff from the winnowing-mill of time: only two, perhaps, are now considered seriously, namely, Hebbel's *Die Nibelungen* and Richard Wagner's *Ring des Nibelungen*. Hebbel in his grandly conceived drama in three parts follows closely the story as we have it in our epic poem the Nibelungenlied, and the skill with which he makes use of its tragic elements shows his dramatic genius at its best. But not even the genius of Hebbel could make these forms of myth and saga live again for us upon a modern stage, and the failure of this work with its wealth of poetic beauty and many scenes of highest dramatic effectiveness to maintain its place as an acting drama is sufficient evidence that the yawning gap that separates the sentiment of the modern world from that of the early centuries in which these sagas grew is not to be bridged over by the drama, however easy and indeed delightful it may be for us to allow ourselves to be transported thither to that romantic land upon the wings of epic story. Wagner in his music-drama in three parts and prelude has followed in the main the saga in its Northern form‡ up to the death of

---

* These will be found in Grimm's Märchen as numbers 60, 90–93, 111, 57, and 97.

† The curious will find a list of these in the introduction to Piper's edition, cited below, *Chapter 7.*

‡ See above, *Chapter 2.*

Siegfried and Brunhild, but to the entire exclusion of the latter part of the story in which Atli (Etzel) figures; his work has accordingly hardly any connection with the Nibelungenlied here offered in translation. Only the pious loyalty of national sentiment can assign a high place in dramatic literature to Wagner's work with its intended imitation of the alliterative form of verse; while his philosophizing gods and goddesses are also but decadent modern representatives of their rugged heathen originals.

6. Modern German Translations

The language of the Nibelungenlied presents about the same difficulty to the German reader of today as that of our English Chaucer to us. Many translations into modern German have accordingly been made to render it accessible to the average reader without special study. In the year 1767 Bodmer in Zurich published a translation into hexameters of a portion of it, and since the investigations of Lachmann raised it to the position of a national epic of first magnitude many more have appeared, both in prose and verse. The best in prose is that by Scherr, of the year 1860. Of the metrical translations that by Simrock, which in its later editions follows pretty closely the text of MS. C, is deservedly the most popular and has passed through a great number of editions. Bartsch has also made a translation based on his edition of MS. B. These modern versions by Simrock and Bartsch reproduce best the metrical quality of the original strophe. Easily obtainable recent translations are those by Junghans (in Reclam's Universalbibliothek) of text C, and by Hahn (Collection Spemann) of text A.

7. English Translations*

Early in last century interest in the Nibelungenlied began to manifest

---

* For a complete list of these, also of magazine articles, etc., relating to the Nibelungenlied, see F. E. Sandbach, The *Nibelungenlied and Gudrun in England*

itself in England. A synopsis of it, with metrical translation of several strophes, appeared in the year 1814 in Weber, Jamieson and Scott's "Illustrations of Northern Antiquities" (London and Edinburgh), in which, according to Lockhart, Sir Walter Scott's hand may perhaps be seen. Carlyle, laboring as a pioneer to spread a knowledge of German literature in England, contributed to the Westminster Review in 1831 his well-known essay on the Nibelungenlied which, though containing an additional mass of rather ill-arranged matter and now antiquated in many particulars, is still well worth reading for its enthusiastic account of the epic itself in the genuine style of the author. Carlyle here reproduces in metrical form a few strophes. He has said elsewhere that one of his ambitions was to make a complete English version of the poem. Since then an endless number of accounts of it, chiefly worthless, has appeared in magazines and elsewhere. The first attempt at a complete metrical translation was made in 1848 by Jonathan Birch, who however only reproduces Lachmann's twenty *lieder*, with some fifty-one strophes added on his own account. His version of the first strophe runs thus:

Legends of by-gone times reveal wonders and prodigies,
Of heroes worthy endless fame, — of matchless braveries, —
Of jubilees and festal sports, — of tears and sorrows great, —
And knights who daring combats fought: — the like I now relate.

In 1850 appeared William Nansom Lettsom's translation of the whole poem according to Braunfels' edition, with the opening strophe turned as follows:

In stories of our fathers high marvels we are told
Of champions well approved in perils manifold.
Of feasts and merry meetings, of weeping and of wail,
And deeds of gallant daring I'll tell you in my tale.

The next metrical rendering is that by A. G. Foster-Barham in the year 1887. His first strophe reads:

Many a wondrous story have the tales of old,
Of feats of knightly glory, and of the Heroes bold,
Of the delights of feasting, of weeping and of wail,
Of noble deeds of daring; you may list strange things in my tale.

In the year 1898 follows still another, by Alice Horton (edited by E.

---

and America, London, 1903.

Bell). This latest translation is based on Bartsch's text of MS. B, and is prefaced by Carlyle's essay. First strophe:

To us, in olden legends,   is many a marvel told
Of praise-deserving heroes,   of labors manifold,
Of weeping and of wailing,   of joy and festival;
Of bold knights' battling shall you   now hear a wondrous tale.

Apart from the many faults of interpretation all of the metrical translations of the Nibelungenlied here enumerated are defective in one all-important respect: they do not reproduce the poem in its *metrical form*. Carlyle and other pioneers we may perhaps acquit of any intention of following the original closely in this regard. None of the translators of the complete poem, however, has retained in the English rendering what is after all the very essence of a poem, — its exact metrical quality. Birch has created an entirely different form of strophe in which all four lines are alike, each containing seven principal accents, with the cæsura, following the fourth foot. Lettsom makes the first serious attempt to reproduce the original strophe. It is evident from the introduction to his translation (see p. xxvi) that he had made a careful study of its form, and he does in fact reproduce the first three lines exactly. Of the fourth line he says: "I have not thought it expedient to make a rule of thus lengthening the fourth lines of the stanzas, though I have lengthened them occasionally"(!). What moved him thus to deprive the stanza of its most striking feature — and one, moreover, that is easily preserved in English — he does not make clear. The versions of Foster-Barham and of Horton and Bell show the same disfigurement, the latter omitting the extra accent of the fourth line, as they say, "for the sake of euphony"(!). It is just this lengthened close of each strophe that gives the Nibelungenlied its peculiar metrical character and contributes not a little to the avoidance of monotony in a poem of over two thousand strophes. In theory the form of the fourth line as it stands in the original is no more foreign to the genius of the English language than to that of modern German, and few of the many Germans giving a modernized version of the epic have been bold enough to lay sacrilegious hands upon it to shorten it.

A brief account of the Nibelungen strophe may not be out of place here, owing to the fact that its character has generally been misunderstood. The origin and evolution of the strophe have been the subject of much discussion, the results of which we need not pause to formulate here. As it appears in actual practice in our poem of about the year 1200, it was as follows: Each strophe consists of four long lines, the first line rhyming with the second, and the third with the fourth. The rhymes are masculine, that is, rhymes on the end syllable. Each line is divided by a clearly marked caesura into two halves; each half of the first three lines and the first half of the fourth line has three accented syllables, the second half of the fourth line has four accented syllables. The first half of each line ends in an unaccented syllabic — or, strictly speaking, in a syllable bearing a secondary accent; that is, each line has what is called a "ringing" caesura. The metrical character of the Nibelungen strophe is thus due to its fixed number of accented syllables. Of unaccented syllables the number may vary within certain limits. Ordinarily each accented syllable is preceded by an unaccented one; that is, the majority of feet are iambic. The unaccented syllable may, however, at times be wanting, or there may, on the other hand, be two or even three of them together. A characteristic of the second half of the last line is that there is very frequently no unaccented syllable between the second and the third accented ones. Among occasional variations of the normal strophe as here described may be mentioned the following: The end-rhyme is in a few instances feminine instead of masculine; while on the other hand the ending of the first half-lines is occasionally masculine instead of feminine, that is, the caesura is not "ringing." In a few scattered instances we find strophes that rhyme throughout in the caesura as well as at the end of lines;* occasionally the first and second lines, or still less frequently the third and fourth, alone have caesural rhyme.† Rhyming of the caesura may be regarded as accidental in most cases, but it is reproduced as exactly as possible in this translation.

In the original the opening strophe, which is altogether more regular than the average and is, moreover, one of the few that have also complete caesural rhyme, is as follows:

Uns ist in alten maeren   wunders vil geseit
von heleden lobebaeren,   von grôzer arebeit,
von fröuden, hochgezîten,   von weinen und von klagen,
von küener recken strîten   muget ir nu wunder hoeren sagen.

Here the only place where the unaccented syllable is lacking before the accented is before *wunders* at the beginning of the second half of the first line. A strophe showing more typical irregularities is, for instance, the twenty-second:

---

*   Strophes *1, 17, 102,* and possibly *841.*
†   Strophes *18, 69, 103, 115, 129, 148, 177, 190, 198, 222, 231, 239, 293, 325, 345, 363, 485, 584, 703, 712, 859, 864, 894, 937, 1022, 1032, 1114, 1225, 1432, 1436, 1460, 1530, 1555, 1597, 1855, 1909, 1944, 1956, 2133, 2200, 2206, 2338.*

In sînen besten zîten,   bî sînen jungen tagen,
man möhte michel wunder   von Sîvride sagen,
waz êren an im wüchse   und wie scoene was sîn lîp.
sît heten in ze minne   diu vil waetlîchen wîp.

Here the rhyme of the first and second lines is still masculine, *tagen* and *sagen* being pronounced *tagn* and *sagn*. The unaccented syllable is lacking, e.g., before the second accent of the second half of line two, also before the first and the third accent of the second half of line four. There are two unaccented syllables at the beginning (*Auftakt*) of the second half of line three. The absence of the unaccented syllable between the second and the third accent of the last half of the fourth line of a strophe, as here, is so frequent in the poem as to amount almost to a rule; it shows an utter misconception, or disregard, of its true character, nevertheless, to treat this last half-line as having only three accented syllables, as all translators hitherto have done.

8. Editions of 'The Nibelungenlied'

1.   MS. A. (Hohenems-Munich).
   Lachmann, *Der Nibelunge Nôt und die Klage,* 5th ed., Berlin, 1878. Several reprints of the text alone later.
2.   MS. B. (St. Gall).
   Bartsch, *Das Nibelungenlied,* 6th ed., Leipzig, 1886. (Vol. 3 of the series Deutsche Classiker des Mittelalters.)
   Piper, *Die Nibelungen.* (Vol. 6 of Kürschner's Deutsche National-Litteratur.)
3.   MS. C. (Donaueschingen).
   Zarncke, *Das Nibelungenlied,* 6th ed., Leipzig, 1887.

The Nibelungenlied

First Adventure

Kriemhild's Dream

To us in olden story   are wonders many told
Of heroes rich in glory,   of trials manifold:
Of joy and festive greeting,   of weeping and of woe,
Of keenest warriors meeting,   shall ye now many a wonder know.

There once grew up in Burgundy   a maid of noble birth,
Nor might there be a fairer   than she in all the earth:
Kriemhild hight the maiden,   and grew a dame full fair,
Through whom high thanes a many   to lose their lives soon
      dooméd were.

'Twould well become the highest   to love the winsome maid,
Keen knights did long to win her,   and none but homage paid.
Beauty without measure,   that in sooth had she,
And virtues wherewith many   ladies else adorned might be.

Three noble lords did guard her,   great as well in might,
Gunther and Gernot,   each one a worthy knight,
And Giselher their brother,   a hero young and rare.
The lady was their sister   and lived beneath the princes' care.

These lords were free in giving,   and born of high degree;
Undaunted was the valor   of all the chosen three.
It was the land of Burgundy   o'er which they did command,
And mighty deeds of wonder   they wrought anon in Etzel's land.

At Worms amid their warriors   they dwelt, the Rhine beside,
And in their lands did serve them   knights of mickle pride,

Who till their days were ended   maintained them high in state.
They later sadly perished   beneath two noble women's hate.

A high and royal lady,   Ute their mother hight,
Their father's name was Dankrat,   a man of mickle might.
To them his wealth bequeathed he   when that his life was done,
For while he yet was youthful   had he in sooth great honor won.

In truth were these three rulers,   as I before did say,
Great and high in power,   and homage true had they
Eke of knights the boldest   and best that e'er were known,
Keen men all and valiant,   as they in battle oft had shown.

There was of Tronje Hagen,   and of that princely line
His brother valiant Dankwart;   and eke of Metz Ortwein;
Then further the two margraves,   Gere and Eckewart;
Of Alzei was Volker,   a doughty man of dauntless heart.

Rumold the High Steward,   a chosen man was he,
Sindold and Hunold   they tended carefully
Each his lofty office   in their three masters' state,
And many a knight beside them   that I the tale may ne'er relate.

Dankwart he was Marshal;   his nephew, then, Ortwein
Upon the monarch waited   when that he did dine;
Sindold was Cup-bearer,   a stately thane was he,
And Chamberlain was Hunold,   masters all in courtesy.

Of the kings' high honor   and their far-reaching might,
Of their full lofty majesty   and how each gallant knight
Found his chiefest pleasure   in the life of chivalry,
In sooth by mortal never   might it full related be.

Amid this life so noble   did dream the fair Kriemhild
How that she reared a falcon,   in beauty strong and wild,
That by two eagles perished;   the cruel sight to see
Did fill her heart with sorrow   as great as in this world might be.

The dream then to her mother   Queen Ute she told,
But she could not the vision   than thus more clear unfold:
"The falcon that thou rearedst,   doth mean a noble spouse:
God guard him well from evil   or thou thy hero soon must lose."

"Of spouse, O darling mother,   what dost thou tell to me?
Without a knight to woo me,   so will I ever be,
Unto my latest hour   I'll live a simple maid,
That I through lover's wooing   ne'er be brought to direst need."

"Forswear it not so rashly,"   her mother then replied.
"On earth if thou wilt ever   cast all care aside,
'Tis love alone will do it;   thou shalt be man's delight,
If God but kindly grant thee   to wed a right good valiant knight."

"Now urge the case, dear mother,"   quoth she, "not further here.
Fate of many another   dame hath shown full clear
How joy at last doth sorrow   lead oft-times in its train.
That I no ruth may borrow,   from both alike I'll far remain."

Long time, too, did Kriemhild   her heart from love hold free,
And many a day the maiden   lived right happily,
Ere good knight saw she any   whom she would wish to woo.
In honor yet she wedded   anon a worthy knight and true.

He was that same falcon   she saw the dream within
Unfolded by her mother.   Upon her nearest kin,
That they did slay him later,   how wreaked she vengeance wild!
Through death of this one hero   died many another mother's child.

Second Adventure
Siegfried

There grew likewise in Netherland   a prince of noble kind,
Siegmund hight his father,   his mother Siegelind —
Within a lordly castle   well known the country o'er,
By the Rhine far downward: Xanten was the name it bore.

Siegfried they did call him,   this bold knight and good;
Many a realm he tested,   for brave was he of mood.
He rode to prove his prowess   in many a land around:
Heigh-ho! what thanes of mettle   anon in Burgundy he found!

In the springtime of his vigor,   when he was young and bold,
Could tales of mickle wonder   of Siegfried be told,
How he grew up in honor,   and how fair he was to see:
Anon he won the favor   of many a debonair lady.

As for a prince was fitting,   they fostered him with care:
Yet how the knightly virtues   to him native were!
'Twas soon the chiefest glory   of his father's land,
That he in fullest measure   endowed with princely worth did stand.

He soon was grown in stature   that he at court did ride.
The people saw him gladly,   lady and maid beside
Did wish that his own liking   might lead him ever there.
That they did lean unto him   the knight was soon right well aware.

In youth they let him never   without safe escort ride;
Soon bade Siegmund and Siegelind   apparel rich provide;
Men ripe in wisdom taught him,   who knew whence honor came.

Thus many lands and people   he won by his wide-honored name.

Now was he of such stature   that he could weapons bear:
Of what thereto he needed   had he an ample share.
Then to think of loving   fair maids did he begin,
And well might they be honored   for wooer Siegfried bold to win.

Then bade his father Siegmund   make known to one and all
That he with his good kinsmen   would hold high festival.
And soon were tidings carried   to all the neighboring kings;
To friends at home and strangers   steeds gave he and rich furnishin

Wherever they found any   who knight was fit to be
By reason of his kindred,   all such were courteously
Unto the land invited   to join the festal throng,
When with the prince so youthful   on them the knightly sword was
		hung.

Of this high time of revelry   might I great wonders tell.
Siegmund and Siegelind   great honor won full well,
Such store of goodly presents   they dealt with generous hand,
That knights were seen full many   from far come pricking to their
		land.

Four hundred lusty squires   were there to be clad
In knight's full garb with Siegfried.   Full many a beauteous maid
At work did never tire,   for dear they did him hold,
And many a stone full precious   those ladies laid within the gold,

That they upon the doublets   embroidered cunningly
Of those soon to be knighted: 't was thus it had to be,
Seats bade the host for many   a warrior bold make right
Against the high midsummer,   when Siegfried won the name of
		knight.

Then went unto the minster   full many a noble knight
And gallant squires beside them.   The elder there with right
Did wait upon the younger,   as once for them was done.
They were all light-hearted,   in hope of pleasure everyone.

God to praise and honor   they sang the mass' song;
There, too, were crowds of people,   a great and surging throng,

When after knightly custom   knighthood received they then,
In such a stately pageant   as scarce might ever be again.

They hastened where they found them   saddled many a steed;
In the court of Siegmund's castle   they tilted with such speed
That far the din resounded   through castle and through hall,
As in the play with clamor   did join the fiery riders all.

Well-tried old knights and youthful   met there in frequent clash,
There was sound of shattered lances   that through the air did crash,
And along before the castle   were splinters seen to fly
From hands of knights a many: each with other there did vie.

The king he bade give over: they led the chargers out:
There was seen all shattered   many a boss well-wrought,
And many a stone full costly   lay there upon the sward
From erstwhile shining shield-bands,   now broken in the jousting
        hard.

The guests all went thereafter   where seats for them were reared;
They by the choicest viands   from weariness were cheered,
And wine, of all the rarest,   that then in plenty flowed.
Upon both friends and strangers   were fitting honors rich bestowed.

In such merry manner   all day did last the feast.
Many a wandering minstrel   knew not any rest,
But sang to win the presents   dealt out with bounteous hand;
And with their praise was honored   far and wide King Siegmund's
        land.

The monarch then did order   Siegfried his youthful son
In fee give lands and castles,   as he erstwhile had done.
To all his sword-companions   he gave with such full hand,
That joyed they o'er the journey   they now had made unto that land.

The festival yet lasted   until the seventh day.
Siegelind after old custom   in plenty gave away
— For so her son she honored —   rich gifts of shining gold:
In sooth deserved she richly   that all should him in honor hold.

Never a wandering minstrel   was unprovided found:
Horses there and raiment   so free were dealt around,

As if to live they had not   beyond it one day more.
I ween a monarch's household   ne'er bestowed such gifts before.

Thus closed the merry feasting   in this right worthy way,
And 't was well known thereafter   how those good knights did say
That they the youthful hero   for king would gladly have;
But this nowise he wished for,   Siegfried the stately knight and
        brave.

While that they both were living,   Siegmund and Siegelind,
No crown their son desired,   — thereto he had no mind.
Yet would he fain be master   o'er all the hostile might
That in the lands around him   opposed the keen and fiery knight.

Third Adventure

How Siegfried Came to Worms

Seldom in sooth, if ever,   the hero's heart was sad.
He heard them tell the story,   how that a winsome maid
There lived afar in Burgundy,   surpassing fair to see:
Great joy she brought him later,   but eke she brought him misery.

Of her exceeding beauty   the fame spread far and near,
And of the thing, moreover,   were knights oft-times aware
How the maid's high spirit   no mortal could command:
The thing lured many a stranger   from far unto King Gunther's
      land.

Although to win her favor   were many wooers bent,
In her own heart would never   Kriemhild thereto consent
That anyone amongst them   for lover she would have:
Still to her was he a stranger   to whom anon her troth she gave.

To true love turned his fancy   the son of Siegelind.
'Gainst his, all others' wooing   was like an idle wind:
Full well did he merit   a lady fair to woo,
And soon the noble Kriemhild   to Siegfried bold was wedded true.

By friends he oft was counseled,   and many a faithful man,
Since to think of wooing   in earnest he began,
That he a wife should find him   of fitting high degree.
Then spoke the noble Siegfried: "In sooth fair Kriemhild shall it be,

"The noble royal maiden   in Burgundy that dwells,
For sake of all her beauty.   Of her the story tells,

Ne'er monarch was so mighty   that, if for spouse he sighed,
'Twere not for him befitting   to take the princess for his bride."

Unto King Siegmund also   the thing was soon made known.
His people talked about it,   whereby to him was shown
The Prince's fixéd purpose.   It grieved him sorely, too,
That his son intent was   the full stately maid to woo.

Siegelind asked and learned it,   the noble monarch's wife.
For her loved son she sorrowed   lest he should lose his life,
For well she knew the humor   of Gunther and his men.
Then gan they from the wooing   strive to turn the noble thane.

Then said the doughty Siegfried: "O father dear to me,
Without the love of woman   would I ever be,
Could I not woo in freedom   where'er my heart is set.
Whate'er be said by any,   I'll keep the selfsame purpose yet."

"Since thou wilt not give over,"   the king in answer said,
"Am I of this thy purpose   inwardly full glad,
And straightway to fulfill it   I'll help as best I can,
Yet in King Gunther's service   is many a haughty-minded man.

"And were there yet none other   than Hagen, warrior-knight,
He with such haughty bearing   is wont to show his might,
That I do fear right sorely   that sad our end may be,
If we set out with purpose   to win the stately maid for thee."

"Shall we by that be hindered?"   outspake Siegfried then;
"Whate'er in friendly fashion   I cannot obtain
I'll yet in other manner   take that, with sword in hand.
I trow from them I'll further   wrest both their vassals and their
          land."

"I grieve to hear thy purpose,"   said Siegmund the king;
"If anyone this story   unto the Rhine should bring,
Then durst thou never after   within that land be seen.
Gunther and Gernot,   — well known to me they long have been.

"By force, however mighty,   no man can win the maid,"
Spake King Siegmund further,   "to me hath oft been said.
But if with knightly escort   thither thou wilt ride,

Good friends — an have we any —   shall soon be summoned to thy
    side."

"No wish," then answered Siegfried,   "it ever was of mine,
That warrior knights should follow   with me unto the Rhine
As if arrayed for battle: 'twould make my heart full sad,
To force in hostile manner   to yield to me the stately maid.

"By my own hand — thus only —   trust I to win my bride;
With none but twelve in company   to Gunther's land I'll ride.
In this, O royal father,   thy present help I pray."
Gray and white fur raiment   had his companions for the way.

Siegelind his mother   then heard the story too,
And grieved she was on hearing   what her dear son would do,
For she did fear to lose him   at hands of Gunther's men.
Thereat with heart full heavy   began to weep the noble queen.

Then came forth Sir Siegfried   where the queen he sought,
And to his weeping mother   thus gently spake his thought:
"No tear of grief thou shouldest   ever shed for me,
For I care not a tittle   for all the warriors that be.

"So help me on my journey   to the land of Burgundy,
And furnish such apparel   for all my knights and me,
As warriors of our station   might well with honor wear.
Then I in turn right truly   to thee my gratitude will swear."

"Since thou wilt not give over,"   Siegelind then replied,
"My only son, I'll help thee   as fits thee forth to ride,
With the best apparel   that riders ever wore,
Thee and thy companions: ye shall of all have goodly store."

Then bowed the youthful Siegfried   the royal dame before,
And said: "Upon the journey   will I take no more,
But twelve good knights only: for these rich dress provide,
For I would know full gladly   how 't doth with Kriemhild betide."

Then sat at work fair women   by night and eke by day,
And rest indeed but little   from busy toil had they,
Until they had made ready   the dress Siegfried should wear.
Firm bent upon the journey,   no other counsel would he hear.

His father bade a costly   garb for him prepare,
That leaving Siegmund's country   he the same might wear.
For all their glittering breastplates   were soon prepared beside,
And helmets firmly welded,   and shining shields long and wide.

Then fast the day grew nearer   when they should thence depart.
Men and likewise women   went sorrowing in heart,
If that they should ever   see more their native land.
With full equipment laden   the sumpter horses there did stand.

Their steeds were stately, furnished   with trappings rich with gold;
It were a task all bootless   to seek for knights more bold
Than were the gallant Siegfried   and his chosen band.
He longed to take departure   straightway for Burgundian land.

Leave granted they with sadness,   both the king and queen,
The which to turn to gladness   sought the warrior keen,
And spake then: "Weep ye shall not   at all for sake of me,
Forever free from doubtings   about my safety may ye be."

Stern warriors stood there sorrowing,   — in tears was many a maid.
I ween their hearts erred nothing,   as sad forebodings said
That 'mongst their friends so many   thereby were doomed to die.
Good cause had they to sorrow   at last o'er all their misery.

Upon the seventh morning   to Worms upon the strand
Did come the keen knights riding.   Bright shone many a band
Of gold from their apparel   and rich equipment then;
And gently went their chargers   with Siegfried and his chosen men.

New-made shields they carried   that were both strong and wide
And brightly shone their helmets   as thus to court did ride
Siegfried the keen warrior   into King Gunther's land.
Of knights before was never   beheld so richly clad a band.

The points of their long scabbards   reached down unto the spur,
And spear full sharply pointed   bore each chosen warrior.
The one that Siegfried carried   in breadth was two good span,
And grimly cut its edges   when driven by the fearless man.

Reins with gold all gleaming   held they in the hand,

The saddle-bands were silken.   So came they to the land.
On every side the people   to gape at them began,
And also out to meet them   the men that served King Gunther ran.

Gallant men high-hearted,   knight and squire too,
Hastened to receive them,   for such respect was due,
And bade the guests be welcome   unto their master's land.
They took from them their chargers,   and shields as well from out
    the hand.

Then would they eke the chargers   lead forth unto their rest;
But straight the doughty Siegfried   to them these words addressed:
"Yet shall ye let our chargers   stand the while near by;
Soon take we hence our journey;   thereon resolved full well am I.

"If that be known to any,   let him not delay,
Where I your royal master   now shall find, to say, —
Gunther, king so mighty   o'er the land of Burgundy."
Then told him one amongst them   to whom was known where that
    might be:

"If that the king thou seekest,   right soon may he be found.
Within that wide hall yonder   with his good knights around
But now I saw him sitting.   Thither do thou repair,
And thou may'st find around him   many a stately warrior there."

Now also to the monarch   were the tidings told,
That within his castle   were knights arrived full bold,
All clad in shining armor   and appareled gorgeously;
But not a man did know them   within the land of Burgundy.

Thereat the king did wonder   whence were come to him
These knights adventure seeking   in dress so bright and trim,
And shields adorned so richly   that new and mighty were.
That none the thing could tell him   did grieve him sorely to hear.

Outspake a knight then straightway,   Ortwein by name was he,
Strong and keen as any   well was he known to be:
"Since we of them know nothing,   bid someone quickly go
And fetch my uncle Hagen: to him thou shalt the strangers show.

"To him are known far kingdoms   and every foreign land,

And if he know these strangers   we soon shall understand."
The king then sent to fetch him: with his train of men
Unto the king's high presence   in stately gear went he then.

What were the king's good pleasure,   asked Hagen grim in war.
"In the court within my castle   are warriors from afar,
And no one here doth know them: if them thou e'er didst see
In any land far distant,   now shalt thou, Hagen, tell to me."

"That will I do, 'tis certain." —   To a window then he went,
And on the unknown strangers   his keen eye he bent.
Well pleased him their equipment   and the rich dress they wore,
Yet ne'er had he beheld them   in land of Burgundy before.

He said that whencesoever   these knights come to the Rhine,
They bear a royal message,   or are of princely line.
"Their steeds are so bedizened,   and their apparel rare:
No matter whence they journey,   high-hearted men in truth they
     are."

Further then spake Hagen: "As far as goes my ken,
Though I the noble Siegfried   yet have never seen,
Yet will I say meseemeth,   howe'er the thing may be,
This knight who seeks adventure,   and yonder stands so proud, is he.

"'Tis some new thing he bringeth   hither to our land.
The valiant Nibelungen   fell by the hero's hand,
Schilbung and Nibelung,   from royal sire sprung;
Deeds he wrought most wondrous   anon when his strong arm he
     swung.

"As once alone the hero   rode without company,
Found he before a mountain   — as hath been told to me —
With the hoard of Nibelung   full many stalwart men;
To him had they been strangers   until he chanced to find them then.

"The hoard of King Nibelung   entire did they bear
Forth from a mountain hollow.   And now the wonder hear,
How that they would share it,   these two Nibelung men.
This saw the fearless Siegfried,   and filled he was with wonder then.

"He came so near unto them   that he the knights espied,

And they in turn him also.   One amongst them said:
'Here comes the doughty Siegfried,   hero of Netherland.'
Since 'mongst the Nibelungen   strange wonders wrought his mighty
    hand.

"Right well did they receive him,   Schilbung and Nibelung,
And straight they both together,   these noble princes young,
Bade him mete out the treasure,   the full valorous man,
And so long time besought him   that he at last the task began.

"As we have heard in story,   he saw of gems such store
That they might not be laden   on wagons full five score;
More still of gold all shining   from Nibelungenland.
'Twas all to be divided   between them by keen Siegfried's hand.

"Then gave they him for hire   King Nibelung's sword.
And sooth to say, that service   brought them but small reward,
That for them there performed   Siegfried of dauntless mood.
His task he could not finish;   thereat they raged as were they wood.

"They had there of their followers   twelve warriors keen,
And strong they were as giants: what booted giants e'en?
Them slew straightway in anger   Siegfried's mighty hand,
And warriors seven hundred   he felled in Nibelungenland

"With the sword full trusty,   Balmung that hight.
Full many a youthful warrior   from terror at the sight
Of that deadly weapon   swung by his mighty hand
Did render up his castle   and pledge him fealty in the land.

"Thereto the kings so mighty,   them slew he both as well.
But into gravest danger   through Alberich he fell,
Who thought for his slain masters   vengeance to wreak straightway,
Until the mighty Siegfried   his wrath with strong arm did stay.

"Nor could prevail against him   the Dwarf, howe'er he tried.
E'en as two wild lions   they coursed the mountainside,
Where he the sightless mantle*   from Alberich soon won.
Then Siegfried, knight undaunted,   held the treasure for his own.

---

* This is the *tarnkappe*, a cloak that made the wearer invisible, and also gave
    him the strength of twelve men.

"Who then dared join the struggle,   all slain around they lay.
Then he bade the treasure   to draw and bear away
Thither whence 'twas taken   by the Nibelungen men.
Alberich for his valor   was then appointed Chamberlain.

"An oath he had to swear him,   he'd serve him as his slave;
To do all kinds of service   his willing pledge he gave" —
Thus spake of Tronje Hagen —   "That has the hero done;
Might as great before him   was never in a warrior known.

"Still know I more about him,   that has to me been told.
A dragon, wormlike monster,   slew once the hero bold.
Then in its blood he bathed him,   since when his skin hath been
So horn-hard, ne'er a weapon   can pierce it, as hath oft been seen.

"Let us the brave knight-errant   receive so courteously
That we in naught shall merit   his hate, for strong is he.
He is so keen of spirit   he must be treated fair:
He has by his own valor   done many a deed of prowess rare."

The monarch spake in wonder: "In sooth thou tellest right.
Now see how proudly yonder   he stands prepared for fight,
He and his thanes together,   the hero wondrous keen!
To greet him we'll go thither,   and let our fair intent be seen."

"That canst thou," out spake Hagen,   "well in honor do.
He is of noble kindred,   a high king's son thereto.
'Tis seen in all his bearing;   meseems in truth, God wot,
The tale is worth the hearing   that this bold knight has hither
    brought."

Then spake the mighty monarch: "Be he right welcome here.
Keen is he and noble,   of fame known far and near.
So shall he be fair treated   in the land of Burgundy."
Down then went King Gunther,   and Siegfried with his men found
    he.

The king and his knights with him   received so well the guest,
That the hearty greeting   did their good will attest.
Thereat in turn the stranger   in reverence bowed low,
That in their welcome to him   they did such courtesy bestow.

"To me it is a wonder,"   straightway spake the host,
"From whence, O noble Siegfried,   come to our land thou dost,
Or what here thou seekest   at Worms upon the Rhine."
Him the stranger answered: "Put thou away all doubts of thine.

"I oft have heard the tiding   within my sire's domain,
How at thy court resided   — and know this would I fain —
Knights, of all the keenest, / — 'tis often told me so —
That e'er a monarch boasted: now come I hither this to know.

"Thyself have I heard also   high praised for knightly worth;
'Tis said a nobler monarch   ne'er lived in all the earth.
Thus speak of thee the people   in all the lands around.
Nor will I e'er give over   until in this the truth I've found.

"I too am warrior noble   and born to wear a crown;
So would I right gladly   that thou of me shouldst own
That I of right am master   o'er people and o'er land.
Of this shall now my honor   and eke my head as pledges stand.

"And art thou then so valiant   as hath to me been told,
I reck not, will he nill he   thy best warrior bold,
I'll wrest from thee in combat   whatever thou may'st have;
Thy lands and all thy castles   shall naught from change of masters
        save."

The king was seized with wonder   and all his men beside,
To see the manner haughty   in which the knight replied
That he was fully minded   to take from him his land.
It chafed his thanes to hear it,   who soon in raging mood did stand.

"How could it be my fortune,"   Gunther the king outspoke,
"What my sire long ruled over   in honor for his folk,
Now to lose so basely   through any vaunter's might?
In sooth 'twere nobly showing   that we too merit name of knight!"

"Nowise will I give over,"   was the keen reply.
"If peace through thine own valor   thy land cannot enjoy,
To me shall all be subject: if heritage of mine
Through thy arm's might thou winnest,   of right shall all
        hence-forth be thine.

"Thy land and all that mine is,　at stake shall equal lie.
Whiche'er of us be victor　when now our strength we try,
To him shall all be subject,　the folk and eke the land."
But Hagen spake against it,　and Gernot too was quick at hand.

"Such purpose have we never,"　Gernot then said,
"For lands to combat ever,　that any warrior dead
Should lie in bloody battle.　We've mighty lands and strong;
Of right they call us master,　and better they to none belong."

There stood full grim and moody　Gernot's friends around,
And there as well amongst them　was Ortwein to be found.
He spake: "This mild peace-making　doth grieve me sore at heart,
For by the doughty Siegfried　attacked all undeserved thou art.

"If thou and thy two brothers　yourselves to help had naught,
And if a mighty army　he too had hither brought,
I trow I'd soon be able　to make this man so keen
His manner now so haughty　of need replace by meeker mien."

Thereat did rage full sorely　the hero of Netherland:
"Never shall be measured　'gainst me in fight thy hand.
I am a mighty monarch,　thou a king's serving-knight;
Of such as thou a dozen　dare not withstand me in the fight."

For swords then called in anger　of Metz Sir Ortwein:
Son of Hagen's sister　he was, of Tronje's line.
That Hagen so long was silent　did grieve the king to see.
Gernot made peace between them:　a gallant knight and keen was he.

Spake he thus to Ortwein:　"Curb now thy wrathful tongue,
For here the noble Siegfried　hath done us no such wrong;
We yet can end the quarrel　in peace, — such is my rede —
And live with him in friendship;　that were for us a worthier deed."

Then spake the mighty Hagen:　"Sad things do I forebode
For all thy train of warriors,　that this knight ever rode
Unto the Rhine thus arméd.　'Twere best he stayed at home;
For from my masters never　to him such wrong as this had come."

But outspake Siegfried proudly,　whose heart was ne'er dismayed:
"An't please thee not, Sir Hagen,　what I now have said,

This arm shall give example   whereby thou plain shall see
How stern anon its power   here in Burgundy will be."

"Yet that myself will hinder,"   said then Gernot.
All his men forbade he   henceforth to say aught
With such unbridled spirit   to stir the stranger's ire.
Then Siegfried eke was mindful   of one most stately maid and fair.

"Such strife would ill befit us,"   Gernot spake again;
"For though should die in battle   a host of valiant men
'Twould bring us little honor   and ye could profit none."
Thereto gave Siegfried answer,   good King Siegmund's noble son:

"Wherefore bides thus grim Hagen,   and Ortwein tardy is
To begin the combat   with all those friends of his,
Of whom he hath so many   here in Burgundy?"
Answer him they durst not,   for such was Gernot's stern decree.

"Thou shalt to us be welcome,"   outspake young Giselher,
"And all thy brave companions   that hither with thee fare.
Full gladly we'll attend thee,   I and all friends of mine."
For the guests then bade they   pour out in store of Gunther's wine.

Then spake the stately monarch: "But ask thou courteously,
And all that we call ours   stands at thy service free;
So with thee our fortune   we'll share in ill and good."
Thereat the noble Siegfried   a little milder was of mood.

Then carefully was tended   all their knightly gear,
And housed in goodly manner   in sooth the strangers were,
All that followed Siegfried;   they found a welcome rest.
In Burgundy full gladly   anon was seen the noble guest.

They showed him mickle honor   thereafter many a day,
And more by times a thousand   than I to you could say.
His might respect did merit,   ye may full well know that.
Scarce a man e'er saw him   who bore him longer any hate.

And when they held their pastime,   the kings with many a man,
Then was he ever foremost;   whatever they began,
None there that was his equal,   — so mickle was his might —
If they the stone were putting,   or hurling shaft with rival knight.

As is the knightly custom,   before the ladies fair
To games they turned for pastime,   these knights of mettle rare;
Then ever saw they gladly   the hero of Netherland.
But he had fixed his fancy   to win one fairest maiden's hand.

In all that they were doing   he'd take a ready part.
A winsome loving maiden   he bore within his heart;
Him only loved that lady,   whose face he ne'er had seen,
But she full oft in secret   of him spake fairest words, I ween.

And when before the castle   they sped in tournament,
The good knights and squires,   oft-times the maiden went
And gazed adown from casement,   Kriemhild the princess rare.
Pastime there was none other   for her that could with this compare.

And knew he she was gazing   whom in his heart he bore,
He joy enough had found him   in jousting evermore.
And might he only see her,   — that can I well believe —
On earth through sight none other   his eyes could such delight
     receive.

Whene'er with his companions   to castle court he went,
E'en as do now the people   whene'er on pleasure bent,
There stood 'fore all so graceful   Siegelind's noble son,
For whom in love did languish   the hearts of ladies many a one.

Eke thought he full often: "How shall it ever be,
That I the noble maiden   with my own eyes may see,
Whom I do love so dearly   and have for many a day?
To me is she a stranger,   which sorely grieves my heart to say."

Whene'er the kings so mighty   rode o'er their broad domain,
Then of valiant warriors   they took a stately train.
With them abroad rode Siegfried,   which grieved those ladies sore:
— He too for one fair maiden   at heart a mickle burden bore.

Thus with his hosts he lingered / — 'tis every tittle true —
In King Gunther's country   a year completely through,
And never once the meanwhile   the lovely maid did see,
Through whom such joy thereafter   for him, and eke such grief
     should be.

Fourth Adventure

How Siegfried Fought with the Saxons

Now come wondrous tidings   to King Gunther's land,
By messengers brought hither   from far upon command
Of knights unknown who harbored   against him secret hate.
When there was heard the story,   at heart in sooth the grief was
    great.

Of these I now will tell you: There was King Luedeger
From out the land of Saxons,   a mighty warrior,
And eke from land of Denmark   Luedegast the king:
Whene'er they rode to battle   went they with mighty following.

Come were now their messengers   to the land of Burgundy,
Sent forth by these foemen   in proud hostility.
Then asked they of the strangers   what tidings they did bring:
And when they heard it, straightway   led them to court before the
    king.

Then spake to them King Gunther: "A welcome, on my word.
Who 'tis that send you hither,   that have I not yet heard:
Now shall ye let me know it,"   spake the monarch keen.
Then dreaded they full sorely   to see King Gunther's angry mien.

"Wilt them, O king, permit us   the tidings straight to tell
That we now have brought thee,   no whit will we conceal,
But name thee both our masters   who us have hither sent:
Luedegast and Luedeger,   — to waste thy land is their intent.

"Their hate hast thou incurréd,   and thou shalt know in sooth

That high enraged against thee　are the monarchs both.
Their hosts they will lead hither　to Worms upon the Rhine;
They're helped by thanes full many —　of this put off all doubts of
　　　thine.

"Within weeks a dozen　their march will they begin;
And if thy friends be valiant,　let that full quick be seen,
To help thee keep in safety　thy castles and thy land:
Full many a shield and helmet　shall here be cleft by warrior's hand.

"Or wilt thou with them parley,　so let it quick be known,
Before their hosts so mighty　of warlike men come down
To Worms upon Rhine river　sad havoc here to make,
Whereby must death most certain　many a gallant knight o'ertake."

"Bide ye now the meanwhile,"　the king did answer kind,
"Till I take better counsel;　then shall ye know my mind.
Have I yet warriors faithful,　from these I'll naught conceal,
But to my friends I'll straightway　these warlike tidings strange
　　　reveal."

The lordly Gunther wondered　thereat and troubled sore,
As he the message pondered　in heart and brooded o'er.
He sent to fetch grim Hagen　and others of his men,
And bade likewise in hurry　to court bring hither Gernot then.

Thus at his word his trusted　advisers straight attend.
He spake: "Our land to harry　foes all unknown will send
Of men a mighty army;　a grievous wrong is this.
Small cause have we e'er given　that they should wish us aught
　　　amiss."

"Our swords ward such things from us,"　Gernot then said;
"Since but the fated dieth,　so let all such lie dead.
Wherefore I'll e'er remember　what honor asks of me:
Whoe'er hath hate against us　shall ever here right welcome be."

Then spake the doughty Hagen:　"Methinks 'twould scarce be good;
Luedegast and Luedeger　are men of wrathful mood.
Help can we never summon,　the days are now so few."
So spake the keen old warrior,　"'Twere well Siegfried the tidings
　　　knew."

The messengers in the borough   were harbored well the while,
And though their sight was hateful,   in hospitable style
As his own guests to tend them   King Gunther gave command,
Till 'mongst his friends he learnéd   who by him in his need would
        stand.

The king was filled with sorrow   and his heart was sad.
Then saw his mournful visage   a knight to help full glad,
Who could not well imagine   what 'twas that grieved him so.
Then begged he of King Gunther   the tale of this his grief to know.

"To me it is great wonder,"   said Siegfried to the king,
"How thou of late hast changéd   to silent sorrowing
The joyous ways that ever   with us thy wont have been."
Then unto him gave answer   Gunther the full stately thane:

"'Tis not to every person   I can the burden say
That ever now in secret   upon my heart doth weigh:
To well-tried friends and steady   are told our inmost woes."
— Siegfried at first was pallid,   but soon his blood like fire up-rose.

He spake unto the monarch: "To thee I've naught denied.
All ills that now do threaten   I'll help to turn aside.
And if but friends thou seekest,   of them the first I'll be,
And trow I well with honor   till death to serve thee faithfully."

"God speed thee well, Sir Siegfried,   for this thy purpose fair:
And though such help in earnest   thy arm should render ne'er,
Yet do I joy at hearing   thou art so true to me.
And live I yet a season,   right heartily repaid 'twill be.

"Know will I also let thee   wherefore I sorrowing stand.
Through messengers from my foemen   have tidings reached my land
That they with hosts of warriors   will ride my country o'er;
Such thing to us did never   thanes of any land before."

"Small cause is that for grieving,"   said then Siegfried;
"But calm thy troubled spirit   and hearken to my rede:
Let me for thee acquire   honor and vantage too,
And bid thou now assemble   for service eke thy warriors true.

"And had thy mighty enemies   to help them now at hand
Good thanes full thirty thousand,   against them all I'd stand,
Had I but one good thousand: put all thy trust in me."
Then answered him King Gunther: "Thy help shall full requited
      be."

"Then bid for me to summon   a thousand of thy men,
Since I now have with me   of all my knightly train
None but twelve knights only;   then will I guard thy land.
For thee shall service faithful   be done alway by Siegfried's hand.

"Herein shall help us Hagen   and eke Ortwein,
Dankwart and Sindold,   those trusted knights of thine;
And with us too shall journey   Volker, the valiant man;
The banner he shall carry: bestow it better ne'er I can.

"Back to their native country   the messengers may go;
They'll see us there right quickly,   let them full surely know,
So that all our castles   peace undisturbed shall have."
Then bade the king to summon   his friends with all their warriors
      brave.

To court returned the heralds   King Luedeger had sent,
And on their journey homeward   full joyfully they went.
King Gunther gave them presents   that costly were and good,
And granted them safe convoy;   whereat they were of merry mood.

"Tell ye my foes," spake Gunther,   "when to your land ye come,
Than making journeys hither   they better were at home;
But if they still be eager   to make such visit here,
Unless my friends forsake me,   cold in sooth shall be their cheer."

Then for the messengers   rich presents forth they bore,
Whereof in sooth to give them   Gunther had goodly store:
And they durst not refuse them   whom Luedeger had sent.
Leave then they took immediate,   and homeward joyfully they went.

When to their native Denmark   the messengers returned,
And the king Luedegast   the answer too had learned,
They at the Rhine had sent him,   — when that to him was told,
His wrath was all unbounded   to have reply in words so bold.

'Twas said their warriors numbered   many a man full keen:
"There likewise among them   with Gunther have we seen
Of Netherland a hero,   the same that Siegfried hight."
King Luedegast was grievéd,   when he their words had heard aright.

When throughout all Denmark   the tidings quick spread o'er,
Then in hot haste they summoned   helpers all the more,
So that King Luedegast,   'twixt friends from far and near,
Had knights full twenty thousand   all furnished well with shield
      and spear.

Then too his men did summon   of Saxony Luedeger,
Till they good forty thousand,   and more, had gathered there,
With whom to make the journey   'gainst the land of Burgundy.
— At home likewise the meanwhile   King Gunther had sent forth
      decree

Mighty men to summon   of his own and brothers twain,
Who against the foemen   would join the armed train.
In haste they made them ready,   for right good cause they had.
Amongst them must thereafter   full many a noble thane lie dead.

To march they quick made ready.   And when they thence would fare,
The banner to the valiant   Volker was given to bear,
As they began the journey   from Worms across the Rhine;
Strong of arm grim Hagen   was chosen leader of the line.

With them there rode Sindold   and eke the keen Hunold
Who oft at hands of Gunther   had won rewards of gold;
Dankwart, Hagen's brother,   and Ortwein beside,
Who all could well with honor   in train of noble warriors ride.

"King Gunther," spake then Siegfried,   "stay thou here at home;
Since now thy knights so gallant   with me will gladly come,
Rest thou here with fair ladies,   and be of merry mood:
I trow we'll keep in safety   thy land and honor as we should.

"And well will I see to it   that they at home remain,
Who fain would ride against thee   to Worms upon the Rhine.
Against them straight we'll journey   into their land so far
That they'll be meeker minded   who now such haughty vaunters
      are."

Then from the Rhine through Hesse   the hosts of knights rode on
Toward the land of Saxons,   where battle was anon.
With fire and sword they harried   and laid the country waste,
So that both the monarchs   full well the woes of war did taste.

When came they to the border   the train-men onward pressed.
With thought of battle-order   Siegfried the thanes addressed:
"Who now shall guard our followers   from danger in the rear?"
In sooth like this the Saxons   in battle worsted never were.

Then said they: "On the journey   the men shall guarded be
By the valiant Dankwart,   — a warrior swift is he;
So shall we lose the fewer   by men of Luedeger.
Let him and Ortwein with him   be chosen now to guard the rear."

Spake then the valiant Siegfried: "Myself will now ride on,
And against our enemies   will keep watch in the van,
Till I aright discover   where they perchance may be."
The son of fair Queen Siegelind   did arm him then immediately.

The folk he left to Hagen   when ready to depart,
And as well to Gernot,   a man of dauntless heart.
Into the land of Saxons   alone he rode away,
And by his hand was severed   many a helmet's band that day.

He found a mighty army   that lay athwart the plain,
Small part of which outnumbered   all those in his own train:
Full forty thousand were they   or more good men of might.
The hero high in spirit   saw right joyfully the sight.

Then had eke a warrior   from out the enemy
To guard the van gone forward,   all arméd cap-a-pie.
Him saw the noble Siegfried,   and he the valiant man;
Each one straight the other   to view with angry mien began.

Who he was I'll tell you   that rode his men before,
— A shield of gold all shining   upon his arm he bore —
In sooth it was King Luedegast   who there the van did guard.
Straightway the noble Siegfried   full eagerly against him spurred.

Now singled out for combat   him, too, had Luedegast.

Then full upon each other   they spurred their chargers fast,
As on their shields they lowered   their lances firm and tight,
Whereat the lordly monarch   soon found himself in sorry plight.

After the shock their chargers   bore the knights so fast
Onward past each other   as flew they on the blast.
Then turned they deftly backward   obedient to the rein,
As with their swords contested   the grim and doughty fighters twain.

When Siegfried struck in anger   far off was heard the blow,
And flew from off the helmet,   as if 'twere all aglow,
The fiery sparks all crackling   beneath his hand around.
Each warrior in the other   a foeman worth his mettle found.

Full many a stroke with vigor   dealt eke King Luedegast,
And on each other's buckler   the blows fell thick and fast.
Then thirty men discovered   their master's sorry plight:
But ere they came to help him   had doughty Siegfried won the fight.

With three mighty gashes   which he had dealt the king
Through his shining breastplate   made fast with many a ring.
The sword with sharpest edges   from wounds brought forth the
     blood,
Whereat King Luedegast   apace fell into gloomy mood.

To spare his life he begged him,   his land he pledged the knight,
And told him straight moreover,   that Luedegast he hight.
Then came his knights to help him,   they who there had seen
How that upon the vanguard   fierce fight betwixt the twain had
     been.

After duel ended,   did thirty yet withstand
Of knights that him attended;   but there the hero's hand
Kept safe his noble captive   with blows of wondrous might.
And soon wrought greater ruin   Siegfried the full gallant knight.

Beneath his arm of valor   the thirty soon lay dead.
But one the knight left living,   who thence full quickly sped
To tell abroad the story   how he the others slew;
In sooth the blood-red helmet   spake all the hapless tidings true.

Then had the men of Denmark   for all their grief good cause,

When it was told them truly   their king a captive was.
They told it to King Luedeger,   when he to rage began
In anger all unbounded: for him had grievous harm been done.

The noble King Luedegast   was led a prisoner then
By hand of mighty Siegfried   back to King Gunther's men,
And placed in hands of Hagen: and when they did hear
That 'twas the king of Denmark   they not a little joyful were.

He bade the men of Burgundy   then bind the banners on.
"Now forward!" Siegfried shouted,   "here shall yet more be done,
An I but live to see it;   ere this day's sun depart,
Shall mourn in land of Saxons   full many a goodly matron's heart.

"Ye warriors from Rhineland,   to follow me take heed,
And I unto the army   of Luedeger will lead.
Ere we again turn backward   to the land of Burgundy
Helms many hewn asunder   by hand of good knights there shall be."

To horse then hastened Gernot   and with him mighty men.
Volker keen in battle   took up the banner then;
He was a doughty Fiddler   and rode the host before.
There, too, every follower   a stately suit of armor wore.

More than a thousand warriors   they there had not a man,
Saving twelve knights-errant.   To rise the dust began
In clouds along the highway   as they rode across the fields,
And gleaming in the sunlight   were seen the brightly shining shields.

Meanwhile eke was nearing   of Saxons a great throng,
Each a broadsword bearing   that mickle was and long,
With blade that cut full sorely   when swung in strong right hand.
'Gainst strangers were they ready   to guard their castles and their
    land.

The leaders forth to battle   led the warriors then.
Come was also Siegfried   with his twelve chosen men,
Whom he with him hither   had brought from Netherland.
That day in storm of battle   was blood-bespattered many a hand.

Sindold and Hunold   and Gernot as well,
Beneath their hands in battle   full many a hero fell,

Ere that their deeds of valor   were known throughout the host.
Through them must many a stately   matron weep for warrior lost.

Volker and Hagen   and Ortwein in the fight
Lustily extinguished   full many a helmet's light
With blood from wounds down flowing, —   keen fighters everyone.
And there by Dankwart also   was many a mickle wonder done.

The knights of Denmark tested   how they could weapons wield.
Clashing there together   heard ye many a shield
And 'neath sharp swords resounding,   swung by many an arm.
The Saxons keen in combat   wrought 'mid their foes a grievous
        harm.

When the men of Burgundy   pressed forward to the fight,
Gaping wounds full many   hewed they there with might.
Then flowing down o'er saddle   in streams was seen the blood,
So fought for sake of honor   these valiant riders keen and good.

Loudly were heard ringing,   wielded by hero's hand,
The sharply-cutting weapons,   where they of Netherland
Their master followed after   into the thickest throng:
Wherever Siegfried led them   rode too those valiant knights along.

Of warriors from Rhine river   could follow not a one.
There could be seen by any   a stream of blood flow down
O'er brightly gleaming helmet   'neath Siegfried's mighty hand,
Until King Luedeger   before him with his men did stand.

Three times hither and thither   had he the host cut through
From one end to the other.   Now come was Hagen too
Who helped him well in battle   to vent his warlike mood.
That day beneath his valor   must die full many a rider good.

When the doughty Luedeger   Siegfried there found,
As he swung high in anger   his arm for blows around
And with his good sword Balmung   knights so many slew,
Thereat was the keen warrior   filled with grief and anger too.

Then mickle was the thronging   and loud the broadswords clashed,
As all their valiant followers   'gainst one another dashed.
Then struggled all the fiercer   both sides the fight to win;

The hosts joined with each other:　'twas frightful there to hear the
　　din.

To the monarch of the Saxons　it had been told before,
His brother was a captive,　which grieved his heart right sore.
He knew not that had done it　fair Siegelind's son,
For rumor said 'twas Gernot.　Full well he learned the truth anon.

King Luedeger struck so mighty　when fierce his anger rose,
That Siegfried's steed beneath him　staggered from the blows,
But forthwith did recover;　then straight his rider keen
Let all his furious mettle　in slaughter of his foes be seen.

There helped him well grim Hagen,　and Gernot in the fray,
Dankwart and Volker;　dead many a knight there lay.
Sindold and Hunold　and Ortwein, doughty thane,
By them in that fierce struggle　was many a valiant warrior slain.

Unparted in storm of battle　the gallant leaders were,
Around them over helmet　flew there many a spear
Through shield all brightly shining,　from hand of mighty thane:
And on the glancing armor　was seen full many a blood-red stain.

Amid the hurly-burly　down fell many a man
To ground from off his charger.　Straight 'gainst each other ran
Siegfried the keen rider　and eke King Luedeger.
Then flew from lance the splinters　and hurled was many a pointed
　　spear.

'Neath Siegfried's hand so mighty　from shield flew off the band.
And soon to win the victory　thought he of Netherland
Over the valiant Saxons,　of whom were wonders seen.
Heigh-ho! in shining mail-rings　many a breach made Dankwart
　　keen!

Upon the shining buckler　that guarded Siegfried's breast
Soon espied King Luedeger　a painted crown for crest;
By this same token knew he　it was the doughty man,
And to his friends he straightway　amid the battle loud began:

"Give o'er from fighting further,　good warriors everyone!
Amongst our foes now see I　Siegmund's noble son,

Of netherland the doughty   knight on victory bent.
Him has the evil Devil   to scourge the Saxons hither sent."

Then bade he all the banners   amid the storm let down.
Peace he quickly sued for: 'Twas granted him anon,
But he must now a hostage   be ta'en to Gunther's land.
This fate had forced upon him   the fear of Siegfried's mighty hand.

They thus by common counsel   left off all further fight.
Hacked full many a helmet   and shields that late were bright
From hands down laid they weary;   as many as there might be,
With stains they all were bloody   'neath hands of the men of
        Burgundy.

Each whom he would took captive,   now they had won the fight.
Gernot, the noble hero,   and Hagen, doughty knight,
Bade bear forth the wounded.   Back led they with them then
Unto the land of Burgundy   five hundred stalwart fighting-men.

The knights, of victory cheated,   their native Denmark sought,
Nor had that day the Saxons   with such high valor fought,
That one could praise them for it,   which caused the warriors pain.
Then wept their friends full sorely   at home for those in battle slain.

For the Rhine then laden   they let their armor be.
Siegfried, the knight so doughty,   had won the victory
With his few chosen followers;   that he had nobly done,
Could not but free acknowledge   King Gunther's warriors everyone.

To Worms sent Gernot riding   now a messenger,
And of the joyous tiding   soon friends at home were ware,
How that it well had prospered   with him and all his men.
Fought that day with valor   for honor had those warriors keen.

The messenger sped forward   and told the tidings o'er.
Then joyfully they shouted   who boded ill before,
To hear the welcome story   that now to them was told.
From ladies fair and noble   came eager questions manifold,

Who all the fair fortune   of King Gunther's men would know.
One messenger they ordered   unto Kriemhild to go.
But that was done in secret: she durst let no one see,

For he was 'mongst those warriors   whom she did love so faithfully.

When to her own apartments   was come the messenger
Joyfully addressed him   Kriemhild the maiden fair:
"But tell me now glad tidings,   and gold I'll give to thee,
And if thou tell'st not falsely,   good friend thou'lt ever find in me.

"How has my good brother   Gernot in battle sped,
And how my other kinsmen?   Lies any of them dead?
Who wrought most deeds of valor?   — That shall thou let me know."
Then spake the messenger truly: "No knight but did high valor
      show.

"But in the dire turmoil   rode rider none so well,
O Princess fair and noble,   since I must truly tell,
As the stranger knight full noble   who comes from Netherland;
There deeds of mickle wonder   were wrought by doughty Siegfried's
      hand.

"Whate'er have all the warriors   in battle dared to do,
Dankwart and Hagen   and the other knights so true,
Howe'er they fought for honor,   'twas naught but idle play
Beside what there wrought Siegfried,   King Siegmund's son, amid
      the fray.

"Beneath their hands in battle   full many a hero fell,
Yet all the deeds of wonder   no man could ever tell,
Wrought by the hand of Siegfried,   when rode he 'gainst the foe:
And weep aloud must women   for friends by his strong arm laid
      low.

"There, too, the knight she loved   full many a maid must lose.
Were heard come down on helmet   so loud his mighty blows,
That they from gaping gashes   brought forth the flowing blood.
In all that maketh noble   he is a valiant knight and good.

"Many a deed of daring   of Metz Sir Ortwein wrought:
For all was evil faring   whom he with broadsword caught,
Doomed to die that instant,   or wounded sore to fall.
And there thy valiant brother   did greater havoc work than all

"That e'er in storm of battle   was done by warrior bold.

Of all those chosen warriors   let eke the truth be told:
The proud Burgundian heroes   have made it now right plain,
That they can free from insult   their country's honor well maintain.

"Beneath their hands was often   full many a saddle bare,
When o'er the field resounding   their bright swords cut the air.
The warriors from Rhine river   did here such victory win
That for their foes 'twere better   if they such meeting ne'er had seen.

"Keen the knights of Tronje   'fore all their valor showed,
When with their stalwart followers   against their foes they rode;
Slain by the hand of Hagen   must knights so many be,
'Twill long be in the telling   here in the land of Burgundy.

"Sindold and Hunold,   Gernot's men each one,
And the valiant Rumold   have all so nobly done,
King Luedeger will ever   have right good cause to rue
That he against thy kindred   at Rhine dared aught of harm to do.

"And deeds of all most wondrous   e'er done by warrior keen
In earliest time or latest,   by mortal ever seen,
Wrought there in lusty manner   Siegfried with doughty hand.
Rich hostages he bringeth   with him unto Gunther's land.

"By his own strength subdued them   the hero unsurpassed
And brought down dire ruin   upon King Luedegast,
Eke on the King of Saxons   his brother Luedeger.
Now hearken to the story   I tell thee, noble Princess fair.

"Them both hath taken captive   Siegfried's doughty hand.
Hostages were so many   ne'er brought into this land
As to the Rhine come hither   through his great bravery."
Than these could never tidings   unto her heart more welcome be.

"With captives home they're hieing,   five hundred men or mo',
And of the wounded dying   Lady shalt thou know,
Full eighty blood-stained barrows   unto Burgundian land,
Most part hewn down in battle   beneath keen Siegfried's doughty
     hand.

"Who message sent defiant   unto the Rhine so late
Must now as Gunther's prisoners   here abide their fate.

Bringing such noble captives   the victors glad return."
Then glowed with joy the princess   when she the tidings glad did
     learn.

Her cheeks so full of beauty   with joy were rosy-red,
That passed he had uninjured   through all the dangers dread,
The knight she loved so dearly,   Siegfried with doughty arm.
Good cause she had for joying   o'er all her friends escaped from
     harm.

Then spake the beauteous maiden: "Glad news thou hast told me,
Wherefor now rich apparel   thy goodly meed shall be,
And to thee shall be given   ten marks of gold as well."
'Tis thus a thing right pleasant   to ladies high such news to tell.

The presents rich they gave him,   gold and apparel rare.
Then hastened to the casement   full many a maiden fair,
And on the street looked downward: hither riding did they see
Many a knight high-hearted   into the land of Burgundy.

There came who 'scaped uninjured,   and wounded borne along,
All glad to hear the greetings   of friends, a joyful throng.
To meet his friends the monarch   rode out in mickle glee:
In joying now was ended   all his full great anxiety.

Then did he well his warriors   and eke the strangers greet;
And for a king so mighty   'twere nothing else but meet
That he should thank right kindly   the gallant men each one,
Who had in storm of battle   the victory so bravely won.

Then of his friends King Gunther   bade tidings tell straightway,
Of all his men how many   were fallen in the fray.
Lost had he none other   than warriors three score:
Then wept they for the heroes,   as since they did for many more.

Shields full many brought they   all hewn by valiant hand,
And many a shattered helmet   into King Gunther's hand.
The riders then dismounted   from their steeds before the hall,
And a right hearty welcome   from friends rejoicing had they all.

Then did they for the warriors   lodging meet prepare,
And for his guests the monarch   bade full well have care.

He bade them take the wounded   and tend them carefully,
And toward his enemies also   his gentle bearing might ye see.

To Luedeger then spake he: "Right welcome art thou here.
Through fault of thine now have I   lost many friends full dear,
For which, have I good fortune,   thou shall right well atone.
God rich reward my liegemen,   such faithfulness to me they've
    shown."

"Well may'st thou thank them, truly,"   spake then Luedeger;
"Hostages so noble   won a monarch ne'er.
For chivalrous protection   rich goods we offer thee,
That thou now right gracious   to us thy enemies shalt be."

"I'll grant you both your freedom,"   spake the king again;
"But that my enemies surely   here by me remain,
Therefor I'll have good pledges   they ne'er shall quit my land,
Save at my royal pleasure."   Thereto gave Luedeger the hand.

Sweet rest then found the weary   their tired limbs to aid,
And gently soon on couches   the wounded knights were laid;
Mead and wine right ruddy   they poured out plenteously:
Than they and all their followers   merrier men there none might be.

Their shields all hacked in battle   secure were laid away;
And not a few of saddles   stained with blood that day,
Lest women weep to see them,   hid they too from sight.
Full many a keen rider   home came aweary from the fight.

The host in gentlest manner   did his guests attend:
The land around with stranger   was crowded, and with friend.
They bade the sorely wounded   nurse with especial care:
Whereby the knights high-hearted   'neath all their wounds knew not
    despair.

Who there had skill in healing   received reward untold,
Silver all unweighéd   and thereto ruddy gold
For making whole the heroes   after the battle sore.
To all his friends the monarch   gave presents rich in goodly store.

Who there again was minded   to take his homeward way
They bade, as one a friend doth,   yet a while to stay.

The king did then take counsel   how to reward each one,
For they his will in battle   like liegemen true had nobly done.

Then outspake royal Gernot: "Now let them homeward go;
After six weeks are over,   — thus our friends shall know —
To hold high feast they're bidden   hither to come again;
Many a knight now lying   sore wounded will be healed ere then.

Of Netherland the hero   would also then take leave.
When of this King Gunther   did tidings first receive,
The knight besought he kindly   not yet his leave to take:
To this he'd ne'er consented   an it were not for Kriemhild's sake.

A prince he was too noble   to take the common pay;
He had right well deserved it   that the king alway
And all his warriors held him   in honor, for they had seen
What by his arm in battle   bravely had accomplished been.

He stayed there yet a little   for the maiden's sake alone,
Whom he would see so gladly.   And all fell out full soon
As he at heart had wished it: well known to him was she.
Home to his father's country   joyously anon rode he.

The king bade at all seasons   keep up the tournament,
And many a youthful rider   forth to the lists there went.
The while were seats made ready   by Worms upon the strand
For all who soon were coming   unto the Burgundian land.

In the meantime also,   ere back the knights returned,
Had Kriemhild, noble lady,   the tidings likewise learned,
The king would hold high feasting   with all his gallant men.
There was a mickle hurry,   and busy were fair maidens then

With dresses and with wimples   that they there should wear.
Ute, queen so stately,   the story too did hear,
How to them were coming   proud knights of highest worth.
Then from enfolding covers   were store of dresses rich brought forth.

Such love she bore her children   she bade rich dress prepare,
Wherewith adorned were ladies   and many a maiden fair,
And not a few young riders   in the land of Burgundy.
For strangers many bade she   rich garments eke should measured be.

Fifth Adventure

How Siegfried first saw Kriembild

Unto the Rhine now daily   the knights were seen to ride,
Who there would be full gladly   to share the festive tide.
To all that thither journeyed   to the king to show them true,
In plenty them were given   steeds and rich apparel too.

And soon were seats made ready   for every noble guest,
As we have heard the story,   for highest and for best,
Two and thirty princes   at the festival.
Then vied with one another   to deck themselves the ladies all.

Never was seen idle   the young Prince Giselher:
The guests and all their followers   received full kindly were
By him and eke by Gernot   and their men everyone.
The noble thanes they greeted   as ever 'tis in honor done.

With gold bright gleaming saddles   unto the land they brought,
Good store of rich apparel   and shields all richly wrought
Unto the Rhine they carried   to that high festival.
And joyous days were coming   for the woúnded warriors all.

They who yet on couches   lay wounded grievously
For joy had soon forgotten   how bitter death would be:
The sick and all the ailing   no need of pity had.
Anent the days of feasting   were they o'er the tidings glad,

How they should make them merry   there where all were so.
Delight beyond all measure,   of joys an overflow,
Had in sooth the people   seen on every hand:

Then rose a mickle joyance   over all King Gunther's land.

Full many a warrior valiant   one morn at Whitsuntide
All gorgeously appareled   was thither seen to ride,
Five thousand men or over,   where the feast should be;
And vied in every quarter   knight with knight in revelry.

Thereof the host was mindful,   for he well did understand
How at heart right warmly   the hero of Netherland
Loved alone his sister,   though her he ne'er had seen,
Who praised for wondrous beauty   before all maidens else had been.

Then spake the thane so noble   of Metz Sir Ortwein:
"Wilt thou full be honored   by every guest of thine,
Then do them all the pleasure   the winsome maids to see,
That are held so high in honor   here in the land of Burgundy.

"What were a man's chief pleasure,   his very joy of life,
An 't were not a lovely maiden   or a stately wife?
Then let the maid thy sister   before thy guests appear."
— Brave thanes did there full many   at heart rejoice the rede to hear.

"Thy words I'll gladly follow,"   then the monarch said,
And all the knights who heard him   ere thereat right glad.
Then told was Queen Ute   and eke her daughter fair,
That they with maids in waiting   unto the court should soon repair.

Then in well-stored wardrobes   rich attire they sought,
And forth from folding covers   their glittering dresses brought,
Armbands and silken girdles   of which they many had.
And zealous to adorn her   was then full many a winsome maid.

Full many a youthful squire   upon that day did try,
By decking of his person,   to win fair lady's eye;
For the which great good fortune   he'd take no monarch's crown:
They longed to see those maidens,   whom they before had never
     known.

For her especial service   the king did order then
To wait upon his sister   a hundred of his men,
As well upon his mother: they carried sword in hand.
That was the court attendance   there in the Burgundian land.

Ute, queen so stately,   then came forth with her:
And with the queen in waiting   ladies fair there were,
A hundred or over,   in festal robes arrayed.
Eke went there with Kriemhild   full many a fair and winsome maid.

Forth from their own apartments   they all were seen to go:
There was a mickle pressing   of good knights to and fro,
Who hoped to win the pleasure,   if such a thing might be,
The noble maiden Kriemhild,   delight of every eye, to see.

Now came she fair and lovely,   as the ruddy sun of morn
From misty clouds emerging.   Straight he who long had borne
Her in his heart and loved her,   from all his gloom was freed,
As so stately there before him   he saw the fair and lovely maid.

Her rich apparel glittered   with many a precious stone,
And with a ruddy beauty   her cheeks like roses shone.
Though you should wish to do so,   you could not say, I ween,
That e'er a fairer lady   in all the world before was seen.

As in a sky all starlit   the moon shines out so bright,
And through the cloudlets peering   pours down her gentle light,
E'en so was Kriemhild's beauty   among her ladies fair:
The hearts of gallant heroes   were gladder when they saw her there.

The richly clad attendants   moved stately on before,
And the valiant thanes high-hearted   stood patiently no more,
But pressed right eager forward   to see the lovely maid:
In noble Siegfried's bosom   alternate joy and anguish swayed.

He thought with heart despairing,   "How could it ever be,
That I should win thy favor?   There hoped I foolishly.
But had I e'er to shun thee,   then were I rather dead."
And oft, to think upon it,   the color from his visage fled.

The noble son of Siegmund   did there so stately stand
As if his form were pictured   by good old master's hand
Upon a piece of parchment.   All who saw, confessed
That he of all good heroes   was the stateliest and the best.

The fair Kriemhild's attendants   gave order to make way

On all sides for the ladies,   and willing thanes obey.
To see their noble bearing   did every warrior cheer;
Full many a stately lady   of gentle manner born was there.

Then outspake of Burgundy   Gernot the valiant knight:
"To him who thus has helped thee   so bravely in the fight,
Gunther, royal brother,   shalt thou like favor show,
A thane before all others;   he's worthy of it well, I trow.

"Let then the doughty Siegfried   unto my sister go
To have the maiden's greetings, / — 'twill be our profit so.
She that ne'er greeted hero   shall greet him courteously,
That thus the stately warrior   for aye our faithful friend may be."

The king's knights hastened gladly   upon his high command
And told these joyous tidings   to the prince of Netherland.
"It is the king's good pleasure   that thou to court shalt go,
To have his sister's greetings;   to honor thee 'tis ordered so."

Then was the thane full valiant   thereat soon filled with joy.
Yea, bore he in his bosom   delight without alloy
At thought that he should straightway   Ute's fair daughter see.
Siegfried anon she greeted   in courteous manner lovingly.

As she saw the knight high-hearted   there before her stand,
Blushed red and spake the maiden,   the fairest of the land:
"A welcome, brave Sir Siegfried,   thou noble knight and good."
As soon as he had heard it,   the hearty greeting cheered his mood.

Before her low he bended;   him by the hand took she,
And by her onward wended   the knight full willingly.
They cast upon each other   fond glances many a one,
The knight and eke the maiden;   furtively it all was done.

Whether he pressed friendly   that hand as white as snow
From the love he bore her,   that I do not know;
Yet believe I cannot   that this was left undone,
For straightway showed the maiden   that he her heart had fully won.

In the sunny summer season   and in the month of May
Had his heart seen never   before so glad a day,
Nor one so fully joyous,   as when he walked beside

That maiden rich in beauty   whom fain he'd choose to be his bride.

Then thought many a warrior: "Were it likewise granted me
To walk beside the maiden,   just as now I see,
Or to lie beside her,   how gladly were that done!"
But ne'er a knight more fully   had gracious lady's favor won.

From all the lands far distant   were guests distinguished there,
But fixed each eye was only   upon this single pair.
By royal leave did Kriemhild   kiss then the stately knight:
In all the world he never   before had known so rare delight.

Then full of strange forebodings,   of Denmark spake the king:
"This full loving greeting   to many woe will bring,
— My heart in secret warns me —   through Siegfried's doughty hand.
God give that he may never   again be seen within my land."

On all sides then 'twas ordered   'fore Kriemhild and her train
Of women make free passage.   Full many a valiant thane
With her unto the minster   in courtly way went on.
But from her side was parted   the full stately knight anon.

Then went she to the minster,   and with her many a maid.
In such rich apparel   Kriemhild was arrayed,
That hearty wishes many   there were made in vain:
Her comely form delighted   the eye of many a noble thane.

Scarce could tarry Siegfried   till mass was sung the while.
And surely did Dame Fortune   upon him kindly smile,
To him she was so gracious   whom in his heart he bore.
Eke did he the maiden,   as she full well deserved, adore.

As after mass then Kriemhild   came to the minster door,
The knight his homage offered,   as he had done before.
Then began to thank him   the full beauteous maid,
That he her royal brothers   did 'gainst their foes so nobly aid.

"God speed thee, Sir Siegfried,"   spake the maiden fair,
"For thou hast well deservéd   that all these warriors are,
As it hath now been told me,   right grateful unto thee."
Then gan he cast his glances   on the Lady Kriemhild lovingly.

"True will I ever serve them,"   — so spake the noble thane —
"And my head shall never   be laid to rest again,
Till I, if life remaineth,   have their good favor won.
In sooth, my Lady Kriemhild,   for thy fair grace it all is done."

Ne'er a day passed over   for a twelve of happy days,
But saw they there beside him   the maiden all did praise,
As she before her kinsmen   to court would daily go:
It pleased the thane full highly   that they did him such honor show.

Delight and great rejoicing,   a mighty jubilee,
Before King Gunther's castle   daily might ye see,
Without and eke within it,   'mongst keen men many a one.
By Ortwein and by Hagen   great deeds and wondrous there were
    done.

Whate'er was done by any,   in all they ready were
To join in way right lusty,   both the warriors rare:
Whereby 'mongst all the strangers   they won an honored name,
And through their deeds so wondrous   of Gunther's land spread far
    the fame.

Who erstwhile lay sore wounded   now were whole again,
And fain would share the pastime,   with all the king's good men;
With shields join in the combat,   and try the shaft so long.
Wherein did join them many   of the merry-making throng.

To all who joined the feasting   the host in plenty bade
Supply the choicest viands: so guarded well he had
'Gainst whate'er reproaches   could rise from spite or spleen.
Unto his guests right friendly   to go the monarch now was seen.

He spake: "Ye thanes high-hearted,   ere now ye part from me,
Accept of these my presents;   for I would willingly
Repay your noble service.   Despise ye not, I pray,
What now I will share with you: 'tis offered in right grateful way."

Straightway they of Denmark   thus to the king replied:
"Ere now upon our journey   home again we ride,
We long for lasting friendship.   Thereof we knights have need,
For many a well-loved kinsman   at hands of thy good thanes lies
    dead."

Luedegast was recovered   from all his wounds so sore,
And eke the lord of Saxons   from fight was whole once more.
Some amongst their warriors   left they dead behind.
Then went forth King Gunther   where he Siegfried might find.

Unto the thane then spake he: "Thy counsel give, I pray.
The foes whom we hold captive   fain would leave straightway,
And long for lasting friendship   with all my men and me.
Now tell me, good Sir Siegfried,   what here seemeth good to thee.

"What the lords bid as ransom,   shall now to thee be told
Whate'er five hundred horses   might bear of ruddy gold,
They'd give to me right gladly,   would I but let them free."
Then spake the noble Siegfried: "That were to do right foolishly.

"Thou shalt let them freely   journey hence again;
And that they both hereafter   shall evermore refrain
From leading hostile army   against thee and thy land,
Therefor in pledge of friendship   let each now give to thee the
     hand."

"Thy rede I'll gladly follow."   Straightway forth they went.
To those who offered ransom   the answer then was sent,
Their gold no one desired   which they would give before.
The warriors battle-weary   dear friends did yearn to see once more.

Full many a shield all laden   with treasure forth they bore:
He dealt it round unmeasured   to friends in goodly store;
Each one had marks five hundred   and some had more, I ween.
Therein King Gunther followed   the rede of Gernot, knight full
     keen.

Then was a great leave-taking,   as they departed thence.
The warriors all 'fore Kriemhild   appeared in reverence,
And eke there where her mother   Queen Ute sat near by.
Gallant thanes were never   dismissed as these so graciously.

Bare were the lodging-places,   when away the strangers rode.
Yet in right lordly manner   there at home abode
The king with friends around him,   full noble men who were.
And them now saw they daily   at court before Kriemhild appear.

Eke would the gallant hero   Siegfried thence depart,
The thing to gain despairing   whereon was set his heart.
The king was told the tidings   how that he would away.
Giselher his brother   did win the knight with them to stay.

"Whither, O noble Siegfried,   wilt thou now from us ride?
Do as I earnest pray thee,   and with these thanes abide,
As guest here with King Gunther,   and live right merrily.
Here dwell fair ladies many: them will he gladly let thee see."

Then spake the doughty Siegfried: "Our steeds leave yet at rest,
The while from this my purpose   to part will I desist.
Our shields once more take from us.   Though gladly home I would,
Naught 'gainst the fond entreaties   of Giselher avail me could."

So stayed the knight full gallant   for sake of friendship there.
In sooth in ne'er another   country anywhere
Had he so gladly lingered: iwis it was that he,
Now whensoe'er he wished it,   Kriemhild the maiden fair could see.

'Twas her surpassing beauty   that made the knight to stay.
With many a merry pastime   they whiled the time away;
But love for her oppressed him,   oft-times grievously.
Whereby anon the hero   a mournful death was doomed to die.

Sixth Adventure

How Gunther Fared to Isenland to Brunhild

Tidings unknown to any   from over Rhine now come,
How winsome maids a many   far yonder had their home.
Whereof the royal Gunther   bethought him one to win,
And o'er the thought the monarch   of full joyous mood was seen.

There was a queenly maiden   seated over sea,
Like her nowhere another   was ever known to be.
She was in beauty matchless,   full mickle was her might;
Her love the prize of contest,   she hurled the shaft with valiant
      knight.

The stone she threw far distant,   wide sprang thereafter too.
Who turned to her his fancy   with intent to woo,
Three times perforce must vanquish   the lady of high degree;
Failed he in but one trial,   forfeited his head had he.

This same the lusty princess   times untold had done.
When to a warrior gallant   beside the Rhine 'twas known,
He thought to take unto him   the noble maid for wife:
Thereby must heroes many   since that moment lose their life.

Then spake of Rhine the master: "I'll down unto the sea
Unto Brunhild journey,   fare as 'twill with me.
For her unmeasured beauty   I'll gladly risk my life,
Ready eke to lose it,   if she may not be my wife."

"I counsel thee against it,"   spake then Siegfried.
"So terrible in contest   the queen is indeed,

Who for her love is suitor   his zeal must dearly pay.
So shalt thou from the journey   truly be content to stay."

"So will I give thee counsel,"   outspake Hagen there,
"That thou beg of Siegfried   with thee to bear
The perils that await thee: that is now my rede,
To him is known so fully   what with Brunhild will be thy need."

He spake: "And wilt thou help me,   noble Siegfried,
To win the lovely maiden?   Do what now I plead;
And if in all her beauty   she be my wedded wife,
To meet thy fullest wishes   honor will I pledge and life."

Thereto answered Siegfried,   the royal Siegmund's son:
"Giv'st thou me thy sister,   so shall thy will be done,
— Kriemhild the noble princess,   in beauty all before.
For toils that I encounter   none other meed I ask thee more."

"That pledge I," spake then Gunther,   "Siegfried, in thy hand.
And comes the lovely Brunhild   thither to this land,
Thereunto thee my sister   for wife I'll truly give,
That with the lovely maiden   thou may'st ever joyful live."

Oaths the knight full noble   upon the compact swore,
Whereby to them came troubles   and dangers all the more,
Ere they the royal lady   brought unto the Rhine.
Still should the warriors valiant   in sorest need and sorrow pine.

With him carried Siegfried   that same mantle then,
The which with mickle trouble   had won the hero keen
From a dwarf in struggle,   Alberich by name.
They dressed them for the journey,   the valiant thanes of lofty fame.

And when the doughty Siegfried   the sightless mantle wore,
Had he within it   of strength as good a store
As other men a dozen   in himself alone.
The full stately princess   anon by cunning art he won.

Eke had that same mantle   such wondrous properties
That any man whatever   might work whate'er he please
When once he had it on him,   yet none could see or tell.
'Twas so that he won Brunhild;   whereby him evil since befell.

"Ere we begin our journey,   Siegfried, tell to me,
That we with fullest honor   come unto the sea,
Shall we lead warriors with us   down to Brunhild's land?
Thanes a thirty thousand   straightway shall be called to hand."

"Men bring we ne'er so many,"   answered Siegfried then.
"So terrible in custom   ever is the queen,
That all would death encounter   from her angry mood.
I'll give thee better counsel,   thane in valor keen and good.

"Like as knights-errant journey   down the Rhine shall we.
Those now will I name thee   who with us shall be;
But four in all the company   seaward shall we fare:
Thus shall we woo the lady,   what fortune later be our share.

"Myself one of the company,   a second thou shalt be,
Hagen be the third one   — so fare we happily;
The fourth let it be Dankwart,   warrior full keen.
Never thousand others   dare in fight withstand us then."

"The tale I would know gladly,"   the king then further said,
"Ere we have parted thither   — of that were I full glad —
What should we of apparel,   that would befit us well,
Wear in Brunhild's presence: that shalt thou now to Gunther tell."

"Weeds the very finest   that ever might be found
They wear in every season   in Brunhild's land:
So shall we rich apparel   before the lady wear,
That we have not dishonor   where men the tale hereafter hear."

Then spake he to the other: "Myself will go unto
My own loving mother,   if I from her may sue
That her fair tendant maidens   help that we be arrayed
As we may go in honor   before the high majestic maid."

Then spake of Tronje Hagen   with noble courtliness:
"Why wilt thou of thy mother   beg such services?
Only let thy sister   hear our mind and mood:
So shall for this our journey   her good service be bestowed."

Then sent he to his sister   that he her would see,

And with him also Siegfried.   Ere that such might be,
Herself had there the fair one   in rich apparel clad.
Sooth to tell, the visit   but little did displease the maid.

Then also were her women   decked as for them was meet.
The princes both were coming: she rose from off her seat,
As doth a highborn lady   when that she did perceive,
And went the guest full noble   and eke her brother to receive.

"Welcome be my brother   and his companion too.
I'd know the story gladly,"   spake the maiden so,
"What ye now are seeking   that ye are come to me:
I pray you straightway tell me   how 't with you valiants twain may
       be."

Then spake the royal Gunther: "Lady, thou shall hear:
Spite of lofty spirits   have we yet a care.
To woo a maid we travel   afar to lands unknown;
We should against the journey   have rich apparel for our own."

"Seat thee now, dear brother,"   spake the princess fair;
"Let me hear the story,   who the ladies are
That ye will seek as suitors   in stranger princes' land."
Both good knights the lady   took in greeting by the hand.

With the twain then went she   where she herself had sat,
To couches rich and costly,   in sooth believe ye that,
Wrought in design full cunning   of gold embroidery.
And with these fair ladies   did pass the time right pleasantly.

Many tender glances   and looks full many a one
Fondly knight and lady   each other cast upon.
Within his heart he bore her,   she was as his own life.
Anon the fairest Kriemhild   was the doughty Siegfried's wife.

Then spake the mighty monarch: "Full loving sister mine,
This may we ne'er accomplish   without help of thine.
Unto Brunhild's country   as suitor now we fare:
'Tis fitting that 'fore ladies   we do rich apparel wear."

Then spake the royal maiden: "Brother dear to me,
In whatsoever manner   my help may given be,

Of that I well assure you,   ready thereto am I.
To Kriemhild 'twere a sorrow   if any should the same deny.

"Of me, O noble brother,   thou shalt not ask in vain:
Command in courteous manner   and I will serve thee fain.
Whatever be thy pleasure,   for that I'll lend my aid
And willingly I'll do it,"   spake the fair and winsome maid.

"It is our wish, dear sister,   apparel good to wear;
That shall now directing   the royal hand prepare;
And let thy maids see to it   that all is done aright,
For we from this same journey   turn not aside for word of wight."

Spake thereupon the maiden: "Now mark ye what I say:
Myself have silks in plenty;   now send us rich supply
Of stones borne on bucklers,   so vesture we'll prepare."
To do it royal Gunther   and Siegfried both right ready were.

"And who are your companions,"   further questioned she,
"Who with you appareled   now for court shall be?"
"I it is and Siegfried,   and of my men are two,
Dankwart and Hagen,   who with us to court shall go.

"Now rightly what we tell thee,   mark, O sister dear:
'Tis that we four companions   for four days may wear
Thrice daily change of raiment   so wrought with skillful hand
That we without dishonor   may take our leave of Brunhild's land."

After fair leave-taking   the knights departed so.
Then of her attendants   thirty maids to go
Forth from her apartments   Kriemhild the princess bade,
Of those that greatest cunning   in such skillful working had.

The silks that were of Araby   white as the snow in sheen,
And from the land of Zazamank   like unto grass so green,
With stones of price they broidered;   that made apparel rare.
Herself she cut them, Kriemhild   the royal maiden debonair.

Fur linings fashioned fairly   from dwellers in the sea
Beheld by people rarely,   the best that e'er might be,
With silken stuffs they covered   for the knights to wear.
Now shall ye of the shining   weeds full many a wonder hear.

From land of far Morocco   and eke from Libya
Of silks the very finest   that ever mortal saw
With any monarch's kindred,   they had a goodly store.
Well showed the Lady Kriemhild   that unto them good will she
      bore.

Since they unto the journey   had wished that so it be,
Skins of costly ermine   used they lavishly,
Whereon were silken pieces   black as coal inlaid.
Today were any nobles   in robes so fashioned well arrayed.

From the gold of Araby   many a stone there shone.
The women long were busy   before the work was done;
But all the robes were finished   ere seven weeks did pass,
When also trusty armor   for the warriors ready was.

When they at length were ready   adown the Rhine to fare,
A ship lay waiting for them   strong built with mickle care,
Which should bear them safely   far down unto the sea.
The maidens rich in beauty   plied their work laboriously.

Then 'twas told the warriors   for them was ready there
The finely wrought apparel   that they were to wear;
Just as they had wished it,   so it had been made;
After that the heroes   there by the Rhine no longer stayed.

To the knights departing   went soon a messenger:
Would they come in person   to view their new attire,
If it had been fitted   short and long aright.
'Twas found of proper measure,   and thanked those ladies fair each
      knight.

And all who there beheld them   they must needs confess
That in the world they never   had gazed on fairer dress:
At court to wear th' apparel   did therefore please them well.
Of warriors better furnished   never could a mortal tell.

Thanks oft-times repeated   were there not forgot.
Leave of parting from them   the noble knights then sought:
Like thanes of noble bearing   they went in courteous wise.
Then dim and wet with weeping   grew thereat two shining eyes.

She spake: "O dearest brother,   still here thou mightest stay,
And woo another woman —   that were the better way —
Where so sore endangered   stood not thus thy life.
Here nearer canst thou find thee   equally a highborn wife."

I ween their hearts did tell them   what later came to pass.
They wept there all together,   whatever spoken was.
The gold upon their bosoms   was sullied 'neath the tears
That from their eyes in plenty   fell adown amid their fears.

She spake: "O noble Siegfried,   to thee commended be
Upon thy truth and goodness   the brother dear to me,
That he come unscathed   home from Brunhild's land."
That plighted the full valiant   knight in Lady Kriemhild's hand.

The mighty thane gave answer: "If I my life retain,
Then shall thy cares, good Lady,   all have been in vain.
All safe I'll bring him hither   again unto the Rhine,
Be that to thee full sicker."   To him did the fair maid incline.

Their shields of golden color   were borne unto the strand,
And all their trusty armor   was ready brought to hand.
They bade their horses bring them: they would at last depart.
— Thereat did fairest women   weep with sad foreboding heart.

Down from lofty casement   looked many a winsome maid,
As ship and sail together   by stirring breeze were swayed.
Upon the Rhine they found them,   the warriors full of pride.
Then outspake King Gunther: "Who now is here the ship to guide?"

"That will I," spake Siegfried;   "I can upon the flood
Lead you on in safety,   that know ye, heroes good;
For all the water highways   are known right well to me."
With joy they then departed   from the land of Burgundy.

A mighty pole then grasped he,   Siegfried the doughty man,
And the ship from shore   forth to shove began.
Gunther the fearless also   himself took oar in hand.
The knights thus brave and worthy   took departure from the land.

They carried rich provisions,   thereto the best of wine

That might in any quarter be found about the Rhine.
Their chargers stood in comfort and rested by the way:
The ship it moved so lightly that naught of injury had they.

Stretched before the breezes were the great sail-ropes tight,
And twenty miles they journeyed ere did come the night,
By fair breezes favored down toward the sea.
Their toil repaid thereafter the dauntless knights full grievously.

Upon the twelfth morning, as we in story hear,
Had they by the breezes thence been carried far,
Unto Castle Isenstein and Brunhild's country:
That to Siegfried only was known of all the company.

As soon as saw King Gunther so many towers rise
And eke the boundless marches stretch before his eyes,
He spake: "Tell me, friend Siegfried, is it known to thee
Whose they are, the castles and the majestic broad country?"

Thereto gave answer Siegfried: "That well to me is known:
Brunhild for their mistress do land and people own
And Isenstein's firm towers, as ye have heard me say.
Ladies fair a many shall ye here behold today.

"And I will give you counsel: be it well understood
That all your words must tally — so methinks 'twere good.
If ere today is over our presence she command,
Must we leave pride behind us, as before Brunhild we stand.

"When we the lovely lady 'mid her retainers see,
Then shall ye, good companions, in all your speech agree
That Gunther is my master and I his serving-man:
'Tis thus that all he hopeth shall we in the end attain."

To do as he had bidden consented straight each one,
And spite of proudest spirit they left it not undone.
All that he wished they promised, and good it proved to be
When anon King Gunther the fair Brunhild came to see.

"Not all to meet thy wishes do I such service swear,
But most 'tis for thy sister, Kriemhild the maiden fair;
Just as my soul unto me she is my very life,

And fain would I deserve it   that she in truth become my wife."

Seventh Adventure

How Gunther Won Brunhild

The while they thus did parley   their ship did forward glide
So near unto the castle   that soon the king espied
Aloft within the casements   many a maiden fair to see.
That all to him were strangers   thought King Gunther mournfully.

He asked then of Siegfried,   who bare him company:
"Know'st thou aught of the maidens,   who the same may be,
Gazing yonder downward   upon us on the tide?
Howe'er is named their master,   minded are they high in pride."

Then spake the valiant Siegfried: "Now thither shalt thou spy
Unseen among the ladies,   then not to me deny
Which, wert thou free in choosing,   thou'dst take to be thy queen."
"That will I do," then answered   Gunther the valiant knight and
      keen.

"I see there one among them   by yonder casement stand,
Clad in snow-white raiment: 'tis she my eyes demand,
So buxom she in stature,   so fair she is to see.
An I were free in choosing,   she it is my wife must be."

"Full well now in choosing   thine eyes have guided thee:
It is the stately Brunhild   the maiden fair to see,
That doth now unto her   thy heart and soul compel."
All the maiden's bearing   pleased the royal Gunther well.

But soon the queen commanded   from casement all to go
Of those her beauteous maidens: they should not stand there so

To be gazed at by the strangers.　　They must obey her word.
What were the ladies doing,　　of that moreover have we heard.

Unto the noble strangers　　their beauty they would show,
A thing which lovely women　　are ever wont to do.
Unto the narrow casements　　came they crowding on,
When they spied the strangers:　　that they might also see, 'twas done.

But four the strangers numbered,　　who came unto that land.
Siegfried the doughty　　the king's steed led in hand:
They saw it from the casements,　　many a lovely maid,
And saw the willing service　　unto royal Gunther paid.

Then held he by the bridle　　for him his gallant steed,
A good and fair-formed charger,　　strong and of noble breed,
Until the royal Gunther　　into the saddle sprung.
Thus did serve him Siegfried:　　a service all forgot ere long.

Then his own steed he also　　led forth upon the shore.
Such menial service had he　　full seldom done before,
That he should hold the stirrup　　for monarch whomsoe'er.
Down gazing from the casements　　beheld it ladies high and fair.

At every point according,　　the heroes well bedight
— Their dress and eke their chargers　　of color snowy white —
Were like unto each other,　　and well-wrought shield each one
Of the good knights bore with him,　　that brightly glimmered in the
　　　sun.

Jeweled well was saddle　　and narrow martingale
As they rode so stately　　in front of Brunhild's Hall,
And thereon bells were hanging　　of red gold shining bright.
So came they to that country,　　as fitting was for men of might,

With spears all newly polished,　　with swords, well-made that were
And by the stately heroes　　hung down unto the spur:
Such bore the valiant riders　　of broad and cutting blade.
The noble show did witness　　Brunhild the full stately maid.

With him came then Dankwart　　and Hagen, doughty thane.
The story further telleth　　how that the heroes twain
Of color black as raven　　rich attire wore,

And each a broad and mighty   shield of rich adornment bore.

Rich stones from India's country   every eye could see,
Impending on their tunics,   sparkle full brilliantly.
Their vessel by the river   they left without a guard,
As thus the valiant heroes   rode undaunted castleward.

Six and fourscore towers   without they saw rise tall,
Three spacious palaces   and molded well a hall
All wrought of precious marble   green as blade of grass,
Wherein the royal Brunhild   with company of fair ladies was.

The castle doors unbolted   were flung open wide
As out toward them   the men of Brunhild hied
And received the strangers   into their Lady's land.
Their steeds they bade take over,   and also shield from out the hand.

Then spake a man-in-waiting: "Give o'er the sword each thane,
And eke the shining armor." —   "Good friend, thou ask'st in vain,"
Spake of Tronje Hagen;   "the same we'd rather wear."
Then gan straightway Siegfried   the country's custom to declare.

"'Tis wont within this castle,   — of that be now aware —
That never any stranger   weapons here shall bear.
Now let them hence be carried: well dost thou as I say."
In this did full unwilling   Hagen, Gunther's man, obey.

They bade the strangers welcome   with drink and fitting rest.
Soon might you see on all sides   full many knights the best
In princely weeds appareled   to their reception go:
Yet did they mickle gazing   who would the keen newcomers know.

Then unto Lady Brunhild   the tidings strange were brought
How that unknown warriors   now her land had sought,
In stately apparel   come sailing o'er the sea.
The maiden fair and stately   gave question how the same might be.

"Now shall ye straight inform me,"   spake she presently,
"Who so unfamiliar   these warrior knights may be,
That within my castle   thus so lordly stand,
And for whose sake the heroes   have hither journeyed to my land."

Then spake to her a servant: "Lady, I well can say
Of them I've ne'er seen any   before this present day:
Be it not that one among them   is like unto Siegfried.
Him give a goodly welcome: so is to thee my loyal rede.

"The next of the companions   he is a worthy knight:
If that were in his power   he well were king of might
O'er wide domains of princes,   the which might reach his hand.
Now see him by the others   so right majestically stand.

"The third of the companions,   that he's a man of spleen,
— Withal of fair-formed body,   know thou, stately Queen, —
Do tell his rapid glances   that dart so free from him.
He is in all his thinking   a man, I ween, of mood full grim.

"The youngest one among them   he is a worthy knight:
As modest as a maiden,   I see the thane of might
Goodly in his bearing   standing so fair to see,
We all might fear if any   affront to him should offered be.

"How blithe soe'er his manner,   how fair soe'er is he,
Well could he cause of sorrow   to stately woman be,
If he gan show his anger.   In him may well be seen
He is in knightly virtues   a thane of valor bold and keen."

Then spake the queen in answer: "Bring now my robes to hand.
And is the mighty Siegfried   come unto this land,
For love of me brought thither,   he pays it with his life.
I fear him not so sorely   that I e'er become his wife."

So was fair Brunhild   straightway well arrayed.
Then went with her thither   full many a beauteous maid,
A hundred good or over,   bedight right merrily.
The full beauteous maidens   would those stranger warriors see.

And with them went the warriors   there of Isenland,
The knights attending Brunhild,   who bore sword in hand,
Five hundred men or over.   Scarce heart the strangers kept
As those knights brave and seemly   down from out the saddle leapt.

When the royal lady   Siegfried espied,
Now mote ye willing listen   what there the maiden said.

"Welcome be thou, Siegfried,   hither unto this land.
What meaneth this thy journey,   gladly might I understand."

"Full mickle do I thank thee,   my Lady, high Brunhild,
That thou art pleased to greet me,   noble Princess mild,
Before this knight so noble,   who stands before me here:
For he is my master,   whom first to honor fitting were.

"Born is he of Rhineland: what need I say more?
For thee 'tis highest favor   that we do hither fare.
Thee will he gladly marry,   an bring that whatsoe'er.
Betimes shalt thou bethink thee: my master will thee never spare.

"For his name is Gunther   and he a mighty king.
If he thy love hath won him,   more wants he not a thing.
In sooth the king so noble   hath bade me hither fare:
And gladly had I left it,   might I to thwart his wishes dare."

She spake: "Is he thy master   and thou his vassal art,
Some games to him I offer,   and dare he there take part,
And comes he forth the victor,   so am I then his wife:
And be it I that conquer,   then shall ye forfeit each his life."

Then spake of Tronje Hagen: "Lady, let us see
Thy games so fraught with peril.   Before should yield to thee
Gunther my master,   that well were something rare.
He trows he yet is able   to win a maid so passing fair."

"Then shall ye try stone-putting   and follow up the cast,
And the spear hurl with me.   Do ye naught here in haste.
For well may ye pay forfeit   with honor eke and life:
Bethink ye thus full calmly,"   spake she whom Gunther would for
      wife.

Siegfried the valiant   stepped unto the king,
And bade him speak out freely   his thoughts upon this thing
Unto the queen so wayward,   he might have fearless heart.
"For to well protect thee   from her do I know an art."

Then spake the royal Gunther: "Now offer, stately Queen,
What play soe'er thou mayest.   And harder had it been,
Yet would I all have ventured   for all thy beauty's sake.

My head I'll willing forfeit or thyself my wife I'll make."

When therefore the Queen Brunhild heard how the matter stood
The play she begged to hasten, as indeed she should.
She bade her servants fetch her therefor apparel trim,
A mail-coat ruddy golden and shield well wrought from boss to
  rim.

A battle-tunic silken the maid upon her drew,
That in ne'er a contest weapon piercéd through,
Of skins from land of Libya, and structure rare and fine;
And brilliant bands embroidered might you see upon it shine.

Meanwhile were the strangers jibed with many a threat;
Dankwart and Hagen, their hearts began to beat.
How here the king should prosper were they of doubtful mood,
Thinking, "This our journey shall bring us wanderers naught of
  good."

le did also Siegfried the thane beyond compare,
Before 'twas marked by any, unto the ship repair,
Where he found his sightless mantle* that did hidden lie,
And slipped into 't full deftly: so was he veiled from every eye.

Thither back he hied him and found great company
About the queen who ordered what the high play should be.
There went he all in secret; so cunningly 'twas done,
Of all around were standing perceived him never anyone.

The ring it was appointed wherein the play should be
'Fore many a keen warrior who the same should see.
More than seven hundred were seen their weapons bear,
That whoso were the victor they might sure the same declare.

Thither was come Brunhild; all arméd she did stand
Like as she were to combat for many a royal land;
Upon her silken tunic were gold bars many a one,
And glowing 'mid the armor her flesh of winsome color shone.

Then followed her attendants and with them thither brought
At once a shield full stately, of pure red gold 'twas wrought,

* See *strophe 97, note.*

With steel-hard bands for facings,   full mickle 'twas and broad,
Wherewith in the contest   would guard herself the lovely maid.

To hold the shield securely   a well-wrought band there was,
Whereon lay precious jewels   green as blade of grass.
Full many a ray their luster   shot round against the gold.
He were a man full valiant   whom this high dame should worthy
     hold.

The shield was 'neath the boss-point,   as to us is said,
Good three spans in thickness,   which should bear the maid.
Of steel 'twas wrought so richly   and had of gold such share,
That chamberlain and fellows   three the same scarce could bear.

When the doughty Hagen   the shield saw thither brought,
Spake the knight of Tronje,   and savage was his thought:
"Where art thou now, King Gunther?   Shall we thus lose our life!
Whom here thou seekst for lover,   she is the very Devil's wife."

List more of her apparel;   she had a goodly store.
Of silk of Azagang   a tunic made she wore,
All bedight full richly;   amid its color shone
Forth from the queen it covered,   full many a sparkling precious
     stone.

Then brought they for the lady,   large and heavy there,
As she was wont to hurl it,   a sharply-pointed spear;
Strong and massive was it,   huge and broad as well,
And at both its edges   it cut with devastation fell.

To know the spear was heavy   list ye wonders more:
Three spears of common measure   'twould make, and something
     o'er.
Of Brunhild's attendants   three scarce the same could bear.
The heart of noble Gunther   thereat began to fill with fear.

Within his soul he thought him: "What pickle am I in?
Of hell the very Devil,   how might he save his skin?
Might I at home in Burgundy   safe and living be,
Should she for many a season   from proffered love of mine be free."

Then spake Hagen's brother   the valiant Dankwart:

"In truth this royal journey   doth sorely grieve my heart.
We passed for good knights one time: what caitiff's death, if we
Here in far-off country   a woman's game are doomed to be!

"It rueth me full sorely   that I came to this land.
And had my brother Hagen   his good sword in hand,
And had I mine to help him,   a bit more gently then,
A little tame of spirit,   might show themselves all Brunhild's men.

"And know it of a certain   to lord it thus they'd cease;
E'en though oaths a thousand   I'd sworn to keep the peace,
Before that I'd see perish   my dear lord shamefully,
Amid the souls departed   this fair maid herself should be."

"Well should we unhampered   quit at last this land,"
Spake his brother Hagen,   "did we in armor stand,
Such as we need for battle,   and bore we broadswords good:
'Twould be a little softened,   this doughty lady's haughty mood."

Well heard the noble maiden   what the warriors spoke.
Back athwart her shoulder   she sent a smiling look:
"Now thinks he him so valiant,   so let them arméd stand;
Their full keen-edged broadswords   give the warriors each in hand."

When they their swords received,   as the maiden said,
The full valiant Dankwart   with joy his face grew red.
"Now play they what them pleaseth,"   cried the warrior brave;
"Gunther is yet a freeman,   since now in hand good swords we
        have."

The royal Brunhild's prowess   with terror was it shown.
Into the ring they bore her   in sooth a ponderous stone,
Great and all unwieldy,   huge it was and round:
And scarce good knights a dozen   together raised it from the
        ground.

To put this was her custom   after trial with the spear.
Thereat the men of Burgundy   began to quake with fear.
"Alack! Alack!" quoth Hagen,   "what seeks the king for bride?
Beneath in hell 'twere better   the Devil had her by his side!"

On her white arms the flowing   sleeves she backward flung,

Then with grasp of power   the shield in hand she swung,
And spear poised high above her.   So did the contest start.
Gunther and Siegfried   saw Brunhild's ire with falling heart.

And were it not that Siegfried   a ready help did bring,
Surely then had perished   beneath her hand the king.
There went he unperceived   and the king's hand did touch.
Gunther at his cunning   artifice was troubled much.

"What is that hath touched me?"   thought the monarch keen.
Then gazed he all around him: none was there to be seen.
A voice spake: "Siegfried is it,   a friend that holds thee dear.
Before this royal maiden   shall thy heart be free from fear.

"Thy shield in hand now give me   and leave it me to bear,
And do thou rightly mark thee   what thou now shalt hear.
Now make thyself the motions,   — the power leave to me."
When he did know him rightly,   the monarch's heart was filled
        with glee.

"Now secret keep my cunning,   let none e'er know the same:
Then shall the royal maiden   here find but little game
Of glory to win from thee,   as most to her is dear.
Behold now how the lady   stands before thee void of fear."

The spear the stately maiden   with might and main did wield,
And huge and broad she hurled it   upon the new-made shield,
That on his arm did carry   the son of Siegelind;
From the steel the sparks flew hissing   as if were blowing fierce the
        wind.

The mighty spear sharp-pointed   full through the shield did crash,
That ye from off the mail-rings   might see the lightning flash.
Beneath its force they stumbled,   did both those men of might;
But for the sightless mantle   they both were killed there outright.

From mouth of the full doughty   Siegfried burst the blood.
Full soon he yet recovered;   then seized the warrior good
The spear that from her strong arm   thus his shield had rent,
And back with force as came it   the hand of doughty Siegfried sent.

He thought: "To pierce the maiden   were but small glory earned,"

And so the spear's sharp edges   backward pointing turned;
Against her mail-clad body   he made the shaft to bound,
And with such might he sent it   full loud her armor did resound.

The sparks as if in stormwind   from mail-rings flew around.
So mightily did hurl it   the son of Siegmund
That she with all her power   could not the shaft withstand.
In sooth it ne'er was speeded   so swiftly by King Gunther's hand.

But to her feet full sudden   had sprung Brunhild fair.
"A shot, O noble Gunther,   befitting hero rare."
She weened himself had done it,   and all unaided he,
Nor wot she one far mightier   was thither come so secretly.

Then did she go full sudden,   wrathful was her mood,
A stone full high she heaved   the noble maiden good,
And the same far from her   with might and main she swung:
Her armor's mail-rings jingled   as she herself thereafter sprung.

The stone, when it had fallen,   lay fathoms twelve from there,
And yet did spring beyond it   herself the maiden fair.
Then where the stone was lying   thither Siegfried went:
Gunther feigned to move it,   but by another arm 'twas sent.

A valiant man was Siegfried   full powerful and tall.
The stone then cast he farther,   and farther sprang withal.
From those his arts so cunning   had he of strength such store
That as he leaped he likewise   the weight of royal Gunther bore.

And when the leap was ended   and fallen was the stone,
Then saw they ne'er another   but Gunther alone.
Brunhild the fair maiden,   red grew she in wrath:
Siegfried yet had warded   from royal Gunther surest death.

Unto her attendants   she spake in loud command,
When she saw 'cross the circle   the king unvanquished stand.
"Come hither quick, my kinsmen,   and ye that wait on me;
Henceforth unto Gunther   shall all be pledged faithfully."

Then laid the knights full valiant   their swords from out the hand;
At feet 'fore mighty Gunther   from Burgundian land
Offered himself in service   full many a valiant knight.

They weened that he had conquered   in trial by his proper might.

He gave her loving greeting,   right courteous was he.
Then by the hand she took him,   the maiden praiseworthy,
In pledge that all around him   was his to have and hold.
Whereat rejoiced Hagen   the warrior valorous and bold.

Into the spacious palace   with her thence to go
Bade she the noble monarch.   When they had done so,
Then still greater honors   unto the knight were shown.
Dankwart and Hagen,   right willingly they saw it done.

Siegfried the valiant,   by no means was he slow,
His sightless mantle did he   away in safety stow.
Then went he again thither   where many a lady sat.
He spake unto the monarch —   full cunningly was done all that:

"Why bidest thus, my master?   Wilt not the play begin,
To which so oft hath challenged   thee the noble queen?
Let us soon have example   what may the trial be."
As knew he naught about it,   did the knight thus cunningly.

Then spake the queen unto him: "How hath this ever been,
That of the play, Sir Siegfried,   nothing thou hast seen,
Wherein hath been the victor   Gunther with mighty hand?"
Thereto gave answer Hagen   a grim knight of Burgundian land.

Spake he: "There dost thou, Lady,   think ill without a cause:
By the ship down yonder   the noble Siegfried was,
The while the lord of Rhineland   in play did vanquish thee:
Thus knows he nothing of it,"   spake Gunther's warrior courteously.

"A joy to me these tidings,"   the doughty Siegfried spoke,
"That so thy haughty spirit   is brought beneath the yoke,
And that yet one there liveth   master to be of thine.
Now shalt thou, noble maiden,   us follow thither to the Rhine."

Then spake the maiden shapely: "It may not yet be so.
All my men and kindred   first the same must know.
In sooth not all so lightly   can I quit my home.
First must I bid my trusty   warriors that they hither come."

Then bade she messengers   quickly forth to ride,
And summoned in her kindred   and men from every side.
Without delay she prayed them   to come to Isenstein,
And bade them all be given   fit apparel rare and fine.

Then might ye see daily   'twixt morn and eventide
Unto Brunhild's castle   many a knight to ride.
"God wot, God wot," quoth Hagen,   "we do an evil thing,
To tarry here while Brunhild   doth thus her men together bring.

"If now into this country   their good men they've brought
— What thing the queen intendeth   thereof know we naught:
Belike her wrath ariseth,   and we are men forlorn —
Then to be our ruin   were the noble maiden born."

Then spake the doughty Siegfried: "That matter leave to me.
Whereof thou now art fearful,   I'll never let it be.
Ready help I'll bring thee   hither unto this land,
Knights of whom thou wotst not   till now I'll bring, a chosen band.

"Of me shalt thou ask not: from hence will I fare.
May God of thy good honor   meanwhile have a care.
I come again right quickly   with a thousand men for thee,
The very best of warriors   hitherto are known to me."

"Then tarry not unduly,"   thus the monarch said.
"Glad we are full fairly   of this thy timely aid."
He spake: "Till I come to thee   full short shall be my stay.
That thou thyself hast sent me   shalt thou unto Brunhild say."

Eighth Adventure

How Siegfried Fared to His Knights, the Nibelungen

Thence went then Siegfried   out through the castle door
In his sightless mantle   to a boat upon the shore.
As Siegmund's son doth board it   him no mortal sees;
And quickly off he steers it   as were it wafted by the breeze.

No one saw the boatman,   yet rapid was the flight
Of the boat forth speeding   driven by Siegfried's might.
They weened that did speed it   a swiftly blowing wind:
No, 'twas Siegfried sped it,   the son of fairest Siegelind.

In that one day-time   and the following night
Came he to a country   by dint of mickle might,
Long miles a hundred distant,   and something more than this:
The Nibelungen were its people   where the mighty hoard was his.

Alone did fare the hero   unto an island vast
Whereon the boat full quickly   the gallant knight made fast.
Of a castle then bethought him   high upon a hill,
And there a lodging sought him,   as wayworn men are wont to still.

Then came he to the portals   that locked before him stood.
They guarded well their honor   as people ever should.
At the door he gan a-knocking,   for all unknown was he.
But full well 'twas guarded,   and within it he did see

A giant who the castle   did guard with watchful eye,
And near him did at all times   his good weapons lie.

Quoth he: "Who now that knocketh   at the door in such strange
     wise?"
Without the valiant Siegfried   did cunningly his voice disguise.

He spake: "A bold knight-errant   am I; unlock the gate.
Else will I from without here   disturbance rare create
For all who'd fain lie quiet   and their rest would take."
Wrathful grew the Porter   as in this wise Siegfried spake.

Now did the giant valorous   his good armor don,
And placed on head his helmet;   then the full doughty man
His shield up-snatched quickly   and gate wide open swung.
How sore was he enraged   as himself upon Siegfried he flung!

'How dared he thus awaken   brave knights within the hall?'
The blows in rapid showers   from his hand did fall.
Thereat the noble stranger   began himself to shield.
For so a club of iron   the Porter's mighty arm did wield,

That splinters flew from buckler,   and Siegfried stood aghast
From fear that this same hour   was doomed to be his last,
So mightily the Porter's   blows about him fell.
To find such faithful warder   did please his master Siegfried well.

So fiercely did they struggle   that castle far within
And hall where slept the Nibelungen   echoed back the din.
But Siegfried pressed the Porter   and soon he had him bound.
In all the land of Nibelungen   the story soon was bruited round.

When the grim sound of fighting   afar the place had filled,
Alberich did hear it,   a Dwarf full brave and wild.
He donned his armor deftly,   and running thither found
This so noble stranger   where he the doughty Porter bound.

Alberich was full wrathy,   thereto a man of power.
Coat of mail and helmet   he on his body wore,
And in his hand a heavy   scourge of gold he swung.
Where was fighting Siegfried,   thither in mickle haste he sprung.

Seven knobs thick and heavy   on the club's end were seen,
Wherewith the shield that guarded   the knight that was so keen
He battered with such vigor   that pieces from it brake.

Lest he his life should forfeit   the noble stranger gan to quake.

The shield that all was battered   from his hand he flung;
And into sheath, too, thrust he   his sword so good and long.
For his trusty chamberlain   he did not wish to slay,
And in such case he could not   grant his anger fullest sway.

With but his hands so mighty   at Alberich he ran.
By the beard then seized he   the gray and aged man,
And in such manner pulled it   that he full loud did roar.
The youthful hero's conduct   Alberich did trouble sore.

Loud cried the valiant steward: "Have mercy now on me.
And might I other's vassal   than one good hero's be,
To whom to be good subject   I an oath did take,
Until my death I'd serve thee."   Thus the man of cunning spake.

Alberich then bound he   as the giant before.
The mighty arm of Siegfried   did trouble him full sore.
The Dwarf began to question: "Thy name, what may it be?"
Quoth he: "My name is Siegfried;   I weened I well were known to
     thee."

"I joy to hear such tidings,"   Dwarf Alberich replied.
"Well now have I found thee   in knightly prowess tried,
And with goodly reason   lord o'er lands to be.
I'll do whate'er thou biddest,   wilt thou only give me free."

Then spake his master Siegfried: "Quickly shalt thou go,
And bring me knights hither,   the best we have to show,
A thousand Nibelungen,   to stand before their lord."
Wherefore thus he wished it,   spake he never yet a word.

The giant and Alberich   straightway he unbound.
Then ran Alberich quickly   where the knights he found.
The warriors of Nibelung   he wakened full of fear.
Quoth he: "Be up, ye heroes,   before Siegfried shall ye appear."

From their couches sprang they   and ready were full soon,
Clothed well in armor   a thousand warriors boon,
And went where they found standing   Siegfried their lord.
Then was a mickle greeting   courteously in act and word.

Candles many were lighted, and sparkling wine he drank.
That they came so quickly, therefor he all did thank.
Quoth he: "Now shall ye with me from hence across the flood."
Thereto he found full ready the heroes valiant and good.

Good thirty hundred warriors soon had hither pressed,
From whom were then a thousand taken of the best.
For them were brought their helmets and what they else did need.
For unto Brunhild's country would he straightway the warriors
  lead.

He spake: "Ye goodly nobles, that would I have you hear,
In full costly raiment shall ye at court appear,
For yonder must there see us full many a fair lady.
Therefore shall your bodies dight in good apparel be."

Upon a morning early went they on their way.
What host of brave companions bore Siegfried company!
Good steeds took they with them and garments rich to wear,
And did in courtly fashion unto Brunhild's country fare.

As gazed from lofty parapet women fair to see,
Spake the queen unto them: "Knows any who they be,
Whom I see yonder sailing upon the sea afar?
Rich sails their ships do carry, whiter than snow they are."

Then spake the king of Rhineland: "My good men they are,
That on my journey hither left I lying near.
I've sent to call them to me: now are they come, O Queen."
With full great amazing were the stately strangers seen.

There saw they Siegfried out on the ship's prow stand
Clad in costly raiment, and with him his good band.
Then spake Queen Brunhild: "Good monarch, let me know,
Shall I go forth to greet them, or shall I greetings high forego?"

He spake: "Thou shalt to meet them before the palace go,
So that we see them gladly they may surely know."
Then did the royal lady fulfill the king's behest.
Yet Siegfried in the greeting was not honored with the rest.

Lodgings were made ready   and their armor ta'en in hand.
Then was such host of strangers   come into that land,
On all sides they jostled   from the great company.
Then would the knights full valiant   homeward fare to Burgundy.

Then spake Queen Brunhild: "In favor would I hold
Who might now apportion   my silver and my gold
To my guests and the monarch's,   for goodly store I have."
Thereto an answer Dankwart,   Giselher's good warrior, gave:

"Full noble royal Lady,   give me the keys to hold.
I trow I'll so divide it,"   spake the warrior bold,
"If blame there be about it,   that shall be mine alone."
That he was not a niggard,   beyond a doubt he soon had shown.

When now Hagen's brother   the treasure did command,
So many a lavish bounty   dealt out the hero's hand,
Whoso mark did covet,   to him was given such store
That all who once were poor men   might joyous live for evermore.

In sooth good pounds a hundred   gave he to each and all.
A host in costly raiment   were seen before the hall,
Who in equal splendor   ne'er before were clad.
When the queen did hear it,   verily her heart was sad.

Then spake the royal lady: "Good King, it little needs,
That now thy chamberlain   of all my stately weeds
Leave no whit remaining,   and squander clean my gold.
Would any yet prevent it,   him would I aye in favor hold.

"He deals with hand so lavish,   in sooth doth ween the thane
That death I've hither summoned;   but longer I'll remain.
Eke trow I well to spend all   my sire hath left to me."
Ne'er found queen a chamberlain   of such passing generosity.

Then spake of Tronje Hagen: "Lady, be thou told,
That the king of Rhineland   raiment hath and gold
So plenteous to lavish   that we may well forego
To carry with us homeward   aught that Brunhild can bestow."

"No; as high ye hold me,"   spake the queen again,
"Let me now have filled   coffers twice times ten

Of gold and silken raiment,   that may deal out my hand,
When that we come over   into royal Gunther's land."

Then with precious jewels   the coffers they filled for her.
The while her own chamberlain   must be standing near:
For no whit would she trust it   unto Giselher's man.
Whereat Gunther and Hagen   heartily to laugh began.

Then spake the royal lady: "To whom leave I my lands?
First must they now be given   in charge from out our hands."
Then spake the noble monarch: "Whomsoe'er it pleaseth thee,
Bid him now come hither,   the same we'll let our Warden be."

One of her highest kindred   near by the lady spied,
— He was her mother's brother —   to him thus spake the maid:
"Now be to thee entrusted   the castles and eke the land,
Until that here shall govern   Gunther the king by his own hand."

Trusty knights two thousand   from her company
Chose she to journey with her   unto Burgundy,
Beyond those thousand warriors   from Nibelungenland.
They made ready for the journey,   and downward rode unto the
      strand.

Six and eighty ladies   led they thence with her,
Thereto good hundred maidens   that full beauteous were.
They tarried no whit longer,   for they to part were fain.
Of those they left behind them,   O how they all to weep began!

In high befitting fashion   quitted she her land:
She kissed of nearest kindred   all who round did stand.
After fair leave-taking   they went upon the sea.
Back to her father's country   came never more that fair lady.

Then heard you on the journey   many a kind of play:
Every pleasant pastime   in plenty had they.
Soon had they for their journey   a wind from proper art:
So with full great rejoicing   did they from that land depart.

Yet would she on the journey   not be the monarch's spouse:
But was their pleasant pastime   reserved for his own house
At Worms within his castle   at a high festival,

Whither anon full joyous   came they with their warriors all.

Ninth Adventure

How Siegfried Was Sent to Worms

When that they had journeyed   full nine days on their way,
Then spake of Tronje Hagen: "Now hear what I shall say.
We tarry with the tidings   for Worms upon the Rhine.
At Burgundy already   should now be messengers of thine."

Then outspake King Gunther: "There hast thou spoken true.
And this selfsame journey,   none were so fit thereto
As thyself, friend Hagen.   So do thou now ride on.
This our high court journey,   none else can better make it known."

Thereto answered Hagen: "Poor messenger am I.
Let me be treasure-warden.   Upon the ships I'll stay
Near by the women rather,   their guardian to be,
Till that we bring them safely   into the land of Burgundy.

"Now do thou pray Siegfried   that he the message bear,
For he's a knight most fitting   this thing to have in care.
If he decline the journey,   then shalt thou courteously,
For kindness to thy sister,   pray that he not unwilling be."

He sent for the good warrior   who came at his command.
He spake: "Since we are nearing   home in my own land,
So should I send a message   to sister dear of mine
And eke unto my mother,   that we are nigh unto the Rhine.

"Thereto I pray thee, Siegfried,   now meet my wish aright,"
Spake the noble monarch: "I'll ever thee requite."
But Siegfried still refused it,   the full valiant man,

Till that King Gunther   sorely to beseech began.

He spake: "Now bear the message,   in favor unto me
And eke unto Kriemhild   a maiden fair to see,
That the stately maiden   help me thy service pay."
When had heard it Siegfried,   ready was the knight straightway.

"Now what thou wilt, command me: 'twill not be long delayed.
This thing will I do gladly   for sake of that fair maid.
Why should I aught refuse her,   who all my heart hath won?
What thou for her commandest,   whate'er it be 'twill all be done."

"Then say unto my mother,   Ute the queen,
That we on our journey   in joyous mood have been.
Let know likewise my brothers   what fortune us befell.
Eke unto all our kinsmen   shalt thou then merry tidings tell.

"Unto my fair sister   shalt thou all confide.
From me bring her fair compliment   and from Brunhild beside,
And eke unto our household   and all my warriors brave.
What my heart e'er did strive for,   how well accomplished it I have!

"And say as well to Ortwein   nephew dear of mine
That he do bid make ready   at Worms beside the Rhine.
And all my other kindred,   to them made known shall be,
With Brunhild I am minded   to keep a great festivity.

"And say unto my sister,   when that she hath learned
That I am to my country   with many a guest returned,
She shall have care to welcome   my bride in fitting way.
So all my thoughts of Kriemhild   will be her service to repay."

Then did Sir Siegfried   straightway in parting greet
High the Lady Brunhild,   as 'twas very meet,
And all her company;   then toward the Rhine rode he.
Nor in this world a better   messenger might ever be.

With four and twenty warriors   to Worms did he ride.
When soon it was reported   the king came not beside,
Then did all the household   of direst news have dread:
They feared their royal master   were left in distant country dead.

Then sprang they from the saddle,   full high they were of mood.
Full soon before them Giselher   the prince so youthful stood,
And Gernot his brother.   How quickly then spake he,
When he the royal Gunther   saw not in Siegfried's company:

"Be thou welcome, Siegfried.   Yet shalt thou tell to me,
Why the king my brother   cometh not with thee.
Brunhild's prowess is it   hath taken him, I ween;
And so this lofty wooing   hath naught but our misfortune been."

"Now cease such ill foreboding.   To you and friends hath sent
My royal companion   his good compliment.
Safe and sound I left him;   myself did he command
That I should be his herald   with tidings hither to your land.

"Quickly shall ye see to it,   how that it may be,
That I the queen and likewise   your fair sister see.
From Gunther and Brunhild   the message will I tell
That hath now been sent them: the twain do find them passing
          well."

Then spake the youthful Giselher: "So shalt thou go to her:
Here dost thou on my sister   a favor high confer.
In sooth she's mickle anxious   how't with my brother be.
The maid doth see thee gladly,   — of that will I be surety."

Then outspake Sir Siegfried: "If serve her aught I can,
That same thing most willing   in truth it shall be done.
Who now will tell the ladies   I would with them confer?"
Then was therein Giselher   the stately knight his messenger.

Giselher the valiant   unto his mother kind
And sister spake the tidings   when he the twain did find:
"To us returned is Siegfried,   the hero of Netherlands
Unto the Rhine he cometh   at my brother Gunther's command.

"He bringeth us the tidings   how't with the king doth fare.
Now shall ye give permission   that he 'fore you appear.
He'll tell the proper tidings   from Isenland o'er the main."
Yet mickle sad forebodings   did trouble still the ladies twain.

They sprang for their attire   and donned it nothing slow.

Then bade they that Siegfried   to court should thither go.
That did he right willing   for he gladly them did see.
Kriemhild the noble maiden   spake to him thus graciously.

"Welcome be, Sir Siegfried,   thou knight right praiseworthy.
Yet where may King Gunther   my noble brother be?
It is through Brunhild's prowess,   I ween, he is forlorn.
Alack of me, poor maiden,   that I into this world was born!"

The valiant knight then answered: "Give me news-bringer's meed
Know ye, fairest ladies,   ye weep without a need.
I left him well and happy,   that would I have you know;
They two have sent me hither   to bear the tidings unto you.

"And offer thee good service   both his bride and he,
My full noble lady,   in love and loyalty.
Now give over weeping,   for straight will they be here."
They had for many a season   heard not a tale to them so dear.

With fold of snow-white garment   then her eyes so bright
Dried she after weeping.   She gan thank the knight
Who of these glad tidings   had been the messenger.
Then was a mickle sorrow   and cause of weeping ta'en from her.

She bade the knight be seated,   which he did willingly.
Then spake the lovely maiden: "It were a joy to me,
Could I the message-bringer   with gold of mine repay.
Thereto art thou too highborn;   I'll serve thee then in other way."

"If I alone were ruler,"   spake he, "o'er thirty lands,
Yet gifts I'd take right gladly,   came they from thy fair hands."
Then spake the virtuous maiden: "In truth it shall be so."
Then bade she her chamberlain   forth for message-money go.

Four and twenty armlets   with stones of precious kind,
These gave she him for guerdon.   'Twas not the hero's mind,
That he himself should keep them: he dealt them all around
Unto her fair attendants   whom he within the chamber found.

Of service, too, her mother   did kindly offer make.
"Then have I more to tell you,"   the keen warrior spake:
"Of what the king doth beg you,   when comes he to the Rhine.

Wilt thou perform it, lady,   then will he e'er to thee incline.

"The noble guests he bringeth,   — this heard I him request,
That ye shall well receive them;   and furthermore his hest,
That ye ride forth to meet him   'fore Worms upon the strand.
So have ye from the monarch   faithfully his high command."

Then spake the lovely maiden: "Full ready there am I.
If I in aught can serve him,   I'll never that deny.
In all good faith and kindness   shall it e'er be done."
Then deeper grew her color   that from increase of joy she won.

Never was royal message   better received before.
The lady sheer had kissed him,   if 'twere a thing to dare.
From those high ladies took he   his leave in courteous wise.
Then did they there in Burgundy   in way as Siegfried did advise.

Sindold and Hunold   and Rumold the thane
In truth were nothing idle,   but wrought with might and main
To raise the sitting-places   'fore Worms upon the strand.
There did the royal Steward   busy 'mid the workers stand.

Ortwein and Gere   thought longer not to bide,
But sent unto their kinsmen   forth on every side.
They told of festive meeting   there that was to be;
And deck themselves to meet them   did the maidens fair to see.

The walls throughout the palace   were dight full richly all,
Looking unto the strangers;   and King Gunther's hall
Full well with seats and tables   for many a noble guest.
And great was the rejoicing   in prospect of the mighty feast.

Then rode from every quarter   hither through the land
The three monarchs' kinsmen,   who there were called to hand,
That they might be in waiting   for those expected there.
Then from enfolding covers   took they store of raiments rare.

Some watchers brought the tidings   that Brunhild's followers were
Seen coming riding hither.   Then rose a mickle stir
Among the folk so many   in the land of Burgundy.
Heigh-ho! What valiant warriors   alike on both parts might you see!

Then spake the fair Kriemhild: "Of my good maidens, ye
Who at this reception   shall bear me company,
From out the chests now seek ye   attire the very best.
So shall praise and honor   be ours from many a noble guest."

Then came the knights also   and bade bring forth to view
The saddles richly furnished   of ruddy golden hue,
That ladies fair should ride on   at Worms unto the Rhine.
Better horse-equipment   could never artisan design.

Heigh-ho! What gold all glancing   from the steeds there shone!
Sparkled from their bridles   full many a precious stone.
Gold-wrought stools for mounting   and shining carpets good
Brought they for the ladies: joyous were they all of mood.

Within the court the heroes   bedight with trappings due
Awaited noble maidens,   as I have told to you.
A narrow band from saddle   went round each horse's breast,
Its beauty none could tell you: of silk it was the very best.

Six and eighty ladies   came in manner meet
Wearing each a wimple.   Kriemhild there to greet
They went, all fair to look on,   in shining garments clad.
Then came eke well appareled   full many a fair and stately maid.

Four and fifty were they   of the land of Burgundy,
And they were eke the noblest   that ever you might see.
Adorned with shining hair-bands   the fair-haired maids came on.
What now the king desired,   that most carefully was done.

Made of stuffs all costly,   the best you might desire,
Before the gallant strangers   wore they such rich attire
As well did fit the beauty   of many amid the throng.
He sure had lost his senses,   who could have wished them any
    wrong.

Of sable and of ermine   many a dress was worn.
Arms and hands a many   did they full well adorn
With rings o'er silken dresses   that there did clothe them well.
Of all the ready-making   none might ever fully tell.

Full many a well-wrought girdle   in long and costly braid

About the shining garments   by many a hand was laid
On dress of precious ferrandine   of silk from Araby.
And full of high rejoicing   were those maids of high degree.

With clasps before her bosom   was many a fair maid
Laced full beauteously.   She might well be sad,
Whose full beaming color   vied not with weeds she wore.
Such a stately company   ne'er possessed a queen before.

When now the lovely maidens   attired you might see,
Soon were those beside them   should bear them company,
Of warriors high-hearted   a full mickle band.
And with their shields they carried   full many an ashen shaft in
     hand.

Tenth Adventure

How Brunhild Was Received at Worms

On yonder side Rhine river   they saw a stately band,
The king and host of strangers,   ride down unto the strand,
And also many a lady   sitting on charger led.
By those who should receive them   was goodly preparation made.

Soon they of Isenland   the ship had entered then,
And with them Siegfried's vassals   the Nibelungen men;
They strained unto the shore   with untiring hand
When they beheld the monarch's   friends upon the farther strand.

Now list ye eke the story   of the stately queen,
Ute, how at her bidding   ladies fair were seen
Forth coming from the castle   to ride her company.
Then came to know each other   full many a knight and fair lady.

The Margrave Gere   but to the castle gate
The bridle held for Kriemhild;   the keen Siegfried did wait
Thenceforward upon her.   She was a beauteous maid.
Well was the knight's good service   by the lady since repaid.

Ortwein the valiant   Queen Ute rode beside,
And many a knight full gallant   was stately lady's guide.
At such a high reception,   that may we say, I ween,
Was ne'er such host of ladies   in company together seen.

With show of rider's talent   the tilt was carried on,
For might the knights full gallant   naught fitting leave undone,
As passed down to the river   Kriemhild the lady bright.

Then helped was many a lady   fair from charger to alight.

The king had then come over   and many a stranger too.
Heigh-ho! What strong shafts splintered   before the ladies flew!
Many a shaft go crashing   heard you there on shield.
Heigh-ho! What din of costly   arms resounded o'er the field.

The full lovely maidens   upon the shore did stand,
As Gunther with the strangers   stepped upon the land;
He himself did Brunhild   by the hand lead on.
Then sparkled towards each other   rich dress and many a shining
     stone.

Then went Lady Kriemhild   with fullest courtesy due,
To greet the Lady Brunhild   and her retinue.
And saw ye each the head-band   with fair hand move aside
When they kissed each other: high courtesy did the ladies guide.

Then spake the maiden Kriemhild,   a highborn lady she:
"Unto this our country   shalt thou right welcome be,
To me and to my mother   and each true friend of mine,
That we here have with us."   Then each did unto each incline.

Within their arms the ladies   oft-times clasped each other.
Like this fond reception   heard ye of ne'er another,
As when both the ladies   there the bride did greet,
Queen Ute and her daughter;   oft-times they kissed her lips so sweet.

When all of Brunhild's ladies   were come upon the strand,
Then was there taken   full fondly by the hand
By the warriors stately   many a fair lady.
Before the Lady Brunhild   the train of fair maids might ye see.

Before their greetings ended   a mickle time was gone,
For lips of rosy color   were kissed there, many a one.
Long stood they together,   the royal ladies high,
And so to look upon them   pleased many a noble warrior's eye.

Then spied with probing eye, too,   who before did hear
That till then was never   aught beheld so fair,
As those two royal ladies: they found it was no lie.
In all their person might ye   no manner of deceit espy.

Who there could spy fair ladies   and judge of beauty rare,
They praised the wife of Gunther   that she was passing fair;
Yet spake again the wise men   who looked with keener gaze,
They rather would to Kriemhild   before Brunhild award the praise.

Then went unto each other   maid and fair lady.
Full many a fair one might ye   in rich adornment see.
There stood rich tents a many,   silken great and small,
Wherewith in every quarter   'fore Worms the field was covered all.

Of the king's high kindred   a mighty press there was.
Then bade they Brunhild   and Kriemhild on to pass,
And with them all the ladies,   where they in shade might be.
Thither did bring them warriors   of the land of Burgundy.

When now the strangers also   on horse sat everyone,
Plenteous knightly tilting   at shield was there begun.
Above the field rose dust-clouds,   as had the country been
All in flames a-burning;   who bore the honors there was seen.

Looked on full many a maiden   as the knights did sport them so.
Meseemeth that Sir Siegfried   full many a to-and-fro
Did ride with his good followers   along 'fore many a tent.
With him of Nibelungen   a thousand stately men there went.

Then came of Tronje Hagen,   whom the king did send;
He bade in pleasing manner   the tourney have an end,
Before in dust be buried   all the ladies fair.
And ready to obey him   soon the courteous strangers were.

Then spake Sir Gernot: "Now let the chargers stand,
Until the air is cooler,   for we must be at hand
As escort for fair ladies   unto the stately hall;
And will the king take saddle,   so let him find you ready all."

When now the sound of tourney   o'er all the field was spent,
Then went for pleasant pastime   'neath many a lofty tent
The knights unto the ladies,   and willing thither hied.
And there they passed the hours   till such time as they thence
        should ride.

Just before the evening when the sun was in the west,
And the air grew cooler, no longer did they rest,
But both knights and ladies unto the castle passed.
And eyes in loving glances on many a beauteous maid were cast.

By hand of goodly warrior many a coat was rent,
For in the country's custom they tourneyed as they went,
Until before the palace the monarch did dismount.
They tended fairest ladies as knights high-spirited are wont.

After fairest greeting the queens did part again.
Dame Ute and her daughter, thither passed the twain
With train of fair attendants unto a hall full wide.
Din of merrymaking heard ye there on every side.

Arranged were sitting-places where the king would be
With his guests at table. By him might ye see
Standing the fair Brunhild. She wore a royal crown
In the monarch's country, the which might well such mistress own.

Seats for all the people at many a spacious board
There were, as saith the story, where victuals rich were stored.
How little there was lacking of all that makes a feast!
And by the monarch saw ye sitting many a stately guest.

The royal host's attendants in basins golden red
Carried water forward. And should it e'er be said
By any that a better service did receive
Ever guests of monarch, I never could such thing believe.

Before the lord of Rhineland with water was waited on,
Unto him Sir Siegfried, as fitting was, had gone;
He called to mind a promise that made by him had been
Ere that the Lady Brunhild afar in Isenland he'd seen.

He spake: "Thou shalt bethink thee what once did plight thy hand,
If that the Lady Brunhild should come unto this land,
Thou'dst give to me thy sister. Where now what thou hast sworn?
In this thy wooing journey not small the labor I have borne."

Then to his guest the monarch: "Well hast thou minded me,
And by this hand shall never false word plighted be.

To gain thy wish I'd help thee   in the way as best I know."
Bidden then was Kriemhild   forth unto the king to go.

With her full beauteous maidens   unto the Hall she passed.
Then sprang the youthful Giselher   adown the steps in haste
"Bid now these many maidens   wend their way again;
None but my sister only   unto the king shall enter in."

Then led they Kriemhild thither   where the king was found,
With him were knights full noble   from many a land around.
Within that Hall so spacious   she waited the king's behest,
What time the Lady Brunhild   betook her likewise to the feast.

Then spake the royal Gunther: "Sister mine full fair,
Redeem the word I've given,   an hold'st thou virtue dear.
Thee to a knight I plighted: An tak'st thou him to man,
Thereby my wish full truly   unto the warrior hast thou done."

Then spake the noble maiden: "Brother full dear to me,
Not long shalt thou entreat me.   In truth I'll ever be
Obedient to thy bidding;   that shall now be done,
And him I'll take full gladly,   my Lord, whom thou giv'st me for
     man."

Before those fair eyes' glances   grew Siegfried's color red.
The knight to Lady Kriemhild   his service offeréd.
Within a ring together   then were led the twain,
And they asked the maiden,   if she to take the knight were fain.

Upon her face not little   was the modest glow;
Nathless to joy of Siegfried   did fortune will it so,
That the maiden would not   refuse the knight her hand.
Eke swore his wife to make her   the noble king of Netherland.

When he to her had plighted,   and eke to him the maid,
Siegfried to embrace her   nothing more delayed,
But clasped in arms full fondly   and oft the lady fair,
And stately knights were witness   how that he kissed the princess
     there.

When that the maids attendant   from thence had ta'en their leave,
In place of honor seated   Siegfried might ye perceive

And by him fairest Kriemhild;   and many a knight at hand
Was seen of the Nibelungen   at Siegfried's service ready stand.

There too was Gunther seated   and with him Queen Brunhild.
At sight of Kriemhild sitting   by Siegfried was she filled
With anger such as never   before her heart did swell:
She wept, and tears in plenty   adown her shining face there fell.

Then spake who ruled the country: "What aileth, lady mine,
That so thou let'st be dimméd   thine eyes that brightly shine?
Be straight of joyous spirit,   for now at thy command
My land and my good castles   and host of stately warriors stand."

"Good cause to me for weeping,"   spake the lady fair.
"For sake of this thy sister   sorrow now I bear,
Whom here behold I seated   by one that serveth thee.
That must forever grieve me,   shall she thus dishonored be."

Then answered her King Gunther: "But for the nonce be still.
At other time more fitting   the thing to thee I'll tell,
Wherefore thus my sister   to Siegfried I did give.
And truly with the hero   may she ever joyous live."

She spake: "Her name and beauty   thus lost it grieveth me.
An knew I only whither,   from hence I'd surely flee,
This night nor e'er hereafter   to share thy royal bed,
Say'st thou not truly wherefore   Kriemhild thus hath Siegfried wed."

Then spake the noble monarch: "Then unto thee be known
That he as stately castles,   lands wide as I, doth own.
And know thou that full surely   a mighty monarch he;
Wherefore the fairest maiden   I grant him thus his wife to be."

Whate'er the king did tell her,   sad was she yet of mood.
Then hastened from the tables   full many a warrior good,
And jousted that the castle   walls gave back the din.
Amid his guests the monarch   waiting longingly was seen.

He deemed 'twere better lying   beside his fair lady.
Of thinking on that plaisance   his mind he could not free,
And what her love would bring him   before the night be past;
He many a glance full tender   upon the Lady Brunhild cast.

The guests they bade give over   in joust who combated,
For that with spouse new-wedded   the monarch would to bed.
Leaving then the banquet,   there together met
Kriemhild and Brunhild: their bitter hate was silent yet.

At hand were their attendants;   they longer tarried not,
And chamberlains full lordly   lights for them had brought.
Then parted eke the followers   of the monarchs twain,
And bearing Siegfried company   went full many a worthy thane.

The lords were both come thither   where that they should lie.
As each one bethought him   of loving victory
To win o'er winsome lady,   merry he grew of mood.
The noble Siegfried's pastime   it was beyond all measure good.

As there Sir Siegfried   by fair Kriemhild lay
And to the maid devoted   himself in such fond way
As noble knight beseemeth,   they twain to him were one,
And not a thousand others   had he then ta'en for her alone.

I'll tell you now no further   how he the lady plied,
But list ye first the story   what Gunther did betide
By Lady Brunhild lying.   In sooth the noble thane
By side of other ladies   a deal more happily had lain.

Withdrawn were now attendants,   man and also maid;
Not long to lock the chamber   within the king delayed.
He weened to have good pleasure   of that fair lady,
Yet was the time still distant   when that she his wife should be.

In gown of whitest linen   unto the bed she passed.
Then thought the knight full noble: "Now have I here at last
All that I e'er desired   as long as I can tell."
Perforce her stately beauty   did please the monarch passing well.

That they should shine more dimly   he placed the lights aside,
Then where did lie the lady   the thane full eager hied.
He placed himself a-nigh her,   his joy right great it was,
As in his arms the monarch   the winsome maid did there embrace.

A loving plaisance had he   with vigor there begun

If that the noble lady　had let the same be done.
She then did rage so sorely　that grieved was he thereat;
He weened to find who loved him,　— instead he found him naught
　　but hate.

Spake she: "Good knight and noble,　from this thing give o'er.
That which thou here hast hope of,　it may be nevermore.
A maid I still will keep me　— well mayest thou know that —
Until I learn that story."　Gunther wrathy grew thereat.

Her gown he wrought to ruin　to win her maidenhead.
Whereat did seize a girdle　the full stately maid,
A strong and silken girdle　that round her sides she wore,
And with the same the monarch　she soon had brought to pains
　　full sore.

His feet and his hands also,　together bound she all,
Unto a nail she bore him　and hung him on the wall.
Him who disturbed her sleeping　in his love she sorely let,
And from her mighty prowess,　he full nigh his death had met.

Then gan he to entreat her,　who master late had been.
"From these my bonds now loose me,　my full noble queen.
Nor trow I e'er, fair lady,　victor o'er thee to be,
And henceforth will I seldom　seek to lie thus nigh to thee."

She recked not how 'twere with him,　as she full softly lay.
There hung he, will he nill he,　the night through unto day,
Until the light of morning　through the windows shone.
Could he e'er boast of prowess,　small now the measure he did own.

"Now tell me, lordly Gunther,　wert thou thereat so sad,
If that in bonds should find thee"　— spake the fairest maid —
"Thy royal men-in-waiting,　bound by lady's hand?"
Then spake the knight full noble:　"Thou should'st in case most evil
　　stand.

"Eke had I little honor　therefrom," continued he.
"For all thy royal honor　let me then go to thee.
Since that my fond embracements　do anger thee so sore,
With these my hands I pledge thee　to touch thy garment
　　nevermore."

Then she loosed him straightway   and he once more stood free.
To the bed he went as erstwhile   where rested his lady.
But far from her he laid him   and well he now forebore
To stir the lady's anger   by touching e'en the gown she wore.

At length came their attendants   who garments fresh did bring,
Whereof was ready for them   good store on that morning.
Yet merry as his folk were,   a visage sad did own
The lord of that proud country,   for all he wore that day a crown.

As was the country's custom,   a thing folk do of right,
Gunther and Brunhild   presently were dight
To go unto the minster   where the mass was sung.
Thither eke came Siegfried,   and in their trains a mighty throng.

As fitted royal honor   for them was thither brought
The crown that each should carry   and garments richly wrought.
There were they consecrated;   and when the same was done,
Saw ye the four together   happy stand and wearing crown.

There was knighted many a squire,   — six hundred or beyond —
In honor of the crowning,   that shall ye understand.
Arose full great rejoicing   in the land of Burgundy
As hand of youthful warrior   did shatter shaft right valiantly.

Then sat in castle casement   maidens fair to see,
And many a shield beneath them   gleamed full brilliantly.
Yet himself had sundered   from all his men the king;
Though joyous every other,   sad-visaged stood he sorrowing.

He and the doughty Siegfried,   how all unlike their mood!
Well wist the thing did grieve him   that noble knight and good.
He went unto the monarch   and straight addressed him so:
"This night how hast thou fared?   In friendship give thou me to
          know."

To his guest the king gave answer: "Than shame and scathe I've
          naught.
The devil's dam I surely   into my house have brought.
When as I thought to have her   she bound me like a thrall;
Unto a nail she bore me   and hung me high upon the wall.

"There hung I sore in anguish   the night through until day
Ere that she would unbind me,   the while she softly lay!
And hast thou friendly pity   know then the grief I bear."
Then spake the doughty Siegfried: "Such grieves me verily to hear.

"The which I'll show thee truly,   wilt thou me not deny.
I'll bring it that tonight she   so near to thee shall lie
That she to meet thy wishes   shall tarry nevermore."
Thereat rejoice did Gunther   to think perchance his trials o'er.

Then further spake Sir Siegfried: "With thee 'twill yet be right.
I ween that all unequal   we twain have fared this night.
To me thy sister Kriemhild   dearer is than life;
Eke shall the Lady Brunhild   be yet this coming night thy wife."

"I'll come unto thy chamber   this night all secretly,"
Spake he, "and wrapped in mantle   invisible I'll be,
That of this my cunning   naught shall any know;
And thy attendants shalt thou   bid to their apartments go.

"The lights I'll all extinguish   held by each page in hand,
By the which same token   shalt thou understand
I present am to serve thee.   I'll tame thy shrewish wife
That thou this night enjoy her,   else forfeit be my caitiff life."

"An thou wilt truly leave me"   — answered him the king —
'My lady yet a maiden,   I joy o'er this same thing.
So do thou as thou willest;   and takest thou her life,
E'en that I'll let pass o'er me,   — to lose so terrible a wife."

"Thereto," spake then Siegfried,   "plight I word of mine,
To leave her yet a maiden.   A sister fair of thine
Is to me before all women   I ever yet have seen."
Gunther believed right gladly   what had by Siegfried plighted been.

Meanwhile the merry pastime   with joy and zest went on.
But all the din and bustle   bade they soon be done,
When band of fairest ladies   would pass unto the hall
'Fore whom did royal chamberlains   bid backward stand the people
    all.

The chargers soon and riders   from castle court were sped.
Each of the noble ladies   by bishop high was led,
When that before the monarchs   they passed to banquet board,
And in their train did follow   to table many a stately lord.

There sat the king all hopeful   and full of merriment;
What him did promise Siegfried,   thereon his mind was bent.
To him as long as thirty   did seem that single day;
To plaisance with his lady,   thither turned his thought alway.

And scarce the time he bided   while that the feast did last.
Now unto her chamber   the stately Brunhild passed,
And for her couch did Kriemhild   likewise the table leave.
Before those royal ladies   what host ye saw of warriors brave!

Full soon thereafter Siegfried   sat right lovingly
With his fair wife beside him,   and naught but joy had he.
His hand she clasped full fondly   within her hand so white,
Until — and how she knew not —   he did vanish from her sight.

When she the knight did fondle,   and straightway saw him not,
Unto her maids attendant   spake the queen distraught:
"Meseemeth a mickle wonder   where now the king hath gone.
His hands in such weird fashion   who now from out mine own
     hath drawn?"

Yet further not she questioned.   Soon had he hither gone
Where with lights were standing   attendants many a one.
The same he did extinguish   in every page's hand;
That Siegfried then was present   Gunther thereby did understand.

Well wist he what he would there;   so bade he thence be gone
Ladies and maids-in-waiting.   And when that was done,
Himself the mighty monarch   fast did lock the door:
Two bolts all wrought securely   he quickly shoved the same before.

The lights behind the curtains   hid he presently.
Soon a play was started   (for thus it had to be),
Betwixt the doughty Siegfried   and the stately maid:
Thereat was royal Gunther   joyous alike and sad.

Siegfried there laid him   by the maid full near.

Spake she: "Let be, now, Gunther,   an hast thou cause to fear
Those troubles now repeated   which befell thee yesternight."
And soon the valiant Siegfried   through the lady fell in sorry plight.

His voice did he keep under   and ne'er a word spake he.
Intently listened Gunther,   and though he naught could see,
Yet knew he that in secret   nothing 'twixt them passed.
In sooth nor knight nor lady   upon the bed had mickle rest.

He did there as if Gunther   the mighty king he were,
And in his arms he pressed her,   the maiden debonair.
Forth from the bed she hurled him   where a bench there stood,
And head of valiant warrior   against a stool went ringing loud.

Up sprang again undaunted   the full doughty man,
To try for fortune better.   When he anew began
Perforce to curb her fury,   fell he in trouble sore.
I ween that ne'er a lady   did so defend herself before.

When he would not give over,   up the maid arose:
"My gown so white thou never   thus shalt discompose.
And this thy villain's manner   shall sore by thee be paid,
The same I'll teach thee truly,"   further spake the buxom maid.

Within her arms she clasped him,   the full stately thane,
And thought likewise to bind him,   as the king yestreen,
That she the night in quiet   upon her couch might lie.
That her dress he thus did rumple,   avenged the lady grievously.

What booted now his prowess   and eke his mickle might?
Her sovereignty of body   she proved upon the knight;
By force of arm she bore him, / — 'twixt wall and mighty chest
(For so it e'en must happen)   him she all ungently pressed.

"Ah me!" — so thought the hero —   "shall I now my life
Lose at hand of woman,   then will every wife
Evermore hereafter   a shrewish temper show
Against her lord's good wishes,   who now such thing ne'er thinks to
        do."

All heard the monarch meanwhile   and trembled for the man.
Sore ashamed was Siegfried,   and a-raging he began.

With might and main he struggled   again to make him free,
Ere which to sorest trouble   'neath Lady Brunhild's hand fell he.

Long space to him it seeméd   ere Siegfried tamed her mood.
She grasped his hand so tightly   that 'neath the nails the blood
Oozéd from the pressure,   which made the hero wince.
Yet the stately maiden   subdued he to obedience since.

Her unrestrainéd temper   that she so late displayed,
All overheard the monarch,   though ne'er a word he said.
'Gainst the bed did press her Siegfried   that aloud she cried,
Ungentle was the treatment   that he meted to the bride.

Then grasped she for a girdle   that round her sides she wore,
And thought therewith to bind him;   but her limbs and body o'er
Strained beneath the vigor   that his strong arm displayed.
So was the struggle ended   — Gunther's wife was vanquishéd.

She spake: "O noble monarch,   take not my life away.
The harm that I have done thee   full well will I repay.
No more thy royal embraces   by me shall be withstood,
For now I well have seen it,   thou canst be lord o'er woman's
        mood."

From the couch rose Siegfried,   lying he left the maid,
As if that he would from him   lay his clothes aside.
He drew from off her finger   a ring of golden sheen
Without that e'er perceivéd   his practice the full noble queen.

Thereto he took her girdle   that was all richly wrought:
If from wanton spirit   he did it, know I not.
The same he gave to Kriemhild: the which did sorrow bear.
Then lay by one another   Gunther and the maiden fair.

Hearty were his embraces   as such king became:
Perforce must she relinquish   her anger and her shame.
In sooth not little pallid   within his arms she grew,
And in that love-surrender   how waned her mighty prowess too!

Then was e'en she not stronger   than e'er another bride;
He lay with fond embraces   the beauteous dame beside.
And had she struggled further,   avail how could it aught?

Gunther, when thus he clasped her,   such change upon her strength
    had wrought.

And with right inward pleasure   she too beside him lay
In warmest love embracings   until the dawn of day!
Meantime now had Siegfried   departure ta'en from there,
And was full well receivéd   by a lady debonair.

Her questioning he avoided   and all whereon she thought,
And long time kept he secret   what he for her had brought,
Until in his own country   she wore a royal crown;
Yet what for her he destined,   how sure at last it was her own.

Upon the morn was Gunther   by far of better mood
Than he had been before it;   joy thus did spread abroad
'Mid host of knights full noble   that from his lands around
To his court had been invited,   and there most willing service found.

The merry time there lasted   until two weeks were spent,
Nor all the while did flag there   the din of merriment
And every kind of joyance   that knight could e'er devise;
With lavish hand expended   the king thereto in fitting wise.

The noble monarch's kinsmen   upon his high command
By gifts of gold and raiment   told forth his generous hand,
By steed and thereto silver   on minstrel oft bestowed.
Who there did gift desire   departed thence in merry mood.

All the store of raiment   afar from Netherland,
The which had Siegfried's thousand   warriors brought to hand
Unto the Rhine there with them,   complete 'twas dealt away,
And eke the steeds well saddled: in sooth a lordly life led they.

Ere all the gifts so bounteous   were dealt the guests among,
They who would straightway homeward   did deem the waiting long.
Ne'er had guests of monarch   such goodly gifts before;
And so as Gunther willed it   the merry feast at last was o'er.

Eleventh Adventure
How Siegfried Came Home with His Wife

When that now the strangers   all from thence were gone,
Spake unto his followers   noble Siegmund's son:
"We shall eke make ready   home to my land to fare."
Unto his spouse was welcome   such news when she the same did
    hear.

She spake unto her husband: "When shall we hence depart?
Not hastily on the journey   I pray thee yet to start.
With me first my brothers   their wide lands shall share."
Siegfried yet it pleased not   such words from Kriemhild to hear.

The princes went unto him   and spake they there all three:
"Now know thou well, Sir Siegfried,   for thee shall ever be
In faithfulness our service   ready while yet we live."
The royal thanes then thanked he   who thus did proof of friendship
    give.

"With thee further share we,"   spake young Giselher,
"The lands and eke the castles   by us that ownéd are.
In wide lands whatsoever   we rule o'er warriors brave,
Of the same with Kriemhild   a goodly portion shalt thou have.

Then spake unto the princes   the son of Siegmund
When he their lofty purpose   did rightly understand:
"God grant your goodly heritage   at peace may ever be,
And eke therein your people.   The spouse in sooth so dear to me."

"May well forego the portion   that ye to her would give.

For she a crown shall carry,　if to such day I live,
And queen more rich than any　that lives she then must be.
What else to her ye offer,　therein I'll meet you faithfully."

Then spake the Lady Kriemhild:　"If wealth thou wilt not choose,
Yet gallant thanes of Burgundy　shalt thou not light refuse.
They're such as monarch gladly　would lead to his own land.
Of these shall make division　with me my loving brothers' hand."

Thereto spake noble Gernot:　"Now take to please thy mind.
Who gladly will go with thee　full many here thou'lt find.
Of thirty hundred warriors　we give thee thousand men
To be thy royal escort."　Kriemhild did summon then

Hagen of Tronje to her　and Ortwein instantly:
And would they and their kinsmen　make her good company?
To hear the same did Hagen　begin to rage full sore.
Quoth he: "E'en royal Gunther　may thus bestow us nevermore.

"Other men that serve thee,　let them follow thee;
Thou know'st the men of Tronje　and what their pledges be:
Here must we by the monarchs　in service true abide;
Hereto as them we followed,　so shall we henceforth keep their side."

And so the thing was ended:　to part they ready make.
A high and noble escort　did Kriemhild to her take,
Maidens two and thirty　and five hundred men also.
In Lady Kriemhild's company　the Margrave Eckewart did go.

Leave took they all together,　squire and also knight,
Maidens and fair ladies,　as was their wont aright.
There parted they with kisses　and eke with clasp of hand:
Right merrily they journeyed　forth from royal Gunther's land.

Their friends did give them escort　upon the way full far.
Night-quarters at every station　they bade for them prepare,
Where they might wish to tarry　as on their way they went.
Then straightway was a messenger　unto royal Siegmund sent,

To him and Siegelind bearing　thereof the joyful sign
That his son was coming　from Worms upon the Rhine
And with him Ute's daughter,　Kriemhild the fair lady.

As this could other message   nevermore so welcome be.

"Well is me!" quoth Siegmund,   "that I the day have known,
When the fair Lady Kriemhild   here shall wear a crown.
Thus higher shall my kingdom   stand in majesty.
My son the noble Siegfried   here himself the king shall be."

Then dealt the Lady Siegelind   velvet red in store,
Silver and gold full heavy   to them the news that bore:
She joyed to hear the story   that there her ear did greet.
Then decked themselves her ladies   all in rich attire meet.

'Twas told, with Siegfried coming   whom they did expect.
Then bade they sitting-places   straightway to erect,
Where he before his kinsmen   a crown in state should wear.
Then men of royal Siegmund   forward rode to meet him there.

Was e'er more royal greeting,   news have I not to hand,
As came the knights full noble   into Siegmund's land.
There the royal Siegelind   to Kriemhild forth did ride
With ladies fair a many,   and followed gallant knights beside

Out a full day's journey   to welcome each high guest.
And little with the strangers   did they ever rest
Until into a castle   wide they came once more,
The same was called Xanten,   where anon a crown they wore.

With smiling lips Dame Siegelind   — and Siegmund eke did this —
To show the love they bore her   full oft did Kriemhild kiss,
And eke the royal Siegfried: far was their sorrow gone.
And all the merry company,   good welcome had they everyone.

The train of strangers bade they   'fore Siegmund's Hall to lead,
And maidens fair a many   down from gallant steed
Helped they there dismounting.   Full many a man was there
To do them willing service   as was meet for ladies fair.

How great soe'er the splendor   erstwhile beside the Rhine,
Here nonetheless was given   raiment yet more fine,
Nor were they e'er attired   in all their days so well.
Full many a wonder might I   of their rich apparel tell.

How there in state resplendent   they sat and had full store,
And how each high attendant   gold-broidered raiment wore,
With stones full rare and precious   set with skill therein!
The while with care did serve them   Siegelind the noble queen.

Then spake the royal Siegmund   before his people so:
"To every friend of Siegfried   give I now to know
That he before these warriors   my royal crown shall wear."
And did rejoice that message   the thanes of Netherland to hear.

His crown to him he tendered   and rule o'er wide domain
Whereof he all was master.   Where'er did reach his reign
Or men were subject to him   bestowed his hand such care
That evil-doers trembled   before the spouse of Kriemhild fair.

In such high honor truly   he lived, as ye shall hear,
And judged as lofty monarch   unto the tenth year,
What time his fairest lady   to him a son did bear.
Thereat the monarch's kinsmen   filled with mickle joyance were.

They soon the same did christen   and gave to him a name,
Gunther, as hight his uncle,   nor cause was that for shame:
Grew he but like his kinsmen   then happy might he be.
As well he did deserve it,   him fostered they right carefully.

In the selfsame season   did Lady Siegelind die,
When was full power wielded   by Ute's daughter high,
As meet so lofty lady   should homage wide receive.
That death her thus had taken   did many a worthy kinsman grieve.

Now by the Rhine yonder,   as we likewise hear,
Unto mighty Gunther   eke a son did bear
Brunhild his fair lady   in the land of Burgundy.
In honor to the hero   Siegfried naméd eke was he.

The child they also fostered   with what tender care!
Gunther the noble monarch   anon did masters rare
Find who should instruct him   a worthy man to grow.
Alas! by sad misfortune   to friends was dealt how fell a blow!

At all times the story   far abroad was told,
How that in right worthy   way the warriors bold

Lived there in Siegmund's country   as noble knights should do.
Likewise did royal Gunther   eke amid his kinsmen true.

Land of the Nibelungen   Siegfried as well did own,
— Amid his lofty kindred   a mightier ne'er was known —
And Schilbung's knights did serve him,   with all that theirs had
    been.
That great was thus his power   did fill with joy the knight full keen.

Hoard of all the greatest   that hero ever won,
Save who erstwhile did wield it,   now the knight did own,
The which before a mountain   he seized against despite,
And for whose sake he further   slew full many a gallant knight.

Naught more his heart could wish for;   yet had his might been less,
Rightly must all people   of the high knight confess,
One was he of the worthiest   that e'er bestrode a steed.
Feared was his mickle prowess,   and, sooth to say, thereof was need.

Twelfth Adventure

How Gunther Bade Siegfried to the Feast

Now all time bethought her   royal Gunther's wife:
"How now doth Lady Kriemhild   lead so haughty life?
In sooth her husband Siegfried   doth homage to us owe,
But now full long unto us   little service he doth show."

That in her heart in secret   eke she pondered o'er.
That they were strangers to her   did grieve her heart full sore,
And so seldom sign of service   came from Siegfried's land.
How it thus was fallen,   that she fain would understand.

She probed then the monarch,   if the thing might be,
That she the Lady Kriemhild   once again might see.
She spake it all in secret   whereon her heart did dwell;
The thing she then did speak of   pleased the monarch passing well.

"How might we bring them hither"   — spake the mighty king —
"Unto this my country?   'Twere ne'er to do, such thing.
They dwell too distant from us,   the quest I fear to make."
Thereto gave answer Brunhild,   and in full crafty wise she spake:

"How high soe'er and mighty   king's man were ever one,
Whate'er should bid his master,   may he not leave undone."
Thereat did smile King Gunther,   as such words spake she:
Ne'er bade he aught of service,   oft as Siegfried he did see.

She spake: "Full loving master,   as thou hold'st me dear,
Help me now that Siegfried   and thy sister fair
Come to this our country,   that them we here may see;

In sooth no thing could ever   unto me more welcome be.

"Thy sister's lofty bearing   and all her courtesy,
Whene'er I think upon it,   full well it pleaseth me,
How we did sit together   when erst I was thy spouse!
Well in sooth with honor   might she the valiant Siegfried choose."

She pleaded with the monarch   so long till answered he:
"Know now that guests none other   so welcome were to me.
To gain thy wish 'tis easy: straight messengers of mine
To both shall message carry,   that hither come they to the Rhine."

Thereto the queen gave answer: "Now further shalt thou say,
When thou them wilt summon,   or when shall be the day
That our dear friends come hither   unto our country.
Who'll bear thy message thither,   shalt thou eke make known to
       me."

"That will I," spake the monarch.   "Thirty of my men
Shall thither ride unto them."   The same he summoned then,
And bade them with the message   to Siegfried's land to fare.
They joyed as gave them Brunhild   stately raiment rich to wear.

Then further spake the monarch: "Ye knights from me shall bring
This message, nor withhold ye   of it anything,
Unto the doughty Siegfried   and eke my sister fair:
In the world could never any   to them a better purpose bear.

"And pray them both that hither   they come unto the Rhine.
With me will e'er my lady   such grace to pay combine,
Ere turn of sun in summer   he and his men shall know
That liveth here full many   to them would willing honor show.

"Unto royal Siegmund   bear greeting fair from me,
That I and my friends ever   to him well-minded be.
And tell ye eke my sister   she shall no wise omit
Hither to friends to journey: ne'er feast could better her befit."

Brunhild and Ute   and ladies all at hand,
They sent a fairest greeting   unto Siegfried's land
To winsome ladies many   and many a warrior brave.

With godspeed from the monarch   and friends the messengers took
  leave.

They fared with full equipment: their steeds did ready stand
And rich were they attired: so rode they from that land
They hastened on the journey   whither they would fare;
Escort safe the monarch   had bidden eke for them prepare.

Their journey had they ended   e'er three weeks were spent.
At the Nibelungen castle,   whither they were sent,
In the mark of Norway   found they the knight they sought,
And weary were the horses   the messengers so far had brought.

Then was told to Siegfried   and to Kriemhild fair
How knights were there arrivéd   who did raiment wear
Like as in land of Burgundy   of wont the warriors dressed.
Thereat did hasten Kriemhild   from couch where she did lying rest.

Then bade eke to a window   one of her maids to go.
She saw the valiant Gere   stand in the court below,
And with him his companions,   who did thither fare.
To hear such joyous tidings,   how soon her heart forgot its care.

She spake unto the monarch: "Look now thitherward
Where with the doughty Gere   stand in the castle yard
Whom to us brother Gunther   adown the Rhine doth send!"
Thereto spake doughty Siegfried: "With greeting fair we'll them
  attend."

Then hastened their retainers   all the guests to meet,
And each of them in special   manner then did greet
The messengers full kindly   and warmest welcome bade.
Siegmund did likewise   o'er their coming wax full glad.

In fitting way was harbored   Gere and his men,
And steeds in charge were taken.   The messengers went then
Where beside Sir Siegfried   the Lady Kriemhild sat.
To court the guests were bidden,   where them did greeting fair await.

The host with his fair lady,   straightway up stood he,
And greeted fairly Gere   of the land of Burgundy
And with him his companions   King Gunther's men also.

Gere, knight full mighty,   bade they to a settle go.

"Allow that first the message   we give ere sit we down;
The while we'll stand, though weary   upon our journey grown.
Tidings bring we to you   what greetings high have sent
Gunther and Brunhild   who live in royal fair content.

"Eke what from Lady Ute   thy mother now we've brought.
The youthful Giselher   and also Sir Gernot
And best among thy kinsmen   have sent us here to thee:
A fairest greeting send they   from the land of Burgundy."

"God give them meed," spake Siegfried;   "Good will and faith withal
I trow full well they harbor,   as with friends we shall;
Likewise doth eke their sister.   Now further shall ye tell
If that our friends belovéd   at home in high estate do dwell.

"Since that we from them parted   hath any dared to do
Scathe to my lady's kinsmen?   That shall ye let me know.
I'll help them ever truly   all their need to bear
Till that their enemies   have good cause my help to fear."

Then spake the Margrave   Gere, a knight full good:
"In all that maketh knighthood   right proud they stand of mood.
Unto the Rhine they bid you   to high festivity:
They'd see you there full gladly,   thereof may ye not doubtful be.

"And bid they eke my Lady   Kriemhild that she too,
When ended is the winter,   thither come with you.
Ere turn of sun in summer   trust they you to see."
Then spake the doughty Siegfried: "That same thing might hardly
      be."

Thereto did answer Gere   of the land of Burgundy:
"Your high mother Ute   hath message sent by me,
Likewise Gernot and Giselher,   that they plead not in vain.
That you they see so seldom   daily hear I them complain.

"Brunhild my mistress   and all her company
Of fair maids rejoice them;   if the thing might be
That they again should see you,   of merry mood they were."
Then joy to hear the tidings   filled the Lady Kriemhild fair.

Gere to her was kinsman.   The host did bid him rest,
Nor long were they in pouring   wine for every guest.
Thither came eke Siegmund   where the strangers he did see,
And in right friendly manner   spake to the men of Burgundy:

"Welcome be, ye warriors,   ye Gunther's men, each one.
Since that fair Kriemhild   Siegfried my son
For spouse did take unto him,   we should you ofter see
Here in this our country,   an ye good friends to us would be."

They spake, whene'er he wished it,   full glad to come were they.
All their mickle weariness   with joy was ta'en away.
The messengers were seated   and food to them they bore,
Whereof did Siegfried offer   unto his guests a goodly store.

Until nine days were over   must they there abide,
When did at last the valiant   knights begin to chide
That they did not ride thither   again unto their land.
Then did the royal Siegfried   summon his good knights to hand.

He asked what they did counsel: should they unto the Rhine?
"Me unto him hath bidden   Gunther, friend of mine,
He and his good kinsmen,   to high festivity.
Thither went I full gladly,   but that his land so far doth lie.

"Kriemhild bid they likewise   that she with me shall fare.
Good friends, now give ye counsel   how we therefor prepare.
And were it armies thirty   to lead in distant land,
Yet must serve them gladly   evermore Siegfried's hand."

Then answer gave his warriors.   "An't pleaseth thee to go
Thither to the festival,   we'll counsel what thou do.
Thou shalt with thousand warriors   unto Rhine river ride.
So may'st thou well with honor   in the land of Burgundy abide."

Then spake of Netherland   Siegmund the king:
"Will ye to the festival,   why hide from me the thing!
I'll journey with you thither,   if it not displeasing be,
And lead good thanes a hundred   wherewith to swell your
        company."

"And wilt thou with us journey,   father full dear to me,"
Spake the valiant Siegfried,   "full glad thereat I'll be.
Before twelve days are over   from these my lands I fare."
To all who'd join the journey   steeds gave they and apparel rare.

When now the lofty monarch   was minded thus to ride
Bade he the noble messengers   longer not to bide,
And to his lady's kinsmen   to the Rhine a message sent,
How that he would full gladly   join to make them merriment.

Siegfried and Kriemhild,   this same tale we hear,
To the messengers gave so richly   that the burden could not bear
Their horses with them homeward,   such wealth in sooth he had.
The horses heavy-laden   drove they thence with hearts full glad.

Siegfried and Siegmund   their people richly clad.
Eckewart the Margrave,   straightway he bade
For ladies choose rich clothing,   the best that might be found,
Or e'er could be procuréd   in all Siegfried's lands around.

The shields and the saddles   gan they eke prepare,
To knights and fair ladies   who with them should fare
Lacked nothing that they wished for,   but of all they were possessed.
Then to his friends led Siegfried   many a high and stately guest.

The messengers swift hasted   homeward on their way,
And soon again came Gere   to the land of Burgundy.
Full well was he receivéd,   and there dismounted all
His train from off their horses   before the royal Gunther's Hall.

Old knights and youthful squires   crowded, as is their way,
To ask of them the tidings.   Thus did the brave knight say:
"When to the king I tell them   then shall ye likewise hear."
He went with his companions   and soon 'fore Gunther did appear.

Full of joy the monarch   did from the settle spring;
And did thank them also   for their hastening
Brunhild the fair lady.   Spake Gunther eagerly:
"How now liveth Siegfried,   whose arm hath oft befriended me?"

Then spake the valiant Gere: "Joy o'er the visage went
Of him and eke thy sister.   To friends was never sent

A more faithful greeting   by good knight ever one,
Than now the mighty Siegfried   and his royal sire have done."

Then spake unto the Margrave   the noble monarch's wife:
"Now tell me, cometh Kriemhild?   And marketh yet her life
Aught of the noble bearing   did her erstwhile adorn?"
"She cometh to thee surely,"   Gere answer did return.

Ute straightway the messengers   to her did command.
Then might ye by her asking   full well understand
To her was joyous tidings   how Kriemhild did betide.
He told her how he found her,   and that she soon would hither ride.

Eke of all the presents   did they naught withhold,
That had given them Siegfried: apparel rich and gold
Displayed they to the people   of the monarchs three.
To him were they full grateful   who thus had dealt so bounteously.

"Well may he," quoth Hagen,   "of his treasure give,
Nor could he deal it fully,   should he forever live:
Hoard of the Nibelungen   beneath his hand doth lie.
Heigh-ho, if came it ever   into the land of Burgundy!"

All the king's retainers   glad they were thereat,
That the guests were coming.   Early then and late
Full little were they idle,   the men of monarchs three.
Seats builded they full many   toward the high festivity.

The valiant knight Hunold   and Sindold doughty thane
Little had of leisure.   Meantime must the twain,
Stands erect full many,   as their high office bade.
Therein did help them Ortwein,   and Gunther's thanks therefor
     they had.

Rumold the High Steward   busily he wrought
Among them that did serve him.   Full many a mighty pot,
And spacious pans and kettles,   how many might ye see!
For those to them were coming   prepared they victuals plenteously.

Thirteenth Adventure

How They Fared to the Feast

Leave we now the ardor   wherewith they did prepare,
And tell how Lady Kriemhild   and eke her maidens fair
From land of Nibelungen   did journey to the Rhine.
Ne'er did horses carry   such store of raiment rich and fine.

Carrying-chests full many   for the way they made ready.
Then rode the thane Siegfried   with his friends in company
And eke the queen thither   where joy they looked to find.
Where now was high rejoicing   they soon in sorest grief repined.

At home behind them left they   Lady Kriemhild's son
That she did bear to Siegfried / — 'twas meet that that be done.
From this their festive journey   rose mickle sorrow sore:
His father and his mother   their child beheld they never more.

Then eke with them thither   Siegmund the king did ride.
Had he e'er had knowledge   what should there betide
Anon from that high journey,   such had he never seen:
Ne'er wrought upon dear kindred   might so grievous wrong have
    been.

Messengers sent they forward   that the tidings told should be.
Then forth did ride to meet them   with gladsome company
Ute's friends full many   and many a Gunther's man.
With zeal to make him ready   unto his guests the king began.

Where he found Brunhild sitting,   thither straight went he.
"How receivéd thee my sister,   as thou cam'st to this country?

Like preparations shalt thou   for Siegfried's wife now make."
"Fain do I that; good reason   have I to love her well," she spake.

Then quoth the mighty monarch: "The morn shall see them here.
Wilt thou go forth to meet them,   apace do thou prepare,
That not within the castle   their coming we await.
Guests more welcome never   greeted I of high estate."

Her maidens and her ladies   straight did she command
To choose them rich apparel,   the best within the land,
In which the stately company   before the guests should go.
The same they did right gladly,   that may ye full surely know.

Then eke to offer service   the men of Gunther hied,
And all his doughty warriors   saw ye by the monarch's side.
Then rode the queen full stately   the strangers forth to meet,
And hearty was the welcome   as she her loving guests did greet.

With what glad rejoicings   the guests they did receive!
They deemed that Lady Kriemhild   did unto Brunhild give
Ne'er so warm a welcome   to the land of Burgundy.
Bold knights that yet were strangers   rejoiced each other there to see.

Now come was also Siegfried   with his valiant men.
The warriors saw ye riding   thither and back again,
Where'er the plain extended,   with huge company.
From the dust and crowding   could none in all the rout be free.

When the monarch of the country   Siegfried did see
And with him also Siegmund,   spake he full lovingly:
"Be ye to me full welcome   and to all these friends of mine.
Our hearts right glad they shall be   o'er this your journey to the
     Rhine."

"God give thee meed," spake Siegmund,   a knight in honor grown.
"Since that my son Siegfried   thee for a friend hath known,
My heart hath e'er advised me   that thee I soon should see."
Thereto spake royal Gunther: "Joy hast thou brought full great to
     me."

Siegfried was there receivéd,   as fitted his high state,
With full lofty honors,   nor one did bear him hate.

There joined in way right courteous   Gernot and Giselher:
I ween so warm a welcome   did they make for strangers ne'er.

The spouse of each high monarch   greeted the other there.
Emptied was many a saddle,   and many a lady fair
By hero's hand was lifted   adown upon the sward.
By waiting on fair lady   how many a knight sought high reward!

So went unto each other   the ladies richly dight;
Thereat in high rejoicing   was seen full many a knight,
That by both the greeting   in such fair way was done.
By fair maidens standing   saw ye warriors many a one.

Each took the hand of other   in all their company;
In courteous manner bending   full many might ye see
And loving kisses given   by ladies debonair.
Rejoiced the men of Gunther   and Siegfried to behold them there.

They bided there no longer   but rode into the town.
The host bade to the strangers   in fitting way be shown,
That they were seen full gladly   in the land of Burgundy.
High knights full many tilting   before fair ladies might ye see.

Then did of Tronje Hagen   and eke Ortwein
In high feats of valor   all other knights outshine.
Whate'er the twain commanded   dared none to leave undone;
By them was many a service   to their high guests in honor shown.

Shields heard ye many clashing   before the castle gate
With din of lances breaking.   Long in saddle sate
The host and guests there with him,   ere that within they went.
With full merry pastime   joyfully the hours they spent.

Unto the Hall so spacious   rode the merry company.
Many a silken cover   wrought full cunningly
Saw ye beyond the saddles   of the ladies debonair
On all sides down hanging.   King Gunther's men did meet them
    there.

Led by the same the strangers   to their apartments passed.
Meanwhile oft her glances   Brunhild was seen to cast
Upon the Lady Kriemhild,   for she was passing fair.

In luster vied her color   with the gold that she did wear.

Within the town a clamor   at Worms on every hand
Arose amid their followers.   King Gunther gave command
To Dankwart his Marshal   to tend them all with care.
Then bade he fitting quarters   for the retinue prepare.

Without and in the castle   the board for all was set:
In sooth were never strangers   better tended yet.
Whatever any wished for   did they straightway provide:
So mighty was the monarch   that naught to any was denied.

To them was kind attention   and all good friendship shown.
The host then at the table   with his guests sat him down.
Siegfried they bade be seated   where he did sit before.
Then went with him to table   full many a stately warrior more.

Gallant knights twelve hundred   in the circle there, I ween,
With him sat at table.   Brunhild the lofty queen
Did deem that never vassal   could more mighty be.
So well she yet was minded,   she saw it not unwillingly.

There upon an evening,   as the king with guests did dine,
Full many a rich attire   was wet with ruddy wine,
As passed among the tables   the butlers to and fro.
And great was their endeavor   full honor to the guests to show.

As long hath been the custom   at high festivity
Fit lodging there was given   to maid and high lady.
From whence soe'er they came there   they had the host's good care;
Unto each guest was meted   of fitting honors fullest share.

When now the night was ended   and came forth the dawn,
From chests they carried with them,   full many a precious stone
Sparkled on costly raiment   by hand of lady sought.
Stately robes full many   forth to deck them then they brought.

Ere dawn was full appeared,   before the Hall again
Came knights and squires many,   whereat arose the din
E'en before the matins   that for the king were sung.
Well pleaséd was the monarch   at joust to see the warriors young.

Full lustily and loudly   many a horn did blare,
Of flutes and eke of trumpets   such din did rend the air
That loud came back the echo   from Worms the city wide.
The warriors high-hearted   to saddle sprung on every side.

Arose there in that country   high a jousting keen
Of many a doughty warrior   whereof were many seen,
Whom there their hearts more youthful   did make of merry mood;
Of these 'neath shield there saw ye   many a stately knight and good.

There sat within the casements   many a high lady
And maidens many with them,   the which were fair to see.
Down looked they where did tourney   many a valiant man.
The host with his good kinsmen   himself a-riding soon began.

Thus they found them pastime,   and fled the time full well;
Then heard they from the minster   the sound of many a bell.
Forth upon their horses   the ladies thence did ride;
Many a knight full valiant   the lofty queens accompanied.

They then before the minster   alighted on the grass.
Unto her guests Queen Brunhild   yet well-minded was.
Into the spacious minster   they passed, and each wore crown.
Their friendship yet was broken   by direst jealousy anon.

When the mass was ended   went they thence again
In full stately manner.   Thereafter were they seen
Joyous at board together.   The pleasure full did last,
Until days eleven   amid the merry-making passed.

Fourteenth Adventure

How the Queens Berated Each Other

Before the time of vespers   arose a mickle stir
On part of warriors many   upon the courtyard there.
In knightly fashion made they   the time go pleasantly;
Thither knights and ladies   went their merry play to see.

There did sit together   the queens, a stately pair,
And of two knights bethought them,   that noble warriors were.
Then spake the fair Kriemhild: "Such spouse in sooth have I,
That all these mighty kingdoms   might well beneath his scepter lie."

Then spake the Lady Brunhild: "How might such thing be?
If that there lived none other   but himself and thee,
So might perchance his power   rule these kingdoms o'er;
The while that liveth Gunther,   may such thing be nevermore."

Then again spake Kriemhild: "Behold how he doth stand
In right stately fashion   before the knightly band,
Like as the bright moon beameth   before the stars of heaven.
In sooth to think upon it   a joyous mood to me is given."

Then spake the Lady Brunhild: "How stately thy spouse be,
Howe'er so fair and worthy,   yet must thou grant to me
Gunther, thy noble brother,   doth far beyond him go:
In sooth before all monarchs   he standeth, shalt thou truly know."

Then again spake Kriemhild: "So worthy is my spouse,
That I not have praised him   here without a cause.
In ways to tell full many   high honor doth he bear:

Believe well may'st thou, Brunhild,   he is the royal Gunther's peer."

"Now guard thee, Lady Kriemhild,   my word amiss to take,
For not without good reason here   such thing I spake.
Both heard I say together,   when them I first did see,
When that erstwhile the monarch   did work his royal will o'er me,

And when in knightly fashion   my love for him he won,
Then himself said Siegfried   he were the monarch's man.
For liegeman thus I hold him,   since he the same did say."
Then spake fair Lady Kriemhild: "With me 'twere dealt in sorry
     way.

"And these my noble brothers,   how could they such thing see,
That I of their own liegeman   e'er the wife should be?
Thus will I beg thee, Brunhild,   as friend to friend doth owe,
That thou, as well befits thee,   shalt further here such words forego."

"No whit will I give over,"   spake the monarch's spouse.
"Wherefore should I so many   a knight full valiant lose,
Who to us in service   is bounden with thy man?"
Kriemhild the fair lady   thereat sore to rage began.

"In sooth must thou forego it   that he should e'er to thee
Aught of service offer.   More worthy e'en is he
Than is my brother Gunther,   who is a royal lord.
So shalt thou please to spare me   what I now from thee have heard.

"And to me is ever wonder,   since he thy liegeman is,
And thou dost wield such power   over us twain as this,
That he so long his tribute   to thee hath failed to pay.
'Twere well thy haughty humor   thou should'st no longer here
     display."

"Too lofty now thou soarest,"   the queen did make reply.
"Now will I see full gladly   if in such honor high
This folk doth hold thy person   as mine own it doth."
Of mood full sorely wrathful   were the royal ladies both.

Then spake the Lady Kriemhild: "That straightway shall be seen.
Since that thou my husband   dost thy liegeman ween,
Today shall all the followers   of both the monarchs know,

If I 'fore wife of monarch   dare unto the minster go.

"That I free-born and noble   shalt thou this day behold,
And that my royal husband,   as now to thee I've told,
'Fore thine doth stand in honor,   by me shall well be shown.
Ere night shalt thou behold it,   how wife of him thou call'st thine
        own

To court shall lead good warriors   in the land of Burgundy.
And ne'er a queen so lofty   as I myself shall be
Was seen by e'er a mortal,   or yet a crown did wear."
Then mickle was the anger   that rose betwixt the ladies there.

Then again spake Brunhild: "Wilt thou not service own,
So must thou with thy women   hold thyself alone
Apart from all my following,   as we to minster go."
Thereto gave answer Kriemhild: "In truth the same I fain will do."

"Now dress ye fair, my maidens,"   Kriemhild gave command.
"Nor shall shame befall me   here within this land.
An have ye fair apparel,   let now be seen by you.
What she here hath boasted   may Brunhild have full cause to rue."

But little need to urge them: soon were they richly clad
In garments wrought full deftly,   lady and many a maid.
Then went with her attendants   the spouse of the monarch high;
And eke appeared fair Kriemhild,   her body decked full gorgeously,

With three and forty maidens,   whom to the Rhine led she,
All clad in shining garments   wrought in Araby.
So came unto the minster   the maidens fair and tall.
Before the hall did tarry   for them the men of Siegfried all.

The people there did wonder   how the thing might be,
That no more together   the queens they thus did see,
And that beside each other   they went not as before.
Thereby came thanes a many   anon to harm and trouble sore.

Here before the minster   the wife of Gunther stood.
And good knights full many   were there of merry mood
With the fair ladies   that their eyes did see.
Then came the Lady Kriemhild   with a full stately company.

Whate'er of costly raiment   decked lofty maids before,
'Twas like a windy nothing   'gainst what her ladies wore.
The wives of thirty monarchs   — such riches were her own —
Might ne'er display together   what there by Lady Kriemhild shown.

Should any wish to do so   he could not say, I ween,
That so rich apparel   e'er before was seen
As there by her maidens   debonair was worn:
But that it grievéd Brunhild   had Kriemhild that to do forborne.

There they met together   before the minster high.
Soon the royal matron,   through mickle jealousy,
Kriemhild to pass no further,   did bid in rage full sore:
"She that doth owe her homage   shall ne'er go monarch's wife
    before."

Then spake the Lady Kriemhild   — angry was her mood:
"An could'st thou but be silent   that for thee were good.
Thyself hast brought dishonor   upon thy fair body:
How might, forsooth, a harlot   ever wife of monarch be?"

"Whom mak'st thou now a harlot?"   the king's wife answered her.
"That do I thee," spake Kriemhild,   "for that thy body fair
First was clasped by Siegfried,   knight full dear to me.
In sooth 'twas ne'er my brother   won first thy maidenhead from
    thee.

"How did thy senses leave thee?   Cunning rare was this.
How let his love deceive thee,   since he thy liegeman is?
And all in vain," quoth Kriemhild,   "the plaint I hear thee bring."
"In sooth," then answered Brunhild,   "I'll tell it to my spouse the
    king."

"What reck I of such evil?   Thy pride hath thee betrayed,
That thou deem'st my homage   should e'er to thee be paid.
Know thou in truth full certain   the thing may never be:
Nor shall I e'er be ready   to look for faithful friend in thee."

Thereat did weep Queen Brunhild: Kriemhild waited no more,
But passed into the minster   the monarch's wife before,
With train of fair attendants.   Arose there mickle hate,

Whereby eyes brightly shining   anon did grow all dim and wet.

However God they worshipped   or there the mass was sung,
Did deem the Lady Brunhild   the waiting all too long,
For that her heart was saddened   and angry eke her mood.
Therefore anon must suffer   many a hero keen and good.

Brunhild with her ladies   'fore the minster did appear.
Thought she: "Now must Kriemhild   further give me to hear
Of what so loud upbraideth   me this free-tongued wife.
And if he thus hath boasted,   amend shall Siegfried make with life."

Now came the noble Kriemhild   followed by warrior band.
Then spake the Lady Brunhild: "Still thou here shalt stand.
Thou giv'st me out for harlot: let now the same be seen.
Know thou, what thus thou sayest   to me hath mickle sorrow been."

Then spake the Lady Kriemhild: "So may'st thou let me go.
With the ring upon my finger   I the same can show:
That brought to me my lover   when first by thee he lay."
Ne'er did Lady Brunhild   know grief as on this evil day.

Quoth she: "This ring full precious   some hand from me did steal,
And from me thus a season   in evil way conceal:
Full sure will I discover   who this same thief hath been."
Then were the royal ladies   both in mood full angry seen.

Then gave answer Kriemhild: "I deem the thief not I.
Well hadst thou been silent,   hold'st thou thine honor high.
I'll show it with this girdle   that I around me wear,
That in this thing I err not: Siegfried hath lain by thee full near."

Wrought of silk of Nineveh   a girdle there she wore,
That of stones full precious   showed a goodly store.
When saw it Lady Brunhild   straight to weep gan she:
Soon must Gunther know it   and all the men of Burgundy.

Then spake the royal matron: "Bid hither come to me
Of Rhine the lofty monarch.   Hear straightway shall he
How that his sister   doth my honor stain.
Here doth she boast full open   that I in Siegfried's arms have lain."

The king came with his warriors,   where he did weeping find
His royal spouse Brunhild,   then spake in manner kind:
"Now tell me, my dear lady,   who hath done aught to thee?"
She spake unto the monarch: "Thy wife unhappy must thou see.

"Me, thy royal consort,   would thy sister fain
Rob of all mine honor.   To thee must I complain:
She boasts her husband Siegfried   hath known thy royal bed."
Then spake the monarch Gunther: "An evil thing she then hath
     said."

"I did lose a girdle: here by her 'tis worn,
And my ring all golden.   That I e'er was born,
Do I rue full sorely   if thou wardest not from me
This full great dishonor: that will I full repay to thee."

Then spake the monarch Gunther: "Now shall he come near,
And hath he such thing boasted,   so shall he let us hear:
Eke must full deny it   the knight of Netherland."
Then straight the spouse of Kriemhild   hither to bring he gave
     command.

When that angry-minded   Siegfried them did see,
Nor knew thereof the reason,   straightway then spake he:
"Why do weep these ladies?   I'd gladly know that thing,
Or wherefore to this presence   I am bidden by the king."

Then spake the royal Gunther: "Sore grieveth me this thing:
To me my Lady Brunhild   doth the story bring,
How that thereof thou boastest   that her fair body lay
First in thy embraces: this doth thy Lady Kriemhild say."

Thereto gave answer Siegfried: "An if she thus hath said,
Full well shall she repent it   ere doth rest my head:
Before all thy good warriors   of that I'll make me free,
And swear by my high honor   such thing hath ne'er been told by
     me."

Then spake of Rhine the monarch: "That shalt thou let us see.
The oath that thou dost offer,   if such perfoŕmed be,
Of all false accusation   shalt thou delivered stand."
In ring to take their station   did he the highborn thanes command.

The full valiant Siegfried   in oath the hand did give.
Then spake the lordly monarch: "Well now do I perceive
How thou art all blameless,   of all I speak thee free;
What here maintains my sister,   the same hath ne'er been done by
        thee."

Thereto gave answer Siegfried: "If gain should e'er accrue
Unto my spouse, that Brunhild   from her had cause to rue,
Know that to me full sorely   'twould endless sorrow be."
Then looked upon each other   the monarchs twain right graciously.

"So should we govern women,"   spake the thane Siegfried,
"That to leave wanton babble   they should take good heed.
Forbid it to thy wife now,   to mine I'll do the same.
Such ill-becoming manner /in sooth doth fill my heart with shame."

No more said many a lady   fair, but thus did part.
Then did the Lady Brunhild   grieve so sore at heart,
That it must move to pity   all King Gunther's men.
To go unto his mistress   Hagen of Tronje saw ye then.

He asked to know her worry,   as he her weeping saw.
Then told she him the story.   To her straight made he vow,
That Lady Kriemhild's husband   must for the thing atone,
Else henceforth should never   a joyous day by him be known.

Then came Ortwein and Gernot   where they together spake,
And there the knights did counsel   Siegfried's life to take.
Thither came eke Giselher,   son of Ute high.
When heard he what they counseled,   spake he free from treachery:

"Ye good knights and noble,   wherefore do ye that?
Ne'er deserved hath Siegfried   in such way your hate,
That he therefor should forfeit   at your hands his life.
In sooth small matter is it   that maketh cause for woman's strife."

"Shall we rear race of bastards?"   Hagen spake again:
"Therefrom but little honor   had many a noble thane.
The thing that he hath boasted   upon my mistress high,
Therefor my life I forfeit,   or he for that same thing shall die."

Then spake himself the monarch: "To us he ne'er did give
Aught but good and honor: let him therefore live.
What boots it if my anger   I vent the knight upon?
Good faith he e'er hath shown us,   and that full willingly hath
         done."

Then outspake of Metz   Ortwein the thane:
"In sooth his arm full doughty   may bring him little gain.
My vengeance full he'll suffer,   if but my lord allow."
The knights — nor reason had they —   against him mortal hate did
         vow.

None yet his words did follow,   but to the monarch's ear
Ne'er a day failed Hagen   the thought to whisper there:
If that lived not Siegfried,   to him would subject be
Royal lands full many.   The king did sorrow bitterly.

Then did they nothing further: soon began the play.
As from the lofty minster   passed they on their way,
What doughty shafts they shattered   Siegfried's spouse before!
Gunther's men full many   saw ye there in rage full sore.

Spake the king: "Now leave ye   such mortal enmity:
The knight is born our honor   and fortune good to be.
Keen is he unto wonder,   hath eke so doughty arm
That, were the contest open,   none is who dared to work him harm."

"Naught shall he know," quoth Hagen.   "At peace ye well may be:
I trow the thing to manage   so full secretly
That Queen Brunhild's weeping   he shall rue full sore.
In sooth shall he from Hagen   have naught but hate for evermore."

Then spake the monarch Gunther: "How might such thing e'er be?"
Thereto gave answer Hagen: "That shalt thou hear from me.
We'll bid that hither heralds   unto our land shall fare,
Here unknown to any,   who shall hostile tidings bear.

"Then say thou 'fore the strangers   that thou with all thy men
Wilt forth to meet the enemy.   He'll offer service then
If that thus thou sayest,   and lose thereby his life,
Can I but learn the story   from the valiant warrior's wife."

The king in evil manner   did follow Hagen's rede,
And the two knights, ere any   man thereof had heed,
Had treachery together   to devise begun.
From quarrel of two women   died heroes soon full many a one.

Fifteenth Adventure

How Siegfried Was Betrayed

Upon the fourth morning   two and thirty men
Saw ye to court a-riding.   Unto King Gunther then
Were tidings borne that ready   he should make for foe —
This lie did bring to women   many, anon full grievous woe.

Leave had they 'fore the monarch's   presence to appear,
There to give themselves out   for men of Luedeger,
Him erstwhile was conquered   by Siegfried's doughty hand
And brought a royal hostage   bound unto King Gunther's land.

The messengers he greeted   and to seat them gave command.
Then spake one amongst them: "Allow that yet we stand
Until we tell the tidings   that to thee are sent.
Know thou that warriors many   on thee to wreak their hate are bent.

"Defiance bids thee Luedegast   and eke Luedeger
Who at thy hands full sorely   erstwhile aggrievéd were:
In this thy land with hostile   host they'll soon appear."
To rage begin the monarch   when such tidings he did hear.

Those who did act thus falsely   they bade to lodge the while.
How himself might Siegfried   guard against such guile
As there they planned against him,   he or ever one?
Unto themselves 'twas sorrow   great anon that e'er 'twas done.

With his friends the monarch   secret counsel sought.
Hagen of Tronje   let him tarry not.
Of the king's men yet were many   who fain would peace restore:

But nowise would Hagen   his dark purpose e'er give o'er.

Upon a day came Siegfried   when they did counsel take,
And there the knight of Netherland   thus unto them spake:
"How goeth now so sorrowful   amid his men the king?
I'll help you to avenge it,   hath he been wronged in anything."

Then spake the monarch Gunther: "Of right do I lament,
Luedegast and Luedeger   have hostile message sent:
They will in open manner   now invade my land."
The knight full keen gave answer: "That in sooth shall Siegfried's
    hand,

"As doth befit thy honor,   know well to turn aside.
As erstwhile to thy enemies,   shall now from me betide:
Their lands and eke their castles   laid waste by me shall be
Ere that I give over: thereof my head be surety.

"Thou and thy good warriors   shall here at home abide,
And let me with my company   alone against them ride.
That I do serve thee gladly,   that will I let them see;
By me shall thy enemies,   — that know thou — full requited be."

"Good tidings, that thou sayest,"   then the monarch said,
As if he in earnest   did joy to have such aid.
Deep did bow before him   the king in treachery.
Then spake Sir Siegfried: "Bring that but little care to thee."

Then serving-men full many   bade they ready be:
'Twas done alone that Siegfried   and his men the same might see.
Then bade he make them ready   the knights of Netherland,
And soon did Siegfried's warriors   for fight appareled ready stand.

"My royal father Siegmund,   here shalt thou remain,"
Spake then Sir Siegfried.   "We come full soon again
If God but give good fortune,   hither the Rhine beside;
Here shalt thou with King Gunther   full merrily the while abide."

Then bound they on the banners   as they thence would fare.
Men of royal Gunther   were full many there,
Who naught knew of the matter,   or how that thing might be:
There with Siegfried saw ye   of knights a mickle company.

Their helms and eke their mail-coats   bound on horse did stand:
And doughty knights made ready   to fare from out that land.
Then went of Tronje Hagen   where he Kriemhild found
And prayed a fair leave-taking,   for that to battle they were bound.

"Now well is me, such husband   I have," Kriemhild said,
"That to my loving kindred   can bring so potent aid,
As my lord Siegfried   doth now to friends of me.
Thereby," spake the high lady,   "may I full joyous-minded be.

"Now full dear friend Hagen,   call thou this to mind,
Good-will I e'er have borne thee,   nor hate in any kind.
Let now therefrom have profit   the husband dear to me.
If Brunhild aught I've injured   may't not to him requited be.

"For that I since have suffered,"   spake the high lady.
"Sore punishment hath offered   therefor the knight to me.
That I have aught e'er spoken   to make her sad of mood,
Vengeance well hath taken   on me the valiant knight and good."

"In the days hereafter shall ye   be reconciled full well.
Kriemhild, belovéd lady,   to me shalt thou tell
How that in Siegfried's person   I may service do to thee.
That do I gladly, lady,   and unto none more willingly."

"No longer were I fearful,"   spake his noble wife,
"That e'er in battle any   should take from him his life,
Would he but cease to follow   his high undaunted mood:
Secure were then forever   the thane full valiant and good."

"Lady," spake then Hagen,   "an hast thou e'er a fear
That hostile blade should pierce him,   now shalt thou give to hear
With what arts of cunning   I may the same prevent.
On horse and foot to guard him   shall ever be my fair intent."

She spake: "Of my kin art thou,   as I eke of thine.
In truth to thee commended   be then dear spouse of mine,
That him well thou guardest   whom full dear I hold."
She told to him a story   'twere better had she left untold.

She spake: "A valorous husband   is mine, and doughty too.

When he the wormlike dragon   by the mountain slew,
In its blood the stately   knight himself then bathed,
Since when from cutting weapons   in battle is he all unscathed.

"Nathless my heart is troubled   when he in fight doth stand,
And full many a spear-shaft   is hurled by hero's hand,
Lest that I a husband   full dear should see no more.
Alack! How oft for Siegfried   must I sit in sorrow sore!

"On thy good-will I rest me,   dear friend, to tell to thee,
And that thy faith thou fully   provest now to me,
Where that my spouse may smitten   be by hand of foe.
This I now shall tell thee,   and on thy honor this I do.

"When from the wounded dragon   reeking flowed the blood,
And therein did bathe him   the valiant knight and good,
Fell down between his shoulders   full broad a linden leaf.
There may he be smitten;   'tis cause to me of mickle grief."

Then spake of Tronje Hagen: "Upon his tunic sew
Thou a little token.   Thereby shall I know
Where I may protect him   when in the fight we strain."
She weened to save the hero,   yet wrought she nothing save his bane.

She spake: "All fine and silken   upon his coat I'll sew
A little cross full secret.   There, doughty thane, shalt thou
From my knight ward danger   when battle rageth sore,
And when amid the turmoil   he stands his enemies before."

"That will I do," quoth Hagen,   "lady full dear to me."
Then weenéd eke the lady   it should his vantage be,
But there alone did Kriemhild   her own good knight betray.
Leave of her took Hagen,   and joyously he went away.

The followers of the monarch   were all of merry mood.
I ween that knight thereafter   never any could
Of treachery be guilty   such as then was he
When that Queen Kriemhild   did rest on his fidelity.

With his men a thousand   upon the following day
Rode thence Sir Siegfried   full joyously away.
He weened he should take vengeance   for harm his friends did bear.

That he might view the tunic   Hagen rode to him full near.

When he had viewed the token   sent Hagen thence away
Two of his men in secret   who did other tidings say:
How that King Gunther's country   had nothing now to fear
And that unto the monarch   had sent them royal Luedeger.

'Twas little joy to Siegfried   that he must turn again
Ere for the hostile menace   vengeance he had ta'en.
In sooth the men of Gunther   could scarce his purpose bend.
Then rode he to the monarch,   who thus began his thanks to lend:

"Now God reward thee for it,   my good friend Siegfried,
That thou with mind so willing   hast holpen me in need.
That shall I e'er repay thee,   as I may do of right.
To thee before all other   friends do I my service plight.

"Now that from battle-journey   free we are once more,
So will I ride a-hunting   the wild bear and the boar
Away to the Vosges forest,   as I full oft have done."
The same had counseled Hagen,   the full dark and faithless man.

"To all my guests here with me   shall now be told
That we ride forth at daybreak: themselves shall ready hold,
Who will join the hunting;   will any here remain
For pastime with fair ladies,   the thing behold I eke full fain."

Then outspake Sir Siegfried   as in manner due:
"If that thou rid'st a-hunting,   go I gladly too.
A huntsman shalt thou grant me   and good hound beside
That shall the game discover;   so with thee to the green I'll ride."

Straightway spake the monarch: "Wilt thou but one alone?
And wilt thou, four I'll grant thee,   to whom full well is known
The forest with the runways   where most the game doth stray,
And who unto the campfires   will help thee back to find thy way."

Unto his spouse then rode he,   the gallant knight and bold.
Full soon thereafter Hagen   unto the king had told
How he within his power   would have the noble thane:
May deed so dark and faithless   ne'er by knight be done again!

Sixteenth Adventure
How Siegfried Was Slain

Gunther and Hagen,   the knights full keen,
Proposed with evil forethought   a hunting in the green:
The boar within the forest   they'd chase with pointed spear,
And shaggy bear and bison.   — What sport to valiant men more
    dear?

With them rode also Siegfried   happy and light of heart:
Their load of rich refreshments   was made in goodly part.
Where a spring ran cooling   they took from him his life,
Whereto in chief had urged them   Brunhild, royal Gunther's wife.

Then went the valiant Siegfried   where he Kriemhild found;
Rich hunting-dress was laden   and now stood ready bound
For him and his companions   across the Rhine to go.
Than this a sadder hour   nevermore could Kriemhild know.

The spouse he loved so dearly   upon the mouth he kissed.
"God grant that well I find thee   again, if so He list,
And thine own eyes to see me.   'Mid kin that hold thee dear
May now the time go gently,   the while I am no longer near."

Then thought she of the story   — but silence must she keep —
Whereof once Hagen asked her: then began to weep
The princess high and noble   that ever she was born,
And wept with tears unceasing   the valiant Siegfried's wife forlorn.

She spake unto her husband: "Let now this hunting be.
I dreamt this night of evil,   how wild boars hunted thee,

Two wild boars o'er the meadow,   wherefrom the flowers grew red.
That I do weep so sorely   have I poor woman direst need.

"Yea, do I fear, Sir Siegfried,   something treacherous,
If perchance have any   of those been wronged by us
Who might yet be able   to vent their enmity.
Tarry thou here, Sir Siegfried: let that my faithful counsel be."

Quoth he: "I come, dear lady,   when some short days are flown.
Of foes who bear us hatred   here know I never one.
All of thine own kindred   are gracious unto me,
Nor know I aught of reason   why they should other-minded be."

"But nay, belovéd Siegfried,   thy death I fear 'twill prove.
This night I dreamt misfortune,   how o'er thee from above
Down there fell two mountains: I never saw thee more.
And wilt thou now go from me,   that must grieve my heart full
        sore."

The lady rich in virtue   within his arms he pressed,
And with loving kisses   her fair form caressed.
From her thence he parted   ere long time was o'er:
Alas for her, she saw him   alive thereafter nevermore.

Then rode from thence the hunters   deep within a wold
In search of pleasant pastime.   Full many a rider bold
Followed after Gunther   in his stately train.
Gernot and Giselher,   — at home the knights did both remain.

Went many a horse well laden   before them o'er the Rhine,
That for the huntsmen carried   store of bread and wine,
Meat along with fishes   and other victualling,
The which upon his table   were fitting for so high a king.

Then bade they make encampment   before the forest green
Where game was like to issue,   those hunters proud and keen,
Who there would join in hunting,   on a meadow wide that spread.
Thither also was come Siegfried: the same unto the king was said.

By the merry huntsmen   soon were watched complete
At every point the runways.   The company then did greet
Siegfried the keen and doughty: "Who now within the green

Unto the game shall guide us,   ye warriors so bold and keen?"

"Now part we from each other,"   answered Hagen then,
"Ere that the hunting   we do here begin!
Thereby may be apparent   to my masters and to me
Who on this forest journey   of the hunters best may be.

"Let then hounds and huntsmen   be ta'en in equal share,
That wheresoever any   would go, there let him fare.
Who then is first in hunting   shall have our thanks this day."
Not longer there together   did the merry hunters stay.

Thereto quoth Sir Siegfried: "Of dogs have I no need,
More than one hound only   of trusty hunting breed
For scenting well the runway   of wild beast through the brake.
And now the chase begin we!"   — so the spouse of Kriemhild spake.

Then took a practiced hunter   a good tracking-hound,
That did bring them where they   game in plenty found,
Nor kept them long awaiting.   Whate'er did spring from lair
Pursued the merry huntsmen,   as still good hunters everywhere.

As many as the hound started   slew with mighty hand
Siegfried the full doughty   hero of Netherland.
So swiftly went his charger   that none could him outrun;
And praise before all others   soon he in the hunting won.

He was in every feature   a valiant knight and true.
The first within the forest   that with his hand he slew
Was a half-grown wild-boar   that he smote to ground;
Thereafter he full quickly   a wild and mighty lion found.

When it the hound had started,   with bow he shot it dead,
Wherewith a pointed arrow   he had so swiftly sped
That the lion after   could forward spring but thrice.
All they that hunted with him   cried Siegfried's praise with merry
     voice.

Soon fell a prey unto him   an elk and bison more,
A giant stag he slew him   and huge ure-oxen four.
His steed bore him so swiftly   that none could him outrun;
Of stag or hind encountered   scarce could there escape him one.

A boar full huge and bristling   soon was likewise found,
And when the same bethought him   to flee before the hound,
Came quick again the master   and stood athwart his path.
The boar upon the hero   full charged straightway in mickle wrath.

Then the spouse of Kriemhild,   with sword the boar he slew,
A thing that scarce another   hunter had dared to do.
When he thus had felled him   they lashed again the hound,
And soon his hunting prowess   was known to all the people round.

Then spake to him his huntsmen: "If that the thing may be,
So let some part, Sir Siegfried,   of the forest game go free;
Today thou makest empty   hillside and forest wild."
Thereat in merry humor   the thane so keen and valiant smiled.

Then they heard on all sides   the din, from many a hound
And huntsmen eke the clamor   so great was heard around
That back did come the answer   from hill and forest tree —
Of hounds had four-and-twenty   packs been set by hunter free.

Full many a forest denizen   from life was doomed to part.
Each of all the hunters   thereon had set his heart,
To win the prize in hunting.   But such could never be,
When they the doughty Siegfried   at the camping-place did see.

Now the chase was ended,   — and yet complete 'twas not.
All they to camp who wended   with them thither brought
Skin of full many an animal   and of game good store.
Heigho! unto the table   how much the king's attendants bore!

Then bade the king the noble   hunters all to warn
That he would take refreshment,   and loud a hunting-horn
In one long blast was winded: to all was known thereby
That the noble monarch   at camp did wait their company.

Spake one of Siegfried's huntsmen: "Master, I do know
By blast of horn resounding   that we now shall go
Unto the place of meeting;   thereto I'll make reply."
Then for the merry hunters   blew the horn right lustily.

Then spake Sir Siegfried: "Now leave we eke the green."

His charger bore him smoothly,   and followed huntsmen keen.
With their rout they started   a beast of savage kind,
That was a bear untaméd.   Then spake the knight to those behind

"For our merry party   some sport will I devise.
Let slip the hound then straightway,   a bear now meets my eyes,
And with us shall he thither   unto the campfire fare.
Full rapid must his flight be   shall he our company forbear."

From leash the hound was loosened,   the bear sprang through the
    brake,
When that the spouse of Kriemhild   did wish him to o'ertake.
He sought a pathless thicket,   but yet it could not be,
As bruin fondly hoped it,   that from the hunter he was free.

Then from his horse alighted   the knight of spirit high,
And gan a running after.   Bruin all unguardedly
Was ta'en, and could escape not.   Him caught straightway the
    knight,
And soon all unwounded   had him bound in fetters tight.

Nor claws nor teeth availed him   for aught of injury,
But bound he was to saddle.   Then mounted speedily
The knight, and to the campfire   in right merry way
For pastime led he bruin,   the hero valiant and gay.

In what manner stately   unto the camp he rode!
He bore a spear full mickle,   great of strength and broad.
A sword all ornamented   hung down unto his spur,
And wrought of gold all ruddy   at side a glittering horn he wore.

Of richer hunting-garments   heard I ne'er tell before.
Black was the silken tunic   that the rider wore,
And cap of costly sable   did crown the gallant knight.
Heigho, and how his quiver   with well-wrought hands was rich
    bedight!

A skin of gleaming panther   covered the quiver o'er,
Prized for its pleasant odor.   Eke a bow he bore,
The which to draw if ever   had wished another man,
A lever he had needed: such power had Siegfried alone.

Of fur of costly otter　his mantle was complete,
With other skins embroidered　from head unto the feet.
And 'mid the fur all shining,　full many a golden seam
On both sides of the valiant　huntsman saw ye brightly gleam.

Balmung, a goodly weapon　broad, he also wore,
That was so sharp at edges　that it ne'er forbore
To cleave when swung on helmet:　blade it was full good.
Stately was the huntsman　as there with merry heart he rode.

If that complete the story　to you I shall unfold,
Full many a goodly arrow　did his rich quiver hold
Whereof were gold the sockets,　and heads a hand-breadth each.
In sooth was doomed to perish　whate'er in flight the same did
　　　reach.

Pricking like goodly huntsman　the noble knight did ride
When him the men of Gunther　coming thither spied.
They hasted out to meet him　and took from him his steed,
As bruin great and mighty　by the saddle he did lead.

When he from horse alighted　he loosed him every band
From foot and eke from muzzle.　Straight on every hand
Began the dogs a howling　when they beheld the bear.
Bruin would to the forest:　among the men was mickle stir.

Amid the clamor bruin　through the campfires sped:
Heigho, how the servants　away before him fled!
O'erturned was many a kettle　and flaming brands did fly:
Heigho, what goodly victuals　did scattered in the ashes lie!

Then sprang from out the saddle　knights and serving-men.
The bear was wild careering:　the king bade loosen then
All the dogs that fastened　within their leashes lay.
If this thing well had ended,　then had there passed a merry day.

Not longer then they waited　but with bow and eke with spear
Hasted the nimble hunters　to pursue the bear,
Yet none might shoot upon him　for all the dogs around.
Such clamor was of voices　that all the mountain did resound.

When by the dogs pursuéd　the bear away did run,

None there that could o'ertake him   but Siegfried alone.
With his sword he came upon him   and killed him at a blow,
And back unto the campfire   bearing bruin they did go.

Then spake who there had seen it,   he was a man of might.
Soon to the table bade they   come each noble knight,
And on a smiling meadow   the noble company sat.
Heigho, with what rare victuals   did they upon the huntsmen wait!

Ne'er appeared a butler   wine for them to pour.
Than they good knights were never   better served before,
And had there not in secret   been lurking treachery,
Then were the entertainers   from every cause of cavil free.

Then spake Sir Siegfried: "A wonder 'tis to me,
Since that from the kitchen   so full supplied are we,
Why to us the butlers   of wine bring not like store:
If such the huntsman's service   a huntsman reckon me no more.

"Meseems I yet did merit   some share of courtesy."
The king who sat at table   spake then in treachery:
"Gladly shall be amended   wherein we're guilty so.
The fault it is of Hagen,   he'd willing see us thirsting go."

Then spake of Tronje Hagen: "Good master, hear me say,
I weened for this our hunting   we did go today
Unto the Spessart forest: the wine I thither sent.
Go we today a-thirsting,   I'll later be more provident."

Thereto replied Sir Siegfried: "Small merit here is thine.
Good seven horses laden   with mead and sparkling wine
Should hither have been conducted.   If aught the same denied,
Then should our place of meeting   have nearer been the Rhine
      beside."

Then spake of Tronje Hagen: "Ye noble knights and bold,
I know here nigh unto us   a spring that's flowing cold.
Be then your wrath appeaséd,   and let us thither go."
Through that same wicked counsel   came many a thane to grievous
      woe.

Sore was the noble Siegfried   with the pangs of thirst:

To bid them rise from table   was he thus the first.
He would along the hillside   unto the fountain go:
In sooth they showed them traitors,   those knights who there did
        counsel so.

On wagons hence to carry   the game they gave command
Which had that day been slaughtered   by Siegfried's doughty hand.
He'd carried off the honors,   all who had seen did say.
Hagen his faith with Siegfried   soon did break in grievous way.

When now they would go thither   to where the linden spread,
Spake of Tronje Hagen: "To me hath oft been said,
That none could follow after   Kriemhild's nimble knight
Or vie with him in running: would that he'd prove it to our sight!"

Then spake of Netherland   bold Siegfried speedily:
"That may ye well have proof of,   will ye but run with me
In contest to the fountain.   When that the same be done,
To him be given honor   who the race hath fairly won."

"Now surely make we trial,"   quoth Hagen the thane.
Thereto the doughty Siegfried: "I too will give you gain,
Afore your feet at starting   to lay me in the grass."
When that he had heard it,   thereat how joyous Gunther was!

And spake again the warrior: "And ye shall further hear:
All my clothing likewise   will I upon me wear,
The spear and shield full heavy   and hunting-dress I'll don."
His sword as well as quiver   had he full quickly girded on.

Doffed they their apparel   and aside they laid it then:
Clothed in white shirts only   saw you there the twain.
Like unto two wild panthers   they coursed across the green:
Yet first beside the fountain   was the valiant Siegfried seen.

No man in feats of valor   who with him had vied.
The sword he soon ungirded   and quiver laid aside,
The mighty spear he leanéd   against the linden tree:
Beside the running fountain   stood the knight stately to see.

To Siegfried naught was lacking   that doth good knight adorn.
Down the shield then laid he   where did flow the burn,

Yet howsoe'er he thirsted   no whit the hero drank
Before had drunk the monarch: therefor he earned but evil thank.

There where ran clear the water   and cool from out the spring,
Down to it did bend him   Gunther the king.
And when his thirst was quenchéd   rose he from thence again:
Eke the valiant Siegfried,   how glad had he done likewise then.

For his courtesy he suffered.   Where bow and sword there lay,
Both did carry Hagen   from him thence away,
And again sprang quickly thither   where the spear did stand:
And for a cross the tunic   of the valiant knight he scanned.

As there the noble Siegfried   to drink o'er fountain bent,
Through the cross he pierced him,   that from the wound was sent
The blood nigh to bespatter   the tunic Hagen wore.
By hand of knight such evil   deed shall wrought be nevermore.

The spear he left projecting   where it had pierced the heart.
In terror as that moment   did Hagen never start
In flight from any warrior   he ever yet had found.
Soon as the noble Siegfried   within him felt the mighty wound,

Raging the knight full doughty   up from the fountain sprang,
The while from 'twixt his shoulders   stood out a spearshaft long.
The prince weened to find there   his bow or his sword:
Then in sooth had Hagen   found the traitor's meet reward.

When from the sorely wounded   knight his sword was gone,
Then had he naught to 'venge him   but his shield alone.
This snatched he from the fountain   and Hagen rushed upon,
And not at all escape him   could the royal Gunther's man.

Though he nigh to death was wounded   he yet such might did wield
That out in all directions   flew from off the shield
Precious stones a many: the shield he clave in twain.
Thus vengeance fain had taken   upon his foe the stately thane.

Beneath his hand must Hagen   stagger and fall to ground.
So swift the blow he dealt him,   the meadow did resound.
Had sword in hand been swinging,   Hagen had had his meed,
So sorely raged he stricken: to rage in sooth was mickle need.

Faded from cheek was color,   no longer could he stand,
And all his might of body   soon complete had waned,
As did a deathly pallor   over his visage creep.
Full many a fairest lady   for the knight anon must weep.

So sank amid the flowers   Kriemhild's noble knight,
While from his wound flowed thickly   the blood before the sight.
Then gan he reviling   — for dire was his need —
Who had thus encompassed   his death by this same faithless deed.

Then spake the sorely wounded: "O ye base cowards twain,
Doth then my service merit   that me ye thus have slain?
To you I e'er was faithful   and so am I repaid.
Alas, upon your kindred   now have ye shame eternal laid.

"By this deed dishonored   hereafter evermore
Are their generations.   Your anger all too sore
Have ye now thus vented   and vengeance ta'en on me.
With shame henceforth be parted   from all good knights' company."

All the hunters hastened   where he stricken lay,
It was in sooth for many   of them a joyless day.
Had any aught of honor,   he mourned that day, I ween,
And well the same did merit   the knight high-spirited and keen.

As there the king of Burgundy   mourned that he should die,
Spake the knight sore wounded: "To weep o'er injury,
Who hath wrought the evil   hath smallest need, I trow.
Reviling doth he merit,   and weeping may he well forego."

Thereto quoth grim Hagen: "Ye mourn, I know not why:
This same day hath ended   all our anxiety.
Few shall we find henceforward   for fear will give us need,
And well is me that from his   mastery we thus are freed."

"Light thing is now thy vaunting,"   did Siegfried then reply.
"Had I e'er bethought me   of this thy infamy
Well had I preservéd   'gainst all thy hate my life.
Me rueth naught so sorely   as Lady Kriemhild my wife.

"Now may God have mercy   that to me a son was born,

That him alack!, the people   in times to come shall spurn,
That those he nameth kinsmen   have done the murderer's deed.
An had I breath," spake Siegfried,   "to mourn o'er this I well had
        need."

Then spake, in anguish praying,   the hero doomed to die:
"An wilt thou, king, to any   yet not good faith deny,
In all the world to any,   to thee commended be
And to thy loving mercy   the spouse erstwhile was wed to me.

"Let it be her good fortune   that she thy sister is:
By all the princely virtues,   I beg thee pledge me this.
For me long time my father   and men henceforth must wait:
Upon a spouse was never   wrought, as mine, a wrong so great."

All around the flowers   were wetted with the blood
As there with death he struggled.   Yet not for long he could,
Because the deadly weapon   had cut him all too sore:
And soon the keen and noble   knight was doomed to speak no
        more.

When the lords perceivéd   how that the knight was dead,
Upon a shield they laid him   that was of gold full red,
And counsel took together   how of the thing should naught
Be known, but held in secret   that Hagen the deed had wrought.

Then spake of them a many: "This is an evil day.
Now shall ye all conceal it   and all alike shall say,
When as Kriemhild's husband   the dark forest through
Rode alone a-hunting,   him the hand of robber slew."

Then spake of Tronje Hagen: "Myself will bring him home.
In sooth I reck but little   if to her ears it come,
Who my Lady Brunhild   herself hath grieved so sore.
It maketh me small worry,   an if she weep for evermore."

Seventeenth Adventure

How Kriemhild Mourned for Siegfried, and How He Was Buried

There till the night they tarried   and o'er the Rhine they went.
By knights in chase might never   more evil day be spent;
For the game that there they hunted   wept many a noble maid.
In sooth by many a valiant   warrior must it since be paid.

Of humor fierce and wanton   list now and ye shall hear,
And eke of direst vengeance.   Hagen bade to bear
Siegfried thus lifeless,   of the Nibelung country,
Unto a castle dwelling   where Lady Kriemhild found might be.

He bade in secret manner   to lay him there before
Where she should surely find him   when she from out the door
Should pass to matins early,   ere that had come the day.
In sooth did Lady Kriemhild   full seldom fail the hour to pray.

When, as was wont, in minster   the bell to worship bade,
Kriemhild, fair lady, wakened   from slumber many a maid:
A light she bade them bring her   and eke her dress to wear.
Then hither came a chamberlain   who Siegfried's corse found
    waiting there.

He saw him red and bloody,   all wet his clothing too.
That it was his master,   in sooth no whit he knew.
On unto the chamber   the light in hand he bore,
Whereby the Lady Kriemhild   did learn what brought her grief full
    sore.

When she with train of ladies   would to the minster go,
Then spake the chamberlain: "Pause, I pray thee now:
Here before thy dwelling   a noble knight lies slain."
Thereat gan Lady Kriemhild   in grief unmeasured sore to plain.

Ere yet that 'twas her husband   she did rightly find,
Had she Hagen's question   begun to call to mind,
How might he protect him: then first did break her heart,
For all her joy in living   did with his death from her depart.

Unto the earth then sank she   ere she a word did say,
And reft of all her pleasure   there the fair lady lay.
Soon had Kriemhild's sorrow   all measure passed beyond:
She shrieked, when past the swooning,   that did the chamber all
          resound.

Then spake her attendants: "What if't a stranger were?"
From out her mouth the heart-blood   did spring from anguish sore.
Then spake she: "It is Siegfried   my husband, other none:
This thing hath counseled Brunhild,   and Hagen's hand the deed
          hath done."

The lady bade them lead her   where did lie the knight,
And his fair head she raiséd   with her hand full white.
Red though it was and bloody   she knew him yet straightway,
As all forlorn the hero   of Nibelungenland there lay.

Then cried the queen in anguish,   whose hand such wealth might
          wield:
"O woe is me for sorrow!   Yet is not thy shield
With blow of sword now battered,   but murdered dost thou lie.
And knew I who hath done it,   by my counsel should he die."

All of her attendants   did weep and wail enow
With their belovéd mistress,   for filled they were with woe
For their noble master   whom they should see no more.
For anger of Queen Brunhild   had Hagen wrought revenge full sore.

Then spake Kriemhild sorrowing: "Hence now the message take,
And all the men of Siegfried   shall ye straightway awake.
Unto Siegmund likewise   tell ye my sorrow deep,
If that he will help me   for the doughty Siegfried weep."

Then ran straightway a messenger   and soon he found at hand,
Siegfried's valiant warriors   of Nibelungenland.
Of joy he all bereft him   with tale that he did bear,
Nor would they aught believe it   till sound of weeping met their ear.

The messenger came eke quickly   where the king did lie,
Yet closed was not in sleeping   the monarch Siegmund's eye:
I ween his heart did tell him   the thing that there had been,
And that his dear son living   might nevermore by him be seen.

"Awake, awake, Lord Siegmund.   Hither hath sent for thee
Kriemhild my mistress.   A wrong now beareth she,
A grief that 'fore all others   unto her heart doth go:
To mourn it shalt thou help her,   for sorely hast thou need thereto."

Up raised himself then Siegmund.   He spake: "What may it be
Of wrong that grieveth Kriemhild,   as thou hast told to me?"
The messenger spake weeping: "Now may I naught withhold:
Know thou that of Netherland   Siegfried brave lies slain and cold."

Thereto gave answer Siegmund: "Let now such mocking be
And tale of such ill tidings   — an thou regardest me —
As that thou say'st to any   now he lieth slain:
An were it so, I never   unto my end might cease to plain."

"Wilt thou now believe not   the tidings that I bear,
So may'st thyself the Lady   Kriemhild weeping hear,
And all of her attendants,   that Siegfried lieth dead."
With terror filled was Siegmund: whereof in very sooth was need.

He and his men a hundred   from their beds they sprang,
Then snatched in hand full quickly   swords both sharp and long,
And toward the sound of weeping   in sorrow sore did speed.
There came a thousand warriors   eke of the valiant knight Siegfried.

When they heard the women weeping   in such sore distress
Thought some, strict custom keeping,   we first must don our dress.
In sooth for very sorrow   their wits no more had they,
For on their hearts a burden   of grief full deep and heavy lay.

Then came the monarch Siegmund   where he Kriemhild espied.

He spake: "Alack that ever   to this country I did ride!
Who in such wondrous manner,   and while good friends are near,
Hath of my child bereft me   and thee of spouse thou hold'st so
      dear?"

"Ah, might I him discover,"   spake the lady high,
"Evermore would mercy   I to him deny.
Such meed of vengeance should he   at my hands receive
That all who call him kinsman   reason good should have to grieve."

Siegmund the monarch   in arms the knight did press,
And of his friends there gathered   so great was the distress,
That from the mighty wailing   palace and wide hall
And Worms the city likewise   with sound of woe re-echoed all.

None was who aught might comfort   the wife of Siegfried there.
They drew the knight's attire   from off his body fair,
From wounds the blood, too, washed they   and laid him on the bier.
Then from all his people   a mighty wailing might ye hear.

Then outspake his warriors   of Nibelungenland:
"Until he be avengéd   rest shall not our hand.
He is within this castle   who the deed hath done."
Then rushed to find their weapons   Siegfried's warriors everyone.

The knights of chosen valor   with shields did thither throng,
Eleven hundred warriors,   that did to train belong
Of Siegmund the monarch.   That his son lay dead,
Would he wreak dire vengeance,   whereof in very sooth was need.

Yet knew they not whom should they   beset in battle then,
If it were not Gunther   and with him his men
With whom their lord Siegfried   unto the hunting rode.
Yet filled with fear was Kriemhild   when she beheld how armed they
      stood.

How great soe'er her sorrow   and stern the grief she bore,
Yet for the Nibelungen   feared she death full sore
From her brother's warriors,   and bade them hold their wrath.
She gave them kindly warning   as friend to friend beloved doth.

Then spake she rich in sorrow: "What thing beginnest thou,

Good my lord Siegmund?   This case thou dost not know.
In sooth hath here King Gunther   so many a valiant knight,
Lost are ye all together,   will ye the thanes withstand in fight."

With shields upraised they ready   for the fight did stand.
But the queen full noble   did straightway give command
To those high knights, and prayed them,   their purpose to give o'er.
That she might not dissuade them,   in sooth to her was sorrow sore.

Spake she thus: "Lord Siegmund,   thou shalt this thing let be
Until more fitting season.   Seek will I e'er with thee
Full to avenge my husband.   Who him from me hath ta'en,
An I shall know him guilty,   in me shall surely find his bane.

"Of warriors proud and mighty   are many here by Rhine,
Therefore will I advise not   the struggle to begin.
For one that we can muster   good thirty men have they;
As unto us their dealing,   God them requite in equal way.

"Here shall ye bide with me   and help my grief to bear;
Soon as dawns the morning,   ye noble knights and rare,
Help me my loved husband   prepare for burial."
"That shall be done full willing,"   spake the doughty warriors all.

To you could never any   full the wonder say,
Of knights and noble ladies,   so full of grief were they,
That the sound of wailing   through the town was heard afar,
Whereat the noble burghers   hastily did gather there.

With the guests they mourned together,   for sore they grieved as
     well.
What was the guilt of Siegfried   none to them might tell,
Wherefore the knight so noble   thus his life should lose.
Then wept with the high ladies   many a worthy burgher's spouse.

Smiths they bade a casket   work full hastily
All of gold and silver   that great and strong should be.
They bade them fast to weld it   with bands of steel full good.
Then saw ye all the people   stand right sorrowful of mood.

Now the night was over,   for day, they said, drew near.
Then bade the noble lady   unto the minster bear

Siegfried her lord full lovéd   for whom she mourned so.
Whoe'er was friend unto him,   him saw ye weeping thither go.

As they brought him to the minster   bells full many rung.
On every hand then heard ye   how priests did chant their song.
Thither with his followers   came Gunther the king
And eke the grim knight Hagen   where was sound of sorrowing.

He spake: "Full loving sister,   alack for grief to thee,
And that from such great evil   spared we might not be!
Henceforth must we ever   mourn for Siegfried's sake."
"That do ye without reason,"   full of woe the lady spake.

"If that ye grievéd for it,   befallen were it not.
For say I may full truly,   me had ye all forgot
There where I thus was parted   from my husband dear.
Would it God," spake Kriemhild,   "that done unto myself it were!"

Fast they yet denied it.   Kriemhild spake again:
"If any speak him guiltless,   let here be seen full plain.
Unto the bier now shall he   before the people go;
Thus the truth full quickly   may we in this manner know."

It is a passing wonder   that yet full oft is seen,
Where blood-bespotted slayer   beside slain corse hath been,
That from the wounds come blood-drops,   as here it eke befell.
Thereby the guilt of Hagen   might they now full plainly tell.

Now ran the wounds all bloody /like as they did before.
Who erstwhile wept full sorely   now wept they mickle more.
Then spake the monarch Gunther: "To thee the truth be known:
Slain hath he been by robbers,   nor is this deed by Hagen done."

"Of these same robbers," spake she,   "full well I understand.
God give that yet may vengeance   wreak some friendly hand.
Gunther and Hagen,   yourselves have done this deed."
Then looked for bloody conflict   the valiant thanes that served
     Siegfried.

Then spake unto them Kriemhild: "Now bear with me my need."
Knights twain came likewise hither   and did find him dead, —
Gernot her brother   and the young Giselher.

With upright hearts then joined they   with the others grief to share.

They mourned for Kriemhild's husband   with hearts all full of woe.
A mass should then be chanted: to the minster forth did go
Man and child and woman   gathered from every side.
E'en they did likewise mourn him   who little lost that Siegfried died.

Gernot and Giselher spake: "O Sister dear,
Now comfort thee in sorrow,   for death is ever near.
Amends we'll make unto thee   the while that we shall live."
In the world might never any   unto her a comfort give.

His coffin was made ready   about the middle day.
From off the bier they raised him   whereupon he lay.
But yet would not the lady   let him be laid in grave.
Therefor must all the people   first a mickle trouble have.

In a shroud all silken   they the dead man wound.
I ween that never any   that wept not might be found.
There mournéd full of sorrow   Ute the queen full high
And all of her attendants   that such a noble knight did die.

When did hear the people   how they in minster sung,
And that he there lay coffined,   came then a mickle throng:
For his soul's reposing   what offerings they bore!
E'en amid his enemies   found he of good friends a store.

Kriemhild the poor lady   to her attendants spake:
"Let them shun no trouble   to suffer for my sake,
Who to him are friendly-minded   and me in honor hold;
For the soul of Siegfried   meted be to them his gold."

Child so small there was not,   did it but reason have,
But offering carried thither.   Ere he was laid in grave,
More than a hundred masses   upon the day they sung,
Of all the friends of Siegfried   was gathered there a mickle throng.

When were the masses over,   the folk departed soon.
Then spake the Lady Kriemhild: "Leave ye me not alone
To pass the night in watching   by this chosen thane now dead,
With whose passing from me   all my joy of life hath fled.

"Three days and three nights further   shall he lie on bier,
Until my heart find quiet   that weeps for spouse so dear.
God perchance commandeth   that death eke me do take:
That were for me poor Kriemhild   fit end of all my woe to make."

Then of the town the people   went to their homes again.
Priests and monks yet bade she   longer there remain,
And all the hero's followers   who willing served alway.
They watched a night all gruesome,   and full of toil was eke the day.

Meat and drink forgetting   abode there many a one.
If any were would take it   'twas unto all made known,
That have they might in plenty: thus did provide Siegmund.
Then for the Nibelungen   did trouble and sore need abound.

The while the three days lasted   — such the tale we hear —
All who could join the chanting,   mickle must they bear
There of toil and trouble.   What gifts to them they bore!
Rich were seen full many   who did suffer need before.

As many poor as found they   who themselves had naught,
By them yet an offering   bade they there be brought,
Of gold of Siegfried's treasure.   Though he no more might live,
Yet for his soul's reposing   marks many thousand did they give.

Land of fruitful income   bestowed Kriemhild around,
Wheresoever cloisters   and worthy folk were found.
Silver and apparel   to the poor she gave in store,
And in good manner showed she   that truest love to him she bore.

Upon the third morning   at the mass' tide
Was there beside the minster   filled the churchyard wide
With country-folk a-weeping   that came from far and near:
In death they yet did serve him   as is meet for friend full dear.

And so it hath been told us,   ere these four days were o'er,
Marks full thirty thousand,   yea, in sooth, and more,
For his soul's reposing   to the poor were given there:
The while that lay all broken   his life and eke his body fair.

When ended was the service   and full the masses sung,
In unrestrained sorrow   there the flock did throng.

They bade that from the minster   he to the grave be borne.
Them that fain had kept him   there beheld ye weep and mourn.

Thence full loud lamenting   did the people with him pass.
Unmoved there never any   nor man nor woman was.
Ere that in grave they laid him   chanted they and read.
What host of priests full worthy   at his burial were gatheréd!

Ere that the wife of Siegfried   was come unto the grave,
With water from the fountain   full oft her face they lave,
So struggled with her sorrow   the faithful lady fair.
Great beyond all measure   was the grief that she did bear.

It was a mickle wonder   that e'er her life she kept.
Many a lady was there   that helped her as she wept.
Then spake the queen full noble: "Ye men that service owe
To Siegfried, as ye love me,   now to me a mercy show.

"Upon this sorrow grant ye   the little grace to me
That I his shining visage   yet once more may see."
So filled she was with anguish   and so long time she sought,
Perforce they must break open   the casket all so fairly wrought.

Where she did see him lying   they then the lady led.
With hand full white and spotless   raised she his fair head;
Then kissed she there all lifeless   the good and noble knight, —
And wept so that for sorrow   ran blood from out her eyes so bright.

Mournful was the parting   that then did rend the twain.
Thence away they bore her,   nor might she walk again,
But in a swoon did senseless   the stately lady lie.
In sooth her winsome body   for sorrow sore was like to die.

When they the knight full noble   now in the grave had laid,
Beheld ye every warrior   beyond all measure sad
That with him was come hither   from Nibelung country.
Full seldom joyous-hearted   might ye royal Siegmund see.

And many were among them   that for sorrow great
Till three days were over   did nor drink nor eat.
Yet might they not their bodies   long leave uncared-for so:
For food they turned from mourning   as people still are wont to do.

Eighteenth Adventure
How Siegmund Fared Home Again

Then went royal Siegmund   where he Kriemhild found.
Unto the queen spake he: "Home must we now be bound.
We ween that guests unwelcome   here are we by the Rhine.
Kriemhild, belovéd lady,   come now to country that is mine.

"Though from us hath been taken   by foul traitor's hand
Thy good spouse and noble   here in stranger land,
Thine be it not to suffer: good friend thou hast in me
For sake of son belovéd: thereof shalt thou undoubting be.

"Eke shalt thou have, good lady,   all the power to hold,
The which erstwhile hath shown thee   Siegfried the thane full bold.
The land and the crown likewise,   be they thine own to call,
And gladly eke shall serve thee   Siegfried's doughty warriors all."

Then did they tell the servants   that they thence would ride,
And straight to fetch the horses   these obedient hied.
'Mid such as so did hate them   it grieved them more to stay:
Ladies high and maidens   were bidden dress them for the way.

When that for royal Siegmund   stood ready horse and man,
Her kinsmen Lady Kriemhild   to beseech began
That she from her mother   would still forbear to go.
Then spake the lofty lady: "That might hardly yet be so.

"How might I forever   look with eyes upon
Him that to me, poor woman,   such evil thing hath done?"
Then spake the youthful Giselher: "Sister to me full dear,

By thy goodness shalt thou   tarry with thy mother here."

"Who in this wise have harmed thee   and so grieved thy heart,
Thyself may'st spurn their service: of what is mine take part."
Unto the knight she answered: "Such thing may never be.
For die I must for sorrow   when that Hagen I should see."

"From need thereof I'll save thee,   sister full dear to me,
For with thy brother Giselher   shalt thou ever be.
I'll help to still thy sorrow   that thy husband lieth dead."
Then spake she sorrow-stricken: "Thereof in sooth had Kriemhild
            need."

When that the youthful Giselher   such kindly offer made,
Then her mother Ute   and Gernot likewise prayed,
And all her faithful kinsmen,   that she would tarry there:
For that in Siegfried's country   but few of her own blood there were.

"To thee they all are strangers,"   did Gernot further say.
Nor lived yet man so mighty   but dead at last he lay.
Bethink thee that, dear sister,   in comfort of thy mood.
Stay thou amid thy kinsmen,   I counsel truly for thy good."

To Giselher she promised   that she would tarry there.
For the men of Siegmund   the horses ready were,
When they thence would journey   to the Nibelungen land:
On carrying-horses laden   the knights' attire did ready stand.

Went the royal Siegmund   unto Kriemhild then;
He spake unto the lady: "Now do Siegfried's men
Await thee by the horses.   Straight shall we hence away,
For 'mid the men of Burgundy   unwilling would I longer stay."

Then spake the Lady Kriemhild: "My friends have counseled me,
That by the love I bear them,   here my home shall be,
For that no kinsmen have I   in the Nibelungen land."
Grieved full sore was Siegmund   when he did Kriemhild understand.

Then spake the royal Siegmund: "To such give not thine ear,
A queen 'mid all my kinsmen,   thou a crown shalt wear
And wield as lordly power   as e'er till now thou hast.
Nor thou a whit shalt forfeit,   that we the hero thus have lost."

"And journey with us thither,   for child's sake eke of thine:
Him shalt thou never, lady,   an orphan leave to pine.
When hath grown thy son to manhood,   he'll comfort thee thy
     mood.
Meanwhile shall ready serve thee   many a warrior keen and good."

She spake: "O royal Siegmund,   I may not thither ride,
For I here must tarry,   whate'er shall me betide,
'Mid them that are my kinsmen,   who'll help my grief to share."
The knights had sore disquiet   that such tidings they must hear.

"So might we say full truly,"   spake they everyone,
"That unto us still greater   evil now were done,
Would'st thou longer tarry   here amid our foes:
In sooth were never journey   of knights to court more full of woes."

"Now may ye free from trouble   in God's protection fare:
I'll bid that trusty escort   shall you have in care
Unto Siegmund's country.   My child full dear to me,
Unto your knights' good mercy   let it well commended be."

When that they well perceived   how she would not depart,
Wept all the men of Siegmund   and sad they were at heart.
In what right heavy sorrow   Siegmund then took leave
Of the Lady Kriemhild!   Full sore thereover must he grieve.

"Woe worth this journey hither,"   the lofty monarch spake.
"Henceforth from merry meeting   shall nevermore o'ertake
King or his faithful kinsmen   what here our meed hath been.
Here 'mid the men of Burgundy   may we never be more seen."

Then spake the men of Siegfried   in open words and plain:
"An might we right discover   who our lord hath slain,
Warriors bent on vengeance   shall yet lay waste this ground.
Among his kin in plenty   may doughty foemen be found."

Anon he kissed Kriemhild   and spake sorrowfully,
When she there would tarry,   and he the same did see:
"Now ride we joy-forsaken   home unto our land.
First now what 'tis to sorrow   do I rightly understand."

From Worms away sans escort   unto the Rhine they rode:
I ween that they full surely   did go in such grim mood,
That had against them any   aught of evil dared,
Hand of keen Nibelungen   had known full well their life to guard.

Nor parting hand they offered   to any that were there.
Then might ye see how Gernot   and likewise Giselher
Did give him loving greeting.   That as their very own
They felt the wrong he suffered,   by the courteous knights and brave
        was shown.

Then spake in words full kindly   the royal knight Gernot:
"God in heaven knoweth   that of guilt I've naught
In the death of Siegfried,   that e'er I e'en did hear
Who here to him were hostile.   Well may I of thy sorrow share."

An escort safe did furnish   the young knight Giselher:
Forth from out that country   he led them full of care,
The monarch with his warriors,   to Netherland their home.
How joyless is the greeting   as thither to their kin they come!

How fared that folk thereafter,   that can I nowise say.
Here heard ye Kriemhild plaining   as day did follow day,
That none there was to comfort   her heart and sorry mood,
Did Giselher not do it;   he faithful was to her and good.

The while the fair Queen Brunhild   in mood full haughty sat,
And weep howe'er did Kriemhild,   but little recked she that,
Nor whit to her of pity   displayed she evermore.
Anon was Lady Kriemhild   eke cause to her of sorrow sore.

Nineteenth Adventure

How the Nibelungen Hoard was Brought to Worms

When that the noble Kriemhild   thus did widowed stand,
Remained there with his warriors   by her in that land
Eckewart the margrave,   and served her ever true.
And he did help his mistress   oft to mourn his master too.

At Worms a house they built her   the minster high beside,
That was both rich and spacious,   full long and eke full wide,
Wherein with her attendants   joyless did she dwell.
She sought the minster gladly,   — that to do she loved full well.

Seldom undone she left it,   but thither went alway
In sorry mood where buried   her loved husband lay.
God begged she in his mercy   his soul in charge to keep,
And, to the thane right faithful,   for him full often did she weep.

Ute and her attendants   all times a comfort bore,
But yet her heart was stricken   and wounded all so sore
That no whit might avail it   what solace e'er they brought.
For lover taken from her   with such grief her heart was fraught,

As ne'er for spouse belovéd   a wife did ever show.
Thereby how high in virtue   she stood ye well might know.
She mourned until her ending   and while did last her life.
Anon a mighty vengeance   wreaked the valiant Siegfried's wife.

And so such load of sorrow   for her dead spouse she bore,
The story sayeth truly,   for years full three or more,

Nor ever unto Gunther   any word spake she,
And meantime eke her enemy   Hagen never might she see.

Then spake of Tronje Hagen: "Now seek'st thou such an end,
That unto thee thy sister   be well-disposéd friend?
Then Nibelungen treasure   let come to this country:
Thereof thou much might'st win thee,   might Kriemhild
      friendly-minded be."

He spake: "Be that our effort.   My brothers' love hath she:
Them shall we beg to win her   that she our friend may be,
And that she gladly see it   that we do share her store."
"I trow it well," spake Hagen,   "may such thing be nevermore."

Then did he Ortwein   unto the court command
And the margrave Gere.   When both were found at hand,
Thither brought they Gernot   and eke young Giselher.
In friendly manner sought they   to win the Lady Kriemhild there.

Then spake of Burgundy   Gernot the warrior strong:
"Lady, the death of Siegfried   thou mournest all too long.
Well will the monarch prove thee   that him he ne'er hath slain.
'Tis heard how that right sorely   thou dost for him unending plain."

She spake: "The king none chargeth: t'was Hagen's hand that slew.
When Hagen me did question   where might one pierce him through,
How might e'er thought come to me   that hate his heart did bear?
Then 'gainst such thing to guard me,"   spake she, "had I ta'en good
      care.

"And kept me from betraying   to evil hands his life,
Nor cause of this my weeping   had I his poor lorn wife.
My heart shall hate forever   who this foul deed have done."
And further to entreat her   young Giselher had soon begun.

When that to greet the monarch   a willing mind spake she,
Him soon with noble kinsmen   before her might ye see.
Yet dare might never Hagen   unto her to go:
On her he'd wrought sore evil,   as well his guilty mind did know.

When she no hatred meted   unto Gunther as before,
By Hagen to be greeted   were fitting all the more.

Had but by his counsel   no ill to her been done,
So might he all undaunted   unto Kriemhild have gone.

Nor e'er was peace new offered   kindred friends among
Sealed with tears so many.   She brooded o'er her wrong.
To all she gave her friendship   save to one man alone.
Nor slain her spouse were ever,   were not the deed by Hagen done.

Small time it was thereafter   ere they did bring to pass
That with the Lady Kriemhild   the mighty treasure was,
That from Nibelungen country   she brought the Rhine unto.
It was her bridal portion   and 'twas fairly now her due.

For it did journey thither   Gernot and Giselher.
Warriors eighty hundred   Kriemhild commanded there
That they should go and fetch it   where hidden it did lie,
And where the good thane Alberich   with friends did guard it
    faithfully.

When saw they coming warriors   from Rhine the hoard to take,
Alberich the full valiant   to his friends in this wise spake:
"We dare not of the treasure   aught from them withhold:
It is her bridal portion,   — thus the noble queen hath told.

"Yet had we never granted,"   spake Alberich, "this to do,
But that in evil manner   the sightless mantle too
With the doughty Siegfried   we alike did lose,
The which did wear at all times   the fair Kriemhild's noble spouse.

"Now alas hath Siegfried   had but evil gain
That from us the sightless mantle   the hero thus hath ta'en,
And so hath forced to serve him   all these lands around."
Then went forth the porter   where full soon the keys he found.

There stood before the mountain   ready Kriemhild's men,
And her kinsmen with them.   The treasure bore they then
Down unto the water   where the ships they sought:
To where the Rhine flowed downward   across the waves the hoard
    they brought.

Now of the treasure further   may ye a wonder hear:
Heavy wains a dozen   scarce the same might bear

In four days and nights together   from the mountain all away,
E'en did each one of them   thrice the journey make each day.

In it was nothing other   than gold and jewels rare.
And if to every mortal   on earth were dealt a share,
Ne'er 'twould make the treasure   by one mark the less.
Not without good reason   forsooth would Hagen it possess.

The wish-rod lay among them,   of gold a little wand.
Whosoe'er its powers   full might understand,
The same might make him master   o'er all the race of men.
Of Alberich's kin full many   with Gernot returned again.

When they did store the treasure   in King Gunther's land,
And to royal Kriemhild   'twas given 'neath her hand,
Storing-rooms and towers   could scarce the measure hold.
Nevermore such wonder   might of wealth again be told.

And had it e'en been greater,   yea a thousandfold,
If but again might Kriemhild   safe her Siegfried hold,
Fain were she empty-handed   of all the boundless store.
Spouse than she more faithful   won a hero nevermore.

When now she had the treasure,   she brought into that land
Knights many from far distance.   Yea, dealt the lady's hand
So freely that such bounty   ne'er before was seen.
High in honor held they   for her goodly heart the queen.

Unto both rich and needy   began she so to give
That fearful soon grew Hagen,   if that she would live
Long time in such high power,   lest she of warriors true
Such host might win to serve her,   that cause would be her strength
        to rue.

Spake Gunther then: "The treasure is hers and freedom too.
Wherefore shall I prevent her,   whate'er therewith she do?
Yea, nigh she did her friendship   from me evermore withhold.
Now reck we not who shareth   or her silver or her gold."

Unto the king spake Hagen: "No man that boasteth wit
Should to any woman   such hoard to hold permit.
By gifts she yet will bring it   that will come the day

When valiant men of Burgundy   rue it with good reason may."

Then spake the monarch Gunther: "To her an oath I swore,
That I would cause of evil   to her be nevermore,
Whereof henceforth I'll mind me: sister she is to me."
Then spake further Hagen: "Let me bear the guilt for thee."

Many they were that kept not   there their plighted word:
From the widow took they   all that mighty hoard:
Every key had Hagen   known to get in hand.
Rage filled her brother Gernot   when he the thing did understand.

Then spake the knight Giselher: "Hagen here hath wrought
Sore evil to my sister: permit this thing I'll not.
And were he not my kinsman,   he'd pay it with his life."
Anew did fall aweeping   then the doughty Siegfried's wife.

Then spake the knight Gernot: "Ere that forever we
Be troubled with this treasure,   let first commanded be
Deep in the Rhine to sink it,   that no man have it more."
In sad manner plaining   Kriemhild stood Giselher before.

She spake: "Belovéd brother,   be mindful thou of me:
What life and treasure toucheth   shalt thou my protector be."
Then spake he to the lady: "That shall sure betide,
When we again come hither: now called we are away to ride."

The monarch and his kinsmen   rode from out the land,
And in his train the bravest   ye saw on any hand:
Went all save Hagen only,   and there he stayed for hate,
That he did bear to Kriemhild,   and full gladly did he that.

Ere that the mighty monarch   was thither come again,
In that while had Hagen   all that treasure ta'en.
Where Loch is by the river   all in the Rhine sank he.
He weened thereof to profit,   yet such thing might never be.

The royal knights came thither   again with many a man.
Kriemhild with her maidens   and ladies then began
To mourn the wrong they suffered,   that pity was to hear.
Fain had the faithful Giselher   been unto her a comforter.

Then spake they all together: "Done hath he grievous wrong."
But he the princes' anger   avoided yet so long
At last to win their favor.   They let him live sans scathe.
Then filled thereat was Kriemhild   as ne'er before with mickle wrath.

Ere that of Tronje Hagen   had hidden thus the hoard,
Had they unto each other   given firm plighted word,
That it should lie concealéd   while one of them might live.
Thereof anon nor could they   to themselves nor unto other give.

With renewéd sorrows   heavy she was of heart
That so her dear-loved husband   perforce from life must part,
And that of wealth they reft her.   Therefor she mourned alway,
Nor ever ceased her plaining   until was come her latest day.

After the death of Siegfried   dwelt she in sorrow then,
— Saith the tale all truly —   full three years and ten,
Nor in that time did ever   for the knight mourn aught the less.
To him she was right faithful,   must all the folk of her confess.

Twentieth Adventure

How King Etzel Sent to Burgundy for Kriemhild

In that same time when ended   was Lady Helke's life,
And that the monarch Etzel   did seek another wife,
To take a highborn widow   of the land of Burgundy
Hun his friends did counsel: Lady Kriemhild hight was she.

Since that was ended   the fair Helke's life,
Spake they: "Wilt thou ever   win for thee noble wife,
The highest and the fairest   that ever king did win,
Take to thee this same lady   that doughty Siegfried's spouse hath
    been."

Then spake the mighty monarch: "How might that come to pass
Since that I am a heathen,   nor named with sign of cross?
The lady is a Christian,   thereto she'll ne'er agree.
Wrought must be a wonder,   if the thing may ever be."

Then spake again his warriors: "She yet may do the same.
For sake of thy great power   and thy full lofty name
Shalt thou yet endeavor   such noble wife to gain.
To woo the stately lady   might each monarch high be fain."

Then spake the noble monarch: "Who is 'mong men of mine,
That knoweth land and people   dwelling far by Rhine?"
Spake then of Bechelaren   the trusty Ruediger:
"I have known from childhood   the noble queen that dwelleth there.

"And Gunther and Gernot,   the noble knights and good,
And hight the third is Giselher: whatever any should

That standeth high in honor   and virtue, doth each one:
Eke from eld their fathers   have in like noble manner done."

Then spake again Etzel: "Friend, now shalt thou tell,
If she within my country   crown might wear full well —
For be she fair of body   as hath been told to me,
My friends for this their counsel   shall ever full requited be."

"She likeneth in beauty   well my high lady,
Helke that was so stately.   Nor forsooth might be
In all this world a fairer   spouse of king soe'er.
Whom taketh she for wooer,   glad of heart and mind he were."

He spake: "Make trial, Ruediger,   as thou hold'st me dear.
And if by Lady Kriemhild   e'er I lie full near,
Therefor will I requite thee   as in best mode I may:
So hast thou then fulfilled   all my wish in fullest way.

"Stores from out my treasure   I'll bid to thee to give,
That thou with thy companions   merry long shalt live,
Of steeds and rich apparel   what thou wilt have to share.
Thereof unto thy journey   I'll bid in measure full prepare."

Thereto did give him answer   the margrave Ruediger:
"Did I thy treasure covet   unworthy thing it were.
Gladly will I thy messenger   be unto the Rhine,
From my own store provided: all have I e'en from hand of thine."

Then spake the mighty monarch: "When now wilt thou fare
To seek the lovely lady?   God of thee have care
To keep thee on thy journey   and eke a wife to me.
Therein good fortune help me,   that she to us shall gracious be."

Then again spake Ruediger: "Ere that this land we quit,
Must we first prepare us   arms and apparel fit,
That we may thus in honor   in royal presence stand.
To the Rhine I'll lead five hundred   warriors, a doughty band.

"Wherever they in Burgundy   me and my men may see,
Shall they all and single   then confess of thee
That ne'er from any monarch   so many warriors went
As now to bear thy message   thou far unto the Rhine hast sent.

"May it not, O mighty monarch,   thee from thy purpose move:
Erstwhile unto Siegfried   she gave her noble love,
Who scion is of Siegmund: him thou here hast seen.
Worthy highest honor   verily the knight had been."

Then answered him King Etzel: "Was she the warrior's wife,
So worthy was of honor   the noble prince in life,
That I the royal lady   therefor no whit despise.
'Tis her surpassing beauty   that shall be joy unto mine eyes."

Then further spake the margrave: "Hear then what I do say:
After days four-and-twenty   shall we from hence away.
Tidings to Gotelinde   I'll send, my spouse full dear,
That I to Lady Kriemhild   myself will be thy messenger."

Away to Bechelaren   sent then Ruediger.
Both sad his spouse and joyous   was the news to hear.
He told how for the monarch   a wife he was to woo:
With love she well remembered   the fair Lady Helke too.

When that the margravine   did the message hear,
In part 'twas sorrow to her,   and weep she must in fear
At having other mistress   than hers had been before.
To think on Lady Helke   did grieve her inmost heart full sore.

Ruediger from Hunland   in seven days did part,
Whereat the monarch Etzel   merry was of heart.
When at Vienna city   all was ready for the way,
To begin the journey   might he longer not delay.

At Bechelaren waited   Gotelinde there,
And eke the young margravine,   daughter of Ruediger,
Was glad at thought her father   and all his men to see.
And many a lovely maiden   looked to the coming joyfully.

Ere that to Bechelaren   rode noble Ruediger
From out Vienna city,   was rich equipment there
For them in fullest measure   on carrying-horses brought,
That went in such wise guarded   that robber hand disturbed them
        not.

When they at Bechelaren   within the town did stand,
His fellows on the journey   did the host command
To lead to fitting quarters   and tend carefully.
The stately Gotelinde,   glad she was her spouse to see.

Eke his lovely daughter   the youthful margravine, —
To her had nothing dearer   than his coming been.
The warriors too from Hunland,   what joy for her they make!
With a laughing spirit   to all the noble maiden spake:

"Be now to us right welcome,   my father and all his men."
Fairest thanks on all sides   saw ye offered then
Unto the youthful margravine   by many a valiant knight.
How Ruediger was minded   knew Gotelinde aright.

When then that night she   by Ruediger lay,
Questioned him the margravine   in full loving way,
Wherefore had sent him thither   the king of Hunland.
He spake: "My Lady Gotelinde,   that shalt thou gladly understand.

"My master now hath sent me   to woo him other wife,
Since that by death was ended   the fair Helke's life.
Now will I to Kriemhild   ride unto the Rhine:
She shall here in Hunland   be spouse to him and stately queen."

"God will it," spake Gotelinde,   "and well the same might be,
Since that so high in honor   ever standeth she.
The death of my good mistress   we then may better bear;
Eke might we grant her gladly   among the Huns a crown to wear."

Then spake to her the margrave: "Thou shalt, dear lady mine,
To them that shall ride with me   thither unto the Rhine,
In right bounteous manner   deal out a goodly share.
Good knights go lighter-hearted   when they well provided fare."

She spake: "None is among them,   an he would take from me,
But I will give whatever   to him may pleasing be,
Ere that ye part thither,   thou and thy good men."
Thereto spake the margrave: "So dost thou all my wishes then."

Silken stuffs in plenty   they from her chamber bore,
And to the knights full noble   dealt out in goodly store,

Mantles lined all richly   from collar down to spur.
What for the journey pleased him   did choose therefrom Sir
      Ruediger.

Upon the seventh morning   from Bechelaren went
The knight with train of warriors.   Attire and armament
Bore they in fullest measure   through the Bavarian land,
And ne'er upon the journey   dared assail them robber band.

Unto the Rhine then came they   ere twelve days were flown,
And there were soon the tidings   of their coming known.
'Twas told unto the monarch   and with him many a man,
How strangers came unto him.   To question then the king began,

If any was did know them,   for he would gladly hear.
They saw their carrying-horses   right heavy burdens bear:
That they were knights of power   knew they well thereby.
Lodgings they made them ready   in the wide city speedily.

When that the strangers   had passed within the gate
Every eye did gaze on   the knights that came in state,
And mickle was the wonder   whence to the Rhine they came.
Then sent the king for Hagen,   if he perchance might know the
      same.

Then spake he of Tronje: "These knights I ne'er have seen,
Yet when we now behold them   I'll tell thee well, I ween,
From whence they now ride hither   unto this country.
An I not straightway know them,   from distant land in sooth they
      be."

For the guests fit lodgings   now provided were.
Clad in rich apparel   came the messenger,
And to the court his fellows   did bear him company.
Sumptuous attire   wore they, wrought full cunningly.

Then spake the doughty Hagen: "As far as goes my ken,
For that long time the noble   knight I not have seen,
Come they in such manner   as were it Ruediger,
The valiant thane from Hunland,   that leads the stately riders here."

Then straightway spake the monarch: "How shall I understand

That he of Bechelaren   should come unto this land?"
Scarce had King Gunther   his mind full spoken there,
When saw full surely Hagen   that 'twas the noble Ruediger.

He and his friends then hastened   with warmest welcoming.
Then saw ye knights five hundred   adown from saddle spring,
And were those knights of Hunland   received in fitting way.
Messengers ne'er beheld ye   attired in so fine array.

Hagen of Tronje,   with voice full loud spake he:
"Unto these thanes full noble   a hearty welcome be,
To the lord of Bechelaren   and his men everyone."
Thereat was fitting honor   done to every valiant Hun.

The monarch's nearest kinsmen   went forth the guests to meet.
Of Metz the knight Sir Ortwein   Ruediger thus did greet:
"The while our life hath lasted,   never yet hath guest
Here been seen so gladly: be that in very truth confessed."

For that greeting thanked they   the brave knights one and all.
With train of high attendants   they passed unto the hall,
Where valiant men a many   stood round the monarch's seat.
The king arose from settle   in courteous way the guests to greet.

Right courteously he greeted   then the messenger.
Gunther and Gernot,   full busy both they were
For stranger and companions   a welcome fit to make.
The noble knight Sir Ruediger   by the hand the king did take.

He led him to the settle   where himself he sat:
He bade pour for the strangers   (a welcome work was that)
Mead the very choicest   and the best of wine,
That e'er ye might discover   in all the lands about the Rhine.

Giselher and Gere   joined the company too,
Eke Dankwart and Volker,   when that they knew
The coming of the strangers: glad they were of mood,
And greeted 'fore the monarch   fair the noble knights and good.

Then spake unto his master   of Tronje the knight:
"Let our thanes seek ever   fully to requite
What erstwhile the margrave   in love to us hath done:

Fair Gotelinde's husband   our gratitude full well hath won."

Thereto spake King Gunther: "Withhold it not I may.
How they both do bear them,   tell me now, I pray,
Etzel and Helke   afar in Hunland."
Then answered him the margrave: "Fain would I have thee
        understand."

Then rose he from the settle   and his men everyone.
He spake unto the monarch: "An may the thing be done,
And is't thy royal pleasure,   so will I naught withhold,
But the message that I bring thee   shall full willingly be told."

He spake: "What tale soever,   doth this thy message make,
I grant thee leave to tell it,   nor further counsel take.
Now shalt thou let us hear it,   me and my warriors too,
For fullest leave I grant thee   thy high purpose to pursue."

Then spake the upright messenger: "Hither to thee at Rhine
Doth faithful service tender   master high of mine;
To all thy kinsmen likewise,   as many as may be:
Eke is this my message   borne in all good will to thee.

"To thee the noble monarch   bids tell his tale of need.
His folk 's forlorn and joyless;   my mistress high is dead,
Helke the full stately   my good master's wife,
Whereby now is orphaned   full many a fair maiden's life,

"Children of royal parents   for whom hath cared her hand:
Thereby doth the country   in plight full sorry stand.
Alack, nor is there other   that them with love may tend.
I ween the time long distant   eke when the monarch's grief shall
        end."

"God give him meed," spake Gunther,   "that he so willingly
Doth offer thus good service   to my kinsmen and to me —
I joy that I his greeting   here have heard this day —
The which with glad endeavor   my kinsmen and my men shall pay."

Thereto the knight of Burgundy,   the valiant Gernot, said:
"The world may ever rue it   that Helke fair lies dead,
So manifold the virtues   that did her life adorn."

A willing testimony   by Hagen to the words was borne.

Thereto again spake Ruediger   the noble messenger:
"Since thou, O king, dost grant it,   shalt thou now further hear
What message 'tis my master   beloved hath hither sent,
For that since death of Helke   his days he hath in sorrow spent.

"'Tis told my lord that Kriemhild   doth widowed live alone,
And dead is doughty Siegfried.   May now such thing be done,
And wilt thou grant that favor,   a crown she then shall wear
Before the knights of Etzel: this message from my lord I bear."

Then spake the mighty monarch   — a king he was of grace —
"My will in this same matter   she'll hear, an so she please.
Thereof will I instruct thee   ere three days are passed by —
Ere I her mind have sounded,   wherefore to Etzel this deny?"

Meanwhile for the strangers   bade they make cheer the best
In sooth so were they tended   that Ruediger confessed
He had 'mong men of Gunther   of friends a goodly store.
Hagen full glad did serve him,   as he had Hagen served of yore.

Thus there did tarry Ruediger   until the third day.
The king did counsel summon   — he moved in wisest way —
If that unto his kinsmen   seemed it fitting thing,
That Kriemhild take unto her   for spouse Etzel the king.

Together all save Hagen   did the thing advise,
And unto King Gunther   spake he in this wise:
"An hast thou still thy senses,   of that same thing beware,
That, be she ne'er so willing,   thou lend'st thyself her will to share."

"Wherefore," spake then Gunther,   "should I allow it not?
Whene'er doth fortune favor   Kriemhild in aught,
That shall I gladly grant her,   for sister dear is she.
Yea, ought ourselves to seek it,   might it but her honor be."

Thereto gave answer Hagen: "Now such words give o'er.
Were Etzel known unto thee   as unto me of yore,
And did'st thou grant her to him,   as 'tis thy will I hear,
Then wouldst thou first have reason   for thy later weal to fear."

"Wherefore?" spake then Gunther.   "Well may I care for that,
E'er to thwart his temper   that so I aught of hate
At his hands should merit,   an if his wife she be."
Thereto gave answer Hagen: "Such counsel hast thou ne'er of me."

Then did they bid for Gernot   and Giselher to go,
For wished they of the royal   twain their mind to know,
If that the mighty monarch   Kriemhild for spouse should take.
Yet Hagen and none other   thereto did opposition make.

Then spake of Burgundy   Giselher the thane:
"Well may'st thou now, friend Hagen,   show upright mind again:
For sorrows wrought upon her   may'st thou her well requite.
Howe'er she findeth fortune,   ne'er should it be in thy despite."

"Yea, hast thou to my sister   so many sorrows done,"
So spake further Giselher,   the full noble thane,
"That fullest reason hath she   to mete thee naught but hate.
In sooth was never lady   than she bereft of joy more great."

"What I do know full certain,   that known to all I make:
If e'er shall come the hour   that she do Etzel take,
She'll work us yet sore evil,   howe'er the same she plan.
Then in sooth will serve her   full many a keen and doughty man."

In answer then to Hagen   the brave Gernot said:
"With us doth lie to leave it   until they both be dead,
Ere that we ride ever   unto Etzel's land.
That we be faithful to her   doth honor meantime sure command."

Thereto again spake Hagen: "Gainsay me here may none.
And shall the noble Kriemhild   e'er sit 'neath Helke's crown,
Howe'er she that accomplish,   she'll do us grievous hurt.
Good knights, therefrom to keep you   doth better with your weal
          consort."

In anger spake then Giselher   the son of Ute the fair:
"None shall yet among us   himself like traitor bear.
What honor e'er befall her,   rejoice thereat should we.
Whate'er thou sayest, Hagen,   true helper shall she find in me."

When that heard it Hagen   straightway waxed he wroth.

Gernot and Giselher   the knights high-minded both,
And Gunther, mighty monarch,   did counsel finally,
If that did wish it Kriemhild,   by them 'twould unopposéd be.

Then spake the margrave Gere: "That lady will I tell
How that of royal Etzel   she may think full well.
In fear are subject to him   brave warriors many a one:
Well may he recompense her   for wrong that e'er to her was done."

Then went the knight full valiant   where he did Kriemhild find,
And straightway spake unto her   upon her greeting kind:
"Me may'st thou gladly welcome   with messengers high meed.
Fortune hath come to part thee   now from all thy bitter need.

"For sake of love he bears thee,   lady, doth seek thy hand
One of all the highest   that e'er o'er monarch's land
Did rule in fullest honor,   or ever crown might wear:
High knights do bring the message,   which same thy brother bids
      thee hear."

Then spake she rich in sorrow: "Now God forbid to thee
And all I have of kinsmen   that aught of mockery
They do on me, poor woman.   What were I unto one,
Who e'er at heart the joyance   of a noble wife hath known?"

Much did she speak against it.   Anon as well came there
Gernot her brother   and the young Giselher.
In loving wise they begged her   her mourning heart to cheer:
An would she take the monarch,   verily her weal it were.

Yet might not then by any   the lady's mind be bent,
That any man soever   to love she would consent.
Thereon the thanes besought her: "Now grant the thing to be,
An dost thou nothing further,   that the messenger thou deign'st to
      see."

"That will I not deny you,"   spake the high lady,
"That the noble Ruediger   I full gladly see,
Such knightly grace adorns him.   Were he not messenger,
And came there other hither   by him I all unspoken were."

She spake: "Upon the morrow   bid him hither fare

Unto this my chamber.   Then shall he fully hear
How that do stand my wishes,   the which I'll tell him true."
Of her full grievous sorrow   was she minded thus anew.

Eke not else desired   the noble Ruediger
Than that by the lady   leave thus granted were:
He knew himself so skillful,   might he such favor earn,
So should he her full certain   from her spoken purpose turn.

Upon the morrow early   when that the mass was sung
Came the noble messengers,   whereof a mickle throng.
They that should Sir Ruediger   to court bear company,
Many a man full stately   in rich apparel might ye see.

Kriemhild, dame high-stated,   — full sad she was of mood —
There Ruediger awaited,   the noble knight and good.
He found her in such raiment   as daily she did wear:
The while were her attendants   in dresses clad full rich and rare,

Unto the threshold went she   the noble guest to meet,
And the man of Etzel   did she full kindly greet.
Twelve knights there did enter,   himself and eleven more,
And well were they received: to her such guests came ne'er before.

The messenger to seat him   and his men they gave command.
The twain valiant margraves   saw ye before her stand,
Eckewart and Gere,   the noble knights and keen,
Such was the lady's sorrow,   none saw ye there of cheerful mien.

They saw before her sitting   full many a lady fair,
And yet the Lady Kriemhild   did naught but sorrow there.
The dress upon her bosom   was wet with tears that fell,
And soon the noble margrave   perceived her mickle grief full well.

Then spake the lofty messenger: "Daughter of king full high,
To me and these my fellows   that bear me company
Deign now the grace to grant us   that we before thee stand
And tell to thee the tidings   wherefore we rode unto thy land."

"That grace to thee is granted,"   spake the lofty queen;
"Whate'er may be thy message,   I'll let it now be seen
That I do hear it gladly: thou'rt welcome messenger."

That fruitless was their errand   deemed the others well to hear.

Then spake of Bechelaren   the noble Ruediger:
"Pledge of true love unto thee   from lofty king I bear,
Etzel who bids thee, lady,   here royal compliment:
He hath to woo thy favor   knights full worthy hither sent.

"His love to thee he offers   full heartily and free:
Fidelity that lasteth   he plighteth unto thee,
As erst to Lady Helke   who o'er his heart held sway.
Yea, thinking on her virtues   hath he full oft had joyless day."

Then spake the royal lady: "O Margrave Ruediger,
If that known to any   my sharp sorrows were,
Besought then were I never   again to take me spouse.
Such ne'er was won by lady   as the husband I did lose."

"What is that sootheth sorrow,"   the valiant knight replied,
"An be't not loving friendship   whene'er that may betide,
And that each mortal choose him   who his delight shall be?
Naught is that so availeth   to keep the heart from sorrow free.

"Wilt thou minded be to love him,   this noble master mine,
O'er mighty crowns a dozen   the power shall be thine.
Thereto of princes thirty   my lord shall give thee land,
The which hath all subdued   the prowess of his doughty hand.

"O'er many a knight full worthy   eke mistress shalt thou be
That my Lady Helke   did serve right faithfully,
And over many a lady   that served amid her train,
Of high and royal lineage,"   spake the keen and valiant thane.

"Thereto my lord will give thee   — he bids to thee make known —
If that beside the monarch   thou deign'st to wear a crown,
Power in fullest measure   that Helke e'er might boast:
The same in lordly manner   shalt thou wield o'er Etzel's host."

Then spake the royal lady: "How might again my life
Have thereof desire   to be a hero's wife?
Hath death in one already   wrought me such sorrows sore,
That joyless must my days be   from this time for evermore."

Then spake the men of Hunland: "O royal high lady,
Thy life shall there by Etzel   so full of honor be
Thy heart 'twill ever gladden   if but may be such thing:
Full many a thane right stately   doth homage to the mighty king.

"Might but Helke's maidens   and they that wait on thee
E'er be joined together   in one royal company,
Well might brave knights to see them   wax merry in their mood.
Be, lady, now persuaded / — 'tis verily thy surest good."

She spake in courteous manner: "Let further parley be
Until doth come the morrow.   Then hither come to me.
So will I give my answer   to bear upon your way."
The noble knights and worthy   must straight therein her will obey.

When all from thence were parted   and had their lodgings sought,
Then bade the noble lady   that Giselher be brought,
And eke with him her mother.   To both she then did tell
That meet for her was weeping,   and naught might fit her mood so
        well.

Then spake her brother Giselher: "Sister, to me 'tis told —
And well may I believe it —   that thy grief manifold
Etzel complete will scatter,   an tak'st thou him for man.
Whate'er be other's counsel,   meseems it were a thing well done."

Further eke spake Giselher: "Console thee well may he.
From Rhone unto Rhine river,   from Elbe unto the sea,
King there is none other   that holds so lordly sway.
An he for spouse do take thee,   gladden thee full well he may."

"Brother loved full dearly,   wherefore dost counsel it?
To mourn and weep forever   doth better me befit.
How may I 'mid warriors   appear in royal state?
Was ever fair my body,   of beauty now 'tis desolate."

Then spake the Lady Ute   her daughter dear unto:
"The thing thy brother counsels,   my loving child, that do.
By thy friends be guided,   then with thee well 'twill be.
Long time it now hath grieved me   thee thus disconsolate to see."

Then prayed she God with fervor   that he might her provide

With store of gold and silver   and raiment rich beside,
As erstwhile when her husband   did live a stately thane:
Since then so happy hour   never had she known again.

In her own bosom thought she: "An shall I not deny
My body to a heathen   — a Christian lady I —
So must I while life lasteth   have shame to be my own.
An gave he realms unnumbered,   such thing by me might ne'er be
       done."

And there withal she left it.   The night through until day,
Upon her couch the lady   with mind full troubled lay.
Nor yet her eyes full shining   of tears at all were free,
Until upon the morrow   forth to matins issued she.

When for mass was sounded,   came there the kings likewise.
Again did they their sister   by faithful word advise
To take for spouse unto her   of Hunland the king.
All joyless was the visage   they saw the lady thither bring.

They bade the men of Etzel   thither lead again,
Who unto their country   fain their leave had ta'en,
Their message won or fruitless,   how that soe'er might be.
Unto the court came Ruediger.   Full eager were his company

By the knight to be informéd   how the thing befell,
And if betimes they knew it   'twould please them all full well,
For weary was the journey   and long unto their land.
Soon did the noble Ruediger   again in Kriemhild's presence stand.

In full earnest manner   then the knight gan pray
The high royal lady   that she to him might say
What were from her the message   to Etzel he should bear.
Naught but denial only   did he from the lady hear,

For that her love might never   by man again be won.
Thereto spake the margrave: "Ill such thing were done.
Wherefore such fair body   wilt thou to ruin give?
Spouse of knight full worthy   may'st thou yet in honor live."

Naught booted how they besought her,   till that Ruediger
Spake in secret manner   in the high lady's ear,

How stood the mind of Kriemhild,   came the tidings unto Hagen's
     ear.

He spake: "Since Kriemhild never   may me in favor hold,
E'en so here must tarry   Siegfried's store of gold.
Wherefore unto mine enemies   such mickle treasure go?
What with the treasure Kriemhild   intendeth, that full well I know.

"Might she but take it thither,   in sooth believe I that,
'Twould be dealt out in largess   to stir against me hate.
Nor own they steeds sufficient   the same to bear away.
'Twill safe be kept by Hagen   — so shall they unto Kriemhild say."

When she did hear the story,   with grief her heart was torn.
Eke unto the monarchs   all three the tale was borne.
Fain would they prevent it: yet when that might not be,
Spake the noble Ruediger   in this wise full joyfully:

"Wherefore, queen full stately,   weep'st thou o'er this gold?
For thee will King Etzel   in such high favor hold
When but his eyes behold thee,   to thee such store he'll give
That ne'er thou may'st exhaust it: that, lady, by my word believe."

Thereto the queen gave answer: "Full noble Ruediger,
Greater treasure never   king's daughter had for share
Than this that Hagen from me   now hath ta'en away."
Then went her brother Gernot   to the chamber where the treasure
     lay.

With force he stuck the monarch's   key into the door,
And soon of Kriemhild's treasure   they from the chamber bore
Marks full thirty thousand   or e'en more plenteously.
He bade the guests to take it,   which pleased King Gunther well to
     see.

Then Gotelinde's husband   of Bechelaren spake:
"An if my Lady Kriemhild   with her complete might take
What treasure e'er came hither   from Nibelungenland,
Ne'er a whit would touch it   mine or my royal lady's hand.

"Now bid them here to keep it,   for ne'er the same I'll touch.
Yea brought I from my country   of mine own wealth so much,

That we upon our journey   may be full well supplied,
And ne'er have lack in outlay   as in state we homeward ride."

Chests well filled a dozen   from the time of old
Had for their own her maidens,   of the best of gold
That e'er ye might discover: now thence away 'twas borne,
And jewels for the ladies   upon the journey to be worn.

Of the might she yet was fearful   of Hagen grim and bold.
Still had she of mass-money   a thousand marks in gold,
That gave she for the soul's rest   of her husband dear.
Such loving deed and faithful   did touch the heart of Ruediger.

Then spake the lady mournful: "Who now that loveth me,
And for the love they bear me   may willing exiles be,
Who with me to Hunland   now away shall ride?
Take they of my treasure   and steeds and meet attire provide."

Then did the margrave Eckewart   answer thus the queen:
"Since I from the beginning   of thy train have been,
Have I e'er right faithful   served thee," spake the thane,
"And to the end I'll ever   thus faithful unto thee remain.

"Eke will I lead with me   five hundred of my men,
Whom I grant to serve thee   in faithful way again.
Nor e'er shall we be parted   till that we be dead."
Low bowing thanked him Kriemhild,   as verily might be his meed.

Forth were brought the horses,   for that they thence would fare.
Then was a mickle weeping   of friends that parted there.
Ute, queen full stately,   and many a lady more
Showed that from Lady Kriemhild   to part did grieve their hearts
        full sore.

A hundred stately maidens   with her she led away,
And as for them was fitting,   full rich was their array.
Many a bitter tear-drop   from shining eye fell down:
Yet joys knew they full many   eke in Etzel's land anon.

Thither came Sir Giselher   and Gernot as well,
And with them train of followers,   as duty did compel.
Safe escort would they furnish   for their dear sister then,

And with them led of warriors   a thousand brave and stately men.

Then came the valiant Gere,   and Ortwein eke came he:
Rumold the High Steward   might not absent be.
Unto the Danube did they   night-quarters meet provide.
Short way beyond the city   did the royal Gunther ride.

Ere from the Rhine they started   had they forward sent
Messengers that full quickly   unto Hunland went,
And told unto the monarch   how that Ruediger
For spouse at length had won him   the highborn queen beyond
        compare.

Twenty-First Adventure

How Kriemhild Fared to the Huns

The messengers leave we riding.   Now shall ye understand
How did the Lady Kriemhild   journey through the land,
And where from her were parted   Gernot and Giselher.
Upon her had they waited   as faithful unto her they were.

As far as to the Danube   at Vergen did they ride,
Where must be the parting   from their royal sister's side,
For that again they homeward   would ride unto the Rhine.
No eye but wet from weeping   in all the company was seen.

Giselher the valiant   thus to his sister said:
"If that thou ever, lady,   need hast of my aid,
And fronts thee aught of trouble,   give me to understand,
And straight I'll ride to serve thee   afar unto King Etzel's land."

Upon the mouth then kissed she   all her friends full dear.
The escort soon had taken   eke leave of Ruediger
And the margrave's warriors   in manner lovingly.
With the queen upon her journey   went many a maid full fair to see.

Four beyond a hundred   there were, all richly clad
In silk of cunning pattern.   Many a shield full broad
On the way did guard the ladies   in hand of valiant thane.
Full many a stately warrior   from thence did backward turn again.

Thence away they hastened   down through Bavarian land.
Soon were told the tidings   how that was at hand
A mickle host of strangers,   where a cloister stands from yore

And where the Inn its torrent   doth into Danube river pour.

At Passau in the city   a lordly bishop bode.
Empty soon each lodging   and bishop's palace stood:
To Bavarian land they hastened   the high guests to meet,
And there the Bishop Pilgrim   the Lady Kriemhild fair did greet.

The warriors of that country   no whit grieved they were
Thus to see follow with her   so many a maiden fair.
Upon those highborn ladies   their eyes with joy did rest,
Full comfortable quarters   prepared they for each noble guest.

With his niece the bishop   unto Passau rode.
When among the burghers   the story went abroad,
That thither was come Kriemhild,   the bishop's niece full fair,
Soon did the towns-people   reception meet for her prepare.

There to have them tarry   was the bishop fain.
To him spake Sir Eckewart: "Here may we not remain.
Unto Ruediger's country   must we journey down.
Thanes many there await us,   to whom our coming well is known."

The tidings now knew likewise   Lady Gotelinde fair.
Herself and noble daughter   did them quick prepare.
Message she had from Ruediger   that he well pleased would be,
Should she unto Lady   Kriemhild show such courtesy,

That she ride forth to meet her,   and bring his warriors true
Upward unto the Ense.   When they the tidings knew,
Saw ye how on all sides   they thronged the busy way.
Forth to meet the strangers   rode and eke on foot went they.

As far as Everdingen   meanwhile was come the queen:
In that Bavarian country   on the way were never seen
Robbers seeking plunder,   as e'er their custom was:
Of fear from such a quarter   had the travelers little cause.

'Gainst that had well provided   the noble margrave:
A band he led that numbered   good thousand warriors brave.
There was eke come Gotelinde,   spouse of Ruediger,
And bearing her high company   full many noble knights there were.

When came they o'er the Traune   by Ense on the green,
There full many an awning   outstretched and tent was seen,
Wherein that night the strangers   should find them welcome rest.
Well was made provision   by Ruediger for each high guest.

Not long fair Gotelinde did in her quarters stay,
But left them soon behind her.   Then coursed upon the way
With merry jingling bridle   many a well-shaped steed.
Full fair was the reception: whereat was Ruediger right glad.

On one side and the other   did swell the stately train
Knights that rode full gaily,   many a noble thane.
As they in joust disported,   full many a maid looked on,
Nor to the queen unwelcome   was the riders' service done.

As rode there 'fore the strangers   the men of Ruediger,
From shaft full many a splinter   saw ye fly in air
In hand of doughty warrior   that jousted lustily.
Them might ye 'fore the ladies   pricking in stately manner see.

Anon therefrom they rested.   Knights many then did greet
Full courteously each other.   Then forth Kriemhild to meet
Went the fair Gotelinde,   by gallant warriors led.
Those skilled in lady's service,   — little there the rest they had.

The lord of Bechelaren   unto his lady rode.
Soon the noble margravine   her high rejoicing showed,
That all safe and sound he   from the Rhine was come again.
The care that filled her bosom   by mickle joy from her was ta'en.

When him she had receivéd,   her on the green he bade
Dismount with all the ladies   that in her train she led.
There saw ye all unidle   many a knight of high estate,
Who with full ready service   upon the ladies then did wait.

Then saw the Lady Kriemhild   the margravine where she stood
Amid her fair attendants: nearer not she rode.
Upon the steed that bore her   the rein she drew full tight,
And bade them straightway help her   adown from saddle to alight.

The bishop saw ye leading   his sister's daughter fair,
And with him eke went Eckewart   to Gotelinde there.

The willing folk on all sides   made way before their feet.
With kiss did Gotelinde   the dame from land far distant greet.

Then spake in manner kindly   the wife of Ruediger;
"Right glad am I, dear lady,   that I thy visage fair
Have in this our country   with mine own eyes seen.
In these times might never   greater joy to me have been."

"God give thee meed," spake Kriemhild,   "Gotelinde, for this grace.
If with son of Botelung   happy may be my place,
May it henceforth be thy profit   that me thou here dost see."
Yet all unknown to either   was that which yet anon must be.

With curtsy to each other   went full many a maid,
The knights a willing service   unto the ladies paid.
After the greeting sat they   adown upon the green;
Knew many then each other   that hitherto had strangers been.

For the ladies they poured refreshment.   Now was come mid-day,
And did those high attendants   there no longer stay,
But went where found they ready   many a spreading tent.
Full willing was the service   unto the noble guests they lent.

The night through until morning   did they rest them there.
They of Bechelaren   meanwhile did prepare
That into fitting quarters   each high guest be brought.
'Twas by the care of Ruediger   that never one did want for aught.

Open ye saw the windows   the castle walls along,
And the burgh at Bechelaren   its gates wide open flung,
As through the guests went pricking,   that there full welcome were.
For them the lord full noble   had bidden quarters meet prepare.

Ruediger's fair daughter   with her attendant train
Came forth in loving manner   to greet the lofty queen.
With her was eke her mother   the stately margravine;
There full friendly greeting   of many a maiden fair was seen.

By the hand they took each other   and thence did pass each pair
Into a Hall full spacious,   the which was builded fair,
And 'neath its walls the Danube   flowed down with rushing tide.

As breezes cool played round them,   might they full happy there
     abide.

What they there did further,   tell it not I can.
That they so long did tarry,   heard ye the knights complain
That were of Kriemhild's company,   who unwilling there abode.
What host of valiant warriors   with them from Bechelaren rode!

Full kindly was the service   did render Ruediger,
Likewise gave Lady Kriemhild   twelve golden armbands rare
To Gotelinde's daughter,   and dress so richly wrought
That finer was none other   that into Etzel's land she brought.

Though Nibelungen treasure   from her erstwhile was ta'en,
Good-will of all that knew her   did she e'er retain
With such little portion   as yet she did command.
Unto her host's attendants   dealt she thereof with bounteous hand.

The Lady Gotelinde   such honors high again
Did pay in gracious manner   to the guests afar from Rhine
That of all the strangers   found ye never one
That wore not rich attire   from her, and many a precious stone.

When they their fast had broken   and would thence depart,
The lady of the castle   did pledge with faithful heart
Unto the wife of Etzel   service true to bear.
Kriemhild caressed full fondly   the margravine's young daughter
     fair.

To the queen then spake the maiden: "If e'er it pleaseth thee,
Well know I that my father   dear full willingly
Unto thee will send me   where thou livest in Hunland."
That faithful was the maiden,   full well did Kriemhild understand.

Now ready were the horses   the castle steps before,
And soon the queen full stately   did take her leave once more
Of the lovely daughter   and spouse of Ruediger.
Eke parted with fair greeting   thence full many a maiden fair.

Each other they full seldom   thereafter might behold.
From Medelick were carried   beakers rich of gold
In hand and eke full many,   wherein was sparkling wine:

Upon the way were greeted   thus the strangers from the Rhine.

High there a lord was seated,   Astold the name he bore,
Who that into Osterland   did lead the way before
As far as to Mautaren   adown the Danube's side.
There did they fitting service   for the lofty queen provide.

Of his niece the bishop   took leave in loving wise.
That she well should bear her,   did he oft advise,
And that she win her honor   as Helke erst had done.
Ah, how great the honor   anon that 'mid the Huns she won!

Unto the Traisem brought they   forth the strangers then.
Fair had they attendance   from Ruediger's men,
Till o'er the country riding   the Huns came them to meet.
With mickle honor did they   then the royal lady greet.

For had the king of Hunland,   Traisem's stream beside,
A full mighty castle,   known afar and wide,
The same hight Traisenmauer: Dame Helke there before
Did sit, such bounteous mistress   as scarce ye ever might see more,

An it were not Kriemhild   who could such bounty show,
That after days of sorrow   the pleasure she might know,
To be held in honor   by Etzel's men each one:
That praise in fullest measure   had she amid those thanes anon.

Afar the might of Etzel   so well was known around,
That at every season   within his court were found
Knights of all the bravest,   whereof ye e'er did hear
In Christian lands or heathen: with him all thither come they were.

By him at every season,   as scarce might elsewhere be,
Knights both of Christian doctrine   and heathen use saw ye.
Yet in what mind soever   did each and every stand,
To all in fullest measure   dealt the king with bounteous hand.

Twenty-Second Adventure

How Etzel Kept the Wedding-Feast with Kriemhild

At Traisenmauer she tarried until the fourth day.
Upon the road the dust-clouds meanwhile never lay.
But rose like smoke of fire around on every side:
Onward then through Austria King Etzel's warriors did ride.

Then eke unto the monarch such tidings now were told,
That at the thought did vanish all his grief of old,
In what high manner Kriemhild should in his land appear.
Then gan the monarch hasten where he did find the lady fair.

Of many a tongue and varied upon the way were seen
Before King Etzel riding full many warriors keen,
Of Christians and of heathen a spreading company.
To greet their coming mistress forth they rode in fair array.

Of Reuss men and Greeks there great was the tale,
And rapid saw ye riding the Wallach and the Pole
On chargers full of mettle that they did deftly guide.
Their own country's custom did they in no wise lay aside.

From the land of Kief rode there full many a thane,
And the wild Petschenegers. Full many a bow was drawn,
As at the flying wild-fowl through air the bolt was sped.
With might the bow was bended as far as to the arrow's head.

A city by the Danube in Osterland doth stand,
Hight the same is Tulna: of many a distant land

Saw Kriemhild there the customs, ne'er yet to her were known.
To many there did greet her sorrow befell through her anon.

Before the monarch Etzel rode a company
Of merry men and mighty, courteous and fair to see,
Good four-and-twenty chieftains, mighty men and bold.
Naught else was their desire save but their mistress to behold.

Then the Duke Ramung from far Wallachia
With seven hundred warriors dashed forth athwart her way:
Their going might ye liken unto birds in flight.
Then came the chieftain Gibeke, with his host a stately sight.

Eke the valiant Hornbog with full thousand men
From the king went forward to greet his mistress then.
After their country's custom in joy they shouted loud;
The doughty thanes of Hunland likewise in merry tourney rode.

Then came a chief from Denmark, Hawart bold and keen,
And the valiant Iring, in whom no guile was seen,
And Irnfried of Thuringia, a stately knight to see:
Kriemhild they greeted that honor high therefrom had she,

With good knights twelve hundred whom led they in their train.
Thither with three thousand came Bloedel eke, the thane
That was King Etzel's brother out of Hunland:
Unto his royal mistress led he then his stately band.

Then did come King Etzel and Dietrich by his side
With all his doughty fellows. In state there saw ye ride
Many a knight full noble, valiant and void of fear.
The heart of Lady Kriemhild did such host of warriors cheer.

Then to his royal mistress spake Sir Ruediger:
"Lady, now give I greeting to the high monarch here.
Whom to kiss I bid thee, grant him such favor then:
For not to all like greeting may'st thou give 'mid Etzel's men."

They lifted then from saddle the dame of royal state.
Etzel the mighty monarch might then no longer wait,
But sprang from off his charger with many a warrior keen:
Unto Kriemhild hasting full joyously he then was seen.

As is to us related,   did there high princes twain
By the lady walking   bear aloft her train,
As the royal Etzel   went forward her to meet,
And she the noble monarch   with kiss in kindly wise did greet.

Aside she moved her wimple,   whereat her visage fair
Gleamed 'mid the gold around it.   Though many a knight stood
     there,
They deemed that Lady Helke   did boast not fairer face.
Full close beside the monarch   his brother Bloedel had his place.

To kiss him then Margrave   Ruediger her did tell,
And eke the royal Gibeke   and Sir Dietrich as well.
Of highest knights a dozen   did Etzel's spouse embrace;
Other knights full many   she greeted with a lesser grace.

All the while that Etzel   stood by Kriemhild so,
Did the youthful riders   as still they're wont to do:
In varied tourney saw ye   each 'gainst the other pass,
Christian knights and heathen,   as for each the custom was.

From men that followed Dietrich   saw ye in kindly wise
Splinters from the lances   flying high arise
Aloft above their bucklers,   from hand of good knight sent!
By the German strangers   pierced was many a shield and rent.

From shaft of lances breaking   did far the din resound.
Together came the warriors   from all the land around,
Eke the guests of the monarch   and many a knight there was.
Thence did the mighty monarch   then with Lady Kriemhild pass.

Stretched a fair pavilion   beside them there was seen:
With tents as well was covered   all around the green,
Where they now might rest them   all that weary were.
By highborn knights was thither   led full many a lady fair.

With their royal mistress,   where in rich cushioned chair
Sat the queen full stately.   'Twas by the margrave's care
That well had been provided,   with all that seeméd good,
A worthy seat for Kriemhild: thereat was Etzel glad of mood.

What was by Etzel spoken,   may I not understand.
In his right hand resting   lay her fair white hand.
They sat in loving fashion,   nor Ruediger would let
The king have secret converse   with Lady Kriemhild as yet.

'Twas bidden that the jousting   on all sides they give o'er.
The din of stately tourney   heard ye then no more.
All the men of Etzel   unto their tents did go,
For every warrior present   did they full spacious lodging show.

And now the day was ended   and they did rest the night
Until beheld they shining   once more the morning light.
Soon on charger mounted   again was many a man:
Heigho, what merry pastime,   the king to honor, they began!

By the Huns the monarch   bade honors high be shown.
Soon rode they forth from Tulna   unto Vienna town,
Where found they many a lady   decked out in fair array:
The same the monarch Etzel's   wife received in stately way.

In very fullest measure   upon them there did wait
Whate'er they might desire.   Of knights the joy was great,
Looking toward the revel.   Lodging then sought each one.
The wedding of the monarch   was in merry wise begun.

Yet not for all might lodging   within the town be had.
All that were not strangers,   Ruediger them bade
That they find them lodgings   beyond the city's bound.
I ween that at all seasons   by Lady Kriemhild's side was found

The noble Sir Dietrich   and many another thane,
Who amid their labors   but little rest had ta'en,
That the guests they harbored   of merry mood should be.
For Ruediger and his companions   went the time full pleasantly.

The wedding time was fallen   upon a Whitsuntide,
When the monarch Etzel   lay Kriemhild beside
In the town at Vienna.   So many men I ween
Through her former husband   had not in her service been.

Many that ne'er had seen her   did her rich bounty take,
And many a one among them   unto the strangers spake:

"We deemed that Lady Kriemhild   of wealth no more had aught
Now hath she by her giving   here full many a wonder wrought."

The wedding-feast it lasted   for days full seventeen.
Ne'er of other monarch   hath any told, I ween,
That wedded with more splendor: of such no tale we hear.
All that there were present,   new-made apparel did they wear.

I ween that far in Netherland   sat she ne'er before
Amid such host of warriors.   And this believe I more:
Was Siegfried rich in treasure,   that yet he ne'er did gain,
As here she saw 'fore Etzel,   so many a high and noble thane.

Nor e'er gave any other   at his own wedding-tide
So many a costly mantle   flowing long and wide,
Nor yet so rich apparel   — so may ye well believe —
As here from hand of Kriemhild   did they one and all receive.

Her friends and eke the strangers   were of a single mind,
That they would not be sparing   of treasure in any kind:
What any from them desired,   they gave with willing hand.
Many a thane from giving   himself of clothing reft did stand.

How by her noble husband   at the Rhine a queen she sat,
Of that she still was minded,   and her eye grew wet thereat.
Yet well she kept it hidden   that none the same might mark.
Now had she wealth of honor   after long years of sorrow dark.

What any did with bounty,   'twas but an idle wind
By side of Dietrich's giving: what Etzel's generous mind
Before to him had given,   complete did disappear.
Eke wrought there many a wonder   the hand of bounteous Ruediger.

Bloedelein the chieftain   that came from Hunland,
Full many a chest to empty   did he then command,
Of gold and eke of silver.   That did they freely give.
Right merrily the warriors   of the monarch saw ye live.

Likewise the monarch's minstrels   Werbel and Schwemmelein,
Won they at the wedding   each alone, I ween,
Marks a good thousand   or even more than that,
Whenas fair Lady Kriemhild   'neath crown by royal Etzel sat.

Upon the eighteenth morning   from Vienna town they went.
Then in knightly pastime   many a shield was rent
By spear full well directed   by doughty rider's hand.
So came the royal Etzel   riding into Hunland.

At Heimburg's ancient castle   they tarried over night.
Tell the tale of people   no mortal ever might,
And the number of good warriors   did o'er the country come.
Ah, what fairest women   were gathered unto Etzel's home!

By Miesenburg's majestic   towers did they embark.
With horses eke and riders   the water all was dark,
As if 'twere earth they trod on,   as far as eye might see.
The way-worn ladies rested   now on board right pleasantly.

Now was lashed together   many a boat full good,
That no harm they suffered   from the waves and flood.
Many a stately awning   likewise above them spread,
Just as if beneath them   had they land and flowery mead.

When to Etzelburg the tidings   soon were borne along,
Therein of men and women   were seen a merry throng.
Who once the Lady Helke   as mistress did obey,
Anon by Lady Kriemhild   lived they many a gladsome day.

There did stand expectant   full many a maid highborn,
That since the death of Helke   had pined all forlorn.
Daughters of seven monarchs   Kriemhild there waiting found,
That were the high adornment   of all King Etzel's country round.

Herrat, a lofty princess,   did all the train obey,
Sister's child to Helke,   in whom high virtues lay,
Betrothéd eke of Dietrich,   of royal lineage born,
Daughter of King Nentwein;   her did high honors eft adorn.

Against the strangers' coming   her heart with joy flowed o'er:
Eke was thereto devoted   of wealth a mickle store.
Who might e'er give the picture,   how the king eft sat on throne?
Nor had with any mistress   the Huns such joyous living known.

As with his spouse the monarch   up from the river came,

Unto the noble Kriemhild   of each they told the name
'Mong them that she did find there: she fairer each did greet.
Ah, how mighty mistress   she long did sit in Helke's seat!

Ready and true the service   to her was offered there.
The queen dealt out in plenty   gold and raiment rare,
Silver eke and jewels.   What over Rhine she brought
With her unto Hunland,   soon thereof retained she naught.

Eke in faithful service   she to herself did win
All the king's warriors   and all his royal kin,
— So that ne'er did Lady Helke   so mighty power wield
As until death to Kriemhild   such host did willing service yield.

Thus stood so high in honor   the court and country round,
That there at every season   was pleasant pastime found
By each, whithersoever   his heart's desire might stand:
That wrought the monarch's favor   and the queen's full bounteous
        hand.

Twenty-Third Adventure
How Kriemhild Thought to Avenge Her Wrong

In full lordly honor,   — truth is that ye hear —
Dwelt they with each other   until the seventh year.
Meanwhile Lady Kriemhild   a son to Etzel bore,
Nor gladder might the monarch   be o'er aught for evermore.

Yet would she not give over,   nor with aught be reconciled,
But that should be baptizéd   the royal Etzel's child
After Christian custom: Ortlieb they did him call.
Thereat was mickle joyance   over Etzel's borders all.

Whate'er of highest virtues   in Lady Helke lay,
Strove the Lady Kriemhild   to rival her each day.
Herrat the stranger maiden   many a grace she taught,
Who yet with secret pining   for her mistress Helke was distraught.

To stranger and to native   full well she soon was known,
Ne'er monarch's country, said they,   did royal mistress own
That gave with freer bounty,   that held they without fear.
Such praise she bore in Hunland,   until was come the thirteenth
    year.

Now had she well perceivéd   how all obeyed her will,
As service to royal mistress   king's knights do render still,
And how at every season   twelve kings 'fore her were seen.
She thought of many a sorrow   that wrought upon her once had
    been.

Eke thought she of lordly power   in Nibelungenland

That she erstwhile had wielded,   and how that Hagen's hand
Of it all had reft her   with her lord Siegfried dead;
She thought for so great evil   how might he ever be repaid.

"'Twould be, might I but bring him   hither into this land."
She dreamed that fondly led her   full often by the hand
Giselher her brother,   full oft in gentle sleep
Thought she to have kissed him,   wherefrom he sorrow soon must
     reap.

I ween the evil demon   was Kriemhild's counselor
That she her peace with Gunther   should sacred keep no more,
Whom she kissed in friendly token   in the land of Burgundy.
Adown upon her bosom   the burning tears fell heavily.

On her heart both late and early   lay the heavy thought,
How that, herself all guiltless,   thereto she had been brought,
That she must share in exile   a heathen monarch's bed.
Through Hagen eke and Gunther   come she was to such sore need.

From her heart such longing   seldom might she dismiss.
Thought she: "A queen so mighty   I am o'er wealth like this,
That I upon mine enemies   may yet avenge me well.
Fain were I that on Hagen   of Tronje yet my vengeance fell.

"For friends that once were faithful   full oft my heart doth long.
Were they but here beside me   that wrought on me such wrong,
Then were in sooth avengéd   my lover reft of life;
Scarce may I bide that hour,"   spake the royal Etzel's wife.

Kriemhild they loved and honored,   the monarch's men each one,
As they that came there with her: well might the same be done.
The treasure wielded Eckewart,   and won good knights thereby.
The will of Lady Kriemhild might   none in all that land deny.

She mused at every season: "The king himself I'll pray," —
That he to her the favor   might grant in friendly way,
To bring her kinsmen hither   unto Hunland.
What vengeful thought she cherished   might none soever
     understand.

As she in stillest night-time   by the monarch lay

(In his arms enclosed he held her,   as he was wont alway
To caress the noble lady: she was to him as life),
Again unto her enemies   turned her thoughts his stately wife.

She spake unto the monarch: "My lord full dear to me,
Now would I pray a favor,   if with thy grace it be,
That thou wilt show unto me   if merit such be mine
That unto my good kinsmen   truly doth thy heart incline."

The mighty monarch answered   (from guile his heart was free):
"Of a truth I tell thee,   if aught of good may be
The fortune of thy kinsmen,   — of that I were full fain,
For ne'er through love of woman   might I friends more faithful
        gain."

Thereat again spake Kriemhild: "That mayst thou well believe,
Full high do stand my kinsmen;   the more it doth me grieve
That they deign so seldom   hither to take their way.
That here I live a stranger,   oft I hear the people say."

Then spake the royal Etzel: "Beloved lady mine,
Seemed not too far the journey,   I'd bid from yond the Rhine
Whom thou wouldst gladly welcome   hither unto my land."
Thereat rejoiced the lady   when she his will did understand.

Spake she: "Wilt thou true favor   show me, master mine,
Then shall thou speed thy messengers   to Worms across the Rhine.
Were but my friends acquainted   what thing of them I would,
Then to this land came hither   full many a noble knight and good."

He spake: "Whene'er thou biddest,   straight the thing shall be.
Thyself mightst ne'er thy kinsmen   here so gladly see,
As I the sons of Ute,   high and stately queen.
It grieveth me full sorely   that strangers here so long they've been.

"If this thing doth please thee,   beloved lady mine,
Then gladly send I thither   unto those friends of thine
As messengers my minstrels   to the land of Burgundy."
He bade the merry fiddlers   lead before him presently.

Then hastened they full quickly   to where they found the king
By side of Kriemhild sitting.   He told them straight the thing,

How they should be his messengers   to Burgundy to fare.
Full stately raiment bade he   for them straightway eke prepare.

Four and twenty warriors   did they apparel well.
Likewise did the monarch   to them the message tell,
How that they King Gunther   and his men should bid aright.
Them eke the Lady Kriemhild   to secret parley did invite.

Then spake the mighty monarch: "Now well my words attend.
All good and friendly greeting   unto my friends I send,
That they may deign to journey   hither to my country.
Few be the guests beside them   that were so welcome unto me.

"And if they be so minded   to meet my will in aught,
Kriemhild's lofty kinsmen,   that they forego it not
To come upon the summer   here where I hold hightide,
For that my joy in living   doth greatly with my friends abide."

Then spake the fiddle-player,   Schwemmelein full bold:
"When thinkst thou in this country   such high feast to hold,
That unto thy friends yonder   tell the same we may?"
Thereto spake King Etzel: "When next hath come midsummer day."

"We'll do as thou commandest,"   spake then Werbelein.
Unto her own chamber   commanded then the queen
To bring in secret manner   the messengers alone.
Thereby did naught but sorrow   befall full many a thane anon.

She spake unto the messengers: "Mickle wealth I give to you,
If my will in this matter   right faithfully ye do,
And bear what tidings send I   home unto our country.
I'll make you rich in treasure   and fair appareled shall ye be.

"And friends of mine so many   as ever see ye may
At Worms by Rhine river,   to them ye ne'er shall say
That any mood of sorrow   in me ye yet have seen.
Say ye that I commend me   unto the knights full brave and keen."

"Pray them that to King Etzel's   message they give heed,
Thereby to relieve me   of all my care and need,
Else shall the Huns imagine   that I all friendless am.
If I but a knight were,   oft would they see me at their home.

"Eke say ye unto Gernot,   brother to me full dear,
To him might never any   disposéd be more fair;
Pray him that he bring hither   unto this country
All our friends most steadfast,   that we thereby shall honored be.

"Say further eke to Giselher   that he do have in mind,
That by his guilt I never   did cause for sorrow find;
Him therefore would I gladly   here with mine own eyes see,
And give him warmest welcome,   so faithful hath he been to me.

"How I am held in honor,   to my mother eke make plain.
And if of Tronje Hagen   hath mind there to remain,
By whom might they in coming   through unknown lands be shown?
The way to Hunland hither   from youth to him hath well been
          known."

No whit knew the messengers   wherefore she did advise
That they of Tronje Hagen   should not in any wise
Leave by the Rhine to tarry.   That was anon their bane:
Through him to dire destruction   was doomed full many a doughty
          thane.

Letters and kindly greeting   now to them they give;
They fared from thence rich laden,   and merrily might live.
Leave then they took of Etzel   and eke his lady fair,
And parted on their journey   dight in apparel rich and rare.

Twenty-Fourth Adventure

How Werbel and Schwemmel Brought the Message

When to the Rhine King Etzel   his messengers had sent,
With hasty flight fresh tidings   from land to land there went:
With messengers full quickly   to his high festival
He bade them, eke and summoned.   To many thereby did death
    befall.

The messengers o'er the borders   of Hunland thence did fare
Unto the land of Burgundy;   thither sent they were
Unto three lordly monarchs   and eke their mighty men.
To Etzel's land to bid them   hastily they journeyed then.

Unto Bechelaren   rode they on their way,
Where found they willing service.   Nor did aught delay
Ruediger to commend him   and Gotelinde as well
And eke their fairest daughter   to them that by the Rhine did dwell.

They let them not unladen   with gifts from thence depart,
So did the men of Etzel   fare on with lighter heart.
To Ute and to her household   sent greeting Ruediger,
That never margrave any   to them more well disposéd were.

Unto Brunhild also   did they themselves commend
With willing service offered   and steadfast to the end.
Bearing thus fair greeting   the messengers thence did fare,
And prayed the noble margravine   that God would have them in
    his care.

Ere the messengers had fully   passed o'er Bavarian ground,

Had the nimble Werbel   the goodly bishop found.
What greetings to his kinsmen   unto the Rhine he sent,
That I cannot tell you;   the messengers yet from him went

Laden with gold all ruddy,   to keep his memory.
Thus spake the Bishop Pilgrim: "'Twere highest joy to me
Might I my sister's children   here see in home of mine,
For that I may but seldom   go unto them to the Rhine."

What were the ways they followed   as through the lands they fared,
That can I nowise tell you.   Yet never any dared
Rob them of wealth or raiment,   for fear of Etzel's hand:
A lofty king and noble,   mighty in sooth was his command.

Before twelve days were over   came they unto the Rhine,
And rode into Worms city   Werbel and Schwemmelein.
Told were soon the tidings   to the kings and their good men,
How that were come strange messengers.   Gunther the king did
        question then.

And spake the monarch further: "Who here may understand
Whence do come these strangers   riding unto our land?"
Yet was never any   might answer to him make,
Until of Tronje Hagen   thus unto King Gunther spake:

"To us hath come strange tidings   to hand this day, I ween,
For Etzel's fiddlers riding   hither have I seen.
The same have by thy sister   unto the Rhine been sent:
For sake of their high master   now give we them fair compliment."

E'en then did ride the messengers   unto the castle door,
And never royal minstrels   more stately went before.
By the monarch's servants   well received they were:
They gave them fitting lodging   and for their raiment had a care.

Rich and wrought full deftly   was the traveling-dress they wore,
Wherein they well with honor   might go the king before;
Yet they at court no longer   would the same garments wear.
The messengers inquired   if any were might wish them there.

In sooth in such condition   many eke were found,
Who would receive them gladly;   to such they dealt around.

Then decked themselves the strangers   in garments richer far,
Such as royal messengers   beseemeth well at court to wear.

By royal leave came forward   to where the monarch sat
The men that came from Etzel,   and joy there was thereat.
Hagen then to meet them   in courteous manner went,
And heartily did greet them,   whereat they gave fair compliment.

To know what were the tidings,   to ask he then began
How did find him Etzel   and each valiant man.
Then answer gave the fiddler: "Ne'er higher stood the land,
Nor the folk so joyous: that shall ye surely understand."

They went unto the monarch.   Crowded was the hall.
There were received the strangers   as of right men shall
Kindly greeting offer   in other monarch's land.
Many a valiant warrior   saw Werbel by King Gunther stand.

Right courteously the monarch   began to greet them then:
"Now be ye both right welcome,   Hunland's merry men,
And knights that give you escort.   Hither sent are ye
By Etzel mighty monarch   unto the land of Burgundy?"

They bowed before the monarch;   then spake Werbelein:
"My dear lord and master,   and Kriemhild, sister thine,
Hither to thy country   give fairest compliment.
In faith of kindly welcome   us unto you they now have sent."

Then spake the lofty ruler: "I joy o'er this ye bring.
How liveth royal Etzel,"   further spake the king,
"And Kriemhild, my sister,   afar in Hunland?"
Then answered him the fiddler: "That shalt thou straightway
        understand.

"That never any people   more lordly life might show
Than they both do joy in,   — that shalt thou surely know, —
Wherein do share their kinsmen   and all their doughty train.
When from them we parted,   of our journey were they fain."

"My thanks for these high greetings   ye bring at his command
And from my royal sister.   That high in joy they stand,
The monarch and his kinsmen,   rejoiceth me to hear.

For, sooth to say, the tidings   asked I now in mickle fear."

The twain of youthful princes   were eke come thitherward,
As soon as they the tidings   from afar had heard.
Right glad were seen the messengers   for his dear sister's sake
By the young Giselher,   who in such friendly manner spake:

"Right hearty were your welcome   from me and brother mine,
Would ye but more frequent   ride hither to the Rhine;
Here found ye friends full many   whom glad ye were to see,
And naught but friendly favors   the while that in this land ye be."

"To us how high thy favor,"   spake Schwemmel, "know we well;
Nor with my best endeavor   might I ever tell
How kindly is the greeting   we bear from Etzel's hand
And from your noble sister,   who doth in highest honor stand.

"Your sometime love and duty   recalleth Etzel's queen,
And how to her devoted   in heart we've ever been,
But first to royal Gunther   do we a message bear,
And pray it be your pleasure   unto Etzel's land to fare.

"To beg of you that favor   commanded o'er and o'er
Etzel mighty monarch   and bids you know the more,
An will ye not your sister   your faces give to see,
So would he know full gladly   wherein by him aggrieved ye be,

"That ye thus are strangers   to him and all his men.
If that his spouse so lofty   to you had ne'er been known,
Yet well he thought to merit   that him ye'd deign to see;
In sooth could naught rejoice him   more than that such thing
        might be."

Then spake the royal Gunther: "A sennight from this day
Shall ye have an answer,   whereon decide I may
With my friends in counsel.   The while shall ye repair
Unto your place of lodging,   and right goodly be your fare."

Then spake in answer Werbel: "And might such favor be
That we the royal mistress   should first have leave to see,
Ute, the lofty lady,   ere that we seek our rest?"
To him the noble Giselher   in courteous wise these words addressed.

"That grace shall none forbid you.   Will ye my mother greet,
Therein do ye most fully   her own desire meet.
For sake of my good sister   fain is she you to see,
For sake of Lady Kriemhild   ye shall to her full welcome be."

Giselher then led him   unto the lofty dame,
Who fain beheld the messengers   from Hunland that came.
She greeted them full kindly   as lofty manner taught,
And in right courteous fashion   told they to her the tale they
    brought.

"Pledge of loyal friendship   sendeth unto thee
Now my lofty mistress,"   spake Schwemmel. "Might it be,
That she should see thee often,   then shalt thou know full well,
In all the world there never   a greater joy to her befell."

Replied the royal lady: "Such thing may never be.
Gladly as would I oft-times   my dearest daughter see,
Too far, alas, is distant   the noble monarch's wife.
May ever yet full happy   with King Etzel be her life.

"See that ye well advise me,   ere that ye hence are gone,
What time shall be your parting;   for messengers I none
Have seen for many seasons   as glad as greet I you."
The twain gave faithful promise   such courtesy full sure to do.

Forthwith to seek their lodgings   the men of Hunland went,
The while the mighty monarch   for trusted warriors sent,
Of whom did noble Gunther   straightway question make,
How thought they of the message.   Whereupon full many spake

That he might well with honor   to Etzel's land be bound,
The which did eke advise him   the highest 'mongst them found,
All save Hagen only,   whom sorely grieved such rede.
Unto the king in secret   spake he: "Ill shall be thy meed.

"What deed we twain compounded   art thou full well aware,
Wherefor good cause we ever   shall have Kriemhild to fear,
For that her sometime husband   I slew by my own hand.
How dare we ever journey   then unto King Etzel's land?"

Replied the king: "My sister   no hate doth harbor more.
As we in friendship kissed her,   vengeance she forswore
For evil that we wrought her,   ere that from hence she rode, —
Unless this message, Hagen,   ill for thee alone forebode."

"Now be thou not deceived,"   spake Hagen, "say what may
The messengers from Hunland.   If thither be thy way,
At Kriemhild's hands thou losest   honor eke and life,
For full long-avenging   is the royal Etzel's wife."

Added then his counsel   the princely Gernot there:
"Though be it thou hast reason   thine own death to fear
Afar in Hunnish kingdom,   should we for that forego
To visit our high sister,   that were in sooth but ill to do."

Unto that thane did likewise   Giselher then say:
"Since well thou know'st, friend Hagen,   what guilt on thee doth
        weigh,
Then tarry here behind us   and of thyself have care,
And let who dares the journey   with us unto my sister fare."

Thereat did rage full sorely   Tronje's doughty thane:
"So shall ye ne'er find any   that were to go more fain,
Nor who may better guide you   than I upon your way.
And will ye not give over,   know then my humor soon ye may."

Then spake the Kitchen Master,   Rumold a lofty thane:
"Here might ye guests and kinsmen   in plenty long maintain
After your own pleasure,   for ye have goodly store.
I ween ye ne'er found Hagen   traitor to you heretofore.

"If heed ye will not Hagen,   still Rumold doth advise
— For ye have faithful service   from me in willing wise —
That here at home ye tarry   for the love of me,
And leave the royal Etzel   afar with Kriemhild to be.

"Where in the world might ever   ye more happy be
Than here where from danger   of every foeman free,
Where ye may go as likes you   in goodliest attire,
Drink wine the best, and stately   women meet your heart's desire.

"And daily is your victual   the best that ever knew

A king of any country.   And were the thing not true,
At home ye yet should tarry   for sake of your fair wife
Ere that in childish fashion   ye thus at venture set your life.

"Thus rede I that ye go not.   Mighty are your lands,
And at home more easy may ye   be freed from hostile hands
Than if ye pine in Hunland.   How there it is, who knows?
O Master, go not thither,   — such is the rede that Rumold owes."

"We'll ne'er give o'er the journey,"   Gernot then did say,
"When thus our sister bids us   in such friendly way
And Etzel, mighty monarch.   Wherefore should we refrain?
Who goes not gladly thither,   here at home may he remain."

Thereto gave answer Hagen: "Take not amiss, I pray,
These my words outspoken,   let befall what may.
Yet do I counsel truly,   as ye your safety prize,
That to the Huns ye journey   armed full well in warlike guise.

"Will ye then not give over,   your men together call,
The best that ye may gather   from districts one and all.
From out them all I'll choose you   a thousand knights full good,
Then may ye reck but little   the vengeful Kriemhild's angry mood."

"I'll gladly heed thy counsel,"   straight the king replied,
And bade the couriers traverse   his kingdom far and wide.
Soon they brought together   three thousand men or more,
Who little weened what mickle   sorrow was for them in store.

Joyful came they riding   to King Gunther's land.
Steeds and equipment for them   all he did command,
Who should make the journey   thence from Burgundy.
Warriors many were there   to serve the king right willingly.

Hagen then of Tronje   to Dankwart did assign
Of their warriors eighty   to lead unto the Rhine.
Equipped in knightly harness   were they soon at hand.
Riding in gallant fashion   unto royal Gunther's land.

Came eke the doughty Volker,   a noble minstrel he,
With thirty goodly warriors   to join the company,
Who wore so rich attire   'twould fit a monarch well.

That he would fare to Hunland,   bade he unto Gunther tell.

Who was this same Volker   that will I let you know:
He was a knight full noble,   to him did service owe
Many a goodly warrior   in the land of Burgundy.
For that he well could fiddle,   named the Minstrel eke was he.

Thousand men chose Hagen,   who well to him were known.
What things in storm of battle   their doughty arm had done,
Or what they wrought at all times,   that knew he full well.
Nor of them might e'er mortal   aught but deeds of valor tell.

The messengers of Kriemhild,   full loath they were to wait,
For of their master's anger   stood they in terror great.
Each day for leave to journey   more great their yearning grew,
But daily to withhold it   crafty Hagen pretext knew.

He spake unto his master: "Well shall we beware
Hence to let them journey   ere we ourselves prepare
In seven days thereafter   to ride to Etzel's land:
If any mean us evil,   so may we better understand.

"Nor may the Lady Kriemhild   ready make thereto,
That any by her counsel   scathe to us may do.
Yet if such wish she cherish,   evil shall be her meed,
For many a chosen warrior   with us shall we thither lead."

Shields well-wrought and saddles,   with all the mickle gear
That into Etzel's country   the warriors should wear,
The same was now made ready   for many a knight full keen.
The messengers of Kriemhild   before King Gunther soon were seen.

When were come the messengers,   Gernot them addressed:
"King Gunther now is minded   to answer Etzel's quest.
Full gladly go we thither   with him to make high-tide
And see our lofty sister,   — of that set ye all doubt aside."

Thereto spake King Gunther: "Can ye surely say
When shall be the high-tide,   or upon what day
We shall there assemble?"   Spake Schwemmel instantly:
"At turn of sun in summer   shall in sooth the meeting be."

The monarch leave did grant them,   ere they should take their way,
If that to Lady Brunhild   they would their homage pay,
His high pleasure was it   they unto her should go.
Such thing prevented Volker,   and did his mistress' pleasure so.

"In sooth, my Lady Brunhild   hath scarce such health today
As that she might receive you,"   the gallant knight did say.
"Bide ye till the morrow,   may ye the lady see."
When thus they sought her presence,   might their wish not granted
     be.

To the messengers right gracious   was the mighty king,
And bade he from his treasure   on shields expansive bring
Shining gold in plenty   whereof he had great store.
Eke richest gifts received they   from his lofty kinsmen more.

Giselher and Gernot,   Gere and Ortwein,
That they were free in giving   soon full well was seen.
So costly gifts were offered   unto each messenger
That they dared not receive them,   for Etzel's anger did they fear.

Then unto King Gunther   Werbel spake again:
Sire, let now thy presents   in thine own land remain.
The same we may not carry,   my master hath decreed
That we accept no bounty.   Of that in sooth we've little need."

Thereat the lord of Rhineland   was seen in high displeasure,
That they should thus accept not   so mighty monarch's treasure?
In their despite yet took they   rich dress and gold in store,
The which moreover with them   home to Etzel's land they bore.

Ere that they thence departed   they Lady Ute sought,
Whereat the gallant Giselher   straight the minstrels brought
Unto his mother's presence.   Kind greetings sent the dame,
And wish that high in honor   still might stand her daughter's name.

Then bade the lofty lady   embroidered silks and gold
For the sake of Kriemhild,   whom loved she as of old,
And eke for sake of Etzel,   unto the minstrels give.
What thus so free was offered   might they in sooth right fain receive.

Soon now had ta'en departure   the messengers from thence,

From knight and fairest lady,   and joyous fared they hence
Unto Suabian country;   Gernot had given behest
Thus far for armed escort,   that none their journey might molest.

When these had parted from them,   safe still from harm were they,
For Etzel's might did guard them   wherever led their way.
Nor ever came there any   that aught to take would dare,
As into Etzel's country   they in mickle haste did fare.

Where'er they friends encountered,   to all they straight made known
How that they of Burgundy   should follow after soon
From Rhine upon their journey   unto the Huns' country.
The message brought they likewise   unto Bishop Pilgrim's see.

As down 'fore Bechelaren   they passed upon their way,
The tidings eke to Ruediger   failed they not to say,
And unto Gotelinde,   the margrave's wife the same.
At thought so soon to see them   was filled with joy the lofty dame.

Hasting with the tidings   each minstrel's courser ran,
Till found they royal Etzel   within his burgh at Gran.
Greeting upon greeting,   which they must all bestow,
They to the king delivered;   with joy his visage was aglow.

When that the lofty Kriemhild   did eke the tidings hear,
How that her royal brothers   unto the land would fare,
In sooth her heart was gladdened;   on the minstrels she bestowed
Richest gifts in plenty,   as she to her high station owed.

She spake: "Now shall ye, Werbel   and Schwemmel, tell to me
Who cometh of my kinsmen   to our festivity,
Who of all were bidden   this our land to seek?
Now tell me, when the message   heard he, what did Hagen speak?"

Answered: "He came to council   early upon a day,
But little was of pleasant   in what he there did say.
When learned he their intention,   in wrath did Hagen swear,
To death 'twere making journey,   to country of the Huns to fare.

"Hither all are coming,   thy royal brothers three,
And they right high in spirit.   Who more shall with them be,
The tale to tell entire   were more than I might do.

To journey with them plighted   Volker the valiant fiddler too."

"'Twere little lost, full truly,"   answered then the queen,
"If by my eyes never   Volker here were seen.
'Tis Hagen hath my favor,   a noble knight is he,
And mickle is my pleasure   that him full soon we here may see."

Her way the Lady Kriemhild   then to the king did take,
And in right joyous manner   unto her consort spake:
"How liketh thee the tidings,   lord full dear to me?
What aye my heart hath yearned for,   that shall now accomplished
      be."

"Thy will my joy was ever,"   the lofty monarch said.
"In sooth for my own kinsmen   I ne'er have been so glad,
To hear that they come hither   unto my country.
To know thy friends are coming,   hath parted sadness far from me."

Straight did the royal provosts   give everywhere decree
That hall and stately palace   well prepared should be
With seats, that unprovided   no worthy guest be left.
Anon by them the monarch   should be of mickle joy bereft.

Twenty-Fifth Adventure
How the Knights All Fared to the Huns

Tell we now no further   how they here did fare.
Knights more high in spirit   saw ye journey ne'er
In so stately fashion   to the land of e'er a king.
Of arms and rich attire   lacked they never anything.

At Rhine the lordly monarch   equipped his warriors well,
A thousand knights and sixty,   as I did hear tell,
And eke nine thousand squires   toward the festivity.
Whom they did leave behind them   anon must mourn full
     grievously.

As at Worms across the courtyard   equipment full they bore
Spake there of Speyer   a bishop old and hoar
Unto Lady Ute: "Our friends have mind to fare
Unto the festivity;   may God their honor have in care."

Then spake unto her children   Ute the noble dame:
"At home ye here should tarry,   ye knights full high in fame.
Me dreamt but yester even   a case of direst need,
How that in this country   all the feathered fowl were dead."

"Who recketh aught of dreamings,"   Hagen then replied,
"Distraught is sure his counsel   when trouble doth betide,
Or he would of his honor   have a perfect care.
I counsel that my master   straight to take his leave prepare.

"Gladly shall we journey   into Etzel's land;
There at their master's service   may good knights ready stand,

     The Nibelungenlied

For that we there shall witness   Kriemhild's festivity."
That Hagen gave such counsel,   rue anon full sore did he.

Yet in sooth far other   than this had been his word,
Had not with bitter mocking   Gernot his anger stirred.
He spake to him of Siegfried   whom Kriemhild loved so,
And said: "Therefore the journey   would Hagen willingly forego."

Then spake of Tronje Hagen: "Through fear I nothing do.
Whenever will ye, Masters,   set straight your hand thereto,
With you I'll gladly journey   unto Etzel's land."
Many a shield and helmet   there hewed anon his mighty hand.

The ships stood ready waiting,   whereunto ample store
Of clothing for the journey   men full many bore,
Nor had they time for resting   till shades of even fell.
Anon in mood full joyous   bade they friends at home farewell.

Tents full large and many   arose upon the green,
Yonder side Rhine river.   But yet the winsome queen
Caressed the doughty monarch   that night, and still did pray
That far from Etzel's country   among his kinsmen might he stay.

When sound of flute and trumpet   arose at break of day,
A signal for their parting,   full soon they took their way.
Each lover to his bosom   did friend more fondly press:
King Etzel's wife full many   did part anon in dire distress.

The sons of stately Ute,   a good knight had they,
A brave man and a faithful.   When they would thence away,
Apart unto the monarch   did he his mind reveal,
And spake: "That ye will journey,   may I naught but sorrow feel."

Hight the same was Rumold,   a man of doughty hand.
He spake: "To whom now leave ye   people here and land?
O that never any   might alter your intent!
Small good, methinks, may follow   message e'er by Kriemhild sent."

"The land to thee entrusted   and eke my child shall be,
And tender care of ladies,   — so hast command from me.
Whene'er thou seest weeping,   do there thy comfort give.
Yea, trust we free from sorrow   at hand of Etzel's wife to live."

For knight and royal master   the chargers ready were,
As with fond embracing   parted many there,
Who long in joy together   a merry life had led.
By winsome dame full many   therefor must bitter tear be shed.

As did those doughty warriors   into the saddle spring,
Might full many a lady   be seen there sorrowing;
For told them well their spirit   that thus so long to part
Did bode a dire peril,   the which must ever cloud the heart.

As mounted stood the valiant   thanes of Burgundy,
Might ye a mickle stirring   in that country see,
Both men and women weeping   on either riverside.
Yet pricked they gaily forward,   let what might their folk betide.

The Nibelungen warriors   in hauberks bright arrayed
Went with them, a thousand,   while at home behind them stayed
Full many a winsome lady,   whom saw they nevermore.
The wounds of doughty Siegfried   still grieved the Lady Kriemhild
     sore.

Their journey they directed   onward to the Main,
Up through East Frankish country,   the men of Gunther's train
Thither led by Hagen,   who well that country knew;
Marshal to them was Dankwart,   a knight of Burgundy full true.

On from East Frankish country   to Schwanefeld they went,
A train of valiant warriors   of high accomplishment,
The monarchs and their kinsmen,   all knights full worthy fame.
Upon the twelfth morning   the king unto the Danube came.

The knight of Tronje, Hagen,   the very van did lead,
Ever to the Nibelungen   a surest help in need.
First the thane full valiant   down leapt upon the ground,
And straightway then his charger   fast unto a tree he bound.

Flooded were the waters   and ne'er a boat was near,
Whereat began the Nibelungen   all in dread to fear
They ne'er might cross the river,   so mighty was the flood.
Dismounted on the shore,   full many a stately knight then stood.

"Ill may it," spake then Hagen,   "fare here with thee,
Lord of Rhine river.   Now thyself mayst see
How flooded are the waters,   and swift the current flows.
I ween, before the morrow   here many a goodly knight we lose."

"How wilt reproach me, Hagen?"   the lofty monarch spake.
I pray thee yet all comfort   not from our hearts to take.
The ford shalt thou discover   whereby we may pass o'er,
Horse and equipment bringing   safely unto yonder shore."

"In sooth, not I," quoth Hagen,   "am yet so weary grown
Of life, that in these waters   wide I long to drown.
Ere that, shall warriors sicken   in Etzel's far country
Beneath my own arm stricken: / — 'tis my intent full certainly.

"Here tarry by the water,   ye gallant knights and good,
The while I seek the boatmen   myself along the flood,
Who will bring us over   into Gelfrat's land."
With that the doughty Hagen   took his trusty shield in hand.

He cap-a-pie was arméd,   as thus he strode away,
Upon his head a helmet   that gleamed with brilliant ray,
And o'er his warlike harness   a sword full broad there hung,
That on both its edges   did fiercely cut, in battle swung.

He sought to find the boatmen   if any might be near,
When sound of falling waters   full soon upon his ear.
Beside a rippling fountain,   where ran the waters cool,
A group of wise mermaidens   did bathe themselves within the pool.

Ware of them soon was Hagen   and stole in secret near,
But fast away they hurried   when they the sound did hear.
That they at all escaped him,   filled they were with glee.
The knight did take their clothing,   yet wrought none other injury.

Then spake the one mermaiden,   Hadburg that hight:
"Hagen, knight full noble,   tell will we thee aright,
An wilt thou, valiant warrior,   our garments but give o'er,
What fortune may this journey   to Hunland have for thee in store."

They hovered there before him   like birds above the flood,
Wherefore did think the warrior   that tell strange things they could,

And all the more believed he   what they did feign to say,
As to his eager question   in ready manner answered they.

Spake one: "Well may ye journey   to Etzel's country.
Thereto my troth I give thee   in full security
That ne'er in any kingdom   might high guests receive
Such honors as there wait you,   — this may ye in sooth believe."

To hear such speech was Hagen   in sooth right glad of heart;
He gave to them their garments,   and straightway would depart.
But when in strange attire   they once more were dight,
Told they of the journey   into Etzel's land aright.

Spake then the other mermaid,   Siegelind that hight:
"I warn thee, son of Aldrian,   Hagen valiant knight,
'Twas but to gain her clothing   my cousin falsely said,
For, comest thou to Hunland,   sorely shalt thou be betrayed.

"Yea, that thou turnest backward   is fitter far, I ween;
For but your death to compass   have all ye warriors keen
Receivéd now the bidding   unto Etzel's land.
Whose doth thither journey,   death leadeth surely by the hand."

Thereto gave answer Hagen: "False speech hath here no gain.
How might it ever happen   that we all were slain
Afar in Etzel's country   through hate of any man?"
To tell the tale more fully   unto him she then began.

Spake again the other: "The thing must surely be,
That of you never any   his home again shall see,
Save only the king's chaplain;   well do we understand
That he unscathed returneth   unto royal Gunther's land."

Then spake the valiant Hagen   again in angry way:
"Unto my royal masters   'twere little joy to say
That we our lives must forfeit   all in Hunland.
Now show us, wisest woman,   how pass we safe to yonder strand."

She spake: "Since from thy purposed   journey thou wilt not turn,
Where upward by the water   a cabin stands, there learn
Within doth dwell a boatman,   nor other find thou mayst."
No more did Hagen question,   but strode away from there in haste.

As went he angry-minded   one from afar did say:
"Now tarry still, Sir Hagen;   why so dost haste away?
Give ear yet while we tell thee   how thou reachest yonder strand.
Master here is Else,   who doth rule this borderland.

"Hight is his brother Gelfrat,   and is a thane full rare,
Lord o'er Bavarian country.   Full ill with you 'twill fare,
Will ye pass his border.   Watchful must ye be,
And eke with the ferryman   'twere well to walk right modestly.

"He is so angry-minded   that sure thy bane 'twill be,
Wilt thou not show the warrior   all civility.
Wilt thou that he transport thee,   give all the boatman's due.
He guardeth well the border   and unto Gelfrat is full true.

"If he be slow to answer,   then call across the flood
That thy name is Amelrich.   That was a knight full good,
Who for a feud did sometime   go forth from out this land.
The ferryman will answer,   when he the name doth understand.

Hagen high of spirit   before those women bent,
Nor aught did say, but silent   upon his way he went.
Along the shore he wandered   till higher by the tide
On yonder side the river   a cabin standing he espied.

He straight began a calling   across the flood amain.
"Now fetch me over, boatman,"   cried the doughty thane.
"A golden armband ruddy   I'll give to thee for meed.
Know that to make this crossing   I in sooth have very need."

Not fitting 'twas high ferryman   his service thus should give,
And recompense from any   seldom might he receive;
Eke were they that served him   full haughty men of mood.
Still alone stood Hagen   on the hither side the flood.

Then cried he with such power   the wave gave back the sound,
For in strength far-reaching   did the knight abound:
"Fetch me now, for Amelrich,   Else's man, am I,
That for feud outbroken   erstwhile from this land did fly."

Full high upon his sword-point   an armband did he hold,

Fair and shining was it   made of ruddy gold,
The which he offered to him   for fare to Gelfrat's land.
The ferryman high-hearted   himself did take the oar in hand.

To do with that same boatman   was ne'er a pleasant thing;
The yearning after lucre   yet evil end doth bring.
Here where thought he Hagen's   gold so red to gain,
Must he by the doughty   warrior's fierce sword be slain.

With might across the river   his oar the boatman plied,
But he who there was naméd   might nowhere be espied.
His rage was all unbounded   when he did Hagen find,
And loud his voice resounded   as thus he spake his angry mind:

"Thou mayst forsooth be calléd   Amelrich by name:
Whom I here did look for,   no whit art thou the same.
By father and by mother   brother he was to me.
Since me thou thus hast cozened,   so yet this side the river be."

"Nay, by highest Heaven,"   Hagen did declare.
"Here am I a stranger   that have good knights in care.
Now take in friendly manner   here my offered pay,
And guide me o'er the ferry;   my favor hast thou thus alway."

Whereat replied the boatman: "The thing may never be.
There are that to my masters   do bear hostility;
Wherefore I never stranger   do lead into this land.
As now thy life thou prizest,   step straightway out upon the strand."

"Deny me not," quoth Hagen,   "for sad in sooth my mood.
Take now for remembrance   this my gold so good,
And carry men a thousand   and horses to yonder shore."
Quoth in rage the boatman: "Such thing will happen nevermore."

Aloft he raised an oar   that mickle was and strong,
And dealt such blow on Hagen,   (but rued he that ere long,)
That in the boat did stumble   that warrior to his knee.
In sooth so savage boatman   ne'er did the knight of Tronje see.

With thought the stranger's anger   the more to rouse anew,
He swung a mighty boat-pole   that it in pieces flew
Upon the crown of Hagen; —   he was a man of might.

Thereby did Else's boatman   come anon to sorry plight.

Full sore enraged was Hagen,   as quick his hand he laid
Upon his sword where hanging   he found the trusty blade.
His head he struck from off him   and flung into the tide.
Known was soon the story   to the knights of Burgundy beside.

While the time was passing   that he the boatman slew,
The waters bore him downward,   whereat he anxious grew.
Ere he the boat had righted   began his strength to wane,
So mightily was pulling   royal Gunther's doughty thane.

Soon he yet had turned it,   so rapid was his stroke,
Until the mighty oar   beneath his vigor broke.
As strove he his companions   upon the bank to gain,
No second oar he found him.   Yet soon the same made fast again.

With quickly snatched shield-strap,   a fine and narrow band.
Downward where stood a forest   he sought again the land,
And there his master found he   standing upon the shore.
In haste came forth to meet him   many a stately warrior more.

The gallant knight they greeted   with right hearty mood.
When in the boat perceived they   reeking still the blood
That from the wound had issued   where Hagen's sword did swing,
Scarce could his companions   bring to an end their questioning.

When that royal Gunther   the streaming blood did see
Within the boat there running,   straightway then spake he:
"Where is now the ferryman,   tell me, Hagen, pray?
By thy mighty prowess   his life, I ween, is ta'en away."

Thereto replied he falsely: "When the boat I found
Where slopeth a wild meadow,   I the same unbound.
Hereabout no ferryman   I today have seen,
Nor ever cause of sorrow   unto any have I been."

The good knight then of Burgundy,   the gallant Gernot, spake:
"Dear friends full many, fear I,   the flood this day will take,
Since we of the boatmen   none ready here may find
To guide us o'er the current.   'Tis mickle sorrow to my mind."

Full loudly cried then Hagen: "Lay down upon the grass,
Ye squires, the horse equipments.   I ween a time there was,
Myself was best of boatmen   that dwelt the Rhine beside.
To Gelfrat's country trow I   to bring you safely o'er the tide."

That they might come the sooner   across the running flood,
Drove they in the horses.   Their swimming, it was good,
For of them never any   beneath the waves did sink,
Though many farther downward   must struggle sore to gain the
          brink.

Their treasure and apparel   unto the boat they bore,
Since by no means the journey   thought they to give o'er.
Hagen was director,   and safely reached the strand
With many a stalwart warrior   bound unto the unknown land.

Gallant knights a thousand   first he ferried o'er,
Whereafter came his own men.   Of others still were more,
For squires full nine thousand   he led unto that land.
That day no whit was idle   that valiant knight of Tronje's hand.

When he them all in safety   o'er the flood had brought,
Of that strange story   the valiant warrior thought,
Which erstwhile had told him   those women of the sea.
Lost thereby the chaplain's   life well-nigh was doomed to be.

Beside his priestly baggage   he saw the chaplain stand,
Upon the holy vestments   resting with his hand.
No whit was that his safety;   when Hagen him did see,
Must the priest full wretched   suffer sorest injury.

From out the boat he flung him   ere might the thing be told,
Whereat they cried together: "Hold, O Master, hold!"
Soon had the youthful Giselher   to rage thereat begun,
And mickle was his sorrow   that Hagen yet the thing had done.

Then outspake Sir Gernot,   knight of Burgundy:
"What boots it thee, Sir Hagen,   that thus the chaplain die?
Dared any else to do it,   thy wrath 'twould sorely stir.
Wherein the priest's offending,   thus thy malice to incur?"

To swim the chaplain struggled.   He thought him yet to free,

If any but would help him.	Yet such might never be,
For that the doughty Hagen	full wrathful was of mood,
He sunk him to the bottom,	whereat aghast each warrior stood.

When that no help forthcoming	the wretched priest might see,
He sought the hither shore,	and fared full grievously.
Though failed his strength in swimming,	yet helped him God's
	own hand,
That he came securely	back again unto the land.

Safe yonder stood the chaplain	and shook his dripping dress.
Thereby perceived Hagen	how true was nonetheless
The story that did tell him	the strange women of the sea.
Thought he: "Of these good warriors	soon the days must ended be."

When that the boat was emptied,	and complete their store
All the monarch's followers	had borne upon the shore,
Hagen smote it to pieces	and cast it on the flood,
Whereat in mickle wonder	the valiant knights around him stood.

"Wherefore dost this, brother,"	then Sir Dankwart spake;
"How shall we cross the river	when again we make
Our journey back from Hunland,	riding to the Rhine?"
Behold how Hagen bade him	all such purpose to resign.

Quoth the knight of Tronje:	"This thing is done by me,
That if e'er coward rideth	in all our company,
Who for lack of courage	from us away would fly,
He beneath these billows	yet a shameful death must die."

One there journeyed with them	from the land of Burgundy,
That was a knight of valor,	Volker by name was he.
He spake in cunning manner	whate'er might fill his mind,
And aught was done by Hagen	did the Fiddler fitting find.

Ready stood their chargers,	the carriers laden well;
At passage of the river	was there naught to tell
Of scathe to any happened,	save but the king's chaplain.
Afoot must he now journey	back unto the Rhine again.

Twenty-Sixth Adventure
How Gelfrat Was Slain by Dankwart

When now they all were gathered   upon the farther strand,
To wonder gan the monarch: "Who shall through this land
On routes aright direct us,   that not astray we fare?"
Then spake the doughty Volker: "Thereof will I alone have care."

"Now hark ye all," quoth Hagen,   "knight and squire too,
And list to friendly counsel,   as fitting is to do.
Full strange and dark the tidings   now ye shall hear from me:
Home nevermore return we   unto the land of Burgundy.

"Thus mermaids twain did tell me,   who spake to me this morn,
That back we come not hither.   You would I therefore warn
That arméd well ye journey   and of all ills beware.
To meet with doughty foemen   well behooveth us prepare.

"I weened to turn to falsehood   what those wise mermaids spake,
Who said that safe this journey   none again should make
Home unto our country   save the chaplain alone:
Him therefore was I minded   today beneath the flood to drown."

From company to company   quickly flew the tale,
Whereon grew many a doughty   warrior's visage pale,
As gan he think in sorrow   how death should snatch away
All ere the journey ended;   and very need for grief had they.

By Moeringen was it   they had the river crossed,
Where also Else's boatman   thus his life had lost.
There again spake Hagen: "Since in such wise by me

Wrath hath been incurréd,   assailed full surely shall we be.

"Myself that same ferryman   did this morning slay.
Far bruited are the tidings.   Now arm ye for the fray,
That if Gelfrat and Else   be minded to beset
Our train today, they surely   with sore discomfiture be met.

"So keen they are, well know I   the thing they'll not forego.
Your horses therefore shall ye   make to pace more slow,
That never man imagine   we flee away in fear."
"That counsel will I follow,"   spake the young knight Giselher.

"Who will guide our vanguard   through this hostile land?"
"Volker shall do it," spake they,   "well doth he understand
Where leadeth path and highway,   a minstrel brave and keen."
Ere full the wish was spoken,   in armor well equipped was seen

Standing the doughty Fiddler.   His helmet fast he bound,
And from his stately armor   shot dazzling light around.
Eke to a staff he fastened   a banner, red of hue.
Anon with royal masters   came he to sorest sorrow too.

Unto Gelfrat meanwhile   had sure tidings flown,
How that was dead his boatman;   the story eke was known
Unto the doughty Else,   and both did mourn his fate.
Their warriors they summoned,   nor must long time for answer wait.

But little space it lasted   — that would I have you know —
Ere that to them hasted   who oft a mickle woe
Had wrought in stress of battle   and injury full sore;
To Gelfrat now came riding   seven hundred knights or more.

When they their foes to follow   so bitterly began,
Led them both their masters.   Yet all too fast they ran
After the valiant strangers   vengeance straight to wreak.
Ere long from those same leaders   did death full many a warrior
       take.

Hagen then of Tronje   the thing had ordered there,
— How of his friends might ever   knight have better care? —
That he did keep the rearguard   with warriors many a one,
And Dankwart eke, his brother;   full wisely the thing was done.

When now the day was over   and light they had no more,
Injury to his followers   gan he to dread full sore.
They shield in hand rode onward   through Bavarian land,
And ere they long had waited   beset they were by hostile band.

On either side the highway   and close upon their rear
Of hoofs was heard the clatter;   too keen the chasers were.
Then spake the valiant Dankwart: "The foe is close at hand.
Now bind we on the helmet,   — wisdom doth the same command."

Upon the way they halted,   nor else they safe had been.
Through the gloom perceived they   of gleaming shields the sheen.
Thereupon would Hagen   longer not delay:
"Who rideth on the highway?" —   That must Gelfrat tell
        straight-way.

Of Bavaria the margrave   thereupon replied:
"Our enemies now seek we,   and swift upon them ride.
Fain would I discover   who hath my boatman slain.
A knight he was of valor,   whose death doth cause me grievous
        pain."

Then spake of Tronje Hagen: "And was the boatman thine
That would not take us over?   The guilt herein is mine.
Myself did slay the warrior,   and had, in sooth, good need,
For that beneath his valor   I myself full nigh lay dead.

"For pay I rich attire   did bid, and gold a store,
Good knight, that to thy country   he should us ferry o'er.
Thereat he raged full sorely   and on me swung a blow
With a mighty boat-pole,   whereat I eke did angry grow.

"For my sword then reached I   and made his rage to close
With a wound all gaping: so thou thy knight didst lose.
I'll give thee satisfaction   as to thee seemeth good."
Straightway began the combat,   for high the twain in valor stood.

"Well know I," spake Gelfrat,   "when Gunther with his train
Rode through this my country   that we should suffer bane
From Hagen, knight of Tronje.   No more shall he go free,
But for my boatman's slaying   here a hostage must he be."

Against their shields then lowered   for the charge the spear
Gelfrat and Hagen;   eager to close they were.
Else and Dankwart   spurred eke in stately way,
Scanning each the other;   then both did valorous arm display.

How might ever heroes   show doughty arm so well?
Backward from off his charger   from mighty tilt there fell
Hagen the valiant,   by Gelfrat's hand borne down.
In twain was rent the breast-piece: to Hagen thus a fall was known.

Where met in charge their followers,   did crash of shafts resound.
Risen eke was Hagen,   who erst unto the ground
Was borne by mighty lance-thrust,   prone upon the grass.
I ween that unto Gelfrat   nowise of gentle mood he was.

Who held their horses' bridles   can I not recount,
But soon from out their saddles   did they all dismount.
Hagen and Gelfrat   straightway did fierce engage,
And all their men around them   did eke a furious combat wage.

Though with fierce onslaught Hagen   upon Gelfrat sprung,
On his shield the noble margrave   a sword so deftly swung
That a piece from off the border   'mid flying sparks it clave.
Well-nigh beneath its fury   fell dead King Gunther's warrior brave.

Unto Dankwart loudly   thereat he gan to cry:
"Help! ho! my good brother!   Encountered here have I
A knight of arm full doughty,   from whom I come not free."
Then spake the valiant Dankwart: "Myself thereof the judge will
     be."

Nearer sprang the hero   and smote him such a blow
With a keen-edged weapon   that he in death lay low.
For his slain brother Else   vengeance thought to take,
But soon with all his followers   'mid havoc swift retreat must make.

Slain was now his brother,   wound himself did bear,
And of his followers eighty   eke had fallen there,
By grim death snatched sudden.   Then must the doughty knight,
From Gunther's men to save him,   turn away in hasty flight.

When that they of Bavaria   did from the carnage flee,
The blows that followed after   resounded frightfully;
For close the knights of Tronje   upon their enemies chased,
Who to escape the fury   did quit the field in mickle haste.

Then spake upon their fleeing   Dankwart the doughty thane:
"Upon our way now let us   backward turn again,
And leave them hence to hasten   all wet with oozing blood.
Unto our friends return we,   this verily meseemeth good."

When back they were returnéd   where did the scathe befall,
Outspake of Tronje Hagen: "Now look ye, warriors all,
Who of our tale is lacking,   or who from us hath been
Here in battle riven   through the doughty Gelfrat's spleen."

Lament they must for warriors   four from them were ta'en.
But paid for were they dearly,   for roundabout lay slain
Of their Bavarian foemen   a hundred or more.
The men of Tronje's bucklers   with blood were wet and tarnished
     o'er.

From out the clouds of heaven   a space the bright moon shone.
Then again spake Hagen: "Bear report let none
To my beloved masters   how we here did fare.
Let them until the morrow   still be free from aught of care."

When they were back returnéd   who bore the battle's stress,
Sore troubled was their company   from very weariness.
"How long shall we keep saddle?"   was many a warrior's quest.
Then spake the valiant Dankwart: "Not yet may we find place of
     rest,

"But on ye all must journey   till day come back again."
Volker, knight of prowess,   who led the foremost train,
Bade to ask the marshal: "This night where shall we be,
That rest them may our chargers,   and eke my royal masters three?"

Thereto spake valiant Dankwart: "The same I ne'er can say,
Yet may we never rest us   before the break of day.
Where then we find it fitting   we'll lay us on the grass."
When they did hear his answer,   what source of grief to all it was!

Still were they unbetrayéd   by reeking blood and red,
Until the sun in heaven   its shining beams down shed
At morn across the hill-tops,   that then the king might see
How they had been in battle.   Spake he then full angrily:

"How may this be, friend Hagen?   Scorned ye have, I ween,
That I should be beside you,   where coats of mail have been
Thus wet with blood upon you.   Who this thing hath done?"
Quoth he: "The same did Else,   who hath this night us set upon.

"To avenge his boatman   did they attack our train.
By hand of my brother   hath Gelfrat been slain.
Then fled Else before us,   and mickle was his need.
Ours four, and theirs a thousand,   remained behind in battle dead."

Now can we not inform you   where resting-place they found.
But cause to know their passing   had the country-folk around,
When there the sons of Ute   to court did fare in state.
At Passau fit reception   did presently the knights await.

The noble monarchs' uncle,   Bishop Pilgrim that was,
Full joyous-hearted was he   that through the land did pass
With train of lusty warriors   his royal nephews three.
That willing was his service,   waited they not long to see.

To greet them on their journey   did friends lack no device,
Yet not to lodge them fully   might Passau's bounds suffice.
They must across the water   where spreading sward they found,
And lodge and tent erected   soon were stretching o'er the ground.

Nor from that spot they onward   might journey all that day,
And eke till night was over,   for pleasant was their stay.
Next to the land of Ruediger   must they in sooth ride on,
To whom full soon the story   of their coming eke was known.

When fitting rest had taken   the knights with travel worn,
And of Etzel's country   they had reached the bourn,
A knight they found there sleeping   that ne'er should aught but
     wake,
From whom of Tronje Hagen   in stealth a mighty sword did take.

Hight in sooth was Eckewart   that same valiant knight.

For what was there befallen   was he in sorry plight,
That by those heroes' passing   he had lost his sword.
At Ruediger's marches   found they meager was the guard.

"O, woe is me dishonored,"   Eckewart then cried;
"Yea, rueth me fully sorely,   this Burgundian ride.
What time was taken Siegfried,   did joy depart from me.
Alack, O Master Ruediger,   how ill my service unto thee!"

Hagen, full well perceiving   the noble warrior's plight,
Gave him again his weapon   and armbands six full bright.
"These take, good knight, in token   that thou art still my friend.
A valiant warrior art thou,   though dost thou lone this border tend."

"May God thy gifts repay thee,"   Eckewart replied,
"Yet rueth me full sorely   that to the Huns ye ride.
Erstwhile slew ye Siegfried   and vengeance have to fear;
My rede to you is truly: "Beware ye well of danger here."

"Now must God preserve us,"   answered Hagen there.
"In sooth for nothing further   have these thanes a care
Than for place of shelter,   the kings and all their band,
And where this night a refuge   we may find within this land.

"Done to death our horses   with the long journey are,
And food as well exhausted,"   Hagen did declare.
"Nor find we aught for purchase;   a host we need instead,
Who would in kindness give us,   ere this evening, of his bread."

Thereto gave answer Eckewart: "I'll show you such a one,
That so warm a welcome   find ye never none
In country whatsoever   as here your lot may be,
An if ye, thanes full gallant,   the noble Ruediger will see.

He dwelleth by the highway   and is most bounteous host
That house e'er had for master.   His heart may graces boast,
As in the lovely May-time   the flowrets deck the mead.
To do good thanes a service   is for his heart most joyous deed."

Then spake the royal Gunther: "Wilt thou my messenger be,
If will my dear friend Ruediger,   as favor done to me,
His hospitable shelter   with all my warriors share,

Therefor full to requite thee   shall e'er hereafter be my care."

"Thy messenger am I gladly,"   Eckewart replied,
And in right willing manner   straight away did ride,
The message thus receivéd   to Ruediger to bear.
Nor did so joyous tidings   for many a season greet his ear.

Hasting to Bechelaren   was seen a noble thane.
The same perceivéd Ruediger,   and spake: "O'er yonder plain
Hither hastens Eckewart,   who Kriemhild's might doth own."
He weened that by some foemen   to him had injury been done.

Then passed he forth the gateway   where the messenger did stand.
His sword he loosed from girdle   and laid from out his hand.
The message that he carried   might he not long withhold
From the master and his kinsmen;   full soon the same to them was
        told.

He spake unto the margrave: "I come at high command
Of the lordly Gunther   of Burgundian land,
And Giselher and Gernot,   his royal brothers twain.
In service true commends him   unto thee each lofty thane.

"The like hath Hagen bidden   and Volker as well
With homage oft-times proffered.   And more have I to tell,
The which King Gunther's marshal   to thee doth send by me:
How that the valiant warriors   do crave thy hospitality."

With smiling visage Ruediger   made thereto reply:
"Now joyeth me the story   that the monarchs high
Do deign to seek my service,   that ne'er refused shall be.
Come they unto my castle,   'tis joy and gladness unto me."

"Dankwart the marshal   hath bidden let thee know
Who seek with them thy shelter   as through thy land they go:
Three score of valiant leaders   and thousand knights right good,
With squires eke nine thousand."   Thereat was he full glad of mood.

"To me 'tis mickle honor,"   Ruediger then spake,
"That through my castle's portals   such guests will entry make,
For ne'er hath been occasion   my service yet to lend.
Now ride ye, men and kinsmen,   and on these lofty knights attend."

Then to horse did hasten   knight and willing squire,
For glad they were at all times   to do their lord's desire,
And keen that thus their service   should not be rendered late.
Unwitting Lady Gotelinde   still within her chamber sate.

Twenty-Seventh Adventure
How They Came to Bechelaren

Then went forth the margrave   where two ladies sate,
His wife beside his daughter,   nor longer did he wait
To tell the joyful tidings   that unto him were brought,
How Kriemhild's royal brothers   his hospitality had sought.

"Dearly lovéd lady,"   spake then Ruediger,
"Full kind be thy reception   to lordly monarchs here,
That now with train of warriors   to court do pass this way.
Fair be eke thy greeting   to Hagen, Gunther's man, this day.

"One likewise with them cometh,   Dankwart by name,
Volker hight the other,   a knight of gallant fame.
Thyself and eke thy daughter   with kiss these six shall greet;
Full courteous be your manner   as ye the doughty thanes shall
     meet."

Gave straight their word the ladies,   and willing were thereto.
From out great chests they gorgeous   attire in plenty drew,
Which they to meet the lofty   strangers thought to wear,
Mickle was the hurry   there of many a lady fair.

On ne'er a cheek might any   but nature's hue be seen.
Upon their head they carried   band of golden sheen,
That was a beauteous chaplet,   that so their glossy hair
By wind might not be ruffled: that is truth as I declare.

At such employment busy   leave we those ladies now.
Here with mickle hurry   across the plain did see

Friends of noble Ruediger   the royal guests to meet,
And them with warmest welcome   unto the margrave's land did
          greet.

When coming forth the margrave   saw their forms appear,
How spake with heart full joyous   the valiant Ruediger!
"Welcome be ye, Sires,   and all your gallant band.
Right glad am I to see you   hither come unto my land."

Then bent the knights before him   each full courteously.
That he good-will did bear them   might they full quickly see.
Hagen had special greeting,   who long to him was known;
To Volker eke of Burgundy   was like highest honor shown.

Thus Dankwart eke he greeted,   when spake the doughty thane:
"While we thus well are harbored,   who then for all the train
Of those that follow with us   shall meet provision make?"
"Yourselves this night right easy   shall rest," the noble margrave
          spake.

"And all that follow with you,   with equipment whatsoe'er
Ye bring into my country   of steed or warlike gear,
So sure shall it be guarded   that of all the sum,
E'en to one spur's value,   to you shall never damage come.

"Now stretch aloft, my squires,   the tents upon the plain.
What here ye have of losses   will I make good again.
Unbridle now the horses   and let them wander free."
Upon their way they seldom   did meet like hospitality.

Thereat rejoiced the strangers.   When thus it ordered was,
Rode the high knights forward.   All round upon the grass
Lay the squires attendant   and found a gentle rest.
I ween, upon their journey   was here provision costliest.

Out before the castle   the noble margravine
Had passed with her fair daughter.   In her train were seen
A band of lovely women   and many a winsome maid,
Whose arms with bracelets glittered,   and all in stately robes arrayed.

The costly jewels sparkled   with far-piercing ray
From out their richest vestments,   and buxom all were they.

Now came the strangers thither   and sprang upon the ground.
How high in noble courtesy   the men of Burgundy were found!

Six and thirty maidens   and many a fair lady,
— Nor might ye ever any   more winsome wish to see —
Went then forth to meet them   with many a knight full keen.
At hands of noble ladies   fairest greeting then was seen.

The margrave's youthful daughter   did kiss the kings all three
As eke had done her mother.   Hagen stood thereby.
Her father bade her kiss him;   she looked the thane upon,
Who filled her so with terror,   she fain had left the thing undone.

When she at last must do it,   as did command her sire,
Mingled was her color,   both pale and hue of fire.
Likewise kissed she Dankwart   and the Fiddler eke anon:
That he was knight of valor   to him was such high favor shown.

The margrave's youthful daughter   took then by the hand
The royal knight Giselher   of Burgundian land.
E'en so led forth her mother   the gallant Gunther high.
With those guests so lofty   walked they there full joyfully.

The host escorted Gernot   to a spacious hall and wide,
Where knights and stately ladies   sate them side by side.
Then bade they for the strangers   pour good wine plenteously:
In sooth might never heroes   find fuller hospitality.

Glances fond and many   saw ye directed there
Upon Ruediger's daughter,   for she was passing fair.
Yea, in his thoughts caressed her   full many a gallant knight;
A lady high in spirit,   well might she every heart delight.

Yet whatsoe'er their wishes,   might none fulfilléd be.
Hither oft and thither   glanced they furtively
On maidens and fair ladies,   whereof were many there.
Right kind the noble Fiddler   disposéd was to Ruediger.

They parted each from other   as ancient custom was,
And knights and lofty ladies   did separating pass
When tables were made ready   within the spacious hall.
There in stately manner   they waited on the strangers all.

To do the guests high honor　likewise the table sought
With them the lofty margravine.　Her daughter led she not,
But left among the maidens,　where fitting was she sat.
That they might not behold her, grieved were the guests in sooth
　　　thereat.

The drinking and the feasting,　when 'twas ended all,
Escorted was the maiden　again into the hall.
Then of merry jesting　they nothing lacked, I ween,
Wherein was busy Volker,　a thane full gallant and keen.

Then spake the noble Fiddler　to all in lofty tone:
"Great mercy, lordly margrave,　God to thee hath shown,
For that he hath granted　unto thee a wife
Of so surpassing beauty,　and thereto a joyous life.

"If that I were of royal　birth," the Fiddler spake,
"And kingly crown should carry,　to wife I'd wish to take
This thy lovely daughter,　— my heart thus prompteth me.
A noble maid and gentle　and fair to look upon is she."

Then outspake the margrave:　"How might such thing be,
That king should e'er desire　daughter born to me?
Exiled from my country　here with my spouse I dwell:
What avails the maiden,　be she favored ne'er so well?"

Thereto gave answer Gernot,　a knight of manner kind:
"If to my desire　I ever spouse would find,
Then would I of such lady　right gladly make my choice."
In full kindly manner　added Hagen eke his voice:

"Now shall my master Giselher　take to himself a spouse.
The noble margrave's daughter　is of so lofty house,
That I and all his warriors　would glad her service own,
If that she in Burgundy　should ever wear a royal crown."

Glad thereat full truly　was Sir Ruediger,
And eke Gotelinde:　they joyed such words to hear.
Anon arranged the heroes　that her as bride did greet
The noble knight Giselher,　as was for any monarch meet.

What thing is doomed to happen,   who may the same prevent?
To come to the assembly   they for the maidens sent,
And to the knight they plighted   the winsome maid for wife,
Pledge eke by him was given,   his love should yet endure with life.

They to the maid allotted   castles and spreading land,
Whereof did give assurance   the noble monarch's hand
And eke the royal Gernot,   'twould surely so be done.
Then spake to them the margrave: "Lordly castles have I none,

"Yet true shall be my friendship   the while that I may live.
Unto my daughter shall I   of gold and silver give
What hundred sumpter-horses   full laden bear away,
That her husband's lofty kinsmen   find honor in the fair array."

They bade the knight and maiden   within a ring to stand,
As was of old the custom.   Of youths a goodly band,
That all were merry-hearted,   did her there confront,
And thought they on her beauty   as mind of youth is ever wont.

When they began to question   then the winsome maid,
Would she the knight for husband,   somewhat she was dismayed,
And yet forego she would not   to have him for her own.
She blushed to hear the question,   as many another maid hath done.

Her father Ruediger prompted   that Yes her answer be,
And that she take him gladly.   Unto her instantly
Sprang the young Sir Giselher,   and in his arm so white
He clasped her to his bosom.   — Soon doomed to end was her
      delight.

Then spake again the margrave: "Ye royal knights and high,
When that home ye journey   again to Burgundy
I'll give to you my daughter,   as fitting is to do,
That ye may take her with you."   They gave their plighted word
      thereto.

What jubilation made they   yet at last must end.
The maiden then was bidden   unto her chamber wend,
And guests to seek their couches   and rest until the day.
For them the host provided   a feast in hospitable way.

When they had feasted fully   and to the Huns' country
Thence would onward journey,   "Such thing shall never be,"
Spake the host full noble,   "but here ye still shall rest.
Seldom hath my good fortune   welcomed yet so many a guest."

Thereto gave answer Dankwart: "In sooth it may not be.
Bread and wine whence hast thou   and food sufficiently,
Over night to harbor   of guests so great a train?"
When the host had heard it,   spake he: "All thy words are vain.

"Refuse not my petition,   ye noble lords and high.
A fortnight's full provision   might I in sooth supply,
For you and every warrior   that journeys in your train.
Till now hath royal Etzel   small portion of my substance ta'en."

Though fain they had declined it,   yet they there must stay
E'en to the fourth morning.   Then did the host display
So generous hand and lavish   that it was told afar.
He gave unto the strangers   horses and apparel rare.

The time at last was over   and they must journey thence.
Then did the valiant Ruediger   with lavish hand dispense
Unto all his bounty,   refused he unto none
Whate'er he might desire.   Well-pleased they parted everyone.

His courteous retainers   to castle gateway brought
Saddled many horses,   and soon the place was sought
Eke by the gallant strangers   each bearing shield in hand,
For that they thence would journey   onward into Etzel's land.

The host had freely offered   rich presents unto all,
Ere that the noble strangers   passed out before the hall.
High in honor lived he,   a knight of bounty rare.
His fair daughter had he   given unto Giselher.

Eke gave he unto Gunther,   a knight of high renown,
What well might wear with honor   the monarch as his own,
— Though seldom gift received he —   a coat of harness rare.
Thereat inclined King Gunther   before the noble Ruediger.

Then gave he unto Gernot   a good and trusty blade,
Wherewith anon in combat   was direst havoc made.

That thus the gift was taken   rejoiced the margrave's wife:
Thereby the noble Ruediger   was doomed anon to lose his life.

Gotelinde proffered Hagen,   as 'twas a fitting thing,
Her gifts in kindly manner.   Since scorned them not the king,
Eke he without her bounty   to the high festivity
Should thence not onward journey.   Yet loath to take the same was
     he.

"Of all doth meet my vision,"   Hagen then spake,
"Would I wish for nothing   with me hence to take
But alone the shield that hanging   on yonder wall I see.
The same I'd gladly carry   into Etzel's land with me."

When the stately margravine   Hagen's words did hear,
Brought they to mind her sorrow,   nor might she stop a tear.
She thought again full sadly   how her son Nudung fell,
Slain by hand of Wittich;   and did her breast with anguish swell.

She spake unto the hero: "The shield to thee I'll give.
O would to God in heaven   that he still did live,
Whose hand erstwhile did wield it!   In battle fell he low,
And I, a wretched mother,   must weep with never-ending woe.

Thereat the noble lady   up from the settle rose,
And soon her arms all snow-white   did the shield enclose.
She bore it unto Hagen,   who made obeisance low;
The gift she might with honor   upon so valiant thane bestow.

O'er it, to keep its color,   a shining cover lay
With precious stones all studded,   nor ever shone the day
Upon a shield more costly;   if e'er a longing eye
Did covet to possess it,   scarce thousand marks the same might buy.

The shield in charge gave Hagen   thence away to bear.
Before his host then Dankwart   himself presented there,
On whom the margrave's daughter   did costly dress bestow.
Wherein anon in Hunland   arrayed full stately he did go.

Whate'er of gifts by any   was accepted there,
Them had his hand ne'er taken,   but that intent all were
To do their host an honor   who gave with hand so free.

By his guests in combat   soon doomed was he slain to be.

Volker the valiant   to Gotelinde came
And stood in courteous manner   with fiddle 'fore the dame.
Sweet melodies he played her   and sang his songs thereby,
For thought he from Bechelaren   to take departure presently.

The margravine bade to her   a casket forth to bear.
And now of presents given   full freely may ye hear.
Therefrom she took twelve armbands   and drew them o'er his hand.
"These shall thou with thee carry,   as ridest thou to Etzel's land,

"And for my sake shalt wear them   when at court thou dost appear,
That when thou hither comest   I may the story hear
How thou hast done me honor   at the high festival."
What did wish the lady,   faithfully performed he all.

Thus to his guests the host spake: "That ye more safely fare,
Myself will give you escort   and bid them well beware
That upon the highway   no ill on you be wrought."
Thereat his sumpter horses   straightway laden forth were brought

The host was well prepared   with five hundred men
With horse and rich attire.   These led he with him then
In right joyous humor   to the high festival.
Alive to Bechelaren   again came never one of all.

Thence took his leave Sir Ruediger   with kiss full lovingly;
As fitting was for Giselher,   likewise the same did he.
With loving arms enfolding   caressed they ladies fair.
To many a maid the parting   did bring anon full bitter tear.

On all sides then the windows   were open wide flung,
As with his train of warriors   the host to saddle sprung.
I ween their hearts did tell them   how they should sorrow deep.
For there did many a lady   and many a winsome maiden weep.

For dear friends left behind him   grieved many a knight full sore.
Whom they at Bechelaren   should behold no more.
Yet rode they off rejoicing   down across the sand
Hard by the Danube river   on their way to Etzel's land.

Then spake to the Burgundians   the gallant knight and bold,
Ruediger the noble: "Now let us not withhold
The story of our coming   unto the Hun's country.
Unto the royal Etzel   might tidings ne'er more welcome be."

Down in haste through Austria   the messenger did ride,
Who told unto the people   soon on every side,
From Worms beyond Rhine river   were high guests journeying.
Nor unto Etzel's people   gladder tidings might ye bring.

Onward spurred the messengers   who did the message bear,
How now in Hunnish country   the Nibelungen were.
"Kriemhild, lofty lady,   warm thy welcome be;
In stately manner hither   come thy loving brothers three."

Within a lofty casement   the Lady Kriemhild stood,
Looking for her kinsmen,   as friend for friend full good.
From her father's country   saw she many a knight;
Eke heard the king the tidings,   and laughed thereat for sheer
        delight.

"Now well my heart rejoiceth,"   spake Lady Kriemhild.
"Hither come my kinsmen   with many a new-wrought shield
And brightly shining hauberk: who gold would have from me,
Be mindful of my sorrow;   to him I'll ever gracious be."

Twenty-Eighth Adventure
How the Burgundians Came to Etzel's Castle

When that the men of Burgundy   were come into the land,
He of Bern did hear it,   the agéd Hildebrand.
He told it to his master,   who sore thereat did grieve;
The knight so keen and gallant   bade he in fitting way receive.

Wolfhart the valiant   bade lead the heroes forth.
In company with Dietrich   rode many a thane of worth,
As out to receive them   across the plain he went,
Where might ye see erected   already many a stately tent.

When that of Tronje Hagen   them far away espied,
Unto his royal masters   full courteously he said:
"Now shall ye, doughty riders,   down from the saddle spring,
And forward go to meet them   that here to you a welcome bring.

"A train there cometh yonder,   well knew I e'en when young.
Thanes they are full doughty   of the land of Amelung.
He of Bern doth lead them,   and high of heart they are;
To scorn their proffered greeting   shall ye in sooth full well beware."

Dismounted then with Dietrich,   (as was meet and right,)
Attended by his squire   many a gallant knight.
They went unto the strangers   and greeted courteously
The knights that far had ridden   from the land of Burgundy.

When then Sir Dietrich   saw them coming near,
What words the thane delivered,   now may ye willing hear,
Unto Ute's children.   Their journey grieved him sore.

He weened that Ruediger knowing   had warned what lay for them
    in store.

"Welcome be ye, Masters,   Gunther and Giselher,
Gernot and Hagen,   welcome eke Volker
And the valiant Dankwart.   Do ye not understand?
Kriemhild yet sore bemoaneth   the hero of Nibelungen land."

"Long time may she be weeping,"   Hagen spake again;
"In sooth for years a many   dead he lies and slain.
To the monarch now of Hunland   should she devoted be:
Siegfried returneth never,   buried now long time is he."

"How Siegfried's death was compassed,   let now the story be:
While liveth Lady Kriemhild,   look ye for injury."
Thus did of Bern Sir Dietrich   unto them declare:
"Hope of the Nibelungen,   of her vengeance well beware."

"Whereof shall I be fearful?"   the lofty monarch spake:
"Etzel hath sent us message,   (why further question make?)
That we should journey hither   into his country.
Eke hath my sister Kriemhild   oft wished us here as guests to see.

"I give thee honest counsel,"   Hagen then did say,
"Now shalt thou here Sir Dietrich   and his warriors pray
To tell thee full the story,   if aught may be designed,
And let thee know more surely   how stands the Lady Kriemhild's
    mind."

Then went to speak asunder   the lordly monarchs three,
Gunther and Gernot,   and Dietrich went he.
"Now tell us true, thou noble   knight of Bern and kind,
If that perchance thou knowest   how stands thy royal mistress'
    mind."

The lord of Bern gave answer: "What need to tell you more?
I hear each day at morning   weeping and wailing sore
The wife of royal Etzel,   who piteous doth complain
To God in heaven that Siegfried   her doughty spouse from her was
    ta'en."

"Then must we e'en abide it,"   was the fearless word

Of Volker the Fiddler,   "what we here have heard.
To court we yet shall journey   and make full clear to all,
If that to valiant warriors   may aught amid the Huns befall."

The gallant thanes of Burgundy   unto court then rode,
And went in stately manner   as was their country's mode.
Full many a man in Hunland   looked eagerly to see
Of what manner Hagen,   Tronje's doughty thane, might be.

For that was told the story   (and great the wonder grew)
How that of Netherland   Siegfried he slew,
That was the spouse of Kriemhild,   in strength without a peer,
Hence a mickle questioning   after Hagen might ye hear.

Great was the knight of stature,   may ye know full true,
Built with breast expansive;   mingled was the hue
Of his hair with silver;   long he was of limb;
As he strode stately forward   might ye mark his visage grim.

Then were the thanes of Burgundy   unto quarters shown,
But the serving-man of Gunther   by themselves alone.
Thus the queen did counsel,   so filled she was with hate.
Anon where they were harbored   the train did meet with direst fate.

Dankwart, Hagen's brother,   marshal was he.
To him the king his followers   commended urgently,
That he provide them plenty   and have of them good care.
The noble knight of Burgundy   their safety well in mind did bear.

By her train attended,   Queen Kriemhild went
To greet the Nibelungen,   yet false was her intent.
She kissed her brother Giselher   and took him by the hand:
Thereat of Tronje Hagen   did tighter draw his helmet's band.

"After such like greeting,"   the doughty Hagen spake,
"Let all watchful warriors   full precaution take:
Differs wide the greeting   on masters and men bestowed.
Unhappy was the hour   when to this festival we rode."

She spake: "Now be ye welcome   to whom ye welcome be.
For sake of friendship never   ye greeting have from me.
Tell me now what bring ye   from Worms across the Rhine,

That ye so greatly welcome   should ever be to land of mine?"

"An I had only known it,"   Hagen spake again,
"That thou didst look for present   from hand of every thane,
I were, methinks, so wealthy   — had I me bethought —
That I unto this country   likewise to thee my gift had brought."

"Now shall ye eke the story   to me more fully say:
The Nibelungen treasure,   where put ye that away?
My own possession was it,   as well ye understand.
That same ye should have brought me   hither unto Etzel's land."

"In sooth, my Lady Kriemhild,   full many a day hath flown
Since of the Nibelungen   hoard I aught have known.
Into the Rhine to sink it   my lords commanded me:
Verily there must it   until the day of judgment be."

Thereto the queen gave answer: "Such was e'en my thought.
Thereof right little have ye   unto me hither brought,
Although myself did own it   and once o'er it held sway.
'Tis cause that I forever   have full many a mournful day."

"The devil have I brought thee,"   Hagen did declare.
"My shield it is so heavy   that I have to bear,
And my plaited armor;   my shining helmet see,
And sword in hand I carry,   — so might I nothing bring for thee."

Then spake the royal lady   unto the warriors all:
"Weapon shall not any   bear into the hall.
To me now for safe keeping,   ye thanes shall give them o'er."
"In sooth," gave answer Hagen,   "such thing shall happen
        nevermore.

"Such honor ne'er I covet,   royal lady mild,
That to its place of keeping   thou shouldst bear my shield
With all my other armor,   — for thou art a queen.
Such taught me ne'er my sire: myself will be my chamberlain."

"Alack of these my sorrows!"   the Lady Kriemhild cried;
"Wherefore will now my brother   and Hagen not confide
To me their shields for keeping?   Someone did warning give.

Knew I by whom 'twas given,   brief were the space that he might
      live."

Thereto the mighty Dietrich   in wrath his answer gave:
"'Tis I who now these noble   lords forewarnéd have,
And Hagen, knight full valiant   of the land of Burgundy.
Now on! thou devil's mistress,   let not the deed my profit be."

Great shame thereat did Kriemhild's   bosom quickly fill;
She feared lest Dietrich's anger   should work her grievous ill.
Naught she spake unto them   as thence she swiftly passed,
But fierce the lightning glances   that on her enemies she cast.

By hand then grasped each, other   doughty warriors twain:
Hight the one was Dietrich,   with Hagen, noble thane.
Then spake in courteous manner   that knight of high degree:
"That ye are come to Hunland,   'tis very sorrow unto me;

"For what hath here been spoken   by the lofty queen."
Then spake of Tronje Hagen: "Small cause to grieve, I ween."
Held converse thus together   those brave warriors twain,
King Etzel which perceiving   thus a questioning began:

"I would learn full gladly,"   — in such wise spake he —
"Who were yonder warrior,   to whom so cordially
Doth greeting give Sir Dietrich.   Meseemeth high his mood.
Whosoe'er his sire,   a thane he is of mettle good."

Unto the king gave answer   of Kriemhild's train a knight:
"Born he was of Tronje,   Aldrian his sire hight.
How merry here his bearing,   a thane full grim is he.
That I have spoken truly,   shalt thou anon have cause to see."

"How may I then perceive it   that fierce his wrath doth glow?"
Naught of basest treachery   yet the king did know,
That anon Queen Kriemhild   'gainst her kinsmen did contrive,
Whereby returned from Hunland   not one of all their train alive.

"Well knew I Aldrian,   he once to me was thane:
Praise and mickle honor   he here by me did gain.
Myself a knight did make him,   and gave him of my gold.
Helke, noble lady,   did him in highest favor hold.

"Thereby know I fully   what Hagen since befell.
Two stately youths as hostage   at my court did dwell,
He and Spanish Walter,   from youth to manhood led.
Hagen sent I homeward;   Walter with Hildegunde fled."

He thought on ancient story   that long ago befell.
His doughty friend of Tronje   knew he then right well,
Whose youthful valor erstwhile   did such assistance lend.
Through him in age he must be   bereft of many a dearest friend.

Twenty-Ninth Adventure
How He Arose Not Before Her

Then parted from each other   the noble warriors twain,
Hagen of Tronje   and Dietrich, lofty thane.
Then did King Gunther's warrior   cast a glance around,
Seeking a companion   the same he eke full quickly found.

As standing there by Giselher   he did Volker see,
He prayed the nimble Fiddler   to bear him company,
For that full well he knew it   how grim he was of mood,
And that in all things was he   a knight of mettle keen and good.

While yet their lords were standing   there in castle yard
Saw ye the two knights only   walking thitherward
Across the court far distant   before the palace wide.
The chosen thanes recked little   what might through any's hate
    betide.

They sate them down on settle   over against a hall,
Wherein dwelt Lady Kriemhild,   beside the palace wall.
Full stately their attire   on stalwart bodies shone.
All that did look upon them   right gladly had the warriors known.

Like unto beasts full savage   were they gaped upon,
The two haughty heroes,   by full many a Hun.
Eke from a casement Etzel's   wife did them perceive:
Once more to behold them   must fair Lady Kriemhild grieve.

It called to mind her sorrow,   and she to weep began,
Whereat did mickle wonder   many an Etzel's man,

What grief had thus so sudden   made her sad of mood.
Spake she: "That hath Hagen,   ye knights of mettle keen and good."

They to their mistress answered: "Such thing, how hath it been?
For that thee right joyous   we but now have seen.
Ne'er lived he so daring   that, having wrought thee ill,
His life he must not forfeit,   if but to vengeance point thy will."

"I live but to requite him   that shall avenge my wrong;
Whate'er be his desire   shall unto him belong.
Prostrate I beseech you,"   — so spake the monarch's wife —
"Avenge me upon Hagen,   and forfeit surely be his life."

Three score of valiant warriors   made ready then straightway
To work the will of Kriemhild   and her best obey
By slaying of Sir Hagen,   the full valiant thane,
And eke the doughty Fiddler;   by shameful deed thus sought they
        gain.

When the queen beheld there   so small their company,
In full angry humor   to the warriors spake she:
"What there ye think to compass,   forego such purpose yet:
So small in numbers never   dare ye Hagen to beset.

"How doughty e'er be Hagen,   and known his valor wide,
A man by far more doughty   that sitteth him beside,
Volker the Fiddler: a warrior grim is he.
In sooth may not so lightly   the heroes twain confronted be."

When that she thus had spoken,   ready soon were seen
Four hundred stalwart warriors;   for was the lofty queen
Full intent upon it   to work them evil sore.
Therefrom for all the strangers   was mickle sorrow yet in store.

When that complete attiréd   were here retainers seen,
Unto the knights impatient   in such wise spake the queen:
"Now bide ye yet a moment   and stand ye ready so,
While I with crown upon me   unto my enemies shall go.

"And list while I accuse him   how he hath wrought me bane,
Hagen of Tronje,   Gunther's doughty thane.
I know his mood so haughty,   naught he'll deny of all.

Nor reck I what of evil   therefrom may unto him befall."

Then saw the doughty Fiddler   — he was a minstrel keen —
Adown the steps descending   the high and stately queen
Who issued from the castle.   When he the queen espied,
Spake the valiant Volker   to him was seated by his side:

"Look yonder now, friend Hagen,   how that she hither hies
Who to this land hath called us   in such treacherous wise.
No monarch's wife I ever   saw followed by such band
Of warriors armed for battle,   that carry each a sword in hand.

"Know'st thou, perchance, friend Hagen,   if hate to thee they bear?
Then would I well advise thee   of them full well beware
And guard both life and honor.   That methinks were good,
For if I much mistake not,   full wrathful is the warriors' mood.

"Of many eke among them   so broad the breasts do swell,
That who would guard him 'gainst them   betimes would do it well.
I ween that 'neath their tunics   they shining mail-coats wear:
Yet might I never tell thee,   'gainst whom such evil mind they bear."

Then spake all wrathful-minded   Hagen the warrior keen:
"On me to vent their fury   is their sole thought, I ween,
That thus with brandished weapons   their onward press we see.
Despite them all yet trow I   to come safe home to Burgundy.

"Now tell me, friend Volker,   wilt thou beside me stand,
If seek to work me evil   here Kriemhild's band?
That let me hear right truly,   as I am dear to thee.
By thy side forever   shall my service faithful be."

"Full surely will I help thee,"   the minstrel straight replied;
"And saw I e'en a monarch   with all his men beside
Hither come against us,   the while a sword I wield
Not fear shall ever prompt me   from thy side one pace to yield."

"Now God in heaven, O Volker,   give thy high heart its meed.
Will they forsooth assail me,   whereof else have I need?
Wilt thou thus stand beside me   as here is thy intent,
Let come all armed these warriors,   on whatsoever purpose bent."

"Now rise we from this settle,"   the minstrel spake once more,
"While that the royal lady   passeth here before.
To her be done this honor   as unto lady high.
Ourselves in equal manner   shall we honor eke thereby."

"Nay, nay! as me thou lovest,"   Hagen spake again,
"For so would sure imagine   here each hostile thane
That 'twere from fear I did it,   should I bear me so.
For sake of never any   will I from this settle go.

"Undone we both might leave it   in sooth more fittingly.
Wherefore should I honor   who bears ill-will to me?
Such thing will I do never,   the while I yet have life.
Nor reck I aught how hateth   me the royal Etzel's wife."

Thereat defiant Hagen   across his knee did lay
A sword that shone full brightly,   from whose knob did play
The light of glancing jasper   greener than blade of grass.
Well perceivéd Kriemhild   that it erstwhile Siegfried's was.

When she the sword espiéd,   to weep was sore her need.
The hilt was shining golden,   the sheath a band of red.
As it recalled her sorrow,   her tears had soon begun;
I ween for that same purpose   'twas thus by dauntless Hagen done.

Eke the valiant Volker   a fiddle-bow full strong
Unto himself drew nearer;   mickle it was and long,
Like unto a broad-sword   full sharp that was and wide.
So sat they all undaunted   the stately warriors side by side.

There sat the thanes together   in such defiant wise
That would never either   from the settle rise
Through fear of whomsoever.   Then strode before their feet
The lofty queen, and wrathful   did thus the doughty warriors greet.

Quoth she: "Now tell me, Hagen,   upon whose command
Barest thou thus to journey   hither to this land,
And knowest well what sorrow   through thee my heart must bear.
Wert thou not reft of reason,   then hadst thou kept thee far from
     here."

"By none have I been summoned,"   Hagen gave reply.

"Three lofty thanes invited   were to this country:
The same I own as masters   and service with them find.
Whene'er they make court journey   'twere strange should I remain
    behind."

Quoth she: "Now tell me further,   wherefore didst thou that
Whereby thou hast deservéd   my everlasting hate?
'Twas thou that slewest Siegfried,   spouse so dear to me,
The which, till life hath ended,   must ever cause for weeping be."

Spake he: "Why parley further,   since further word were vain?
E'en I am that same Hagen   by whom was Siegfried slain,
That deft knight of valor.   How sore by him 'twas paid
That the Lady Kriemhild   dared the fair Brunhild upbraid!

"Beyond all cavil is it,   high and royal dame,
Of all the grievous havoc   I do bear the blame.
Avenge it now who wisheth,   woman or man tho't be.
An I unto thee lie not,   I've wrought thee sorest injury."

She spake: "Now hear, ye warriors,   how denies he not at all
The cause of all my sorrow.   Whate'er may him befall
Reck I not soever,   that know ye, Etzel's men."
The overweening warriors   blank gazed upon each other then.

Had any dared the onset,   seen it were full plain
The palm must be awarded   to the companions twain,
Who had in storm of battle   full oft their prowess shown.
What that proud band designed   through fear must now be left
    undone.

Outspake one of their number: "Wherefore look thus to me?
What now I thought to venture   left undone shall be,
Nor for reward of any   think I my life to lose;
To our destruction lures us   here the royal Etzel's spouse."

Then spake thereby another: "Like mind therein have I.
Though ruddy gold were offered   like towers piléd high,
Yet would I never venture   to stir this Fiddler's spleen.
Such are the rapid glances   that darting from his eyes I've seen.

"Likewise know I Hagen   from youthful days full well,

Nor more about his valor   to me need any tell.
In two and twenty battles   I the knight have seen,
Whereby sorest sorrow   to many a lady's heart hath been.

"When here they were with Etzel,   he and the knight of Spain
Bore storm of many a battle   in many a warlike train
For sake of royal honor,   so oft thereof was need.
Wherefore of right are honors   high the valiant Hagen's meed.

"Then was yet the hero   but a child in years;
Now how hoary-headed   who were his youthful feres,
To wisdom now attainéd,   a warrior grim and strong,
Eke bears he with him Balmung,   the which he gained by mickle
        wrong."

Therewith the matter ended,   and none the fight dared start,
Whereat the Lady Kriemhild   full heavy was of heart.
Her warriors thence did vanish,   for feared they death indeed
At hands of the Fiddler,   whereof right surely was there need.

Outspake then the Fiddler: "Well we now have seen,
That enemies here do greet us,   as we forewarned have been.
Back unto the monarchs   let us straight repair,
That none against our masters   to raise a hostile hand may dare.

"How oft from impious purpose   doth fear hold back the hand,
Where friend by friend doth only   firm in friendship stand,
Until right sense give warning   to leave the thing undone.
Thus wisdom hath prevented   the harm of mortals many a one."

"Heed I will thy counsel,"   Hagen gave reply.
Then passed they where   the monarchs found they presently
In high state received   within the palace court.
Loud the valiant Volker   straight began after this sort

Unto his royal masters: "How long will ye stand so,
That foes may press upon you?   To the king ye now shall go,
And from his lips hear spoken   how is his mind to you."
The valiant lords and noble   consorted then by two and two.

Of Bern the lofty Dietrich   took by the hand
Gunther the lordly monarch   of Burgundian land;

Irnfried escorted Gernot,   a knight of valor keen,
And Ruediger with Giselher   going unto the court was seen.

Howe'er with fere consorted   there any thane might be,
Volker and Hagen   ne'er parted company,
Save in storm of battle   when they did reach life's bourne,
'Twas cause that highborn ladies   anon in grievous way must mourn.

Unto the court then passing   with the kings were seen.
Of their lofty retinue   a thousand warriors keen,
And threescore thanes full valiant   that followed in their train;
The same from his own country   had doughty Hagen with him
        ta'en.

Hawart and eke Iring,   chosen warriors twain,
Saw ye walk together   in the royal train.
By Dankwart and Wolfhart,   a thane of high renown,
Was high courtly bearing   there before the others shown.

When the lord of Rhineland   passed into the hall,
Etzel mighty monarch   waited not at all,
But sprang from off his settle   when he beheld him nigh.
By monarch ne'er was given   greeting so right heartily.

"Welcome be, Lord Gunther,   and eke Sir Gernot too,
And your brother Giselher.   My greetings unto you
I sent with honest purpose   to Worms across the Rhine;
And welcome all your followers   shall be unto this land of mine.

"Right welcome be ye likewise,   doughty warriors twain,
Volker the full valiant,   and Hagen dauntless thane,
To me and to my lady   here in my country.
Unto the Rhine to greet you   many a messenger sent she."

Then spake of Tronje Hagen: "Thereof I'm well aware,
And did I with my masters   not thus to Hunland fare,
To do thee honor had I   ridden unto thy land."
Then took the lofty monarch   the honored strangers by the hand.

He led them to the settle   whereon himself he sat,
Then poured they for the strangers   — with care they tended that —
In goblets wide and golden   mead and mulberry wine,

And bade right hearty welcome   unto the knights afar from Rhine.

Then spake the monarch Etzel: "This will I freely say:
Naught in this world might happen   to bring my heart more joy,
Than that ye lofty heroes   thus are come to me.
The queen from mickle sadness   thereby make ye likewise free.

"To me 'twas mickle wonder   wherein had I transgressed,
That I for friends had won me   so many a noble guest,
Yet ye had never deignéd   to come to my country.
'Tis now turned cause of gladness   that you as guests I here may see."

Thereto gave answer Ruediger,   a knight of lofty mind:
"Well mayst thou joy to see them;   right honor shalt thou find
And naught but noble bearing   in my high mistress' kin.
With them for guest thou likewise   many a stately thane dost win."

At turn of sun in summer   were the knights arrived
At mighty Etzel's palace.   Ne'er hath monarch lived
That lordly guests did welcome   with higher compliment.
When come was time of eating,   the king with them to table went.

Amid his guests more stately   a host was seated ne'er.
They had in fullest measure   of drink and goodly fare;
Whate'er they might desire,   they ready found the same.
Tales of mickle wonder   had spread abroad the heroes' fame.

Thirtieth Adventure
How They Kept Guard

And now the day was ended   and nearing was the night.
Came then the thought with longing   unto each way-worn knight,
When that they might rest them   and to their beds be shown.
'Twas mooted first by Hagen   and straight was answer then made
     known.

To Etzel spake then Gunther: "Fair days may God thee give!
To bed we'll now betake us,   an be it by thy leave;
We'll come betimes at morning,   if so thy pleasure be."
From his guests the monarch   parted then full courteously.

Upon the guests on all sides   the Huns yet rudely pressed,
Whereat the valiant Volker   these words to them addressed:
"How dare ye 'fore these warriors   thus beset the way?
If that ye desist not,   rue such rashness soon ye may.

"Let fall will I on someone   such stroke of fiddle-bow,
That eyes shall fill with weeping   if he hath friend to show.
Why make not way before us,   as fitting were to do!
Knights by name ye all are,   but knighthood's ways unknown to
     you."

When outspake the Fiddler   thus so wrathfully
Backward glanced bold Hagen   to see what this might be.
Quoth he: "He redes you rightly,   this keen minstrel knight.
Ye followers of Kriemhild,   now pass to rest you for the night.

"The thing whereof ye're minded   will none dare do, I ween.

If aught ye purpose 'gainst us,   on the morrow be that seen,
And let us weary strangers   the night in quiet pass;
I ween, with knights of honor   such evermore the custom was."

Then were led the strangers   into a spacious hall
Where they found prepared   for the warriors one and all
Beds adorned full richly,   that were both wide and long.
Yet planned the Lady Kriemhild   to work on them the direst wrong.

Rich quilted mattress covers   of Arras saw ye there
Lustrous all and silken,   and spreading sheets there were
Wrought of silk of Araby,   the best might e'er be seen.
O'er them lay rich embroidered   stuffs that cast a brilliant sheen.

Coverlets of ermine   full many might ye see,
With sullen sable mingled,   whereunder peacefully
They should rest the night through   till came the shining day.
A king with all retinue   ne'er, I ween, so stately lay.

"Alack for these night-quarters!"   quoth young Giselher,
"Alack for my companions   who this our journey share!
How kind so e'er my sister's   hospitality,
Dead by her devising,   I fear me, are we doomed to be."

"Let now no fears disturb you,"   Hagen gave reply;
"Through the hours of sleeping   keep the watch will I.
I trust full well to guard you   until return the day,
Thereof be never fearful;   let then preserve him well who may."

Inclined they all before him   thereat to give him grace.
Then sought they straight their couches;   in sooth 'twas little space
Until was softly resting   every stately man.
But Hagen, valiant hero,   the while to don his armor gan.

Spake then to him the Fiddler,   Volker a doughty thane:
"I'll be thy fellow, Hagen,   an wilt thou not disdain,
While watch this night thou keepest,   until do come the morn."
Right heartily the hero   to Volker then did thanks return.

"God in heaven requite thee,   Volker, trusty fere.
In all my time of trouble   wished I none other near,
None other but thee only,   when dangers round me throng.

I'll well repay that favor,   if death withhold its hand so long."

Arrayed in glittering armor   both soon did ready stand;
Each did take unto him   a mighty shield in hand,
And passed without the portal   there to keep the way.
Thus were the strangers guarded,   and trusty watchers eke had they.

Volker the valiant,   as he sat before the hall,
Leaned his trusty buckler   meanwhile against the wall,
Then took in hand his fiddle   as he was wont to do:
All times the thane would render   unto his friends a service true.

Beneath the hall's wide portal   he sat on bench of stone;
Than he a bolder fiddler   was there never none.
As from his chords sweet echoes   resounded through the hall,
Thanks for glad refreshment   had Volker from the warriors all.

Then from the strings an echo   the wide hall did fill,
For in his fiddle-playing   the knight had strength and skill.
Softer then and sweeter   to fiddle he began
And wiled to peaceful slumber   many an anxious brooding man.

When they were wrapped in slumber   and he did understand,
Then took again the warrior   his trusty shield in hand
And passed without the portal   to guard the entrance tower,
And safe to keep his fellows   where Kriemhild's crafty men did
        lower.

About the hour of midnight,   or earlier perchance,
The eye of valiant Volker   did catch a helmet's glance
Afar from out the darkness: the men of Kriemhild sought
How that upon the strangers   might grievous scathe in stealth be
        wrought.

Quoth thereat the Fiddler: "Friend Hagen, 'tis full clear
That we do well together   here this watch to share.
I see before us yonder   men arméd for the fight;
I ween they will attack us,   if I their purpose judge aright."

"Be silent, then," spake Hagen,   "and let them come more nigh.
Ere that they perceive us   shall helmets sit awry,
By good swords disjointed   that in our hands do swing.

Tale of vigorous greeting   shall they back to Kriemhild bring."

Amid the Hunnish warriors   one full soon did see,
That well the door was guarded;   straightway then cried he:
"The thing we here did purpose   'tis need we now give o'er,
For I behold the Fiddler   standing guard before the door.

"Upon his head a helmet   of glancing light is seen,
Welded strong and skillful,   dintless, of clearest sheen.
The mail-rings of his armor   do sparkle like the fire,
Beside him stands eke Hagen;   safe are the strangers from our ire."

Straightway they back returned.   When Volker that did see,
Unto his companion   wrathfully spake he:
"Now let me to those caitiffs   across the courtyard go;
What mean they by such business,   from Kriemhild's men I fain
          would know."

"No, as thou dost love me,"   Hagen straight replied;
"If from this hall thou partest,   such ill may thee betide
At hands of these bold warriors   and from the swords they bear,
That I must haste to help thee,   though here our kinsmen's bane it
          were.

"Soon as we two together   have joined with them in fight,
A pair or two among them   will surely hasten straight
Hither to this hall here,   and work such havoc sore
Upon our sleeping brethren,   as must be mournéd evermore."

Thereto gave answer Volker: "So much natheless must be,
That they do learn full certain   how I the knaves did see,
That the men of Kriemhild   hereafter not deny
What they had wrought full gladly   here with foulest treachery."

Straightway then unto them   aloud did Volker call:
"How go ye thus in armor,   ye valiant warriors all?
Or forth, perchance, a-robbing,   Kriemhild's men, go ye?
Myself and my companion   shall ye then have for company."

Thereto no man gave answer.   Wrathful grew his mood:
"Fie, ye caitiff villains,"   spake the hero good,
"Would ye us so foully   have murdered while we slept?

With knights so high in honor   full seldom thus hath faith been
    kept."

Then unto Queen Kriemhild   were the tidings borne,
How her men did fail their purpose: 'twas cause for her to mourn.
Yet otherwise she wrought it,   for grim she was of mood:
Anon through her must perish   full many a valorous knight and
    good.

Thirty-First Adventure

How They Went to Mass

"So cool doth grow my armor,"   Volker made remark,
"I ween but little longer   will endure the dark.
By the air do I perceive it,   that soon will break the day."
Then waked they many a warrior   who still in deepest slumber lay.

When brake the light of morning   athwart the spacious hall,
Hagen gan awaken   the stranger warriors all,
If that they to the minster   would go to holy mass.
After the Christian custom,   of bells a mickle ringing was.

There sang they all uneven,   that plainly might ye see
How Christian men and heathen   did not full well agree.
Each one of Gunther's warriors   would hear the service sung,
So were they all together   up from their night-couches sprung.

Then did the warriors lace them   in so goodly dress,
That never heroes any,   that king did e'er possess,
More richly stood attired;   that Hagen grieved to see.
Quoth he: "Ye knights, far other   here must your attire be.

"Yea, know among you many   how here the case doth stand.
Bear ye instead of roses   your good swords in hand,
For chaplets all bejeweled   your glancing helmets good,
Since we have well perceivéd   how is the angry Kriemhild's mood.

"Today must we do battle,   that will I now declare.
Instead of silken tunic   shall ye good hauberks wear,
And for embroidered mantle   a trusty shield and wide,

That ye may well defend you,   if ye must others' anger bide.

"My masters well belovéd,   knights and kinsmen true,
'Tis meet that ye betake you   unto the minster too,
That God do not forsake you   in peril and in need,
For certain now I make you   that death is nigh to us indeed.

"Forget ye not whatever   wrong ye e'er have done,
But there 'fore God right meekly   all your errors own;
Thereto would I advise you,   ye knights of high degree,
For God alone in heaven   may will that other mass ye see."

Thus went they to the minster,   the princes and their men.
Within the holy churchyard   bade them Hagen then
Stand all still together   that they part not at all.
Quoth he: "Knows not any   what may at hands of Huns befall.

"Let stand, good friends, all ready,   your shields before your feet,
That if ever any   would you in malice greet,
With deep-cut wound ye pay him;   that is Hagen's rede,
That from men may never   aught but praises be your meed."

Volker and Hagen,   the twain thence did pass
Before the broad minster.   Therein their purpose was
That the royal Kriemhild   must meet them where they stood
There athwart her pathway.   In sooth full grim she was of mood.

Then came the royal Etzel   and eke his spouse full fair.
Attired were the warriors   all in raiment rare
That following full stately   with her ye might see;
The dust arose all densely   round Kriemhild's mickle company.

When the lofty monarch   thus all armed did see
The kings and their followers,   straightway then cried he:
"How see I in this fashion   my friends with helm on head?
By my troth I sorrow   if ill to them have happenéd.

"I'll gladly make atonement   as doth to them belong.
Hath any them affronted   or done them aught of wrong,
To me 'tis mickle sorrow,   well may they understand.
To serve them am I ready,   in whatsoever they command."

Thereto gave answer Hagen: "Here hath wronged us none.
'Tis custom of my masters   to keep their armor on
Till full three days be over,   when high festival they hold.
Did any here molest us,   to Etzel would the thing be told."

Full well heard Kriemhild likewise   how Hagen gave reply.
Upon him what fierce glances   flashed furtively her eye!
Yet betray she would not   the custom of her country,
Though well she long had known it   in the land of Burgundy.

How grim soe'er and mighty   the hate to them she bore,
Had any told to Etzel   how stood the thing before,
Well had he prevented   what there anon befell.
So haughty were they minded   that none to him the same would tell.

With the queen came forward   there a mighty train,
But no two handbreadths yielded   yet those warriors twain
To make way before her.   The Huns did wrathful grow,
That their mistress passing   should by them be jostled so.

Etzel's highborn pages   were sore displeased thereat,
And had upon the strangers   straightway spent their hate,
But that they durst not do it   their high lord before.
There was a mickle pressing,   yet naught of anger happened more.

When they thence were parting   from holy service done,
On horse came quickly prancing   full many a nimble Hun.
With the Lady Kriemhild   went many a maiden fair,
And eke to make her escort   seven thousand knights rode there.

Kriemhild with her ladies   within the casement sat
By Etzel, mighty monarch,   — full pleased he was thereat.
They wished to view the tourney   of knights beyond compare.
What host of strangers riding   thronged the court before them there!

The marshal with the squires   not in vain ye sought,
Dankwart the full valiant: with him had he brought
His royal master's followers   of the land of Burgundy.
For the valiant Nibelungen   the steeds well saddled might ye see.

When their steeds they mounted,   the kings and all their men,
Volker thane full doughty,   gave his counsel then,

That after their country's fashion   they ride a mass mellay.
His rede the heroes followed   and tourneyed in full stately way.

The knight had counsel given   in sooth that pleased them well;
The clash of arms in mellay   soon full loud did swell.
Many a valiant warrior   did thereto resort,
As Etzel and Kriemhild   looked down upon the spacious court.

Came there unto the mellay   six hundred knights of those
That followed Dietrich's bidding,   the strangers to oppose.
Pastime would they make them   with the men of Burgundy,
And if he leave had granted,   had done the same right willingly.

In their company rode there   how many a warrior bold!
When unto Sir Dietrich   then the thing was told,
Forbade he that 'gainst Gunther's   men they join the play.
He feared lest harm befall them,   and well his counsel did he weigh.

When of Bern the warriors   thence departed were,
Came they of Bechelaren,   the men of Ruediger,
Bearing shield five hundred,   and rode before the hall;
Rather had the margrave   that they came there not at all.

Prudently then rode he   amid their company
And told unto his warriors   how they might plainly see,
That the men of Gunther   were in evil mood:
Did they forego the mellay,   please him better far it would.

When they were thence departed,   the stately knights and bold,
Came they of Thuringia,   as hath to us been told,
And of them of Denmark   a thousand warriors keen.
From crash of spear up-flying   full frequent were the splinters seen.

Irnfried and Hawart   rode into the mellay,
Whom the gallant men of Rhineland   received in knightly play:
Full oft the men of Thuringia   they met in tournament,
Whereby the piercing lance-point   through many a stately shield was
        sent.

Eke with three thousand warriors   came Sir Bloedel there.
Etzel and Kriemhild   were of his coming ware,
As this play of chivalry   before them they did see.

Now hoped the queen that evil   befall the men of Burgundy.

Schrutan and Gibecke   rode into the mellay,
Eke Ramung and Hornbog   after the Hunnish way;
Yet must they come to standstill   'fore the thanes of Burgundy.
High against the palace   wall the splintered shafts did fly.

How keen soe'er the contest,   'twas naught but knightly sport.
With shock of shields and lances   heard ye the palace court
Loud give back the echo   where Gunther's men rode on.
His followers in the jousting   on every side high honor won.

So long they held such pastime   and with so mickle heat
That through the broidered trappings   oozed clear drops of sweat
From the prancing chargers   whereon the knights did ride.
In full gallant manner   their skill against the Huns they tried.

Then outspake the Fiddler,   Volker deft of hand:
"These knights, I ween, too timid   are 'gainst us to stand.
Oft did I hear the story   what hate to us they bore;
Than this a fairer season   to vent it, find they nevermore."

"Lead back unto the stables,"   once more spake Volker then,
"Now our weary chargers;   we'll ride perchance again
When comes the cool of evening,   if fitting time there be.
Mayhap the queen will honor   award to men of Burgundy."

Beheld they then prick hither   one dressed in state so rare
That of the Huns none other   might with him compare.
Belike from castle tower   did watch his fair lady;
So gay was his apparel   as it some knight's bride might be.

Then again quoth Volker: "How may I stay my hand?
Yonder ladies' darling   a knock shall understand.
Let no man here deter me,   I'll give him sudden check.
How spouse of royal Etzel   thereat may rage, I little reck."

"Nay, as thou dost love me,"   straight King Gunther spake;
"All men will but reproach us   if such affront we make.
The Huns be first offenders,   for such would more befit."
Still did the royal Etzel   in casement by Queen Kriemhild sit.

"I'll add unto the mellay,"   Hagen did declare;
"Let now all these ladies   and knights be made aware
How we can ride a charger;   'twere well we make it known,
For, come what may, small honor   shall here to Gunther's men be
        shown."

Once more the nimble Volker   into the mellay spurred,
Whereat full many a lady   soon to weep was heard.
His lance right through the body   of that gay Hun he sent:
'Twas cause that many a woman   and maiden fair must sore lament.

Straight dashed into the mellay   Hagen and his men.
With three score of his warriors   spurred he quickly then
Forward where the Fiddler   played so lustily.
Etzel and Kriemhild   full plainly might the passage see.

Then would the kings their minstrel   — that may ye fairly know —
Leave not all defenseless   there amid the foe.
With them a thousand heroes   rode forth full dexterously,
And soon had gained their purpose   with show of proudest chivalry.

When in such rude fashion   the stately Hun was slain,
Might ye hear his kinsmen   weeping loud complain.
Then all around did clamor: "Who hath the slayer been?"
"None but the Fiddler was it,   Volker the minstrel keen."

For swords and for shields then   called full speedily
That slain margrave's kinsmen   of the Hun's country.
To avenge him sought they   Volker in turn to slay.
In haste down from the casement   royal Etzel made his way.

Arose a mighty clamor   from the people all;
The kings and men of Burgundy   dismounted 'fore the hall,
And likewise their chargers   to the rear did send.
Came then the mighty Etzel   and sought to bring the strife to end.

From one of that Hun's kinsmen   who near by him did stand
Snatched he a mighty weapon   quick from out his hand,
And therewith backward smote them,   for fierce his anger wrought.
"Shall thus my hospitality   unto these knights be brought to
        naught?"

"If ye the valiant minstrel   here 'fore me should slay,"
Spake the royal Etzel,   "it were an evil day.
When he the Hun impaléd   I did observe full well,
That not through evil purpose   but by mishap it so befell.

"These my guests now must ye   ne'er disturb in aught."
Himself became their escort.   Away their steeds were brought
Unto the stables   by many a waiting squire,
Who ready at their bidding   stood to meet their least desire.

The host with the strangers   into the palace went,
Nor would he suffer any   further his wrath to vent.
Soon were the tables ready   and water for them did wait.
Many then had gladly   on them of Rhineland spent their hate.

Not yet the lords were seated   till some time was o'er.
For Kriemhild o'er her sorrow   meantime did trouble sore.
She spake: "Of Bern, O Master,   thy counsel grant to me,
Thy help and eke thy mercy,   for here in sorry plight I be."

To her gave answer Hildebrand,   a thane right praiseworthy:
"Who harms the Nibelungen   shall ne'er have help of me,
How great soe'er the guerdon.   Such deed he well may rue,
For never yet did any   these gallant doughty knights subdue."

Eke in courteous manner   Sir Dietrich her addressed:
"Vain, O lofty mistress,   unto me thy quest.
In sooth thy lofty kinsmen   have wronged me not at all,
That I on thanes so valorous   should thus with murderous purpose
    fall.

"Thy prayer doth thee small honor,   O high and royal dame,
That upon thy kinsmen   thou so dost counsel shame.
Thy grace to have they deeméd   when came they to this land.
Nevermore shall Siegfried   avengéd be by Dietrich's hand."

When she no guile discovered   in the knight of Bern,
Unto Bloedel straightway   did she hopeful turn
With promise of wide marches   that Nudung erst did own.
Slew him later Dankwart   that he forgot the gift full soon.

Spake she: "Do thou help me,   Sir Bloedel, I pray.

Yea, within the palace   are foes of mine this day,
Who erstwhile slew Siegfried,   spouse full dear to me.
Who helps me to avenge it,   to him I'll e'er beholden be."

Thereto gave answer Bloedel: "Lady, be well aware,
Ne'er to do them evil   'fore Etzel may I dare,
For to thy kinsmen, lady,   beareth he good will.
Ne'er might the king me pardon,   wrought I upon them aught of
        ill."

"But nay, Sir Bloedel, my favor   shall thou have evermore.
Yea, give I thee for guerdon   silver and gold in store,
And eke a fairest lady,   that Nudung erst should wed:
By her fond embraces   may'st thou well be comforted.

"The land and eke the castles,   all to thee I'll give;
Yea, may'st thou, knight full noble,   in joyance ever live,
Call'st thou thine the marches,   wherein did Nudung dwell.
Whate'er this day I promise,   fulfill it all I will full well."

When understood Sir Bloedel   what gain should be his share,
And pleased him well the lady   for that she was so fair,
By force of arms then thought he   to win her for his wife.
Thereby the knight aspirant   was doomed anon to lose his life.

"Unto the hall betake thee,"   quoth he unto the queen,
"Alarum I will make thee   ere any know, I ween.
Atone shall surely Hagen   where he hath done thee wrong:
To thee I'll soon give over   King Gunther's man in fetters strong."

"To arms, to arms!" quoth Bloedel,   "my good warriors all:
In their followers' quarters   upon the foe we'll fall.
Herefrom will not release me   royal Etzel's wife.
To win this venture therefore   fear not each one to lose his life."

When at length Queen Kriemhild   found Bloedel well content
To fulfill her bidding,   she to table went
With the monarch Etzel   and eke a goodly band.
Dire was the treason   she against the guests had planned.

Since in none other manner   she knew the strife to start,
(Kriemhild's ancient sorrow   still rankled in her heart),

Bade she bring to table   Etzel's youthful son:
By woman bent on vengeance   how might more awful deed be done?

Went upon the instant   four of Etzel's men,
And soon came bearing Ortlieb,   the royal scion, then
Unto the princes' table,   where eke grim Hagen sate.
The child was doomed to perish   by reason of his deadly hate.

When the mighty monarch   then his child did see,
Unto his lady's kinsmen   in manner kind spake he:
"Now, my good friends, behold ye   here my only son,
And child of your high sister: may it bring you profit everyone.

"Grow he but like his kindred,   a valiant man he'll be,
A mighty king and noble,   doughty and fair to see.
Live I but yet a little,   twelve lands shall he command;
May ye have faithful service   from the youthful Ortlieb's hand.

"Therefore grant me favor,   ye good friends of mine;
When to your country ride ye   again unto the Rhine,
Shall ye then take with you   this your sister's son,
And at your hands may ever   by the child full fair be done.

"Bring him up in honor   until to manhood grown.
If then in any country   hath wrong to you been done,
He'll help you by his valor   vengeance swift to wreak."
Eke heard the Lady Kriemhild   royal Etzel thus to speak.

"Well might these my masters   on his faith rely,
Grew he e'er to manhood," Hagen made reply:
"Yet is the prince, I fear me,   more early doomed of fate.
'Twere strange did any see me   ever at court on Ortlieb wait."

The monarch glanced at Hagen,   sore grieved at what he heard;
Although the king full gallant   thereto spake ne'er a word,
Natheless his heart was saddened   and heavy was his mind.
Nowise the mood of Hagen   was to merriment inclined.

It grieved all the princes   and the royal host
That of his child did Hagen   make such idle boast.
That they must likewise leave it   unanswered, liked they not:

They little weaned what havoc   should by the thane anon be
    wrought.

Thirty-Second Adventure
How Bloedel Was Slain

The knights by Bloedel summoned   soon armed and ready were,
A thousand wearing hauberks   straightway did repair
Where Dankwart sat at table   with many a goodly squire.
Soon knight on knight was seeking   in fiercest way to vent his ire.

When there Sir Bloedel   strode unto the board,
Dankwart the marshal   thus spoke courteous word:
"Unto this hall right welcome   good Sir Bloedel be.
What business hast thou hither   is cause of wonder yet to me."

"No greeting here befits thee,"   spake Bloedel presently,
"For that this my coming   now thy end must be,
Through Hagen's fault, thy brother,   who Siegfried erstwhile slew
To the Huns thou mak'st atonement,   and many another warrior
        too."

"But nay, but nay, Sir Bloedel,"   Dankwart spake thereto,
"For so should we have reason   our coming here to rue.
A child I was and little   when Siegfried lost his life,
Nor know I why reproacheth   me the royal Etzel's wife."

"In sooth I may the story   never fully tell.
Gunther and Hagen was it   by whom the deed befell.
Now guard you well, ye strangers,   for doomed in sooth are ye,
Unto Lady Kriemhild   must your lives now forfeit be."

"An so thou wilt desist not,"   Dankwart declared,
"Regret I my entreaty,   my toil were better spared."

The nimble thane and valiant   up from the table sprung,
And drew a keen-edged weapon,   great in sooth that was and long.

Then smote he with it Bloedel   such a sudden blow
That his head full sudden   before his feet lay low.
"Be that thy wedding-dower,"   the doughty Dankwart spake,
"Along with bride of Nudung   whom thou would'st to thy bosom
        take.

"Tomorrow may she marry,   but some other one:
Will he have bridal portion,   e'en so to him be done."
A Hun that liked not treason   had given him to know
How that the queen upon him   thought to work so grievous woe.

When the men of Bloedel   saw thus their master slain,
To fall upon the strangers   would they longer not refrain.
With swords swung high above them   upon the squires they flew
In a grimmest humor.   Soon many must that rashness rue.

Full loudly cried then Dankwart   to all his company:
"Behold ye, noble squires,   the fate that ours must be.
Now quit yourselves with valor,   for evil is our pass,
Though fair to us the summons   hither from Lady Kriemhild was!"

They, too, reached down before them,   who no weapons bore,
And each a massive footstool   snatched from off the floor,
For the Burgundian squires   no whit were they dismayed;
And by the selfsame weapons   was many a dint in helmet made.

How fierce they fought to shield them   the strangers one and all!
E'en their arméd foemen   drove they from the hall.
Or smote dead within it   hundreds five or more;
All the valiant fighters   saw ye drenched with ruddy gore.

Ere long the wondrous tidings   some messenger did tell
Unto Etzel's chieftain   — fierce did their anger swell —
How that slain was Bloedel   and knights full many a one;
The which had Hagen's brother   with his lusty squires done.

The Huns, by anger driven,   ere Etzel was aware,
Two thousand men or over,   did quick themselves prepare.
They fell upon those squires   — e'en so it had to be —

And never any living   they left of all that company.

A mickle host they faithless   unto those quarters brought,
But lustily the strangers   'gainst their assailants fought.
What booted swiftest valor?   Soon must all lie dead.
A dire woe thereafter   on many a man was visited.

Now may ye hear a wondrous   tale of honor told:
Of squires full nine thousand   soon in death lay cold,
And eke good knights a dozen   there of Dankwart's band.
Forlorn ye saw him only   the last amid his foemen stand.

The din at last was ended   and lulled the battle-sound,
When the valiant Dankwart   did cast a glance around.
"Alack for my companions,"   cried he, "now from me reft.
Alack that I now only   forlorn amid my foes am left."

The swords upon his body   fell full thick and fast,
Which rashness many a warrior's   widow mourned at last.
His shield he higher lifted   and drew the strap more low:
Down coats of ring-made armor   made he the ebbing blood to flow.

"O woe is me!" spake Dankwart,   the son of Aldrian.
"Now back, ye Hunnish fighters,   let me the open gain,
That the air give cooling   to me storm-weary wight."
In splendid valor moving   strode forward then anew the knight.

As thus he battle-weary   through the hall's portal sprang,
What swords of new-come fighters   upon his helmet rang!
They who not yet had witnessed   what wonders wrought his hand,
Rashly rushed they forward   to thwart him of Burgundian land.

"Now would to God," quoth Dankwart,   "I found a messenger
Who to my brother Hagen   might the tidings bear,
That 'fore host of foemen   in such sad case am I!
From hence he'd surely help me,   or by my side he slain would lie."

Then Hunnish knights gave answer: "Thyself the messenger
Shalt be, when to thy brother   thee a corse we bear.
So shall that thane of Gunther   first true sorrow know.
Upon the royal Etzel   here hast thou wrought so grievous woe."

Quoth he: "Now leave such boasting   and yield me passage free,
Else shall mail-rings a many   with blood bespattered be.
Myself will tell the tidings   soon at Etzel's court,
And eke unto my masters   of this my travail make report."

Etzel's men around him   belabored he so sore
That they at sword-point   durst not withstand him more.
Spears shot into his shield he   so many there did stop
That he the weight unwieldy   must from out his hand let drop.

Then thought they to subdue him   thus of his shield bereft,
But lo! the mighty gashes   wherewith he helmets cleft!
Must there keen knights full many   before him stagger down,
High praise the valiant Dankwart   thereby for his valor won.

On right side and on left side   they still beset his way,
Yet many a one too rashly   did mingle in the fray.
Thus strode he 'mid the foemen   as doth in wood the boar
By yelping hounds beleaguered;   more stoutly fought he ne'er before.

As there he went, his pathway   with reeking blood was wet.
Yea, never any hero   more bravely battled yet
When by foes surrounded,   than he did might display.
To court did Hagen's brother   with splendid valor make his way.

When stewards and cup-bearers   heard how sword-blades rung,
Many a brimming goblet   from their hands they flung
And eke the viands ready   that they to table bore;
Thus many doughty foemen   withstood him where he sought the
        door.

"How now, ye stewards?"   cried the weary knight;
"'Twere better that ye tended   rather your guests aright,
Bearing to lords at table   choice food that fitteth well,
And suffered me these tidings   unto my masters dear to tell."

Whoe'er before him rashly   athwart the stairway sprung,
On him with blow so heavy   his mighty sword he swung,
That soon faint heart gave warning   before his path to yield.
Mickle wonder wrought he   where sword his doughty arm did wield.

Thirty-Third Adventure

How the Burgundians Fought with the Huns

Soon as the valiant Dankwart   stood beneath the door,
Bade he Etzel's followers   all make way before.
With blood from armor streaming   did there the hero stand;
A sharp and mighty weapon   bore he naked in his hand.

Into the hall then Dankwart   cried with voice full strong:
"At table, brother Hagen,   thou sittest all too long.
To thee and God in heaven   must I sore complain:
Knights and squires also   lie within their lodging slain."

Straight he cried in answer: "Who hath done such deed?"
"That hath done Sir Bloedel   and knights that he did lead.
Eke made he meet atonement,   that may'st thou understand:
His head from off his body   have I struck with mine own hand."

"'Tis little cause for sorrow,"   Hagen spake again,
"When they tell the story   of a valiant thane,
That he to death was smitten   by knight of high degree.
The less a cause for weeping   to winsome women shall it be.

"Now tell me, brother Dankwart,   how thou so red may'st be;
From thy wounds thou sufferest,   I ween, full grievously.
Lives he within this country   who serves thee in such way,
Him must the devil shelter,   or for the deed his life shall pay."

"Behold me here all scatheless.   My gear is wet with blood,
From wounds of others, natheless,   now hath flowed that flood,
Of whom this day so many   beneath my broadsword fell:

Must I make solemn witness,   ne'er knew I full the tale to tell."

He answered: "Brother Dankwart,   now take thy stand before,
And Huns let never any   make passage by the door.
I'll speak unto these warriors,   as needs must spoken be:
Dead lie all our followers,   slain by foulest treachery."

"Must I here be chamberlain,"   replied the warrior keen,
"Well know I such high monarchs   aright to serve, I ween.
So will I guard the stairway   as sorts with honor well."
Ne'er to the thanes of Kriemhild   so sorry case before befell.

"To me 'tis mickle wonder,"   Hagen spake again,
"What thing unto his neighbor   whispers each Hunnish thane.
I ween they'd forego the service   of him who keeps the door,
And who such high court tidings   to his friends of Burgundy bore.

"Long since of Lady Kriemhild   the story I did hear,
How unavenged her sorrow   she might no longer bear.
A memory-cup now quaff we   and pay for royal cheer!
The youthful lord of Hunland   shall make the first installment
     here."

Thereat the child Ortlieb   doughty Hagen slew,
That from the sword downward   the blood to hand-grip flew,
And into lap of Kriemhild   the severed head down rolled.
Then might ye see 'mid warriors   a slaughter great and grim unfold.

By both hands swiftly wielded,   his blade then cut the air
And smote upon the tutor   who had the child in care,
That down before the table   his head that instant lay:
It was a sorry payment   wherewith he did the tutor pay.

His eye 'fore Etzel's table   a minstrel espied:
To whom in hasty manner   did wrathful Hagen stride,
Where moved it on the fiddle   his right hand off smote he;
"Have that for thy message   unto the land of Burgundy."

"Alack my hand!" did Werbel   that same minstrel moan;
"What, Sir Hagen of Tronje,   have I to thee done?
I bore a faithful message   unto thy master's land.
How may I more make music   thus by thee bereft of hand?"

Little in sooth recked Hagen,   fiddled he nevermore.
Then in the hall all wrathful   wrought he havoc sore
Upon the thanes of Etzel   whereof he many slew;
Ere they might find exit,   to death then smote he not a few.

Volker the full valiant   up sprang from board also:
In his hand full clearly   rang out his fiddle-bow,
For mightily did fiddle   Gunther's minstrel thane.
What host of foes he made him   because of Hunnish warriors slain!

Eke sprang from the table   the lofty monarchs three,
Who glad had stilled the combat   ere greater scathe might be.
Yet all their art availed not   their anger to assuage,
When Volker and Hagen   so mightily began to rage.

When the lord of Rhineland   saw how his toil was vain,
Gaping wounds full many   himself did smite amain
Through rings of shining mail-coats   there upon the foe.
He was a valiant hero,   as he full gallantly did show.

Strode eke into the combat   Gernot a doughty thane;
By whom of Hunnish warriors   full many a one was slain
With a sword sharp-edgéd   he had of Ruediger;
Oft sent to dire ruin   by him the knights of Etzel were.

The youthful son of Ute   eke to the combat sprang,
And merrily his broadsword   upon the helmets rang
Of many a Hunnish warrior   there in Etzel's land;
Feasts of mickle wonder   wrought Giselher with dauntless hand.

How bold soe'er was any,   of kings and warrior band,
Saw ye yet the foremost   Giselher to stand
There against the foemen,   a knight of valor good;
Wounded deep full many   made he to fall in oozing blood.

Eke full well defend them   did Etzel's warriors too.
There might ye see the strangers   their gory way to hew
With swords all brightly gleaming   adown that royal hall;
Heard ye there on all sides   loudly ring the battle-call.

Join friends within beleaguered   would they without full fain,

Yet might they at the portal but little vantage gain.
Eke they within had gladly gained the outer air;
Nor up nor down did Dankwart suffer one to pass the stair.

There before the portal surged a mighty throng,
And with a mickle clangor on helm the broadsword rung.
Thus on the valiant Dankwart his foes did sorely press,
And soon his trusty brother was anxious grown o'er his distress.

Full loudly cried then Hagen unto Volker:
"Trusty fere, behold'st thou my brother standing there,
Where on him Hunnish warriors their mighty blows do rain?
Good friend, save thou my brother ere we do lose the valiant
   thane."

"That will I do full surely," thereat the minstrel spake.
Adown the hall he fiddling gan his way to make;
In his hand full often a trusty sword rang out,
While grateful knights of Rhineland acclaimed him with a mickle
   shout.

Soon did the valiant Volker Dankwart thus address:
"Hard this day upon thee hath weighed the battle's stress.
That I should come to help thee thy brother gave command;
Keep thou without the portal, I inward guarding here will stand."

Dankwart, thane right valiant, stood without the door
And guarded so the stairway that none might pass before.
There heard ye broadswords ringing, swung by warrior's hand,
While inward in like manner wrought Volker of Burgundian land.

There the valiant Fiddler above the press did call:
"Securely now, friend Hagen, closed is the hall.
Yea, so firmly bolted is King Etzel's door
By hands of two good warriors, as thousand bars were set before,"

When Hagen thus of Tronje the door did guarded find,
The warrior far renownéd swung his shield behind;
He first for harm receivéd revenge began to take,
Whereat all hope of living did soon his enemies forsake.

When of Bern Sir Dietrich rightly did perceive

How the doughty Hagen   did many a helmet cleave,
The king of Amelungen   upon a bench leaped up;
Quoth he: "Here poureth Hagen   for us exceeding bitter cup."

Great fear fell eke on Etzel,   as well might be the case,
(What trusty followers snatched they   to death before his face!)
For well nigh did his enemies   on him destruction bring.
There sat he all confounded.   What booted him to be a king?

Cried then aloud to Dietrich   Kriemhild, the high lady:
"Now help me, knight so noble,   that hence with life I flee,
By princely worth, I pray thee,   thou lord of Amelung's land;
If here do reach me Hagen,   straight find I death beneath his hand."

"How may my help avail thee,   noble queen and high?"
Answered her Sir Dietrich,   "Fear for myself have I.
Too sorely is enraged   each knight in Gunther's band,
To no one at this season   may I lend assisting hand."

"But nay, but nay, Sir Dietrich,   full noble knight and keen,
What maketh thy bright chivalry,   let it this day be seen,
And bring me hence to safety,   else am I death's sure prey."
Good cause was that on Kriemhild's   bosom fear so heavy lay.

"So will I here endeavor   to help thee as I may;
Yet shalt thou well believe me,   hath passed full many a day
Since saw I goodly warriors   of so bitter mood.
'Neath swords behold I flowing   through helmets plenteously the
    blood."

Lustily then cried he,   the warrior nobly born,
That his voice rang loudly   like blast from bison's horn,
That all around the palace   gave back the lusty sound;
Unto the might of Dietrich   never limit yet was found.

When did hear King Gunther   how called the doughty man
Above the storm of combat,   to hearken he began.
Quoth he: "The voice of Dietrich   hath fallen upon mine ear;
I ween some of his followers   before our thanes have fallen here.

"High on the board I see him;   he beckons with the hand.
Now my good friends and kinsmen   of Burgundian land,

Stay ye your hands from conflict,   let us hear and see
If done upon the chieftain   aught by my men of scathe there be."

When thus King Gunther   did beg and eke command,
With swords in stress of battle   stayed they all the hand.
'Twas token of his power   that straight the strife did pause.
Then him of Bern he questioned   what of his outcry were the cause.

He spake: "Full noble Dietrich,   what here on thee is wrought
By any of my warriors?   For truly is my thought
To make a full atonement   and amends to thee.
If here hath wronged thee any,   'twere cause of mickle grief to me."

Then answered him Sir Dietrich: "Myself do nothing grieve.
Grant me with thy protection   but this hall to leave
And quit the dire conflict,   with them that me obey.
Then surely will I ever   seek thy favor to repay."

"How plead'st thou thus so early?"   Wolfhart was heard;
"The Fiddler so securely   the door not yet hath barred,
But it so wide we'll open   to pass it through, I trow."
"Now hold thy peace," quoth Dietrich,   "wrought but little here
     hast thou."

Then spake the royal Gunther: "That grant I thee to do,
Forth from the hall lead many   or lead with thee few,
An if my foes it be not;   here stay they everyone.
Upon me here in Hunland   hath grievous wrong by them been
     done."

When heard he Gunther's answer   he took beneath his arm
The noble Queen Kriemhild,   who dreaded mickle harm.
On the other side too led he   Etzel with him away;
Eke went thence with Dietrich   six hundred knights in fair array.

Then outspake the margrave,   the noble Ruediger:
"If leave to any others   be granted forth to fare,
Of those who glad would serve you,   give us the same to see.
Yea, peace that's never broken   'twixt friends 'tis meet should ever
     be."

Thereto gave answer Giselher   of the land of Burgundy:

"Peace and unbroken friendship   wish we e'er with thee,
With thee and all thy kinsmen,   as true thou ever art.
We grant thee all untroubled   with thy friends from hence to part."

When thus Sir Ruediger   from the hall did pass,
A train of knights five hundred   or more with him there was,
Of them of Bechelaren,   kinsmen and warriors true,
Whose parting gave King Gunther   anon full mickle cause to rue.

When did a Hunnish warrior   Etzel's passing see
'Neath the arm of Dietrich,   to profit him thought he.
Smote him yet the Fiddler   such a mighty blow,
That 'fore the feet of Etzel   sheer on the floor his head fell low.

When the country's monarch   had gained the outer air,
Turned he looking backward   and gazed on Volker.
"Alack such guests to harbor!   Ah me discomfited!
That all the knights that serve me   shall before their might lie dead.

"Alack their coming hither!"   spake the king once more.
"Within, a warrior fighteth   like to wild forest boar;
Hight the same is Volker,   and a minstrel is also;
To pass the demon scatheless   I to fortune's favor owe.

"Evil sound his melodies,   his strokes of bow are red,
Yea, beneath his music   full many a knight lies dead.
I know not what against us   hath stirred that player's ire,
For guests ne'er had I any   whereby to suffer woe so dire."

None other would they suffer   to pass the door than those.
Then 'neath the hall's high roof tree   a mighty din arose.
For evil wrought upon them   those guests sore vengeance take.
Volker the doughty Fiddler,   what shining helmets there he brake!

Gunther, lofty monarch,   thither turned his ear.
"Hear'st thou the music, Hagen,   that yonder Volker
Doth fiddle for the Hun-men,   when near the door they go?
The stroke is red of color,   where he doth draw the fiddle-bow."

"Mickle doth it rue me,"   Hagen spake again,
"That in the hall far severed   I am from that bold thane.
I was his boon companion   and he sworn friend to me:

Come we hence ever scatheless,   trusty feres we yet shall be.

"Behold now, lofty sire,   the faith of Volker bold!
With will he seeks to win him   thy silver and thy gold.
With fiddle-bow he cleaveth   e'en the steel so hard,
Bright-gleaming crests of helmets   are scattered by his mighty sword.

"Never saw I fiddler   so dauntless heart display,
As the doughty Volker   here hath done this day.
Through shield and shining helmet   his melodies ring clear;
Give him to ride good charger   and eke full stately raiment wear."

Of all the Hunnish kindred   that in the hall had been,
None now of all their number   therein to fight was seen.
Hushed was the din of battle   and strife no more was made:
From out their hands aweary   their swords the dauntless warriors
        laid.

Thirty-Fourth Adventure

How They Cast Out the Dead

From toil of battle weary   rested the warriors all.
Volker and Hagen   passed out before the hall,
And on their shields did lean them,   those knights whom naught could daunt.
Then with full merry converse   gan the twain their foes to taunt.

Spake meanwhile of Burgundy   Giselher the thane:
"Not yet, good friends, may ye   think to rest again.
Forth from the hall the corses   shall ye rather bear.
Again we'll be assailéd,   that would I now in sooth declare.

"Beneath our feet no longer   here the dead must lie.
But ere in storm of battle   at hand of Huns to die,
We'll deal such wounds around us   as 'tis my joy to see.
Thereon," spake Giselher,   "my heart is fixed right steadfastly."

"I joy in such a master,"   Hagen spake again:
"Such counsel well befitteth   alone so valiant thane
As my youthful master   hath shown himself this day.
Therefor, O men of Burgundy,   everyone rejoice ye may."

Then followed they his counsel   and from the hall they bore
Seven thousand bodies   and cast them from the door.
Adown the mounting stairway   all together fell,
Whereat a sound of wailing   did from mourning kinsmen swell.

Many a man among them   so slight wound did bear
That he were yet recovered   had he but gentle care,

Who yet falling headlong   now surely must be dead.
Thereat did grieve their kinsmen   as verily was sorest need.

Then outspake the Fiddler,   Volker a hero bold:
"Now do I find how truly   hath to me been told
That cowards are the Hun-men   who do like women weep.
Rather should be their effort   their wounded kin alive to keep."

These words deemed a margrave   spoken in kindly mood.
He saw one of his kinsmen   weltering in his blood.
In his arms he clasped him   and thought him thence to bear,
But as he bent above him   pierced him the valiant minstrel's spear.

When that beheld the others   all in haste they fled,
Crying each one curses   on that same minstrel's head.
From the ground then snatched he   a spear with point full keen,
That 'gainst him up the stairway   by a Hun had hurléd been.

Across the court he flung it   with his arm of might
Far above the people.   Then did each Hunnish knight
Seek him safer quarters   more distant from the hall.
To see his mighty prowess   did fill with fear his foemen all.

As knights full many thousand   far 'fore the palace stood,
Volker and Hagen   gan speak in wanton mood
"Unto King Etzel,   nor did they aught withhold;
Wherefrom anon did sorrow   o'ertake those doughty warriors bold.

"'Twould well beseem," quoth Hagen,   "the people's lofty lord
Foremost in storm of battle   to swing the cutting sword,
As do my royal masters   each fair example show.
Where hew they through the helmets   their swords do make the
     blood to flow."

To hear such words brave Etzel   snatched in haste his shield.
"Now well beware of rashness,"   cried Lady Kriemhild,
"And offer to thy warriors   gold heaped on shield full high:
If yonder Hagen reach thee,   straightway shalt thou surely die."

So high was the king's mettle   that he would not give o'er,
Which case is now full seldom   seen in high princes more;
They must by shield-strap tugging   him perforce restrain.

Grim of mood then Hagen   began him to revile again.

"It was a distant kinship,"   spake Hagen, dauntless knight,
"That Etzel unto Siegfried   ever did unite,
And husband he to Kriemhild   was ere thee she knew.
Wherefore, O king faint-hearted,   seek'st thou such thing 'gainst me
      to do?"

Thereto eke must listen   the noble monarch's spouse,
And grievously to hear it   did Kriemhild's wrath arouse.
That he 'fore men of Etzel   durst herself upbraid;
To urge them 'gainst the strangers   she once more her arts essayed.

Cried she: "Of Tronje Hagen   whoso for me will slay,
And his head from body severed   here before me lay,
For him the shield of Etzel   I'll fill with ruddy gold,
Eke lands and lordly castles   I'll give him for his own to hold."

"I wot not why they tarry,"   — thus the minstrel cried;
"Ne'er saw I heroes any   so their courage hide,
When to them was offered,   like this, reward so high.
'Tis cause henceforth that Etzel   for aye to them goodwill deny."

"Who in such craven manner   do eat their master's bread,
And like caitiffs fail him   in time of greatest need,
Here see I standing many   of courage all forlorn,
Yet would be men of valor;   all time be they upheld to scorn."

Thirty-Fifth Adventure

How Iring Was Slain

Cried then he of Denmark,   Iring the margrave:
"Fixed on things of honor   my purpose long I have,
And oft in storm of battle,   where heroes wrought, was I.
Bring hither now my armor,   with Hagen I'll the combat try."

"I counsel thee against it,"   Hagen then replied,
"Or bring a goodly company   of Hun-men by thy side.
If peradventure any   find entrance to the hall,
I'll cause that nowise scatheless   down the steps again they fall."

"Such words may not dissuade me,"   Iring spake once more;
"A thing of equal peril   oft have I tried before.
Yea, will I with my broadsword   confront thee all alone.
Nor aught may here avail thee   thus to speak in haughty tone."

Soon the valiant Iring   armed and ready stood,
And Irnfried of Thuringia   a youth of mettle good,
And eke the doughty Hawart,   with thousand warriors tried.
Whate'er his purpose, Iring   should find them faithful by his side.

Advancing then with Iring   did the Fiddler see
All clad in shining armor   a mighty company,
And each a well-made helmet   securely fastened wore.
Thereat the gallant Volker   began to rail in anger sore.

"Seest thou, friend Hagen,   yonder Iring go,
Who all alone to front thee   with his sword did vow?
Doth lying sort with honor?   Scorned the thing must be.

A thousand knights or over   here bear him arméd company."

"Now make me not a liar,"   cried Hawart's man aloud,
"For firm is still my purpose   to do what now I vowed,
Nor will I turn me from it   through any cause of fear.
Alone I'll stand 'fore Hagen,   awful howsoe'er he were."

On ground did throw him Iring   before his warriors' feet,
That they leave might grant him   alone the knight to meet.
Loath they were to do it;   well known to them might be
The haughty Hagen's prowess   of the land of Burgundy.

Yet so long besought he   that granted was their leave;
When they that followed with him   did his firm mind perceive,
And how 'twas bent on honor,   they not restrained him.
Then closed the two chieftains   together in a combat grim.

Iring of Denmark   raised his spear on high,
And with the shield he covered   himself full skillfully;
He upward rushed on Hagen   unto the hall right close,
When round the clashing fighters   soon a mighty din arose.

Each hurled upon the other   the spear with arm of might,
That the firm shields were piercéd   e'en to their mail-coats bright,
And outward still projecting   the long spear-shafts were seen.
In haste then snatched their broadswords   both the fighters grim
        and keen.

In might the doughty Hagen   and prowess did abound,
As Iring smote upon him   the hall gave back the sound.
The palace all and towers   re-echoed from their blows,
Yet might that bold assailant   with victory ne'er the combat close.

On Hagen might not Iring   wreak aught of injury.
Unto the doughty Fiddler   in haste then turnéd he.
Him by his mighty sword-strokes   thought he to subdue,
But well the thane full gallant   to keep him safe in combat knew.

Then smote the doughty Fiddler   so lustily his shield
That from it flew its ornaments   where he the sword did wield.
Iring must leave unconquered   there the dauntless man;
Next upon King Gunther   of Burgundy in wrath he ran.

There did each in combat   show him man of might;
Howe'er did Gunther and Iring   yet each the other smite,
From wounds might never either   make the blood to flow,
So sheltered each his armor,   well wrought that was and strong enow.

Gunther left he standing,   upon Gernot to dash,
And when he smote ring-armor   the fire forth did flash.
But soon had he of Burgundy,   Gernot the doughty thane,
Well nigh his keen assailant   Iring of Denmark slain.

Yet from the prince he freed him,   for nimble was he too.
Four of the men of Burgundy   the knight full sudden slew
Of those that followed with them   from Worms across the Rhine.
Thereupon might nothing   the wrath of Giselher confine.

"God wot well, Sir Iring,"   young Giselher then cried,
"Now must thou make requital   for them that here have died
'Neath thy hand so sudden."   He rushed upon him so
And smote the knight of Denmark   that he might not withstand the blow.

Into the blood down fell he   staggering 'neath its might,
That all who there beheld it   might deem the noble knight
Sword again would never   wield amid the fray.
Yet 'neath the stroke of Giselher   Iring all unwounded lay.

Bedazed by helmet's sounding   where ringing sword swung down,
Full suddenly his senses   so from the knight were flown:
That of his life no longer   harbored he a thought.
That the doughty Giselher   by his mighty arm had wrought.

When somewhat was subsided   the din within his head
From mighty blow so sudden   on him was visited,
Thought he: "I still am living   and bear no mortal wound.
How great the might of Giselher,   till now unwitting, have I found."

He hearkened how on all sides   his foes around did stand;
Knew they what he did purpose,   they had not stayed their hand.
He heard the voice of Giselher   eke in that company,
As cunning he bethought him   how yet he from his foes might flee.

Up from the blood he started   with fierce and sudden bound;
By grace alone of swiftness   he his freedom found.
With speed he passed the portal   where Hagen yet did stand,
And swift his sword he flourished   and smote him with his doughty
      hand.

To see such sight quoth Hagen: "To death thou fall'st a prey;
If not the Devil shield thee,   now is thy latest day."
Yet Iring wounded Hagen   e'en through his helmet's crown.
That did the knight with Waske,   a sword that was of far renown.

When thus Sir Hagen   the smart of wound did feel,
Wrathfully he brandished   on high his blade of steel.
Full soon must yield before him   Hawart's daring man,
Adown the steps pursuing   Hagen swiftly after ran.

O'er his head bold Iring   his shield to guard him swung,
And e'en had that same stairway   been full three times as long,
Yet had he found no respite   from warding Hagen's blows.
How plenteously the ruddy   sparks above his helm arose!

Unscathed at last came Iring   where waited him his own.
Soon as was the story   unto Kriemhild known,
How that in fight on Hagen   he had wrought injury,
Therefor the Lady Kriemhild   him gan to thank full graciously.

"Now God requite thee, Iring,   thou valiant knight and good,
For thou my heart hast comforted   and merry made my mood.
Red with blood his armor,   see I yonder Hagen stand."
For joy herself did Kriemhild   take his shield from out his hand.

"Small cause hast thou to thank him,"   thus wrathful Hagen spake;
"For gallant knight 'twere fitting   trial once more to make.
If then returned he scatheless,   a valiant man he were.
The wound doth boot thee little   that now from his hand I bear.

"That here from wound upon me   my mail-coat see'st thou red,
Shall bring woeful reprisal   on many a warrior's head.
Now is my wrath arouséd   in full 'gainst Hawart's thane.
As yet in sooth hath Iring   wrought on me but little bane."

Iring then of Denmark   stood where fanned the wind.

He cooled him in his armor   and did his helm unbind.
Then praised him all the people   and spoke him man of might,
Whereat the margrave's bosom   swelled full high with proud delight.

"Now hearken friends unto me,"   Iring once more spake;
"Make me straightway ready,   new trial now to make
If I this knight so haughty   may yet perchance subdue."
New shield they brought, for Hagen   did his erstwhile asunder hew.

Soon stood again the warrior   in armor all bedight.
In hand a spear full massy   took the wrathful knight,
Wherewith on yonder Hagen   he thought to vent his hate.
With grim and fearful visage   on him the vengeful thane did wait.

Yet not abide his coming   might Hagen longer now.
Adown he rushed upon him   with many a thrust and blow,
Down where the stairway ended   for fierce did burn his ire.
Soon the might of Iring   must 'neath his furious onset tire,

Their shields they smote asunder   that the sparks began
To fly in ruddy showers.   Hawart's gallant man
Was by sword of Hagen   wounded all so sore
Through shield and shining cuirass,   that whole he found him
      never more.

When how great the wound was   Iring fully knew,
Better to guard his helm-band   his shield he higher drew.
The scathe he first receivéd   he deemed sufficient quite,
Yet injury far greater   soon had he from King Gunther's knight.

From where it lay before him   Hagen a spear did lift
And hurled it upon Iring   with aim so sure and swift,
It pierced his head, and firmly   fixed the shaft did stand;
Full grim the end that met him   'neath the doughty Hagen's hand.

Backward Iring yielded   unto his Danish men.
Ere for the knight his helmet   they undid again,
From his head they drew the spear-point;   to death he was anigh.
Wept thereat his kinsmen,   and sore need had verily.

Came thereto Queen Kriemhild   and o'er the warrior bent,
And for the doughty Iring   gan she there lament.

She wept to see him wounded,   and sorely grieved the queen.
Then spake unto his kinsmen   the warrior full brave and keen.

"I pray thee leave thy moaning,   royal high lady.
What avails thy weeping?   Yea, soon must ended be
My life from wounds outflowing   that here I did receive.
To serve thyself and Etzel   will death not longer grant me leave."

Eke spake he to them of Thuringia   and to them of Danish land:
"Of you shall never any   receive the gift in hand
From your royal mistress   of shining gold full red.
Whoe'er withstandeth Hagen   death calleth down upon his head."

From cheek the color faded,   death's sure token wore
Iring the gallant warrior: thereat they grieved full sore.
Nor more in life might tarry   Hawart's valiant knight:
Enraged the men of Denmark   again did arm them for the fight.

Irnfried and Hawart   before the hall then sprang
Leading thousand warriors.   Full furious a clang
Of weapons then on all sides   loud and great ye hear.
Against the men of Burgundy   how hurled they many a mighty
        spear!

Straight the valiant Irnfried   the minstrel rushed upon,
But naught but grievous injury   'neath his hand he won:
For the noble Fiddler   did the landgrave smite
E'en through the well-wrought helmet;   yea, grim and savage was the
        knight.

Sir Irnfried then in answer   the valiant minstrel smote,
That must fly asunder   the rings of his mailed coat
Which showered o'er his cuirass   like sparks of fire red.
Soon must yet the landgrave   fall before the Fiddler dead.

Eke were come together   Hawart and Hagen bold,
And saw he deeds of wonder   who did the sight behold.
Swift flew the sword and fiercely   swung by each hero's hand.
But soon lay Hawart prostrate   before him of Burgundian land.

When Danish men and Thuringians   beheld their masters fall,
Fearful was the turmoil   that rose before the hall

As to the door they struggled,   on dire vengeance bent.
Full many a shield and helmet   was there 'neath sword asunder rent.

"Now backward yield," cried Volker   "and let them pass within;
Thus only are they thwarted   of what they think to win.
When but they pass the portals   are they full quickly slain.
With death shall they the bounty   of their royal mistress gain."

When thus with pride o'erweening   they did entrance find,
The head of many a warrior   was so to earth inclined,
That he must life surrender   'neath blows that thickly fell.
Well bore him valiant Gernot   and eke Sir Giselher as well.

Four knights beyond a thousand   were come into the house;
The light from sword-blades glinted,   swift swung with mighty souse.
Not one of all their number   soon might ye living see;
Tell might ye mickle wonders   of the men of Burgundy.

Thereafter came a stillness,   and ceased the tumult loud.
The blood in every quarter   through the leak-holes flowed,
And out along the corbels   from men in death laid low.
That had the men of Rhineland   wrought with many a doughty
     blow.

Then sat again to rest them   they of Burgundian land,
Shield and mighty broadsword   they laid from out the hand.
But yet the valiant Fiddler   stood waiting 'fore the door,
If peradventure any   would seek to offer combat more.

Sorely did King Etzel   and eke his spouse lament,
Maidens and fair ladies   did sorrow sore torment.
Death long since upon them,   I ween, such ending swore.
To fall before the strangers   was doomed full many a warrior more.

Thirty-Sixth Adventure
How the Queen Bade Set Fire to the Hall

"Now lay ye off the helmets,"   the words from Hagen fell:
"I with a boon companion   will be your sentinel.
And seek the men of Etzel   to work us further harm,
For my royal masters   full quickly will I cry alarm."

Then freed his head of armor   many a warrior good.
They sate them on the corses,   that round them in the blood
Of wounds themselves had dealt them,   prostrate weltering lay.
Now to his guests so lofty   scant courtesy did Etzel pay.

Ere yet was come the even,   King Etzel did persuade,
And eke the Lady Kriemhild,   that once more essayed
The Hunnish knights to storm them.   Before them might ye see
Good twenty thousand warriors,   who soon for fight must ready be.

Then with a furious onset   the strangers they attacked.
Dankwart, Hagen's brother,   who naught of courage lacked,
Sprang out 'mid the besiegers   to ward them from the door.
'Twas deemed a deadly peril,   yet scatheless stood he there before.

Fierce the struggle lasted   till darkness brought an end.
Themselves like goodly heroes   the strangers did defend
Against the men of Etzel   all the long summer day.
What host of valiant warriors   before them fell to death a prey!

At turn of sun in summer   that havoc sore was wrought,
When the Lady Kriemhild   revenge so dire sought
Upon her nearest kinsmen   and many a knight beside,

Wherefore with royal Etzel   never more might joy abide.

As day at last was ending   sad they were of heart.
They deemed from life 'twere better   in sudden death to part
Than be thus long tormented   by great o'erhanging dread.
That respite now be granted,   the knights so proud and gallant
          prayed.

They prayed to lead the monarch   hither to them there.
As heroes blood-bespotted,   and stained from battle-gear,
Forth from the hall emergéd   the lofty monarchs three.
They wist not to whom complainéd   might their full grievous
          sorrows be.

Etzel and Kriemhild   they soon before them found,
And great was now their company   from all their lands around.
Spake Etzel to the strangers: "What will ye now of me?
Ye hope for end of conflict,   but hardly may such favor be.

"This so mighty ruin   that ye on me have wrought,
If death thwart not my purpose,   shall profit you in naught.
For child that here ye slew me   and kinsmen dear to me,
Shall peace and reconcilement   from you withheld forever be."

Thereto gave answer Gunther: "To that drove sorest need.
Lay all my train of squires   before thy warriors dead
Where they for night assembled.   How bore I so great blame?
Of friendly mind I deemed thee,   as trusting in thy faith I came."

Then spake eke of Burgundy   the youthful Giselher:
"Ye knights that still are living   of Etzel, now declare
Whereof ye may reproach me!   How hath you harmed my hand?
For in right friendly manner   came I riding to this land."

Cried they: "Well is thy friendship   in burgh and country known
By sorrow of thy making.   Gladly had we foregone
The pleasure of thy coming   from Worms across the Rhine.
Our country hast thou orphaned,   thou and brother eke of thine."

In angry mood King Gunther   unto them replied:
"An ye this mighty hatred   appeased would lay aside,
Borne 'gainst us knights here homeless,   to both a gain it were

For Etzel's wrath against us   we in sooth no guilt do bear."

The host then to the strangers: "Your sorrow here and mine
Are things all unequal.   For now must I repine
With honor all bespotted   and 'neath distress of woe.
Of you shall never any   hence from my country living go."

Then did the doughty Gernot   unto King Etzel say:
"God then in mercy move thee   to act in friendly way.
Slay us knights here homeless,   yet grant us down to go
To meet thee in the open: thine honor biddeth thus to do.

"Whate'er shall be our portion,   let that straightway appear.
Men hast thou yet so many   that, should they banish fear,
Not one of us storm-weary   might keep his life secure.
How long shall we here friendless   this woeful travail yet endure?"

By the warriors of Etzel   their wish nigh granted was,
And leave well nigh was given   that from the hall they pass.
When Kriemhild knew their purpose,   high her anger swelled,
And straightway such a respite   was from the stranger knights
        withheld.

"But nay, ye Hunnish warriors!   what ye have mind to do,
Therefrom now desist ye,   — such is my counsel true;
Nor let foes so vengeful   pass without the hall,
Else must in death before them   full many of your kinsmen fall.

"If of them lived none other   but Ute's sons alone,
My three noble brothers,   and they the air had won
Where breeze might cool their armor,   to death ye were a prey.
In all this world were never   born more valiant thanes than they."

Then spake the youthful Giselher: "Full beauteous sister mine,
When to this land thou bad'st me   from far beside the Rhine,
I little deemed such trouble   did here upon me weait.
Whereby have I deservéd   from the Huns such mortal hate?

"To thee I ever faithful   was, nor wronged thee e'er.
In such faith confiding   did I hither fare,
That thou to me wert gracious,   O noble sister mine.
Show mercy now unto us,   we must to thee our lives resign."

"No mercy may I show you,   — unmerciful I'll be.
By Hagen, knight of Tronje,   was wrought such woe to me,
That ne'er is reconcilement   the while that I have life.
That must ye all atone for,"   — quoth the royal Etzel's wife.

"Will ye but Hagen only   to me as hostage give,
Then will I not deny you   to let you longer live.
Born are ye of one mother   and brothers unto me,
So wish I that compounded   here with these warriors peace may be."

"God in heaven forfend it,"   Gernot straightway said;
"E'en though we were a thousand,   lay we all rather dead,
We who are thy kinsmen,   ere that warrior one
Here we gave for hostage.   Never may such thing be done."

"Die must we all," quoth Giselher,   "for such is mortal's end.
Till then despite of any,   our knighthood we'll defend.
Would any test our mettle,   here may he trial make.
For ne'er, when help he needed,   did I a faithful friend forsake."

Then spake the valiant Dankwart,   a knight that knew no fear;
"In sooth stands not unaided   my brother Hagen here.
Who here have peace denied us   may yet have cause to rue.
I would that this ye doubt not,   for verily I tell you true."

The queen to those around her: "Ye gallant warriors, go
Now nigher to the stairway   and straight avenge my woe.
I'll ever make requital   therefor, as well I may.
For his haughty humor   will I Hagen full repay.

"To pass without the portal   let not one at all,
For at its four corners   I'll bid ignite the hall.
So will I fullest vengeance   take for all my woe."
Straightway the thanes of Etzel   ready stood her hest to do.

Who still without were standing   were driven soon within
By sword and spear upon them,   that made a mighty din.
Yet naught might those good warriors   from their masters take,
By their faith would never   each the other's side forsake.

To burn the hall commanded   Etzel's wife in ire,

And tortured they those warriors   there with flaming fire;
Full soon with wind upon it   the house in flames was seen.
To any folk did never   sadder plight befall, I ween.

Their cries within resounded: "Alack for sorest need!
How mickle rather lay we   in storm of battle dead.
'Fore God 'tis cause for pity,   for here we all must die!
Now doth the queen upon us   vengeance wreak full grievously."

Among them spake another: "Our lives we here must end.
What now avails the greeting   the king to us did send?
So sore this heat oppresseth   and parched with thirst my tongue,
My life from very anguish   I ween I must resign ere long."

Then quoth of Tronje Hagen: "Ye noble knights and good,
Whoe'er by thirst is troubled,   here let him drink the blood.
Than wine more potent is it   where such high heat doth rage,
Nor may we at this season   find us a better beverage."

Where fallen knight was lying,   thither a warrior went.
Aside he laid his helmet,   to gaping wound he bent,
And soon was seen a-quaffing   therefrom the flowing blood.
To him though all unwonted,   yet seemed he there such drinking
        good.

"Now God reward thee, Hagen,"   the weary warrior said,
"That I so well have drunken,   thus by thy teaching led.
Better wine full seldom   hath been poured for me,
And live I yet a season   I'll ever faithful prove to thee."

When there did hear the others   how to him it seeméd good,
Many more beheld ye   eke that drank the blood.
Each thereby new vigor   for his body won,
And eke for lover fallen   wept many a buxom dame anon.

The flaming brands fell thickly   upon them in the hall,
With upraised shields they kept them   yet scatheless from their fall,
Though smoke and heat together   wrought them anguish sore.
Beset were heroes never,   I ween, by so great woe before.

Then spake of Tronje Hagen: "Stand nigh unto the wall,
Let not the brands all flaming   upon your helmets fall.

Into the blood beneath you   tread them with your feet.
In sooth in evil fashion   us doth our royal hostess greet."

In trials thus enduréd   ebbed the night away.
Still without the portal   did the keen Fiddler stay
And Hagen his good fellow,   o'er shield their bodies leant;
They deemed the men of Etzel   still on further mischief bent.

Then was heard the Fiddler: "Pass we into the hall,
For so the Huns shall fondly   deem we are perished all
Amid the mickle torture   we suffer at their hand.
Natheless shall they behold us   boun for fight before them stand."

Spake then of Burgundy   the young Sir Giselher:
"I ween 'twill soon be dawning,   for blows a cooler air.
To live in fuller joyance   now grant us God in heaven.
To us dire entertainment   my sister Kriemhild here hath given."

Spake again another: "Lo! how I feel the day.
For that no better fortune   here await us may,
So don, ye knights, your armor,   and guard ye well your life.
Full soon, in sooth, we suffer   again at hands of Etzel's wife."

Fondly Etzel fancied   the strangers all were dead,
From sore stress of battle   and from the fire dread;
Yet within were living   six hundred men so brave,
That never thanes more worthy   a monarch for liegemen might
      have.

The watchers set to watch them   soon full well had seen
How still lived the strangers,   spite what wrought had been
Of harm and grievous evil,   on the monarchs and their band.
Within the hall they saw them   still unscathed and dauntless stand.

Told 'twas then to Kriemhild   how they from harm were free.
Whereat the royal lady   quoth, such thing ne'er might be
That any still were living   from that fire dread.
"Nay, believe I rather   that within they all lie dead."

Gladly yet the strangers   would a truce compound,
Might any grace to offer   amid their foes be found.
But such appeared not any   in them of Hunnish land.

Well to avenge their dying   prepared they then with willing hand.

About the dawn of morning   greeted they were again
With a vicious onslaught,   that paid full many a thane.
There was flung upon them   many a mighty spear,
While gallantly did guard them   the lofty thanes that knew not fear.

The warriors of Etzel   were all of eager mood,
And Kriemhild's promised bounty   win for himself each would;
To do the king's high bidding   did likewise urge their mind.
'Twas cause full soon that many   were doomed swift death in fight
    to find.

Of store of bounty promised   might wonders great be told,
She bade on shields to carry   forth the ruddy gold,
And gave to him that wished it   or would but take her store;
In sooth a greater hire   ne'er tempted 'gainst the foe before.

A mickle host of warriors   went forth in battle-gear.
Then quoth the valiant Volker: "Still may ye find us here.
Ne'er saw I move to battle   warriors more fain,
That to work us evil   the bounty of the king have ta'en."

Then cried among them many: "Hither, ye knights, more nigh!
Since all at last must perish,   'twere better instantly;
And here no warrior falleth   but who fore-doomed hath been."
With well-flung spears all bristling   full quickly then their shields
    were seen.

What need of further story?   Twelve hundred stalwart men,
Repulsed in onset gory,   still returned again;
But dealing wounds around them   the strangers cooled their mood,
And there stood all unvanquished.   Flowing might ye see the blood

From deep wounds and mortal,   whereof were many slain.
For friends in battle fallen   heard ye loud complain;
Slain were all those warriors   that served the mighty king,
Whereat from loving kinsmen   arose a mickle sorrowing.

Thirty-Seventh Adventure

How the Margrave Ruediger Was Slain

At morning light the strangers   had wrought high deed of fame,
When the spouse of Gotelinde   unto the courtyard came.
To behold on both sides   such woe befallen there,
Might not refrain from weeping   sorely the faithful Ruediger.

"O woe is me!" exclaimed he,   "that ever I was born.
Alack that this great sorrow   no hand from us may turn!
Though I be ne'er so willing,   the king no peace will know,
For he beholds his sorrow   ever great and greater grow."

Then did the kindly Ruediger   unto Dietrich send,
If to the lofty monarchs   they yet might truce extend.
The knight of Bern gave message: "How might such thing be?
For ne'er the royal Etzel   granteth to end it peacefully."

When a Hunnish warrior   saw standing Ruediger
As from eyes sore weeping   fell full many a tear,
To his royal mistress spake he: "Behold how stands he there
With whom here by Etzel   none other may in might compare,

"And who commandeth service   of lands and people all.
How many lordly castles   Ruediger his own doth call,
That unto him hath given   the bounty of the king!
Not yet in valorous conflict   saw'st thou here his sword to swing.

"Methinks, but little recks he,   what may here betide,
Since now in fullest measure   his heart is satisfied.
'Tis told he is, surpassing   all men, forsooth, so keen,

But in this time of trials   his valor ill-displayed hath been."

Stood there full of sorrow   the brave and faithful man,
Yet whom he thus heard speaking   he cast his eyes upon.
Thought he: "Thou mak'st atonement,   who deem'st my mettle cold.
Thy thought here all too loudly   hast thou unto the people told."

His fist thereat he doubled   and upon him ran,
And smote with blow so mighty   there King Etzel's man
That prone before him straightway   fell that mocker dead.
So came but greater sorrow   on the royal Etzel's head.

"Hence thou basest caitiff,"   cried then Ruediger;
"Here of pain and sorrow   enough I have to bear.
Wherefore wilt thou taunt me   that I the combat shun?
In sooth had I the utmost   of harm upon the strangers done,

"For that good reason have I   to bear them hate indeed,
But that myself the warriors   as friends did hither lead.
Yea, was I their safe escort   into my master's land;
So may I, man most wretched,   ne'er raise against them hostile
      hand."

Then spake the lofty Etzel   unto the margrave:
"What aid, O noble Ruediger,   here at thy hands we have!
Our country hath so many   already doomed to die,
We need not any other: now hast thou wrought full wrongfully."

Returned the knight so noble: "My heart he sore hath grieved,
And reproached me for high honors   at thy hand received
And eke for gifts unto me   by thee so freely made;
Dearly for his slander   hath the base traducer paid."

When had the queen come hither   and had likewise seen
How on the Hunnish warrior   his wrath had vented been,
Incontinent she mourned it,   and tears bedimmed her sight.
Spake she unto Ruediger: "How dost thou now our love requite,

"That for me and thy master   thou bring'st increase of woe?
Now hast thou, noble Ruediger,   ever told us so,
How that thou life and honor   for our sake wouldst dare.

Eke heard I thanes full many   proclaim thee knight beyond
    compare.

"Of the oath I now remind thee   that thou to me didst swear,
When counsel first thou gavest   to Etzel's land to fare,
That thou wouldst truly serve me   till one of us were dead:
Of that I wretched woman   never stood so sore in need."

"Nor do I, royal mistress,   deny that so I sware
That I for thy well-being   would life and honor dare:
But eke my soul to forfeit,   — that sware I not indeed.
'Tis I thy royal brothers   hither to this land did lead."

Quoth she: "Bethink thee, Ruediger,   of thy fidelity
And oath once firmly plighted   that aught of harm to me
Should ever be avengéd,   and righted every ill."
Replied thereto the margrave: "Ne'er have I failed to work thy will."

Etzel the mighty monarch   to implore him then began,
And king and queen together   down knelt before their man,
Whereat the good margrave   was seen in sorest plight,
And gan to mourn his station   in piteous words the faithful knight.

"O woe is me most wretched,"   he sorrow-stricken cried,
"That forced I am my honor   thus to set aside,
And bonds of faith and friendship   God hath imposed on me.
O Thou that rul'st in heaven!   come death, I cannot yet be free.

"Whate'er it be my effort   to do or leave undone,
I break both faith and honor   in doing either one;
But leave I both, all people   will cry me worthy scorn.
May He look down in mercy   who bade me wretched man be born!"

With many a prayer besought him   the king and eke his spouse,
Wherefore was many a warrior   soon doomed his life to lose
At hand of noble Ruediger,   when eke did die the thane.
Now hear ye how he bore him,   though filled his heart with sorest
    pain.

He knew how scathe did wait him   and boundless sorrowing,
And gladly had refuséd   to obey the king
And eke his royal mistress.   Full sorely did he fear,

That if one stranger slew he,   the scorn of all the world he'd bear.

Then spake unto the monarch   the full gallant thane:
"O royal sire, whatever   thou gavest, take again,
The land and every castle,   that naught remain to me.
On foot a lonely pilgrim   I'll wander to a far country."

Thereto replied King Etzel: "Who then gave help to me?
My land and lordly castles   give I all to thee,
If on my foes, O Ruediger,   revenge thou wilt provide.
A mighty monarch seated,   shalt thou be by Etzel's side."

Again gave answer Ruediger: "How may that ever be?
At my own home shared they   my hospitality.
Meat and drink I offered   to them in friendly way,
And gave them of my bounty: how shall I seek them here to slay ?

"The folk belike will fancy   that I a coward be.
Ne'er hath faithful service   been refused by me
Unto the noble princes   and their warriors too;
That e'er I gained their friendship,   now 'tis cause for me to rue.

"For spouse unto Sir Giselher   gave I a daughter mine,
Nor into fairer keeping   might I her resign,
Where truth were sought and honor   and gentle courtesy:
Ne'er saw I thane so youthful   virtuous in mind as he."

Again gave answer Kriemhild: "O noble Ruediger,
To me and royal Etzel   in mercy now give ear
For sorrows that o'erwhelm us.   Bethink thee, I implore,
That monarch never any   harbored so evil guests before."

Spake in turn the margrave   unto the monarch's wife:
"Ruediger requital   must make today with life
For that thou and my master   did me so true befriend.
Therefore must I perish;   now must my service find an end.

"E'en this day, well know I,   my castles and my land
Must surely lose their master   beneath a stranger's hand.
To thee my wife and children   commend I for thy care,
And with all the lorn ones   that wait by Bechelaren's towers fair."

"Now God reward thee, Ruediger,"   thereat King Etzel quoth.
He and the queen together,   right joyful were they both.
"To us shall all thy people   full commended be;
Eke trow I by my fortune   no harm shall here befall to thee."

For their sake he ventured   soul and life to lose.
Thereat fell sore to weeping   the royal Etzel's spouse.
He spake: "I must unto you   my plighted word fulfill.
Alack! beloved strangers,   whom to assail forbids my will."

From the king there parting   ye saw him, sad of mood,
And passed unto his warriors   who at small distance stood.
"Don straightway now your armor,   my warriors all," quoth he.
"Alas! must I to battle   with the valiant knights of Burgundy."

Then straightway for their armor   did the warriors call.
A shining helm for this one,   for that a shield full tall
Soon did the nimble squires   before them ready hold.
Anon came saddest tidings   unto the stranger warriors bold.

With Ruediger there saw ye   five hundred men arrayed,
And noble thanes a dozen   that came unto his aid,
Thinking in storm of battle   to win them honor high.
In sooth but little knew they   how death awaited them so nigh.

With helm on head advancing   saw ye Sir Ruediger.
Swords that cut full keenly   the margrave's men did bear,
And eke in hand each carried   a broad shield shining bright.
Boundless was the Fiddler's   sorrow to behold the sight.

When saw the youthful Giselher   his bride's sire go
Thus with fastened helmet,   how might he ever know
What he therewith did purpose   if 'twere not only good?
Thereat the noble monarchs   right joyous might ye see of mood.

"I joy for friends so faithful,"   spake Giselher the thane,
"As on our journey hither   we for ourselves did gain.
Full great shall be our vantage   that I found spouse so dear,
And high my heart rejoiceth   that plighted thus to wed we were."

"Small cause I see for comfort,"   thereto the minstrel spake.
"When saw ye thanes so many   come a truce to make

With helmet firmly fastened   and bearing sword in hand?
By scathe to us will Ruediger   service do for tower and land."

The while that thus the Fiddler   had spoken to the end,
His way the noble Ruediger   unto the hall did wend.
His trusty shield he rested   on the ground before his feet,
Yet might he never offer   his friends in kindly way to greet.

Loudly the noble margrave   cried into the hall:
"Now guard you well, ye valiant   Nibelungen all.
From me ye should have profit: now have ye harm from me.
But late we plighted friendship: broken now these vows must be."

Then quailed to hear such tidings   those knights in sore distress,
For none there was among them   but did joy the less
That he would battle with them   for whom great love they bore.
At hand of foes already   had they suffered travail sore.

"Now God in heaven forfend it,"   there King Gunther cried,
"That from mercy to us   thou so wilt turn aside,
And the faithful friendship   whereof hope had we.
I trow in sooth that never   may such thing be done by thee."

"Desist therefrom I may not,"   the keen knight made reply,
"But now must battle with you,   for vow thereto gave I.
"Now guard you, gallant warriors,   as fear ye life to lose:
From plighted vow release me   will nevermore King Etzel's spouse."

"Too late thou turnst against us,"   spake King Gunther there.
"Now might God requite thee,   O noble Ruediger,
For the faith and friendship   thou didst on us bestow,
If thou a heart more kindly   even to the end wouldst show.

"We'd ever make requital   for all that thou didst give, —
I and all my kinsmen,   wouldst thou but let us live, —
For thy gifts full stately,   as faithfully thou here
To Etzel's land didst lead us: know that, O noble Ruediger."

"To me what pleasure were it,"   Ruediger did say,
"With full hand of my treasure   unto you to weigh
And with a mind right willing   as was my hope to do!
Thus might no man reproach me   with lack of courtesy to you."

"Turn yet, O noble Ruediger."   Gernot spake again,
"For in so gracious manner   did never entertain
Any host the stranger,   as we were served by thee;
And live we yet a little,   shall thou well requited be."

"O would to God, full noble   Gernot," spake Ruediger,
"That ye were at Rhine river   and that dead I were
With somewhat saved of honor,   since I must be your foe!
Upon good knights was never   wrought by friends more bitter woe."

"Now God requite thee, Ruediger,"   Gernot gave reply,
"For gifts so fair bestowéd.   I rue to see thee die,
For that in thee shall perish   knight of so gentle mind.
Here thy sword I carry,   that gav'st thou me in friendship kind.

"It never yet hath failed me   in this our sorest need,
And 'neath its cutting edges   many a knight lies dead.
'Tis strong and bright of luster,   cunning wrought and well.
I ween, whate'er was given   by knight it doth in worth excel.

"An wilt thou not give over   upon us here to fall,
And if one friend thou slayest   here yet within this hall,
With this same sword thou gavest,   I'll take from thee thy life.
I sorrow for thee Ruediger,   and eke thy fair and stately wife."

"Would God but give, Sir Gernot,   that such thing might be,
That thou thy will completely   here fulfilled mightst see,
And of thy friends not any   here his life should lose!
Yea, shalt thou live to comfort   both my daughter and my spouse."

Then out spake of Burgundy   the son of Ute fair:
"How dost thou so, Sir Ruediger?   All that with me are
To thee are well disposéd.   Thou dost an evil thing,
And wilt thine own fair daughter   to widowhood too early bring.

"If thou with arméd warriors   wilt thus assail me here,
In what unfriendly manner   thou makest to appear
How that in thee I trusted   beyond all men beside,
When thy fairest daughter   erstwhile I won to be my bride."

"Thy good faith remember,   O Prince of virtue rare,

If God from hence do bring thee,"   — so spake Ruediger:
"Forsake thou not the maiden   when bereft of me,
But rather grant thy goodness   be dealt to her more graciously."

"That would I do full fairly,"   spake Giselher again.
"But if my lofty kinsmen,   who yet do here remain,
Beneath thy hand shall perish,   severed then must be
The friendship true I cherish   eke for thy daughter and for thee."

"Then God to us give mercy,"   the knight full valiant spake.
Their shields in hand then took they,   as who perforce would make
Their passage to the strangers   into Kriemhild's hall.
Adown the stair full loudly   did Hagen, knight of Tronje, call:

"Tarry yet a little,   O noble Ruediger,
For further would we parley,"   — thus might ye Hagen hear —
"I and my royal masters,   as presseth sorest need.
What might it boot to Etzel   that we strangers all lay dead.

"Great is here my trouble,"   Hagen did declare:
"The shield that Lady Gotelinde   gave to me to bear
Hath now been hewn asunder   by Hun-men in my hand.
With friendly thought I bore it   hither into Etzel's land.

"Would that God in heaven   might grant in kindliness,
That I a shield so trusty   did for my own possess
As in thy hand thou bearest,   O noble Ruediger!
In battle-storm then need I   never hauberk more to wear."

"Full glad I'd prove my friendship   to thee with mine own shield,
Dared I the same to offer   before Lady Kriemhild.
But take it, natheless, Hagen,   and bear it in thy hand.
Would that thou mightst take it   again unto Burgundian land!"

When with mind so willing   he offered him his shield,
Saw ye how eyes full many   with scalding tears were filled;
For the last gift was it   that was offered e'er
Unto any warrior   by Bechelaren's margrave, Ruediger.

How grim soe'er was Hagen   and stern soe'er of mind,
That gift to pity moved him   that there the chieftain kind,
So near his latest moment,   did on him bestow.

From eyes of many another   began likewise the tears to flow.

"Now God in heaven requite thee,   O noble Ruediger!
Like unto thee none other   warrior was there e'er,
Unto knights all friendless   so bounteously to give.
God grant in his mercy   thy virtue evermore to live.

"Woe's me to hear such tiding,"   Hagen did declare.
"Such load of grief abiding   already do we bear,
If we with friends must struggle,   to God our plaint must be."
Thereto replied the margrave: "'Tis cause of sorrow sore to me."

"To pay thee for thy favor,   O noble Ruediger,
Howe'er these lofty warriors   themselves against thee bear,
Yet never thee in combat   here shall touch my hand,
E'en though complete thou slayest   them from out Burgundian
        land."

Thereat the lofty Ruediger   'fore him did courteous bend.
On all sides was lamenting   that no man might end
These so great heart-sorrows   that sorely they must bear.
The father of all virtue   fell with noble Ruediger.

Then eke the minstrel Volker   from hall down glancing said:
"Since Hagen thus, my comrade,   peace with thee hath made,
Lasting truce thou likewise   receivest from my hand.
Well hast thou deserved it   as fared we hither to this land.

"Thou, O noble margrave,   my messenger shalt be.
These arm-bands ruddy golden   thy lady gave to me,
That here at this high festival   I the same should wear.
Now mayst thyself behold them   and of my faith a witness bear."

"Would God but grant,"   spake Ruediger, "who ruleth high in
        heaven,
That to thee by my lady   might further gift be given!
I'll gladly tell thy tidings   to spouse full dear to me,
An I but live to see her: from doubt thereof thou mayst be free."

When thus his word was given,   his shield raised Ruediger.
Nigh to madness driven   bode he no longer there,
But ran upon the strangers   like to a valiant knight.

Many a blow full rapid smote the margrave in his might.

Volker and Hagen made way before the thane,
As before had promised to him the warriors twain.
Yet found he by the portal so many a valiant man
That Ruediger the combat with mickle boding sore began.

Gunther and Gernot with murderous intent
Let him pass the portal, as knights on victory bent.
Backward yielded Giselher, with sorrow all undone;
He hoped to live yet longer, and therefore Ruediger would shun.

Straight upon their enemies the margrave's warriors sprung,
And following their master was seen a valiant throng.
Swords with cutting edges did they in strong arm wield,
'Neath which full many a helmet was cleft, and many a fair
  wrought shield.

The weary strangers likewise smote many a whirring slash,
Wherefrom the men of Bechelaren felt deep and long the gash
Through the shining ring-mail e'en to their life's core.
In storm of battle wrought they glorious deeds a many more.

All his trusty followers now eke had gained the hall,
On whom Volker and Hagen did soon in fury fall,
And mercy unto no man save Ruediger they showed.
The blood adown through helmets, where smote their swords, full
  plenteous flowed.

How right furiously were swords 'gainst armor driven!
On shields the well-wrought mountings from their wards were riven,
And fell their jeweled facings all scattered in the blood.
Ne'er again might warriors show in fight so grim a mood.

The lord of Bechelaren through foemen cut his way,
As doth each doughty warrior in fight his might display.
On that day did Ruediger show full plain that he
A hero was undaunted, full bold and eke full praiseworthy.

Stood there two knights right gallant, Gunther and Gernot,
And in the storm of battle to death full many smote.
Eke Giselher and Dankwart, never aught recked they

How many a lusty fighter   saw 'neath their hand his latest day.

Full well did show him Ruediger   a knight of mettle true,
Doughty in goodly armor.   What warriors there he slew!
Beheld it a Burgundian,   and cause for wrath was there.
Not longer now was distant   the death of noble Ruediger.

Gernot, knight full doughty,   addressed the margrave then,
Thus speaking to the hero: "Wilt thou of all my men
Living leave not any,   O noble Ruediger?
That gives me grief unmeasured;   the sight I may not longer bear.

"Now must thy gift unto me   prove thy sorest bane,
Since of my friends so many   thou from me hast ta'en.
Now hither turn to front me,   thou bold and noble knight:
As far as might may bear me   I trust to pay thy gift aright."

Ere that full the margrave   might make his way to him,
Must rings of glancing mail-coats   with flowing blood grow dim.
Then sprang upon each other   those knights on honor bent,
And each from wounds deep cutting   sought to keep him all
      unshent.

Their swords cut so keenly   that might withstand them naught.
With mighty arm Sir Ruediger   Gernot then smote
Through the flint-hard helmet,   that downward flowed the blood.
Therefor repaid him quickly   the knight of keen and valiant mood.

The gift he had of Ruediger   high in hand he swung,
And though to death was wounded   he smote with blow so strong
That the good shield was cloven   and welded helmet through.
The spouse of fair Gotelinde,   then his latest breath he drew.

In sooth so sad requital   found rich bounty ne'er.
Slain fell they both together,   Gernot and Ruediger,
Alike in storm of battle,   each by the other's hand.
Sore was the wrath of Hagen   when he the harm did understand.

Cried there the lord of Tronje: "Great is here our loss.
In death of these two heroes   such scathe befalleth us,
Wherefor land and people   shall repine for aye.
The warriors of Ruediger   must now to us the forfeit pay."

"Alack for this my brother,   snatched by death this day!
What host of woes unbidden   encompass me alway!
Eke must I moan it ever   that noble Ruediger fell.
Great is the scathe to both sides   and great the sorrowing as well."

When then beheld Sir Giselher   his lover's sire dead,
Must all that with him followed   suffer direst need.
There Death was busy seeking   to gather in his train,
And of the men of Bechelaren   came forth not one alive again.

Gunther and Giselher   and with them Hagen too,
Dankwart and Volker,   doughty thanes and true,
Went where found they lying   the two warriors slain,
Nor at the sight the heroes   might their grief and tears restrain.

"Death robbeth us right sorely,"   spake young Sir Giselher:
"Yet now give o'er your weeping   and let us seek the air,
That the ringed mail grow cooler   on us storm-weary men.
God in sooth will grant us   not longer here to live, I ween."

Here sitting, and there leaning   was seen full many a thane,
Resting once more from combat,   the while that all lay slain
The followers of Ruediger.   Hushed was the battle's din.
At length grew angry Etzel,   that stillness was so long within.

"Alack for such a service!"   spake the monarch's wife;
"For never 'tis so faithful   that our foes with life
Must to us make payment   at Ruediger's hand.
He thinks in sooth to lead them   again unto Burgundian land.

"What boots it, royal Etzel,   that we did ever share
With him what he desired?   The knight doth evil there.
He that should avenge us,   the same a truce doth make."
Thereto the stately warrior   Volker in answer spake:

"Alas 'tis no such case here,   O high and royal dame.
Dared I but give the lie to   one of thy lofty name,
Thou hast in fiendish manner   Ruediger belied.
He and all his warriors   have laid all thoughts of truce aside.

"With so good heart obeyed he   his royal master's will

That he and all his followers   here in death lie still.
Look now about thee, Kriemhild,   who may thy hests attend.
Ruediger the hero   hath served thee faithful to the end.

"Wilt thou my words believe not,   to thee shall clear be shown."
To cause her heart a sorrow,   there the thing was done.
Wound-gashed they bore the hero   where him the king might see.
Unto the thanes of Etzel   ne'er might so great sorrow be.

When did they the margrave   a corse on bier behold,
By chronicler might never   written be nor told
All the wild lamenting   of women and of men,
As with grief all stricken   out-poured they their hearts' sorrow then.

Royal Etzel's sorrow   there did know no bound.
Like to the voice of lion   echoing rang the sound
Of the king's loud weeping,   wherein the queen had share.
Unmeasured they lamented   the death of noble Ruediger.

Thirty-Eighth Adventure
How All Sir Dietrich's Knights Were Slain

On all sides so great sorrow   heard ye there around,
That palace and high tower   did from the wail resound.
Of Bern a man of Dietrich   eke the same did hear,
And speedily he hastened   the tidings to his lord to bear.

Spake he unto his master: "Sir Dietrich give me ear.
What yet hath been my fortune,   never did I hear
Lamenting past all measure,   as at this hour hath been.
Scathe unto King Etzel   himself hath happenéd, I ween.

"Else how might they ever   all show such dire need?
The king himself or Kriemhild,   one of them lieth dead,
By the doughty strangers   for sake of vengeance slain.
Unmeasured is the weeping   of full many a stately thane."

Then spake of Bern Sir Dietrich: "Ye men to me full dear,
Now haste ye not unduly.   The deeds performéd here
By the stranger warriors   show sore necessity.
That peace with them I blighted,   let it now their profit be."

Then spake the valiant Wolfhart: "Thither will I run
To make question of it   what they now have done,
And straight will tidings bring thee,   master full dear to me,
When yonder I inform me,   whence may so great lamenting be."

Answer gave Sir Dietrich: "Fear they hostility,
The while uncivil questioning   of their deed there be,
Lightly are stirred to anger   good warriors o'er the thing.

Yea, 'tis my pleasure, Wolfhart,   thou sparest them all such
    questioning.

Helfrich he then commanded   thither with speed to go
That from men of Etzel   he might truly know,
Or from the strangers straightway,   what thing there had been.
As that, so sore lamenting   of people ne'er before was seen.

Questioned then the messenger: "What hath here been wrought?"
Answered one among them: "Complete is come to naught
What of joy we cherished   here in Hunnish land.
Slain here lieth Ruediger,   fallen 'neath Burgundian hand.

"Of them that entered with him   not one doth longer live."
Naught might ever happen   Helfrich more to grieve,
Nor ever told he tidings   so ruefully before.
Weeping sore the message   unto Dietrich then he bore.

"What the news thou bringst us?"   Dietrich spake once more;
"Yet, O doughty Helfrich,   wherefore dost weep so sore?"
Answered the noble warrior: "With right may I complain:
Yonder faithful Ruediger   lieth by the Burgundians slain."

The lord of Bern gave answer: "God let not such thing be!
That were a mighty vengeance,   and eke the Devil's glee.
Whereby had ever Ruediger   from them deserved such ill?
Well know I to the strangers   was ever well disposed his will."

Thereto gave answer Wolfhart: "In sooth have they this done,
Therefor their lives shall forfeit   surely, everyone.
And make we not requital,   our shame for aye it were;
Full manifold our service   from hand of noble Ruediger."

Then bade the lord of Amelungen   the case more full to learn.
He sat within a casement   and did full sadly mourn.
He prayed then that Hildebrand   unto the strangers go,
That he from their own telling   of the case complete might know.

The warrior keen in battle,   Master Hildebrand,
Neither shield nor weapon   bore he in his hand,
But would in chivalrous manner   unto the strangers go.
His sister's son reviled him   that he would venture thus to do.

Spake in anger Wolfhart: "Goest thou all weaponless,
Must I of such action   free my thought confess:
Thou shalt in shameful fashion   hither come again;
Goest thou arméd thither,   will all from harm to thee refrain."

So armed himself the old man   at counsel of the young.
Ere he was ware of it,   into their armor sprung
All of Dietrich's warriors   and stood with sword in hand.
Grieved he was, and gladly   had turned them Master Hildebrand.

He asked them whither would they.   "Thee company we'll bear,
So may, perchance, less willing   Hagen of Tronje dare,
As so oft his custom,   to give thee mocking word."
The thane his leave did grant them   at last when he their speech
      had heard.

Keen Volker saw approaching,   in armor all arrayed,
Of Bern the gallant warriors   that Dietrich's word obeyed,
With sword at girdle hanging   and bearing shield in hand.
Straight he told the tidings   to his masters of Burgundian land.

Spake the doughty Fiddler: "Yonder see I come near
The warriors of Dietrich   all clad in battle gear
And decked their heads with helmets,   as if our harm they mean.
For us knights here homeless   approacheth evil end, I ween."

Meanwhile was come anigh them   Master Hildebrand.
Before his foot he rested   the shield he bore in hand,
And soon began to question   the men of Gunther there:
"Alack, ye gallant warriors,   what harm hath wrought you Ruediger?

"Me did my master Dietrich   hither to you command:
If now the noble margrave   hath fallen 'neath the hand
Of any knight among you,   as word to us is borne,
Such a mighty sorrow   might we never cease to mourn."

Then spake of Tronje Hagen: "True is the tale ye hear.
Though glad I were, if to you   had lied the messenger,
And if the faithful Ruediger   still his life might keep,
For whom both man and woman   must ever now in sorrow weep!"

When they for sooth the passing　of the hero knew,
Those gallant knights bemoaned him　like faithful friends and true;
On Dietrich's lusty warriors　saw ye fall the tear
Adown the bearded visage,　for sad of heart in truth they were.

Of Bern then a chieftain,　Siegstab, further cried:
"Of all the mickle comfort　now an end is made,
That Ruediger erst prepared us　after our days of pain.
The joy of exiled people　here lieth by you warriors slain."

Then spake of Amelungen　the thane Wolfwein:
"If that this day beheld I　dead e'en sire of mine,
No more might be my sorrow　than for this hero's life.
Alack! who bringeth comfort　now to the noble margrave's wife?"

Spake eke in angry humor　Wolfhart a stalwart thane:
"Who now shall lead our army　on the far campaign,
As full oft the margrave　of old hath led our host?
Alack! O noble Ruediger,　that in such manner thee we've lost!"

Wolfbrand and Helfrich　and Helmnot with warriors all
Mournéd there together　that he in death must fall.
For sobbing might not further　question Hildebrand.
He spake: "Now do, ye warriors,　according to my lord's command.

"Yield unto us Ruediger's　corse from out the hall,
In whose death to sorrow　hath passed our pleasure all;
And let us do him service　for friendship true of yore
That e'er for us he cherished　and eke for many a stranger more.

"We too from home are exiles　like unto Ruediger.
Why keep ye us here waiting?　Him grant us hence to bear,
That e'en though death hath reft him　our service he receive,
Though fairer had we paid it　the while the hero yet did live."

Thereto spake King Gunther:　"No service equal may
That which, when death hath reft him,　to friend a friend doth pay.
Him deem I friend right faithful,　whoe'er the same may do.
Well make ye here requital　for many a service unto you."

"How long shall we beseech you," spake Wolfhart the thane;
"Since he that best consoled us　by you now lieth slain,

And we, alas, no longer   his living aid may have,
Grant us hence to bear him   and lay the hero in his grave."

Thereto answered Volker: "Thy prayer shall all deny.
From out the hall thou take him,   where doth the hero lie
'Neath deep wounds and mortal   in blood now smitten down.
So may by thee best service   here to Ruediger be shown."

Answered Wolfhart boldly: "Sir Fiddleman, God wot
Thou shalt forbear to stir us,   for woe on us thou'st wrought.
Durst I despite my master,   uncertain were thy life;
Yet must we here keep silence,   for he did bid us shun the strife."

Then spake again the Fiddler: "'Tis all too much of fear,
For that a thing's forbidden,   meekly to forbear.
Scarce may I deem it valor   worthy good knight to tell."
What said his faithful comrade,   did please the doughty Hagen well.

"For proof be not o'er-eager,"   Wolfhart quick replied,
"Else so I'll tune thy fiddle   that when again ye ride
Afar unto Rhine river,   sad tale thou tellest there.
Thy haughty words no longer   may I now with honor bear."

Spake once more the Fiddler: "If e'er the harmony
Of my fiddle-strings thou breakest,   thy helmet's sheen shall be
Made full dim of luster   by stroke of this my hand,
Howe'er fall out my journey   homeward to Burgundian land."

Then would he rush upon him   but that him did restrain
Hildebrand his uncle   who seizéd him amain.
"I ween thou would'st be witless,   by youthful rage misled.
My master's favor had'st thou   evermore thus forfeited."

"Let loose the lion, Master,   that doth rage so sore.
If but my sword may reach him,"   spake Volker further more,
"Though he the world entire   by his own might had slain,
I'll smite him that an answer   never may he chant again."

Thereat with anger straightway   the men of Bern were filled.
Wolfhart, thane right valiant,   grasped in haste his shield,
And like to a wild lion   out before them sped.
By friends a goodly number   full quickly was he followéd.

Though by the hall went striding   ne'er so swift the thane,
O'ertook him Master Hildebrand   ere he the steps might gain,
For nowise would he let him   be foremost in the fray.
In the stranger warriors   worthy foemen soon found they.

Straight saw ye upon Hagen   rush Master Hildebrand,
And sword ye heard give music   in each foeman's hand.
Sore they were enragéd,   as ye soon were ware,
For from their swinging broadswords   whirred the ruddy sparks in
        air.

Yet soon the twain were parted   in the raging fight:
The men of Bern so turned it   by their dauntless might.
Ere long then was Hildebrand   from Hagen turned away,
While that the doughty Wolfhart   the valiant Volker sought to slay.

Upon the helm the Fiddler   he smote with blow so fierce
That the sword's keen edges   unto the frame did pierce.
With mighty stroke repaid him   the valiant minstrel too,
And so belabored Wolfhart   that thick the sparks around him flew.

Hewing they made the fire   from mail-rings scintillate,
For each unto the other   bore a deadly hate.
Of Bern the thane Wolfwein   at length did part the two, —
Which thing might none other   than man of mickle prowess do.

Gunther, knight full gallant,   received with ready hand
There the stately warriors   of Amelungen land.
Eke did young Giselher   of many a helmet bright,
With blood all red and reeking,   cause to grow full dim the light.

Dankwart, Hagen's brother,   was a warrior grim.
What erstwhile in combat   had been wrought by him
Against the men of Etzel   seemed now as toying vain,
As fought with flaming ire   the son of valiant Aldrian.

Ritschart and Gerbart,   Helfrich and Wichart
Had oft in storm of battle   with valor borne their part,
As now 'fore men of Gunther   they did clear display.
Likewise saw ye Wolfbrand   glorious amid the fray.

There old Master Hildebrand   fought as he were wode.
Many a doughty warrior   was stricken in the blood
By the sword that swinging   in Wolfhart's hand was seen.
Thus took dire vengeance   for Ruediger those knights full keen.

Havoc wrought Sir Siegstab   there with might and main.
Ho! in the hurly-burly   what helms he cleft in twain
Upon the crowns of foemen,   Dietrich's sister's son!
Ne'er in storm of battle   had he more feats of valor done.

When the doughty Volker   there aright had seen
How many a bloody rivulet   was hewn by Siegstab keen
From out the well-wrought mail-rings,   the hero's ire arose.
Quick he sprang toward him,   Siegstab then his life must lose.

Ere long time was over,   'neath the Fiddler's hand,
Who of his art did give him   such share to understand
That beneath his broadsword   smitten to death he lay.
Old Hildebrand avenged him   as bade his mighty arm alway.

"Alack that knight so loved,"   spake Master Hildebrand,
"Here should thus lie fallen   'neath Volker's hand.
Now lived his latest hour   in sooth this Fiddler hath."
Filled was the hero Hildebrand   straightway with a mighty wrath.

With might smote he Volker   that severed flew the band
E'en to the hall's wide limit   far on either hand
From shield and eke from helmet   borne by the Fiddler keen;
Therewith the doughty Volker   reft of life at last had been.

Pressed eager to the combat   Dietrich's warriors true,
Smiting that the mail-rings   afar from harness flew,
And that the broken sword-points   soaring aloft ye saw,
The while that reeking blood-stains   did they from riven helmets
        draw.

There of Tronje Hagen   beheld Volker dead.
In that so bloody carnage   'twas far the sorest need
Of all that did befall him   in death of friend and man.
Alack! for him what vengeance   Hagen then to wreak began!

"Therefrom shall profit never   Master Hildebrand.

Slain hath been here my helper   'neath the warrior's hand,
The best of feres in battle   that fortune ever sent."
His shield upraised he higher   and hewing through the throng he
          went.

Next saw ye Dankwart   by doughty Helfrich slain,
Gunther and Giselher   did full sorely plain,
When they beheld him fallen   where fiercely raged the fray.
For his death beforehand   dearly did his foemen pay.

The while coursed Wolfhart   thither and back again,
Through Gunther's men before him   hewing wide a lane.
Thrice in sooth returning   strode he down the hall,
And many a lusty warrior   'neath his doughty hand must fall.

Soon the young Sir Giselher   cried aloud to him:
"Alack, that I should ever   find such foeman grim!
Sir knight, so bold and noble,   now turn thee here to me.
I trow to end thy coursing,   the which will I no longer see."

To Giselher then turned him   Wolfhart in the fight,
And gaping wounds full many   did each the other smite.
With such a mighty fury   he to the monarch sped
That 'neath his feet went flying   the blood e'en high above his head.

With rapid blows and furious   the son of Ute fair
Received the valiant Wolfhart   as came he to him there.
How strong soe'er the thane was,   his life must ended be.
Never king so youthful   might bear himself more valiantly.

Straight he smote Wolfhart   through well-made cuirass,
That from the wound all gaping   the flowing blood did pass.
Unto death he wounded   Dietrich's liegeman true,
Which thing in sooth might never   any save knight full gallant do.

When the valiant Wolfhart   of the wound was ware,
His shield flung he from him   and high with hand in air
Raised he a mighty weapon   whose keen edge failéd not.
Through helmet and through mail-rings   Giselher with might he
          smote.

Grimly each the other   there to death had done.

Of Dietrich's men no longer   lived there ever one.
When old Master Hildebrand   Wolfhart's fall had seen,
In all his life there never   such sorrow him befell, I ween.

Fallen now were Gunther's   warriors everyone,
And eke the men of Dietrich.   Hildebrand the while had gone
Where Wolfhart had fallen   down in pool of blood.
In his arms then clasped he   the warrior of dauntless mood.

Forth from the hall to bear him   vainly did he try:
But all too great the burden   and there he still must lie.
The dying knight looked upward   from his bloody bed
And saw how that full gladly   him his uncle thence had led.

Spake he thus mortal wounded: "Uncle full dear to me,
Now mayst thou at such season   no longer helpful be.
To guard thee well from Hagen   indeed me seemeth good,
For bears he in his bosom   a heart in sooth of grimmest mood.

"And if for me my kinsmen   at my death would mourn,
Unto the best and nearest   by thee be message borne
That for me they weep not,   — of that no whit is need.
At hand of valiant monarch   here lie I gloriously dead.

"Eke my life so dearly   within this hall I've sold,
That have sore cause for weeping   the wives of warriors bold.
If any make thee question,   then mayst thou freely say
That my own hand nigh hundred   warriors hath slain today."

Now was Hagen mindful   of the minstrel slain,
From whom the valiant Hildebrand   erstwhile his life had ta'en.
Unto the Master spake he: "My woes shalt thou repay.
Full many a warrior gallant   thou hast ta'en from us hence away."

He smote upon Hildebrand   that loud was heard the tone
Of Balmung resounding   that erst did Siegfried own,
But Hagen bold did seize it   when he the hero slew.
The old warrior did guard him,   as he was knight of mettle true.

Dietrich's doughty liegeman   with broadsword did smite
That did cut full sorely,   upon Tronje's knight;
Yet had the man of Gunther   never any harm.

Through his cuirass well-jointed   Hagen smote with mighty arm.

Soon as his wound perceivéd   the aged Hildebrand,
Feared he more of damage   to take from Hagen's hand;
Across his back full deftly   his shield swung Dietrich's man,
And wounded deep, the hero   in flight 'fore Hagen's fury ran.

Now longer lived not any   of all that goodly train
Save Gunther and Hagen,   doughty warriors twain.
With blood from wound down streaming   fled Master Hildebrand,
Whom soon in Dietrich's presence,   saw ye with saddest tidings
     stand.

He found the chieftain sitting   with sorrow all distraught,
Yet mickle more of sadness   unto him he brought.
When Dietrich saw how Hildebrand   cuirass all blood-red wore,
With fearful heart he questioned,   what the news to him he bore.

"Now tell me, Master Hildebrand,   how thus wet thou be
From thy life-blood flowing,   or who so harmeth thee.
In hall against the strangers   thou'st drawn thy sword, I ween.
'Twere well my straight denial   here by these had honored been."

Replied he to his master: "From Hagen cometh all.
This deep wound he smote me   there within the hall
When I from his fury   thought to turn away.
'Tis marvel that I living   saved me from the fiend this day."

Then of Bern spake Dietrich: "Aright hast thou thy share,
For thou didst hear me friendship   unto these knights declare,
And now the peace hast broken,   that I to them did give.
If my disgrace it were not,   by this hand no longer shouldst thou
     live."

"Now be not, Master Dietrich,   so sorely stirred to wrath.
On me and on my kinsmen   is wrought too great a scathe.
Thence sought we Ruediger   to bear all peacefully,
The which by men of Gunther   to us no whit would granted be."

"Ah, woe is me for sorrow!   Is Ruediger then dead,
In all my need there never   such grief hath happenéd.
The noble Gotelinde   is cousin fair to me.

Alack for the poor orphans   that there in Bechelaren must be!"

Grief and anguish filled him   o'er Ruediger thus slain,
Nor might at all the hero   the flowing tears restrain.
"Alack for faithful helper   that death from me hath torn.
King Etzel's trusty liegeman   never may I cease to mourn.

"Canst thou, Master Hildebrand,   true the tidings say,
Who might be the warrior   that Ruediger did slay?"
"That did the doughty Gernot   with mighty arm," he said:
"Eke at hand of Ruediger   lieth the royal hero dead."

Spake he again to Hildebrand: "Now let my warriors know,
That straightway they shall arm them,   for thither will I go.
And bid to fetch hither   my shining mail to me.
Myself those knights will question   of the land of Burgundy."

"Who here shall do thee service?"   spake Master Hildebrand;
"All that thou hast yet living,   thou seest before thee stand.
Of all remain I only;   the others, they are dead."
As was in sooth good reason,   filled the tale his soul with dread,

For in his life did never   such woe to him befall.
He spake: "Hath death so reft me   of my warriors all,
God hath forsaken Dietrich,   ah me, a wretched wight!
Sometime a lofty monarch   I was, high throned in wealth and
     might."

"How might it ever happen?"   Dietrich spake again,
"That so worthy heroes   here should all be slain
By the battle-weary   strangers thus beset?
Ill fortune me hath chosen,   else death had surely spared them yet.

"Since that fate not further   to me would respite give,
Then tell me, of the strangers   doth any longer live?"
Answered Master Hildebrand: "God wot, never one
Save Hagen, and beside him   Gunther lofty king alone."

"Alack, O faithful Wolfhart,   must I thy death now mourn,
Soon have I cause to rue me   that ever I was born.
Siegstab and Wolfwein   and eke Wolfbrand!
Who now shall be my helpers   in the Amelungen land?

"Helfrich, thane full valiant,   and is he likewise slain?
For Gerbart and Wichart   when shall I cease to plain?
Of all my life's rejoicing   is this the latest day.
Alack that die for sorrow   never yet a mortal may!"

Thirty-Ninth Adventure
How Gunther and Hagen and Kriemhild Were Slain

Himself did then Sir Dietrich   his armor take in hand,
To don the which did help him   Master Hildebrand.
The doughty chieftain meanwhile   must make so loud complain
That from high palace casement   oft came back the sound again.

Natheless his proper humor   soon he did regain,
And arméd full in anger   stood the worthy thane;
A shield all wrought full firmly   took he straight in hand,
And forth they strode together,   he and Master Hildebrand.

Spake then of Tronje Hagen: "Lo, where doth hither wend
In wrath his way Sir Dietrich.   'Tis plain he doth intend
On us to wreak sore vengeance   for harm befallen here.
Today be full decided   who may the prize for valor bear!

"Let ne'er of Bern Sir Dietrich   hold him so high of might
Nor deem his arm so doughty   and terrible in fight
That, will he wreak his anger   on us for sorest scathe," —
Such were the words of Hagen,   — "I dare not well withstand his
    wrath."

Upon these words defiant   left Dietrich Hildebrand,
And to the warriors hither   came where both did stand
Without before the palace,   and leaning respite found.
His shield well proved in battle   Sir Dietrich lowered to the ground.

Addressed to them Sir Dietrich   these words of sorrowing:

"Wherefore hast thou such evil,   Gunther mighty king,
Wrought 'gainst me a stranger?   What had I done to thee,
Of my every comfort   in such manner reft to be?

"Seemed then not sufficient   the havoc unto you
When from us the hero   Ruediger ye slew,
That now from me ye've taken   my warriors one and all?
Through me did so great sorrow   ne'er to you good knights befall.

"Of your own selves bethink you   and what the scathe ye bore,
The death of your companions   and all your travail sore,
If not your hearts, good warriors,   thereat do heavy grow.
That Ruediger hath fallen,   — ah me! how fills my heart with woe!

"In all this world to any   more sorrow ne'er befell,
Yet have ye minded little   my loss and yours as well.
Whate'er I most rejoiced in   beneath your hands lies slain;
Yea, for my kinsmen fallen   never may I cease to plain."

"No guilt lies here upon us,"   Hagen in answer spake.
"Unto this hall hither   your knights their way did take,
With goodly train of warriors   full arméd for the fight.
Meseemeth that the story   hath not been told to thee aright."

"What shall I else believe in?   To me told Hildebrand
How, when the knights that serve me   of Amelungenland
Did beg the corse of Ruediger   to give them from the hall,
Naught offered ye but mockings   unto the valiant warriors all."

Then spake the King of Rhineland: "Ruediger to bear away
Came they in company hither;   whose corse to them deny
I bade, despiting Etzel,   nor with aught malice more,
Whereupon did Wolfhart   begin to rage thereat full sore."

Then spake of Bern the hero: "'Twas fated so to be.
Yet Gunther, noble monarch,   by thy kingly courtesy
Amends make for the sorrow   thou here on me hast wrought,
That so thy knightly honor   still unsullied be in aught.

"Then yield to me as hostage   thyself and eke thy man;
So will I surely hinder,   as with best might I can,
That any here in Hunland   harm unto thee shall do:

Henceforward shalt thou find me   ever well disposed and true."

"God in heaven forfend it,"   Hagen spake again,
"That unto thee should yield them   ever warriors twain
Who in their strength reliant   all armed before thee stand,
And yet 'fore foes defiant   may freely swing a blade in hand."

"So shall ye not," spake Dietrich,   "proffered peace forswear,
Gunther and Hagen.   Misfortune such I bear
At both your hands, 'tis certain   ye did but do aright,
Would ye for so great sorrow   now my heart in full requite.

"I give you my sure promise   and pledge thereto my hand
That I will bear you escort   home unto your land;
With honors fit I'll lead you,   thereon my life I set,
And for your sake sore evil   suffered at your hands forget."

"Ask thou such thing no longer,"   Hagen then replied.
"For us 'twere little fitting   the tale be bruited wide,
That twain of doughty warriors   did yield them 'neath thy hand.
Beside thee is none other   now but only Hildebrand."

Then answered Master Hildebrand: "The hour may come, God wot,
Sir Hagen, when thus lightly   disdain it thou shalt not
If any man such offer   of peace shall make to thee.
Welcome might now my master's   reconciliation be."

"I'd take in sooth his friendship,"   Hagen gave reply,
"Ere that I so basely   forth from a hall would fly.
As thou hast done but lately,   O Master Hildebrand.
I weened with greater valor   couldst thou 'fore a foeman stand."

Thereto gave answer Hildebrand: "From thee reproach like that?
Who was then on shield so idle   'fore the Waskenstein that sat,
The while that Spanish Walter   friend after friend laid low?
Such valor thou in plenty   hast in thine own self to show."

Outspake then Sir Dietrich: "Ill fits it warriors bold
That they one another   like old wives should scold.
Thee forbid I, Hildebrand,   aught to parley more.
Ah me, most sad misfortune   weigheth on my heart full sore.

"Let me hear, Sir Hagen,"   Dietrich further spake,
"What boast ye doughty warriors   did there together make,
When that ye saw me hither   come with sword in hand?
Thought ye then not singly   me in combat to withstand?"

"In sooth denieth no one,"   bold Sir Hagen spake,
"That of the same with sword-blow   I would trial make,
An but the sword of Niblung   burst not within my hand.
Yea, scorn I that to yield us   thus haughtily thou mak'st demand."

When Dietrich now perceivéd   how Hagen raged amain,
Raise his shield full quickly   did the doughty thane.
As quick upon him Hagen   adown the perron sprang,
And the trusty sword of Niblung   full loud on Dietrich's armor
     rang.

Then knew full well Sir Dietrich   that the warrior keen
Savage was of humor,   and best himself to screen
Sought of Bern the hero   from many a murderous blow,
Whereby the valiant Hagen   straightway came he well to know.

Eke fear he had of Balmung,   a strong and trusty blade.
Each blow meanwhile Sir Dietrich   with cunning art repaid,
Till that he dealt to Hagen   a wound both deep and long,
Whereat give o'er the struggle   must the valiant knight and strong.

Bethought him then Sir Dietrich: "Through toil thy strength has
     fled,
And little honor had I   shouldst thou lie before me dead.
So will I yet make trial   if I may not subdue
Thee unto me as hostage."   Light task 'twas not the same to do.

His shield down cast he from him   and with what strength he found
About the knight of Tronje   fast his arms he wound.
In such wise was subduéd   by him the doughty knight;
Gunther the noble monarch   did weep to see his sorry plight.

Bind Hagen then did Dietrich,   and led him where did stand
Kriemhild the royal lady,   and gave into her hand
Of all the bravest warrior   that ever weapon bore.
After her mickle sorrow   had she merry heart once more.

For joy before Sir Dietrich   bent royal Etzel's wife:
"Blessed be thou ever   in heart while lasteth life.
Through thee is now forgotten   all my dire need;
An death do not prevent me,   from me shall ever be thy meed."

Then spake to her Sir Dietrich,   "Take not his life away,
High and royal lady,   for full will he repay
Thee for the mickle evil   on thee have wrought his hands.
Be it not his misfortune   that bound before thee here he stands."

Then bade she forth lead Hagen   to dungeon keep near by,
Wherein he lay fast bolted   and hid from every eye.
Gunther, the noble monarch,   with loudest voice did say:
"The knight of Bern who wrongs me,   whither hath he fled away?"

Meanwhile back towards him   the doughty Dietrich came,
And found the royal Gunther   a knight of worthy name.
Eke he might bide longer   but down to meet him sprang,
And soon with angry clamor   their swords before the palace rang.

How famed soe'er Sir Dietrich   and great the name he bore,
With wrath was filled King Gunther,   and eke did rage full sore
At thought of grievous sorrow   suffered at his hand:
Still tell they as high wonder   how Dietrich might his blows
        withstand.

In store of doughty valor   each did nothing lack.
From palace and from tower   the din of blows came back
As on well-fastened helmets   the lusty swords came down,
And royal Gunther's valor   in the fight full clear was shown.

The knight of Bern yet tamed him   as Hagen erst befell,
And oozing through his armor   the blood was seen to swell
From cut of sharpest weapon   in Dietrich's arm that swung.
Right worthily King Gunther   had borne him after labors long.

Bound was then the monarch   by Sir Dietrich's hand,
Albeit bonds should suffer   ne'er king of any land.
But deemed he, if King Gunther   and Hagen yet were free,
Secure might never any   from their searching vengeance be.

When in such manner Dietrich   the king secure had bound

By the hand he led him where Kriemhild he found.
At sight of his misfortune did sorrow from her flee:
Quoth she: "Welcome Gunther from out the land of Burgundy."

He spake: "Then might I thank thee, sister of high degree,
When that some whit more gracious might thy greeting be.
So angry art thou minded ever yet, O queen,
Full spare shall be thy greeting to Hagen and to me, I ween."

Then spake of Bern the hero: "Ne'er till now, O queen,
Given o'er as hostage have knights so worthy been,
As I, O lofty lady, in these have given to thee:
I pray thee higher evils to spare them now for sake of me."

She vowed to do it gladly. Then forth Sir Dietrich went
With weeping eyes to see there such knights' imprisonment.
In grimmest ways thereafter wreaked vengeance Etzel's wife:
Beneath her hand those chosen warriors twain must end their life.

She let them lie asunder the less at ease to be,
Nor did each the other thenceforward ever see
Till that unto Hagen her brother's head she bore.
In sooth did Kriemhild vengeance wreak upon the twain full sore.

Forth where she should find Hagen the queen her way did take,
And in right angry manner she to the warrior spake:
"An thou wilt but restore me that thou hast ta'en from me,
So may'st thou come yet living home to the land of Burgundy."

Answered thereto grim Hagen: "'Twere well thy breath to save,
Full high and royal lady. Sworn by my troth I have
That I the hoard will tell not; the while that yet doth live
Of my masters any, the treasure unto none I'll give."

"Then ended be the story," the noble lady spake.
She bade them from her brother straightway his life to take.
His head they struck from off him, which by the hair she bore
Unto the thane of Tronje. Thereat did grieve the knight full sore.

When that he in horror his master's head had seen,
Cried the doughty warrior unto Kriemhild the queen:
"Now is thy heart's desire at length accomplishéd.

And eke hath all befallen   as my foreboding heart hath said.

"Dead lieth now the noble   king of Burgundy,
Also youthful Giselher   and Sir Gernot eke doth he.
The treasure no one knoweth   but God and me alone,
Nor e'er by thee, she-devil,   shall its hiding place be known."

Quoth she: "But ill requital   hast thou made to me.
Yet mine the sword of Siegfried   now henceforth shall be,
The which when last I saw him,   my loved husband bore,
In whom on me such sorrow   through guilt of thine doth weigh
      full sore."

She drew it from the scabbard,   nor might he say her nay,
Though thought she from the warrior   his life to take away.
With both hands high she raised it   and off his head struck she,
Whereat did grieve King Etzel   full sore the sorry sight to see.

"To arms!" cried then the monarch: "here lieth foully slain
Beneath the hand of woman   of all the doughtiest thane
That e'er was seen in battle   or ever good shield bore!
Though foeman howsoever,   yet grieveth this my heart full sore."

Quoth then the aged Hildebrand: "Reap no gain she shall,
That thus she dared to slay him.   Whate'er to me befall,
And though myself in direst   need through him have been,
By me shall be avengéd   the death of Tronje's knight full keen."

In wrathful mood then Hildebrand   unto Kriemhild sprung,
And 'gainst the queen full swiftly   his massy blade he swung.
Aloud she then in terror   'fore Hildebrand did wail,
Yet that she shrieked so loudly,   to save her what might that avail?

So all those warriors fated   by hand of death lay strewn,
And e'en the queen full lofty   in pieces eke was hewn.
Dietrich and royal Etzel   at length to weep began,
And grievously they mournéd   kinsmen slain and many a man.

Who late stood high in honor   now in death lay low,
And fate of all the people   weeping was and woe.
To mourning now the monarch's   festal tide had passed,
As falls that joy to sorrow   turneth ever at the last.

Nor can I tell you further   what later did befall,
But that good knights and ladies   saw ye mourning all,
And many a noble squire,   for friends in death laid low.
Here hath the story ending,   — that is the Nibelungen woe.